PILOT
WHO KNOWS THE
WATERS

A LORD HANI MYSTERY

N . L .   H O L M E S

WayBack Press
P.O.Box 16066
Tampa, FL
⌷

Pilot Who Knows the Waters
Copyright © 2022 by N. L. Holmes

The Lord Hani Mysteries™2020

Quotes from "The Instructions of Any" and from "Hymn to Amun-Ra" from *Ancient Egyptian Literature* by Miriam Lichtheim, University of California Press (1976).

Cover art and map© by Streetlight Graphics.
Author photo© by Kipp Baker.

Dedicated to the women of my writers' group, the best traveling companions a writer ever had.

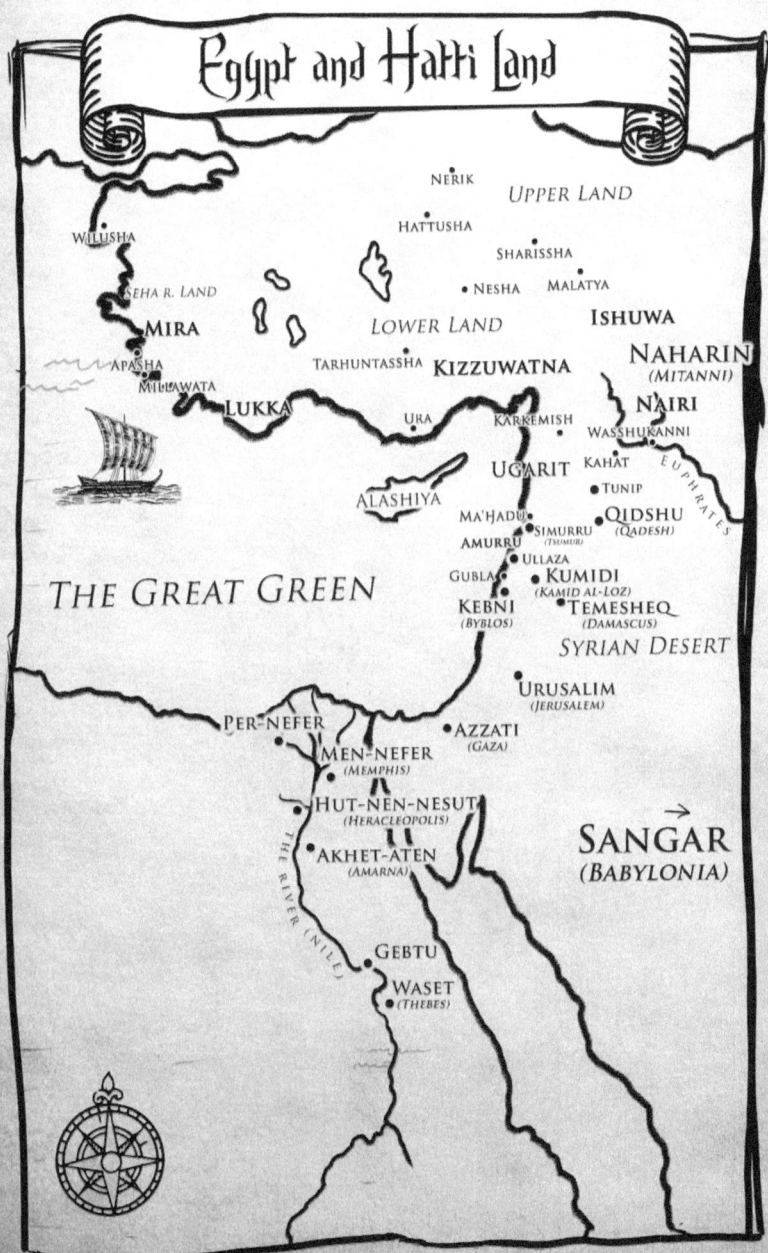

Egypt and Hatti Land

NERIK

UPPER LAND

HATTUSHA

WILUSHA

SHARISSHA

SEHA R. LAND

NESHA   MALATYA

MIRA

LOWER LAND   **ISHUWA**

APASHA   TARHUNTASSHA   **KIZZUWATNA**   **NAHARIN**
MILLAWATA   (MITANNI)

LUKKA   URA   **N'AIRI**

KARKEMISH   WASSHUKANNI

UGARIT   KAHAT
E U P H R A T E S

ALASHIYA   TUNIP

MA'HADU   **QIDSHU**
SIMURRU   (QADESH)
AMURRU   (TSUMUR)

THE GREAT GREEN   ULLAZA

GUBLA   **KUMIDI**
(KAMID AL-LOZ)

KEBNI   **TEMESHEQ**
(BYBLOS)   (DAMASCUS)

SYRIAN DESERT

URUSALIM
(JERUSALEM)

PER-NEFER   **AZZATI**
(GAZA)

MEN-NEFER
(MEMPHIS)

HUT-NEN-NESUT
(HERACLEOPOLIS)   **SANGAR**
(BABYLONIA)

AKHET-ATEN
(AMARNA)

THE RIVER (NILE)

GEBTU

WASET
(THEBES)

HISTORICAL NOTES

Our story opens around the year 1335 BCE. The visit of Hani to Hattusha to obtain a Hittite bridegroom for the queen of Egypt is historical, although we don't know which queen it was. Some scholars think she was the widow of Tut-ankh-aten, others one of the queens that preceded his reign. I have accepted the latter scenario. Historically, Shuppiluliuma's reception of Hani's first delegation probably took place while he was still in the field in Mitanni, but in the interests of compacting the action, I have had him return to his capital first.

The Egyptian phrase for "queen" was "king's wife", presupposing the normal situation of a male king. But since the "king" was simply whoever sat on the throne and wielded supreme power, that title could also be applied to a woman. In that case, she would take on many of the masculine signs of kingship, like the false beard. Especially under the Amarna revolution, the joined male and female principles were a potent symbol, and the royal couple together shared many duties. Thus, Nefert-iti or any other female ruler might take a "queen" (in this case, her daughter) to carry out the public duties of the king's wife, despite the inappropriate gender.

The letter Hani recites to the Hittite king is real. We know, as well, that Hattusha-ziti was sent to reconnoiter the political situation in Egypt, and that Prince Zannanza died or was killed on his way to meet his bride, precipitating a long border war between the Hittites and Egypt that culminates in the Battle of Kadesh. This entire episode, including Hani's meeting with the king, is described for us in a later Hittite document. Other parts of the plot are fictional, except for the enmity between Har-em-heb, who gains young King Tut-ankh-aten/amen's confidence, and the boy's grandfather Ay. The child who takes the throne under the name "Living Image of the Aten" will soon change it to "Living Image of Amen."

Both Har-em-heb and Ay will succeed Tut-ankh-amen on the throne when he dies young. Ay rules for only four years, then Har-em-heb takes his place for an unknown but considerably longer period of time. It is he who will tear down the hated capital Akhet-aten and deface the monuments of Akh-en-aten, expunging him from the lists of kings. Still childless, he is succeeded by his adjutant Pa-ra-mes-su, who changes his name to Ramesses (I).

Although the new king is designated immediately after the death of his predecessor, the ceremonies that confirm his kingship go on for a full year. I have conflated one of the coronation ceremonies with the Ipet or Opet festival, enacted yearly to reinforce the king's power through a ritual crowning, climaxed by the bestowal of a divine ka or identity.

Readers of the *Empire at Twilight* series will remember

the Hittite capital, Hattusha. The great causeway leading up to the citadel had not been built in the time of Hani. Shuppiluliuma I, a usurper, is credited with making Hatti Land a real empire, although kings of previous generations had pushed outside its limited borders. Hatti (Kheta) would become one of the major players in the Late Bronze Age, usually rivals of Egypt but eventually an ally.

In the Bronze Age, lions were to be found all around the eastern Mediterranean, from Egypt to Turkey and probably into Greece. Our hunt takes place in the mountains of Lebanon, in the great forests of cedars which exist today only in a few specimens.

The Egyptians believed the soul had five parts, which would be reunited, along with the body, in the afterlife - hence the importance of preserving the physical remains by mummification. Otherwise, the deceased would be unable to enjoy his blessed eternity, which seemed to have been physical as well as spiritual. Thus, to have one's body destroyed by burning, for example, was a particularly horrible fate. Hence also the custom of "opening the mouth" of the deceased to awaken their senses in the afterlife.

And finally, Egyptian women typically nursed their children for three or four years, which provided a kind of natural family planning (although they also had various forms of contraceptive).

CHARACTERS

(Persons marked with an * are purely fictitious)

HANI'S FAMILY

A'a*: gatekeeper of Hani's family.

Amen-hotep known as **Aha***: Hani and Nub-nefer's elder son.

Amen-em-hut: Nub-nefer's brother, Third Prophet of Amen.

Baket-iset*: Hani's eldest daughter.

Bener-ib*: Neferet's partner and fellow *sunet*.

Amen-hotep known as **Hani**: a diplomat.

In-hapy*: Maya's mother, a royal goldsmith.

Mai-her-pri*: Maya's third child and second son.

Amen-mes known as **Maya***: Hani's dwarf secretary and son-in-law, married to Sat-hut-haru.

Meret-seger*: the former palace handmaid now employed by Hani. Her tongue was cut out to prevent her telling anyone the secret of the young king's birth.

Meryet-amen*: Mery-ra's widowed lady friend.

Mery-ra: Hani's father.

Mut-nodjmet*: Pipi's daughter, the wife of Pa-kiki. The name is shared by Har-em-heb's wife.

Pa-ra-em-heb known as **Pipi***: Hani's brother.

Nedjem-ib*: Pipi's wife.

Neferet*: Hani and Nub-nefer's youngest daughter, a physician to the royal women.

Nub-nefer*: Hani's wife, a chantress of Amen.

Amen-em-ope known as **Pa-kiki*** (The Monkey): Hani and Nub-nefer's younger son.

Sat-hut-haru*: also known as Sati, Hani and Nub-nefer's second daughter, married to Maya.

Amen-hotep known as **Tepy***: Maya and Sat-hut-haru's eldest son.

Web-khet*: Maya and Sati's youngest daughter.

OTHER CHARACTERS

Ah-mes*: grandson of Ptah-mes by his son Djehuty-mes, child of the royal Kap (the young companions raised with the king).

Ankhet-khepru-ra Nefer-nefru-aten: Nefert-iti, Aken-aten's wife and successor on the throne.

Apeny: Ptah-mes's first wife.

Ay: King Ankhet-khepru-ra's father, known as the God's Father, a cavalry commander.

Djefat-nebty*: former physician of the royal women; the teacher of Neferet and Bener-ib and wife of Pentju.

Djehuty-mes: elder son of Ptah-mes, priest of Amen-Ra.

Har-em-heb: infantry commander, married to Ay's daughter Mut-nodjmet.

Hattusha-ziti: emissary of the Hittite king.

Hemet-min*: widow of Ipy.

Hu-may*: eldest son of Ipy, an apprentice goldsmith.

Huy: younger son of Ptah-mes.

Ipy*: In-hapy's chief goldsmith, deceased.

Kurunuwa*: Hattusha-ziti's secretary.

Mai: first prophet (high priest) of Amen-Ra under Amen-hotep III. A leader of the anti-Atenist forces.

Menna*: army officer and friend of Hani, who once saved Menna's life.

Meryet-aten: eldest daughter of Akh-en-aten and Nefert-iti, who served as her mother's queen after the death of her own husband, the coregent Akh-khepru-ra Smenkh-kha-ra. A leader of the anti-Atenist forces.

Mut-em-wia: eldest daughter of Ptah-mes, chantress of Amen-ra.

Neb-khepru-ra Tut-ankh-aten: successor and presumed son of Nefert-iti and Akhe-en-aten, who took the throne at the age of ten.

Pa-ra-mes-su: an army officer and adjutant to General Har-em-heb.

Pa-shedu*: a journeyman goldsmith.

Pentju: former royal physician under Akh-en-aten and vizier of the Upper Kingdom under Tut-ankh-aten.

Pi-ay*: In-hapy's senior goldsmith.

Pirwa*: son of the governor of Ura and Hani's guide.

Ptah-mes known as **Maya:** treasurer of the kingdom, Hani's friend and former superior, now married to Neferet. A member of the old Theban nobility. I have conflated the historical characters of Ptah-mes, vizier and high priest of Amen-Ra under Amen-hotep III, with Maya, Tut-ankh-aten's treasurer.

Shuppiluliuma I: considered the founder of the Hittite Empire, he usurped the throne and expanded Kheta Land's territories extensively.

Si-mut: second prophet of Amen-Ra under Amen-hotep III. A leader of the anti-Atenist forces.

Tarrupishni*: governor of the port of Ura.

GLOSSARY OF PLACES, TERMS, AND GODS

Alashiya: the island kingdom of Cyprus.

Amen-Ra: **Amen**, the Hidden One, was a local god of Thebes. When a Theban dynasty came to power in Egypt, Amen became the high god of the entire country and was merged with the all-important sun god **Ra**.

Ammit: a monster that waited at the balance where hearts were weighed in the afterworld. If one failed to measure up to *ma'at*, it was tossed to Ammit, who devoured it, annihilating it forever.

the Aten: god of the visible sun-disk, whose worship replaced those of Egypt's other gods under the pharaoh Akh-en-aten.

Bes: lion-like dwarf god, protector of women and children.

cloison: a fine strip of metal on edge, soldered to a background, that separates one color from another in the enamel technique called cloisonné.

deben: a 91-gram weight of silver or copper, cast in the form of a large ring, that was used as a kind of metal standard for payments, generally made in kind.

Djehuty: Thoth, the patron god of scribes and judge of souls in the afterlife.

doum palm: a kind of palmetto that bears large, edible fruit.

Geb: god of the earth.

Gebtu: modern Qift, a town at the juncture of the Nile and the Wadi-hammamat, leading to the Red Sea.

Great House (Per-a'o): the palace and by extension, the government and especially the king (cf. our expression "the White House"). Our word *pharaoh* comes from this term.

hapiru: a mixed group of social outcasts (runaway slaves, displaced peoples, and the landless poor) who lived at the margins of settlement in the Levant, harassing farmers, robbing caravans, and even attacking cities.

harper's song: a kind of funeral song that often expressed a cynical or agnostic view of death and the afterlife.

Haru: the solar hawk god, "the one on high", son of Osir. The living king was considered to be the incarnation of Haru.

Haru lock: a braided lock of hair hanging from the side of an otherwise shaven head, often worn by children.

Hattusha: the capital of the Hittite empire, located at modern Boğazköy (Turkey).

Ipet-isut: the great temple of Amun-Ra at Waset (Karnak). On the occasion of certain festivals, it was the northern pole of a procession leading to the "southern Ipet" a mile away in Luxor.

iteru: a unit of distance equalling about one mile.

ka: One of the elements of the human (or divine) soul which survived death. It seemed to be the vital essence and determined the nature of the person, human or divine. The king was thought to have a divine *ka*, renewed annually in the Ipet Festival.

Kemet: the Black Land, the Egyptians' name for their country because of the rich, dark alluvium of the Nile Valley. Also called the Two Lands.

khat: the mortal remains of the dead. It was considered necessary to the afterlife, hence the care with which bodies were embalmed.

Kheta Land: Egyptian term for the homeland of the Hittite empire (**Hatti Land**), centered in northern Anatolia (modern Turkey).

Khonsu the Traveler: the moon, son of Amen-Ra and patron of travelers.

Kidjuwadna (Kizzuwatna in Hittite): a mountainous kingdom in what is today eastern Turkey that had just been annexed by Kheta Land at the time of our story.

Luwian: the Indo-European language spoken most commonly in the Hittite empire. Closely resembled Neshite.

ma'at: the concept of truth, justice, and cosmic order. With a capital M, the goddess who personified all these.

Marasshantiya River: today's Kizilirmak River, which outlines the Hittite homeland.

Master of the Double House of Silver and Gold: the title of the royal treasurer, although much of the king's wealth was in commodities.

Master of the King's Stables: an honorary title granted to the historical Hani.

Men-nefer: one of Egypt's traditional capitals, located not far from modern Cairo.

menut: mourning dove

Meret-seger and **Wadjet:** the goddess of the Western tombs—the "lover of silence"—and "the green one", protector of Lower Egypt, both represented as cobras.

Mizri: the name by which most of its neighbors knew Egypt (cf. modern Arabic *Misr* and Hebrew *Mizraim*).

Neshite: Hittite, the Indo-European language of the ruling class in the Hittite empire.

Osir: divine king of the underworld, with whom the dead were believed to be configured. Hence, any deceased person.

Pa-yom A'a-en-mukhed: the Red Sea.

Per-nefer: a seaport in the Nile Delta near modern Tell el-Dab'a.

Pwenet (or **Punt**): a land on the Horn of Africa (probably Eritrea) with which Egypt traded in the New Kingdom.

quern: a flat grindstone on short legs used to grind flour by hand.

the River: the Nile, which, curiously enough, was never personified as a god or goddess.

sedge nuts: the tuber-like roots of a grassy plant that grows along the Nile.

Sekhmet: lion-headed goddess of plague and healing. According to her legend, she once grew so angry with humans that she determined to destroy them completely and drink their blood. She was tricked by dying beer red. Mistaking it for blood, she drank it and became so drunk that she passed out, forgetting her terrible mission.

sole friend of the king: a high honorific title.

Ta-nehesy: Nubia, today's Sudan, just south of Egypt. At our period, it was an Egyptian-administered territory.

tawananna: the religious and political title of the Hittite queen, held for life, even if her husband should die before her.

Tsumur: the local name for the capital of the Syrian vassal kingdom of Amurru (A'amu); in Egyptian, Simurru. Once part of Egypt's empire (see *The Crocodile Makes No Sound*), it now belonged to the Hittites.

Ura: a port on the south coast of modern Turkey which had just been annexed by Kheta from the formerly independent kingdom of Kidjuwadna (Kizzuwatna in Hittite).

***wab* priests:** "pure" priests, one of the lower categories of men of the gods.

Waset: City of the Scepter, one of Egypt's traditional capitals and seat of the cult of Amen-Ra. Today's Karnak and Luxor.

weshket: a broad collar of beads that lay on the shoulders.

CHAPTER 1

S PRING—HARVEST SEASON FOR WHEAT AND barley— had poured itself generously over the Two Lands, and on the farm, the laborers were bent over, sickles in hand, a line of white, red, and black, moving methodically across the vast golden fields. Despite Hani's misgivings about the politics of the kingdom, he had to confess life was good. The harvest would be rich that year. His granaries would be full. He might even have to build another one.

His wife, Nub-nefer, slipped an arm around his waist and said in a dreamy voice, "It's been so nice to have you here in Waset, my love, and it's been so good for the grandchildren. I hope the king never gets around to reassigning overseas missions."

They were standing in the road between the house and its vegetable gardens and the broader fields of grain. The sky stretched overhead, a vast, piercingly blue canopy like lapis lazuli, shot with the bright flash of pigeon wings as a flock settled in the stubble to glean. Hani drew a deep breath of satisfaction, squeezing Nub-nefer to his side.

Perhaps the queen had decided against her special assignment for him after all. Months had passed since she had summoned him to say, "Be ready," and still no word had come that would send him on the long voyage north to Kheta Land.

In the same way, Hani's lessons with the crown prince had ended as other subjects with which the lad needed to be familiar arose. *Familiar but certainly not expert. How much of a foreign language can one learn in a year? I'm afraid, as Sen-nedjem said, the boy's going to be half-learned.* Prince Tut-ankh-aten's tutor had never seemed enthusiastic about turning any part of the lad's education over to anyone else, and perhaps he had finally had his way. But the upshot was Hani had been able to enjoy a few months of nearly uninterrupted leisure with his family.

And Waset had become an especially exciting place to be in the last year because the liturgies at the Ipet-isut, the great shrine of Amen-Ra, had resumed. Hani glanced sideways at his wife, whose serene gaze told him how her years of anger and anxiety had melted away. Once more, she had taken up her duties as a chantress of the Hidden One. Her brother had emerged from hiding and was again praising Amen-Ra in his office of Third Prophet. One could easily believe all the chaos of the last reign was over and that good times were on their way back, surging irresistibly up the river toward them like the golden barque of the Hidden One on festival days.

"Maybe we should turn back. What do you think?" Nub-nefer asked. "The girls may be getting worried about us."

Hani doubted it, but he smiled tenderly at his wife. "Of

course, my dear. It's hot out here in the full sun anyway. A suntan won't hurt me, but I'm sure you don't want one."

They turned and, their hands linked like a pair of newlyweds', began their leisurely walk back toward the farmhouse.

The couple had only gone a few cubits before a cloud of dust appeared ahead, bursting from the farmyard, which soon resolved itself into the running figure of their grandson, Tepy. The ten-year-old pounded down the road toward them, his elbows pumping, his Haru-lock flying. A chill of fear seized Hani by the throat. *Dear gods, has something happened to Sati or one of the children?*

But Tepy skidded to a halt in front of his grandparents, his eyes bright with excitement not fear. Panting, he cried, "Gamfather, there's a messenger from the queen at the house! He told me to get you right away!"

Nub-nefer shot her husband an anxious glance. She knew as well as Hani what that meant.

Hani could feel his happiness draining away like the receding waters of the Inundation, leaving cold trepidation in its wake. "Thanks, son," he said to Tepy with a forced smile. "Let's see what the queen wants."

The three picked up their pace and made their way through the rows of lettuce, onions, and freshly planted cowpeas and into the low-walled enclosure around the house. Geese scattered, squawking their indignation, as the humans entered, while Tepy danced around in anticipation of something momentous.

In the salon, Sat-hut-haru sat with her children and her sister-in-law and cousin Mut-nofret. Baket-iset, Hani's eldest girl, lay immobile but bright-eyed and lovely, as she had for more than half her life after a terrible crime had left her paralyzed. The young mothers sprang to their feet, and only then did Hani see in the shadows of the small room a rather splendidly dressed gentleman rising at the same time. Under a long court wig, his face had that look of sleek impassivity that said "high-level royal functionary." The man's hands were clasped loosely in front of him, but he didn't look altogether at ease.

"Papa," Baket-iset cried, her voice pleasant, but relief was only too obvious beneath it. "This man has brought you a message from the King's Great Wife. He looked for you in Waset, but the servants told him you were up here."

Hani advanced toward the messenger and, being unclear about the man's rank, greeted him with a sketchy sort of bow. "You've had a long journey. I'm sorry you had to come this extra distance. How may I help you?"

The man's expression grew a little tart, as if he, too, were sorry about the additional *iterus*. "Our lady has a message for your ears only, Lord Hani. Where can we speak?"

Hani was on the verge of telling him, "These people can hear anything you have to say," but already, Nub-nefer had discreetly begun to round up the children and their toys.

She said, "We'll go up to the roof, where there's more breeze. You men say whatever you have to say right here."

In a minute, the three women and the little ones had hustled up the stairs, and the servants carried Baket's couch up after them. Tepy gave a look of curiosity and longing over his shoulder as he trailed in their wake.

With the disappearance of the family, a nervous silence fell. Finally, the messenger said in a low voice, "I'm sure you know what this is about, my lord. The queen our lady wants you to be advised that the time has come to make your... ahem... journey." He fixed Hani with his painted eyes as if to convey without words what they both realized that meant.

Hani knew only too well. A chill ran on spider feet up his backbone. He said in an equally guarded tone, "Is she satisfied that Lord Ay won't oppose us? He's aware of her intention, of course."

The messenger tipped his head. "There's an uprising in Ta-nehesy. The God's Father Lord Ay and General Har-em-heb have gone south to put it down."

So that's why Queen Meryet-aten has chosen this precise moment to send me north. "Very well. I'll leave immediately. Does she want me to meet with her before I go?"

"No, my lord. She wants you to get outside the borders of the kingdom as soon as possible. Gifts of exchange, your military escort, and seagoing ships await you at Per-nefer. Speak to the garrison commander there."

"I have no reply, then. But I invite you to stay the night here before you start back to the capital."

The man bobbed a grateful bow, his cool expression thawing. "Appreciated, Lord Hani."

Hani called a servant to show the man to a guest room—that seemed more appropriate than a pallet in the servants' quarters—and stumped heavily up the stairs and onto the roof terrace. "Nub-nefer, my dove. A word with you?"

She rose from where she sat on her heels on the smooth packed-clay surface, playing cat's-cradle with little Henut-sen. Her eyes were anxious behind her smile.

The two of them retreated to the stairwell, where Hani took his wife by the shoulders. "The queen has finally sent me on that mission I told you about."

Hope flared across Nub-nefer's golden face, and her great kohl-edged eyes grew fierce. "At last! Now the Aten will go back where he came from, and the Hidden One will reign again."

It warmed Hani's heart to see his wife's indomitable faith. Still, he wasn't so sure he saw good things following from this journey. His mission was to bring back to Kemet a bridegroom for the queen so that as soon as her mother, the she-king, should die—and Queen Meryet-aten apparently had reason to think that would be sooner rather than later—the girl would share the throne with him and reinstate the old cults. But the bridegroom would be a Hittite prince, which was so unimaginable that Hani could still hardly believe the young queen was going through with it. Kheta was the rival of the Two Lands. While Hani wasn't opposed to more friendly relations between the kingdoms, there would be many who would be scandalized by the plan, even devotees of the Hidden One. He only hoped it didn't end in disaster. Surely the Black Land had lived through more than its share over the past fourteen years.

"I need to leave immediately. I told the messenger he could stay the night, but as soon as I can pack, I'm taking off. I'll pick up Maya in Waset."

"All right, my dearest. Write to us often. I'll send the other children your love."

"Maybe I'll see Aha when I pass through Akhet-aten." *Or maybe not. This is hardly news I'd want him to think too closely about.* Aha, Hani's firstborn, was a devotee of the

Aten. "And Neferet and Bener-ib. I guess Pa-kiki will be on his way to Ta-nehesy with our friend Har-em-heb." Hani looked around, suddenly missing a familiar face. "Where is Father?"

"He must be outside somewhere. Baket said a messenger brought him a letter, and he went to the garden to read it. You surely want to say goodbye to him. As old as he is, one never knows."

That thought sat, chill as the walls of a deep well, in Hani's gut. He had started reflecting on it more and more. His beloved father, while healthy and strong for his age, was seventy-four, a ripe sum of years. As much as Hani hated the thought, Mery-ra wouldn't live forever. *And if I were to be gone when he passes over into the West?* Hani wasn't sure he could forgive himself. "I'll be sure to see him before I go."

Now, Hani told himself. *Before I get involved in packing.*

He set off through the farmyard. Near the low wall that separated the little yard from the agricultural fields, Hani's father stood, his back turned, seemingly reading something. Mery-ra was an older version of Hani—broad to the point of squat, with powerful shoulders and a cheerful, square-jowled face. Hani felt overcome with a burning wave of tenderness. *No one could have had a better parent.*

Mery-ra turned as Hani approached, and he slipped whatever he had been reading behind his back. Hani thought from the glimpse he caught that it looked like a clay tablet.

"Why, Hani, my boy. I thought you were out in the fields." The old man clapped him jovially on the shoulder and smiled his welcome, but his eyes shifted sideways in a guilty glance.

"What are you up to, Father?" Hani couldn't resist a teasing grin.

"Oh, just a letter from an old friend. What leads you to prowl around the garden, son?"

Hani's smile grew tight. "A messenger just came from the queen."

Mery-ra's thick black eyebrows rose. "I wondered whose big boat that was, tying up."

"She's ready for my mission to Kheta."

Mery-ra's eyes widened then narrowed in what might have been a considering look. After a moment, he said, "Ah, my boy, this could be dangerous. You need protection."

"Menna and Pa-ra-mes-su will be leading the escort," Hani assured him. "They're both loyal to the queen."

"Soldiers, yes, but who's going to be your eyes and ears?"

Hani had a sense he knew where his father was leading and said firmly, "Maya. I need you to protect the women in our absence—which will certainly be a number of months."

"It seems to me, my boy, that what you need is a battle-tried emissary at your side to feel people out. Someone with long experience dealing with foreigners. One who speaks Neshite." Mery-ra looked up at Hani with a sly grin that bared the gap between his front teeth.

But Hani was adamant. "No, Father. This is going to be a very hard journey—we'll be traveling as fast as we can with the fewest number of breaks. And the gods know how many people will be out to stop us from getting to Hattusha."

"All the more reason you need me. I've been to Hattusha." Mery-ra crossed his arms, triumphant.

Hani jerked back in surprise. "You have? I didn't know that."

"You were only four at the time. Trust me, son. There's plenty you don't know."

"No. Absolutely no. This is dangerous. And by the Lord Djehuty, it's an official mission for the queen. I can't just bring my relatives along for a lark." Hani had an unpleasant feeling that his father had already considered such an objection.

Sure enough, Mery-ra said smugly, "You'll have staff, won't you? I'm a better scribe than most of those youngsters, whose script looks like they've written it with their left feet."

Knowing he was defeated, Hani shook his head, lips compressed and face hot with the pressure of all the ripostes that wanted to fly out. "Then we both need to pack. I'm leaving by midafternoon, and anyone who isn't ready will be left behind."

"That's my boy. You'll be amazed at how useful your old papa is. People don't take a venerable gentleman all that seriously. They'll reveal things to me you'd never get out of them."

The two men set off toward the house stride for stride while the geese and ducks scattered at their feet. Hani knew better than to hope to change his father's mind. He couldn't imagine what had put the idea into Mery-ra's head, but there would be no moving him. Mery-ra was as cheerfully stubborn as his granddaughter Neferet. And Hani could imagine that the old man would probably be helpful. *Still, the danger...*

29

❖

In Waset, they picked up Maya, who had gone home to supervise some workmen at the house while the rest of the family enjoyed their time at Lord Hani's farm. Although Maya had expected the call to leave the Two Lands eventually, it had caught him by surprise. He trudged up the gangplank of Hani's boat, feeling mildly disgruntled. The first thing he said to his father-in-law was "I didn't get a chance to say goodbye to Sati and the children."

"She knows where we've gone, son. You can write to her when we put in to shore tonight."

Maya sighed in resignation. Then behind Hani's back, he saw Lord Mery-ra, his hands on his hips, looking pleased with himself. Maya's eyes widened with surprise. "My lord. Are you accompanying us to Per-nefer?"

Mery-ra toddled forward and laid a conspiratorial hand on his son's shoulder. He said to Maya with a grin that split his cheeks, "I'm accompanying you to Hattusha."

Maya stared from one man to the other. He didn't know what to say and eventually managed to stammer, "O-Oh?"

Unseen by his father behind him, Lord Hani rolled his eyes. "Yes. He's familiar with the city and has invited himself along as part of my staff."

As much as he loved the old man, Maya's heart chilled, suddenly grown as heavy as a rock. He had looked forward to the uniquely close relationship to his father-in-law a long journey opened to him. They would have been on the deck of a ship for endless weeks together, with only each other to talk to, play word games with, and plan their course of action. They would have shared the experience of making land in exotic places together, forming memories that only the two of them would laugh over afterward, and faced danger at each other's side.

Now, of course, Lord Hani would talk to and confide in his father. The two highborn men would share the jokes, enriched by their lifetime of familiarity. Lord Mery-ra would be sent on delicate fact-finding missions instead of Maya. Maya would be pushed to the side. He would be reduced to a mere secretary. And even there, who knew. Perhaps the old man would supplant him as Hani's amanuensis.

Disappointment crushed Maya to the ground, and he could scarcely make his face smile. "How wonderful. Welcome, my lord."

Hani caught Maya's eye with a penetrating look and quirked his mouth a little—in amusement or compassion or both—as if he could read his son-in-law's thoughts. "We'll join our party at Per-nefer. The commandant has staff and an escort waiting for us and all the diplomatic gifts the queen has gathered for the negotiations. Meantime, we might as well enjoy our last sight of Kemet for a while."

The three men found a seat under the tented sunshade toward the stern. Hani's small yacht, which he had bought from his brother Pipi to save Pipi from bankruptcy, had no cabin, unlike the much larger vessel of Lord Ptah-mes, his former superior. But it was still a vast improvement over a public ferry—cleaner, more private, and decidedly more appropriate for the Master of the King's Stable. The sailors were well fed and respectful. And the voyagers could stop or even reverse course anytime they liked.

Besides, Maya reminded himself, fellow travelers would stare enviously at the jaunty, expensive-looking boat, painted bright red and green with a grinning Bes-head on the prow, and ask themselves what dignitary was passing.

They sat for a bit, cross-legged on the deck in the small square of shade, while Maya chewed over his disappointment.

All at once, he remembered something he had meant to tell his father-in-law. "My mother said to let you know her chief workman was found murdered, my lord. A fellow named Ipy. You've seen some of his work."

"I'm sorry to hear that," Hani replied in a tone of genuine sorrow. "He was a real artist."

"Right now, of all times, when her workshop is straining to complete a big royal order, which I suspect is for the king's tomb. And Mother had planned to leave the workshop to Ipy when she retires."

Maya had suffered pangs of guilt over that revelation. It should have been he, her only son, who carried on the family business of royal goldsmith. But of course, he had chosen the career of a scribe. As In-hapy approached old age and the inevitable loss of keen eyesight that signaled the end of a jeweler's career, she didn't know what to do. She didn't want to close the shop and take jobs away from the men and boys who worked for her. Maya felt somehow obliquely to blame. A good son would have abandoned his ambitions to support his parent in her later years. It occurred to him that that was why he was in such a self-pitying mood.

"She, er, she was hoping we could find out who killed him—not that that would bring him back, but... you know. For his family's sake," Maya added. His conscience throbbing like a boil, he had almost stayed behind in order to perform this service for his mother. But the lure of adventure and prestige had been too strong.

And now, Lord Mery-ra.

Hani said reluctantly, "As much as I'd love to help her, I don't see how we can, Maya. It will be months before we get done with this mission. Unless you want to turn back."

There they were—the words Maya had dreaded to hear.

"No, no. Official business comes first," he said hastily. "I just wanted you to know."

Eventually, squinting as he gazed across the bright water, Lord Mery-ra said, "It'll take us... What? A week or more to reach the coast of the Great Green?"

"I would think so," Hani said. "On the 'more' side, probably."

"Then how many weeks to Kheta Land? Is the capital on the coast?" Maya asked.

"By no means. It's very far north, in the highlands. Days'—maybe weeks'—journey from the port at Ura." Lord Mery-ra's little brown eyes twinkled. "Unless they've moved Hattusha in the last fifty years."

Lord Hani laughed and shook his head.

"And if we put in farther east and have to go all the way through the land of Kidjuwadna, the mountains are even worse. You think you've seen mountains in A'amu— these are the grandfathers to those little hillocks." Mery-ra chuckled at the memory.

Maya thought glumly, *Are we going to be listening to reminiscences the whole way? Reminders that some of us haven't been to Hattusha?* He felt for the Bes amulet hanging around his neck, as if to send up a prayer for help.

Lord Hani took a deep breath of the fine air. "You

know," he said, "I don't think we're going to reach the capital before nightfall after all. We'll just stop in Seyawt or wherever we've gotten when dusk comes. There was no real reason I needed to go to Akhet-aten except to say goodbye to the girls." His daughter and her friend were physicians to the ladies of the court.

"And we can write our wives tonight, right, my lord?" Maya asked.

But Mery-ra looked sly. "Ah, who will read the letters to them, though? All of us literate fellows are here."

Hani gave a snort of laughter. "It was your choice to abandon them, Father. Aren't you ashamed? Maybe Amen-em-hut, now that he's back among the living. Or we'll have to have Pipi join them for a few months."

All we need is for the indiscreet Lord Pipi to start asking where the rest of us are. Lord Hani's brother, also a scribe, was always begging to help Hani in his investigations. "Surely there's a neighborhood scribe somewhere around," Maya said.

"No doubt," Hani said cheerfully. His eyes were fixed over the water, on the flight of some kind of big bird with its long legs trailing. Then he turned back to Maya with a more serious expression. "I think we need to write a letter to Lord Ay, my friend. He made a point of telling me to let him know when we took off. I'm assuming it will reach him in the field too late for him to do anything about it." He lifted an eyebrow.

Mery-ra slitted his eyes suspiciously. "What's he up to, the old fox? He can't really want this mission to succeed."

"I'm sure I don't know, Father. But whatever he has

in mind, we're right in the middle of it. Don't say I didn't warn you."

✦

The journey downriver took every bit as long as Hani had foreseen—his new yacht might be more comfortable than a ferry, but it was no faster. By the time the men reached Per-nefer on the coast of the Great Green, they were already tired of being confined to a small deck. In relief, they disembarked at that last Egyptian port in the estuary of the River and struck off into the town to find the local commandant. There, they would change to a seagoing vessel for the second leg of the journey and send Hani's little boat back upstream.

The worst is yet to come. Hani sighed. *That endless voyage from one end to the other of the Great Green, across the heaving waves.*

He had to admit that, despite his reservations, his father was a delightful addition to the traveling party. As a former military scribe, Mery-ra was accustomed to bearing difficult conditions without complaint, and his unshakably cheerful and humorous presence helped to lighten the hours. Hani observed, to his amusement, that Maya had been disgruntled at first—he was transparently jealous when it came to Hani's favor—but he was back to himself, won over despite his insecurities.

The commandant of the port garrison was a burly man in his thirties with a big slab of a nose and ears to match. Firmly in the camp of the Hidden One, he seemed willing to put the queen's orders before any the king might have given him. The man drew Hani and his small entourage discreetly into his office.

"My lords, we've gathered here everything you'll need. I'll introduce you to your staff and show you the gifts our lady has put aside for you whenever you're ready. Two young officers you already know will be leading the escort of a hundred troops."

"That's very generous," Hani said.

"Your cargo will be valuable, Lord Hani. Going... but even more valuable coming back." The commandant fixed Hani with a knowing stare. "May the King of the Gods watch over you, my lord. There will be those who will want to stop you."

Hani thanked the man sincerely and let himself be led to the treasure room, where the diplomatic gifts were being kept. Mery-ra and Maya trailed after him in silence.

"We do have Lady Meryet-aten's letters, don't we? Signed with her seal?" Hani whispered to his secretary.

"Yes, my lord. In Egyptian and in Akkadian."

"Good man."

Their young guide led them down a maze of hallways to a ponderous bronze-strapped door sealed with a lump of clay and a string. From its bracket on the wall, he unmounted a torch, broke the clay door seal, and let the men into the room. Hani took the torch and held it up. In the small pool of orange light, he saw the rich glint of gold vessels, bolts of fine linen, elephant tusks, leopard pelts, bundles of ostrich plumes, and inlaid chests. It was a fabulous treasure—like a glimpse into a storehouse of the gods—one that should soften the heart of the Great King of Kheta Land, no matter how obdurate he might prove to be.

"These pieces"—the soldier carefully opened a small enameled casket—"are especially for the prince, I'm told. The servant who brought them said not to touch them. It will tarnish the silver."

Hani saw by the flickering light of the torch a pair of magnificent cuff bracelets made of gold and silver, inlaid with turquoise, carnelian, and lapis in what appeared to be writing. Awed, he sucked in a breath. They were the only things in the treasure trove he wouldn't have minded having for his own—not that he wore much jewelry. But their value could have ransomed a king.

"This is perfect," Hani said to the soldier. "I'll want a detailed list of everything, of course."

"I'll have it ready for you, my lord."

"Could we see Menna and Pa-ra-mes-su this afternoon, or are they busy organizing their men?"

The young soldier assured him the officers of the escort would be more than happy to meet with him, and with a brisk clap of a fist across his chest in salute, he turned and disappeared down the darkening corridor.

Once they were alone, Maya gave an appreciative whistle.

"Our queen was serious about those diplomatic gifts, wasn't she?" Mery-ra said with a waggle of his eyebrows. "She must have raided the treasury. If anybody knows what we're carrying, I'm not sure a hundred men is enough."

"Meryet-aten is trying to convince the king of Kheta to do something pretty extraordinary. This should help sweeten the request." In silence, Hani pondered the dangers of traveling with such objects. Certainly, they were safer at sea than they would have been on the Way of Haru, but the increasingly large delegation would have to take two or even more ships, without a doubt. Hani wasn't sure what he thought about separating himself from the gifts for which he was responsible.

"Lord Hani!" came an ebullient voice from behind him.

Hani turned to see the welcome face of Menna, a man whose life he had saved as a young soldier and who was now devoted to him. Menna—who had to be forty, Hani suspected—had been promoted to regiment commander some while back, but he was the same old lean, dark-skinned, bucktoothed fellow as always, his wide, frank eyes creased with joy. Behind him stood the good-looking Pa-ra-mes-su, General Har-em-heb's adjutant, with his predatory nose. It spoke eloquently of the importance of their mission that Har-em-heb had relinquished him in the middle of the Nubian campaign.

With genuine affection, Hani embraced both the men in turn, and Menna nodded respectfully to Hani's father then said, "We have handpicked troops for you, Lord Hani. Each of them is sworn to fight for the glory of the Hidden One."

"Excellent, Menna. I can't tell you how much better I feel with you two on guard. I'm afraid we may encounter opposition, whether from the Hittites or our own government."

Menna raised an eyebrow in acknowledgement. "Our men are all ready to go, my lord. We have three vessels secured, and we'll split our forces so that each ship has an escort at sea, then when we stop for the night, we'll rejoin one another. Once we're on land, of course, we'll all be there to protect you."

"Do you know your way through Kheta, son?" asked Mery-ra.

"We don't, my lord," Menna admitted. "We'll have to depend on local guides. Surely the king will contact us as soon as he discovers an armed party of foreigners entering his territory."

Contact us or shoot us full of arrows, Hani thought grimly.

Beaming, Mery-ra said, "Lucky for you and Pa-ra-mes-su, I've been to Kheta. I can guide you."

"Fifty years ago, Father. Things might conceivably have changed." Hani shot him a dry grin.

"Well, the mountains and valleys will be in the same spots, won't they?"

"Your help will be appreciated," Pa-ra-mes-su said diplomatically.

The two officers took their leave, and Hani and his party made their way back to the rooms that had been assigned to them.

"Who's ready for dinner?" Hani asked more cheerfully than he felt. "It's our last Egyptian meal for weeks. I hope the commandant has a good cook. What I wouldn't give for Nub-nefer's fried fish or meat pies with cumin!"

Some benevolent god must have heard Hani, because when their meal was delivered to the chamber, it contained both steaming meat pies, fresh from the oven, and small fishes fried to a delicious crisp along with stewed leeks and plenty of bread. And best of all were the little cones of honey and ground sedge nuts.

As Hani bit in, the saliva fountained up appreciatively in his mouth. "Ah!" he cried. "Our commandant has an *excellent* cook. They're almost as good as Nub-nefer's."

"Why don't we just stay at Per-nefer for the rest of our lives?" Mery-ra asked with a chuckle. He brushed crumbs off his belly where they had sprinkled with his first bite of pastry. "My recollection of Hittite food is that it was pretty dull."

His mouth full of leeks, Maya said, "How are we going to divide the men on the ships, my lord? Will the three of us be together?" A wrinkle of anxiety pleated the secretary's brow.

"I think we three and the treasure should be together, with about a third of the troops. We won't be attacked on the water, surely. The rest of the staff and the other soldiers will travel together, and we'll all spend the night on deck when we dock in the evening."

"You know, there are such things as pirates, son," Mery-ra said, suddenly serious. "Maybe it would be safer to divide the treasure among the three ships. Surely you can trust our young officers to oversee its guard."

Hani considered that, gnawing his lip. "I think you're right, Father. If we're attacked, we don't want to lose everything. That would end our mission right there." He reached out for the last fish and threw it into his mouth. "I'll talk to Menna and Pa-ra-mes-su in the morning and see what they think."

Once they had reduced the little tables to a litter of bones, crumbs, and fruit peels, Hani rose and stretched with a satisfying roar. "I vote for going to bed. 'Man ignores how the morrow will be,' but I predict it will start early."

CHAPTER 2

MAYA TRIED TO RETAIN AN event or two that could be embellished for his Tales. The family always loved to hear about his and Lord Hani's adventures, and some day, Maya hoped to write them down. But before long, the next few weeks began to blur in his mind: sailing the featureless water by day. A painfully burnished blue sky. Conversation growing spottier and spottier as the three scribes ran out of new things to say. Pulling onto the land at night in one or another interchangeable harbor, with a close-packed, whitewashed town looming above them. Sunset over the water, creating a slick of ruddy light across the deck. Cold picnic meals brought by one of the soldiers from the local market. Seagulls, endless seagulls. Only Lord Hani continued to watch them with interest.

Maya wondered that he had ever found ocean voyages so thrilling. He could remember his first trip north to the vassal state of Gubla many years ago and how every detail was etched in gold, indelibly, on his memory. This journey, he thought would never end. It was the longest three weeks of his life.

Finally, a large, misty body of land rose out of the sea to their left, and Lord Mery-ra, pointing, said excitedly, "There's Alashiya. We're almost to Kheta."

"Or more properly, Kidjuwadna, which is where we'll land. Lord Ptah-mes sent me word at Kebni when we stopped there that Kidjuwadna has been in revolt. Let's hope that's been resolved, or they may refuse us passage inland." Lord Hani didn't sound worried.

But Maya pushed back his wig and scratched his head uneasily. "Why do we have to go through Kidjuwadna's port?"

"Because Kheta is completely cut off from the sea," said Hani. "Its only coasts are those of its vassals. You can see why they've been so aggressively conquering new territory under this king—they have very few resources of their own."

"Except for rocks," Lord Mery-ra said with a knowing wink.

Maya rolled his eyes inwardly. *I know, I know. You're the only one of us who's been here.* But he had to admit Lord Mery-ra had been as generous as his son in helping Maya learn a few words of the Hittites' barbaric language, with its harsh gutturals and slushy esses.

As Alashiya's great island evaporated into the misty horizon behind them, Maya began to tingle once more with the excitement of the unknown ahead. A stiff headwind was blowing, and he faced into it, snuffing the salty air, darkened with what he fancied was the smell of land ahead. The gulls had grown more numerous and more frantic.

One could almost imagine they were towing the ship to its destination.

The three men stood watching the horizon before them as the vessel leaped forward over increasingly choppy water. Lord Hani, in concentrated silence, had cupped his hands around his eyes as if to block the glare and focus his sight.

Finally, some time in midafternoon, he cried out, "There it is, gentlemen. The port of Ura. We're here."

The town was not as strange as Maya had feared, despite the fact that Kheta was practically the ends of the earth. It had a busy waterfront, familiar enough, where ships rocked at berth, and longshoremen carried cargo to the shore through the shallow green water, churning it into muddy foam. Crowds of people in a variety of garments moved about, shouting orders in their own tongues. There were more foreigners than Maya remembered in Per-nefer. Behind the embarcadero rose a town of stone and mudbrick that had about it something deeply exotic—the heavy, exposed girders that marked the stories, the round, projecting ends of roof beams, and the scalloped crenellations of the fortress that crowned the hills. Indeed, the hills themselves and the fierce mountains that rose behind them like a menacing purple shadow proclaimed the otherness of the place.

"We can't unload our gifts until I find the local governor and get his permission to enter the kingdom. We do have soldiers, after all." Lord Hani observed the shore as their ship slid into shallow water, and the sailors dropped the stone anchors. Maya watched, too, goggle eyed. The trip was his first to a truly foreign land, altogether outside the borders of Egypt's control. His boredom was abating fast, and a kind of tingling in his middle reminded him that he was, in fact, on a great adventure such as few of his countrymen would ever experience. And it wasn't without danger.

At Lord Hani's side, Lord Mery-ra breathed in the salty air deeply. "Ah, just as I remember it. Those aren't the biggest mountains, but they're impressive. You won't believe the terrain in this kingdom."

The three scribes trooped down the bouncing gangplank while the officers kept guard over the treasure. A prosperous-looking man dressed like the Hittite Maya had encountered a year or two ago in Djahy was standing on the quay with a wooden tablet in his hands, watching the unlading of a squat commercial ship and making notes with his stylus. *A merchant, no doubt.*

Lord Hani approached him and called in Neshite, the language of the place, "You, my lord—I'm looking for directions. Can you help me?"

The man glanced up. He appeared to be about Hani's age, a tall personage with a ruddy, clean-shaven face and long brown hair topped with a cap. When he replied, it was not in quite the same tongue.

Naturally, we picked a foreigner, Maya thought.

But the man seemed to understand them quite well, and although Maya could barely recognize a word here and there, Hani appeared to comprehend his reply. The broad gesture up the hillside was clear.

After thanking the man, the scribes turned back to the wharf. As they walked, Hani said, "The governor's residence is that castle on the hilltop. We'll need to hire some donkeys."

"What language was he speaking, my lord?" Maya asked, scratching his head. "Or was it just some strange accent?"

Lord Mery-ra said, "It's Luwian, the language of the Hittites' predecessors in this land. I think there's more of it down here than of Neshite." Seeing Maya's confusion, he explained, "The Luwians outnumber the men of Kheta, so their language is the one people in the street use most commonly."

"So I learned Neshite for nothing?" Maya cried, disappointed.

Hani threw back his head and laughed. "No, no. The two languages are so similar that people who speak one can understand the other. And Neshite is the court language, so it's more important to know that. Of course, official documents are written in Akkadian."

"Which you write quite well," Mery-ra added handsomely.

Maya's ruffled feathers subsided.

At the foot of the gangplank, they could see Menna hanging over the gunwales above them. "What word, my lords?" he called out.

"We're heading up to that fortress on the hill, and we need donkeys. Do any of your men speak the local language?"

Menna grinned. "I doubt it, my lord. Unless we've got a Hittite spy somewhere among the troops."

"I can go ask, son," Mery-ra offered. "Everybody must

need transportation for their cargo—there have to be donkeys around. How many do we need?"

Hani handed over a little bag that clinked alluringly. "Find us twenty, Father. Maybe Maya can go with you." He shot his secretary a sly wink. "He can practice his Neshite. As for me, I'll pay a little visit to the local dignitary."

While Lord Hani remained to organize the debarkation, Mery-ra and Maya set off down the quay, edging between the busy longshoremen and sailors, until they saw a small train of donkeys being loaded with sacks. Lord Mery-ra drew up to one of the workers and asked, "Where can we find some pack animals, my good man?"

"These are my master's own," the fellow replied. "But there's a stable just in there"—he gestured toward the thick of the town—"near the market. They'll sell you some."

They set off inland down the street the man had indicated, Maya craning his neck around, round-eyed with wonder. The farther behind they left the quay, the less familiar things looked. Like the cities of Kharu and unlike all but the poorest of his homeland, the place was tightly packed, the houses very close together with no gardens to space them—even sharing walls. It was a busy place, with streams of passersby dressed in colorful woolen tunics, either very short or halfway down the calf, wide belts, and close-fitted caps on their long hair. The women were so heavily dressed one could hardly appreciate their shape. And everyone seemed gigantically tall.

"Do you spot anything that looks like a stable?" Mery-ra asked under his breath.

Maya shaded his eyes with a hand and stared around. Perhaps Hittite stables didn't look the same as those of home, but he recognized nothing. "No, my lord. What do we do now?"

"Let's go a little farther. If we don't find anything, we may have to ask again."

They set off once more, Maya seeing very little from his position at the bottom of the crowd. Lord Mery-ra toddled along at his side, his head swinging first one way then another. Before long, they came to an open space thronged with people that was clearly a market. The noise level rose considerably, with the cries of merchants, the gabble of shoppers, and the thud of boxes and bags heaved to the ground. A not-very-pleasant smell of fish, bloody cuts of meat, and unknown spices filled the air along with that of sweaty people dressed in wool. There were certainly donkeys around.

And at last, they saw a *lot* of donkeys roped together in a picket line, bearing the noise and jostling with admirable long-suffering. The merchant called out the praises of his living wares enthusiastically, and although Maya didn't catch every word, he recognized "beautiful boys." Several people seemed to be haggling with the man's assistants. Donkeys apparently sold well in the city of offloaded ships.

"Ah," Lord Mery-ra cried in satisfaction. "Here we are." He pushed his way to the front of the crowd, trying to catch the merchant's attention, with Maya elbowing through the crush of bodies in his wake.

The merchant's eyes lit on those of Mery-ra. "Ah, these foreign gentlemen. Here are the best donkeys you'll find in the whole of Hatti Land, my lords." He shook the felty ear of the animal nearest him in a companionable gesture and fixed the two men with a sly, amicable smile. "Where are you from, friends?"

"From Mizri," Lord Mery-ra said genially, using the foreign version of Kemet's name. "We represent our government on a mission to your king. Do you have twenty donkeys well trained as pack animals?"

"Anything for you, my lord, even if I have to deplete my own herd." The merchant yelled for one of his assistants and gestured behind him with a hand in what Maya assumed to be an order to bring donkeys.

Lord Mery-ra watched the merchant narrowly, and once the fellow's back was turned, he asked the customer beside him in an undertone, "Is he honest?"

The man shrugged and grinned. "His animals are good. But don't pay too much for them."

He mentioned what he thought was a fair price, and Mery-ra clapped him on the back in affable gratitude. "I appreciate your frankness, my friend. Here's to trade and friendship between our two nations."

The merchant's assistant led a string of donkeys through the crowd while the merchant danced around, pointing out their finer attributes—strong backs, healthy coats, and well-cared-for legs and hooves. To the animals' annoyance, he parted their lips to display the great yellow teeth. "Young and strong, my lord. Worthy of the embassage of your great kingdom. Are you bringing Our Sun gifts?"

This seemed to Maya a rather too-probing question, and he was relieved when Lord Mery-ra said with an innocent smile, "We're a large party. A lot of soldiers."

At first, the merchant asked far too much for the animals, but Maya assumed one was expected to haggle for such a purchase, and haggle Mery-ra did, with a gusto and humor that suggested—falsely—that he did all the family marketing. Eventually, the donkeys were theirs for rather less than what the shopper had suggested was a fair price, and the two scribes led the animals forth, each holding the line for half of them.

Maya had never actually dealt with donkeys before, although, like everyone, he saw them all the time in the street. They seemed dozy and docile, but he was mindful of their considerable weight and hard hooves clopping at his heels—and those formidable teeth at his shoulder. However, they regained the docks with their purchases, untrampled and unbitten. Lord Hani, they found, had left to see the governor alone, and Maya forced back his disappointment.

❦

The governor's residence was a real fortress, set well up on a steep hill above the port. Hani recollected that Kidjuwadna was still a reluctant vassal of Kheta. Perhaps such a redoubt was necessary. If not, it provided an eloquent symbol of Hittite domination.

He had decided to unpack the litter and travel in style, as behooved a representative of the queen of the Two Lands, so he arrived with a certain amount of ceremony at the gate, a strangely arched affair in a substantial tower.

Soldiers in fringed white tunics lowered their spears as he approached.

"I am an ambassador from the King's Great Wife of Mizri," Hani said in Neshite, summoning an appropriate bit of diplomatic pomposity. "I wish to speak to your governor about passage to Hattusha."

They permitted him to enter, and Hani proceeded through a courtyard filled with milling soldiers and scribes to the residence itself. He noticed from the corner of his eye that he had attracted a few curious stares, but he marched with an easy air up to the open doorway, where an official of some sort stood as if waiting for him. *Perhaps he's always there, in case someone seeks an audience.*

Hani announced himself once more, and the man led him directly to the governor's office.

The governor sat at a heavy table strewn with clay tablets. He looked up, unsurprised, at Hani's entrance. He was a little younger than Hani, a rather small man for this tall people, wiry and sharp-faced, but there was an honest, intelligent look about him that pleased Hani.

"So here you are," the man said, rising. "My people have reported on your arrival. We don't get many Egyptians on our shores."

Hani responded with a respectful bow and offered his diplomatic credentials. "My name is Hani son of Mery-ra, my lord. I represent the Great Queen of my country, who desires a word with your king and his royal wife. A word of amity that I think will please them. We have brought gifts appropriate to their majesty."

"And my name is Prince Taruppishni, the governor of Ura." The governor nodded back, a thin smile of understanding on his lips. "You also have soldiers, if I'm not mistaken."

"I do, my prince. Which is the main reason I wanted to pay my respects. To reassure you we're not here as a conquering force. They're present only to assure the safety of our gifts." Hani grinned. He could see the governor

50

understood as well as he the sometimes-tense relationship between the two nations.

Taruppishni nodded and came around the table to stand before Hani, one fist on his hip. "I think we can assist you there, although I understand the desire to send an impressive delegation to honor Our Sun." He spread his hands in a welcoming gesture. "Please be my guest overnight. Perhaps we can discuss the matter of a guide, since Hattusha is a goodly distance from Ura, and some routes are more dangerous than others." He shot Hani a sharp, amused glance. "There have been a few unfortunate episodes of bad manners among the people of this area."

"I'm sure you have them under control now," Hani said blandly.

The prince's smile deepened. "The might of Hatti is irresistible. Have you been able to provide yourself with pack animals and drivers?"

"I have men looking for donkeys right now, my prince. But our soldiers can double as muleteers."

"I hope you don't pay too much for the animals. We could have provided you with some. I can certainly lend you professional donkey drivers."

Hani tipped his head in grateful acknowledgment. "As to the guide, my father, who is among us, is pretty well instructed in the ways of your kingdom, my lord. He was once sent here as a military scribe."

"Ah." The governor lifted an eyebrow. "That must have been a number of years ago."

After a few more amiable exchanges, Hani took his leave and headed back to the port, where the other members of his delegation waited for his return.

Maya and Mery-ra were standing at the top of the gangplank, and a small crowd of other staff members milled about, some hanging over the gunwales, fanning themselves with their wigs. Hani still didn't have their measure. None of them were men he knew, but the queen and Lord Mai had considered them loyal and competent.

Hani dismounted from his litter on the dock and waved. "All is well. We're to stay at the governor's residence tonight." He trudged noisily up the bouncing plank. "Where are our officers?"

"Menna is below, supervising the removal of the gifts, and Pa-ra-mes-su is out watching the donkeys being loaded. No light-fingered barbarians are going to lift our diplomatic gifts." Mery-ra grinned and drew his son toward him. "How did it go? Is the governor suspicious of our intentions?"

"I would say not. I'm sure he rather liked the idea of rich presents for his king. He's a member of the royal family, I think."

"I bet he's asking himself what under the sun we're doing here, though," Maya said. "Up to now, the Great House has hardly even responded to their overtures of friendship. Isn't that so, Lord Hani?"

"It was certainly true under Nefer-khepru-ra. I'm not sure where Lord Ay stands—I mean his daughter, of course." They all knew that the king's father exercised enormous power over her decisions. "I suppose, given their attitude toward cooperation, the men of Kheta won't be disappointed at our appearance."

Maya laughed. "They'll never guess the full reason for our coming. Never in a million years."

"I find it hard to believe myself," Mery-ra said, with a lift of his eyebrows. He looked suddenly thoughtful and stared out into space. "Indeed, I do."

Before Hani went to see Menna below, he stood for a moment on deck, gazing out over the town. The temperature was hot, but the air was mellowed and moistened by the sea, and the sky was the gauzy turquoise of an early-summer midmorning. The clay-colored jumble of the city lay still half empurpled with the shadow of the mountains in the east—a veiled place, not quite easily read. Foreign. At least the white-and-gray gulls, flapping, strutting, and screeching all along the shore and rising in indignant clouds were familiar. *And people,* Hani told himself, *are the same everywhere.*

He pondered his mission and how much he believed in the desperate effort to assure a princely consort for the queen, who fancied herself a she-king like her mother. *How might the men of Kheta Land exploit her desperation?* And all because she didn't accept the legitimacy of the Haru in the nest, Prince Tut-ankh-aten—whom Hani knew to be completely royal, a more legitimate heir than his half sister. *Should I somehow make this known?* he wondered in an agony of doubt. But it was too late for that. Now, he had only to ask himself how far he was willing to stretch the truth should the Hittites ask him directly if there were no heir.

❖

Hani awoke the next morning a little stiff. The night had been unexpectedly chilly, and he had never quite found a comfortable position to sleep in. Mery-ra was snoring away, sprawled on his back in his own bed. The two men had shared a room, and Maya had been quartered among the secretarial staff—which Hani could well imagine would have put him in a huffy mood.

Hani indulged in a gigantic stretch but muffled the usual roar out of deference to his father's dreams. He got dressed quietly and, still tying his kilt, headed downstairs to walk around a bit in the courtyard of the residence until the rest of his party had awakened.

It was a fine morning for traveling—the summer sun was climbing in a flawless sky and the night's chill fast burning away along with the faint mist that blurred the town and port below. A thin cry drew Hani's eyes to the heavens, where he saw a hunting eagle high, high above, floating down from the mountains. The bird in his sky was already bathed in light that had yet to reach the castle. Hani drew a deep breath of admiration.

"My lord," Maya said from behind him.

Hani turned to see his secretary trundling toward him across the court, still rubbing the slumber from his eyes. "Ah, Maya, my son. You're up early."

"I couldn't sleep," Maya said in a surly voice. "One of those damned secretaries snorted and snored all night long. It was like trying to sleep in a carpenter's shop."

Hani laughed. "We'll probably be camping tonight somewhere in the mountains. That should be quiet enough. You may long for the governor's residence and ten men alongside you."

Maya gave a dubious snort. Then changing the subject abruptly as if it had been on his mind all along, he said,

"You know, my lord, Sat-hut-haru will probably have given birth by the time we get home from this trip."

"Something to look forward to, eh?" Hani grinned, but then he shot his son-in-law a sideways glance and said diffidently, "This is really none of my business, Maya, but speaking from my own family experience, you might want to let her nurse the children herself."

Maya looked surprised. "Isn't that a little working-class? I can afford a wet nurse for three or four years."

"No, no. Nub-nefer did it. It helps to space the children out. We had the first two just a year apart, and it was hard on her. Sati might appreciate a little rest." *I hope I don't come across as an overprotective, interfering father,* he thought.

But Maya, his brow furrowed, appeared to be considering Hani's words without rancor. "I'll see what she'd like to do. But we do want a big family, Lord Hani."

"Of course you do. And I want lots of grandchildren. But it's hard on Sati if they come too close together. That's all I'm trying to say."

Hani's forehead was already damp. The nursing habits of another man's wife were a delicate subject, even if she was Hani's daughter. He was relieved to see his father emerging from the door of the governor's residence. "Ah, Father. About time you were up."

"Oh, I was awake when you left the room, son. Just lying in bed, thinking." Mery-ra glanced around and lowered his voice. "You need someone to intervene on your behalf at court here, someone who'll put the king in a favorable mood. He may find a request such as you're bringing a little hard to believe unless someone vouches for you."

"Well, what can I do about it? None of us has any

contacts here. I think our gifts are intended to convince this Shuppiluliuma of our serious intent." The same concern had occurred to him, but it had been so long since Kemet and Hatti had enjoyed diplomatic relations that no one really stood in a place between the two.

Mery-ra cleared his throat modestly. "I've been here, you know."

A mixture of affection and annoyance drew a smile to Hani's lips. He gave Mery-ra's arm a shake. "After fifty years, I suspect not many of your contacts are still among us, Father. And anyway, you were just a military scribe, not an ambassador."

The old man gave a noncommittal hum, and Hani could see Maya roll his eyes on the other side of him.

"I may have been something more than an officer's secretary, my boy. Let's just say I knew people above me in rank."

"You were a spy, then?" Hani asked, grinning. Other whispers of that suspicion had entered his ears before.

Mery-ra raised an ambiguous eyebrow and clasped his hands over his belly as if to signal that not a word would pass his lips.

Hani said, "I think our friend Prince Hattusha-ziti might be a possible go-between. I don't know what position he holds in the government here, but he was obviously trusted enough to be sent on a mission of rapprochement." The Hittite had sought Hani out in Djahy the previous year, hoping to open peace talks between their two kingdoms.

"I'm just saying don't overlook an obvious resource."

Maya blew a huge breath out his nose, but he managed to keep his voice neutral. "It might look offensive to approach the prince even before we contacted his king, Lord Mery-ra. We're here as the messengers between one ruler and another."

As day had risen, the courtyard was filling up with people, and Hani didn't want to pursue a sensitive discussion in such a public place.

To his relief, the governor of the port approached them from the direction of the residence, a young man in a fringed white tunic and leather leggings at his heels. "Lord Hani," Taruppishni called. "Your officers tell me you're preparing to move out after breakfast. I offer this fine lad to be your guide and interpreter, if you need one—your Neshite is certainly good, but sometimes there are subtleties and issues of court etiquette. I can vouch for him. He's my son." He smiled proudly and clapped the boy on the shoulder.

"We would be honored, my prince. I'm sure his services will be invaluable. What's your name, young friend?"

"Pirwa, my lord."

"He's working his way up through the ranks," his father said as if to explain the simple soldier's garb. "I think his presence will save you some explanations as you cross the interior."

"We thank you, Prince Taruppishni. I assure you we'll take good care of this lad of yours." Hani smiled benevolently.

The governor gave his son a slap on the back and took his leave.

Hani turned to Pirwa. "We look forward to traveling with you. It's generous of your father to lend us your services."

The youth bobbed in a slight bow. "He wants to see friendship between our kingdoms. So do I. So do we all."

Glad to hear that, Hani thought, encouraged. He looked at the boy who was to be their guide. Pirwa was rather taller than his father, a fresh-faced fellow of less than twenty years. *He might still be in the Haru lock at home.* But he was sturdy in a wiry way, with long, wavy brown hair and frank greenish-brown eyes in a sharp-nosed, lightly freckled face. Although there was nothing similar in their appearance, his open expression reminded Hani of his own second son, Pa-kiki.

Hani eyed him with a fatherly gaze as the boy turned to go then reminded himself not to be too quick to like people. They all had an agenda. He said to himself half seriously, *I wonder whether he's a guide or a spy.*

※

Before the sun was halfway up the cloudless sky, they set off inland. Hani was sure word of their approach had already reached the king of Kheta. The Hittites had made occasional overtures during the reign of the late Nefer-khepru-ra, but he had been either opposed or uninterested. Perhaps the rebuff had offended the great kingdom in the north. Or maybe they would be glad that their advances were finally being met with eagerness.

For all Mery-ra's stories about the mountains of Kheta, the terrain they crossed was somewhere between rough wooded hills and high pasture. But he'd been right about the rocks. It was as if Geb, the earth, had been scraped to the bones, and great upthrusts of black stone interrupted the landscape out of nowhere. Agriculture must have been phenomenally difficult, and for the most part, it was sheep Hani saw wandering the steep moors.

They had packed up all the chariots of state to spare the horses until they drew nearer to the capital, and Hani's staff rode on the supply carts, as did Hani, Maya, and Mery-ra. The soldiers trudged alongside over the hard road, the donkeys at their heels. Hani had to admit the roads were well-built and maintained. The bridges they passed over were strong and expertly engineered. *These people are plenty civilized—we mustn't underestimate them.* He saw a pair of hawks circling overhead in pursuit of prey, and it occurred to him that they themselves were probably being watched just as avidly from some hilltop.

The days unrolled to the clopping of hooves and the rumble of wheels. Mostly, the party camped at night, but occasionally, their evening stops coincided with a town. There, Hani and Pirwa never failed to meet with the mayor or the governor, and Hani showed his credentials. Less and less frequently did the master of the place show any surprise at their appearance.

One afternoon, Mery-ra leaned over to Hani and said loudly above the grumbling of the carts, "We're nearly there, my son. We've been lucky—neither bandits nor any of our angry countrymen stalking us."

"May your words continue to be true, Father. The value of our gifts makes us as much of a target as our political aims."

In fact, there's something almost suspicious about the peacefulness with which we've made this journey, Hani thought uneasily. *Things are proceeding too well. Is Ay really going to let this happen?* Hani gazed about him at the forests closing around them again. The air of the open lands was that baking breath of full summer, shimmering with heat and the dusty scent of herbs and the subtle perfume of plane trees, so that the shade was welcome as they entered deeper into the shadowy woods. The trees were enormous, ages old—oaks, plane, and linden.

"It's full of game, my lord," young Pirwa said, walking alongside them. "There are deer, wolves, boars, and sometimes even lions."

"I'm glad you didn't tell us earlier, when we were camping." Hani chuckled. *If we had been hunting for our food along the way, I would have discovered that, but one can never tell who owns the land here. It's better that we bought our supplies. There's no point in provoking an international incident.* "How far are we from Hattusha, my boy?"

"We'll be coming to the high plateau soon, then there's the Marasshantiya River, then we're near to the capital. It's not far—a few days at most."

And that's when the real danger begins, Hani thought gloomily. *We have to convince the king to take an enormous risk with one of his sons. How will I manage to avoid telling him there's a rival for the throne?* He said to Pirwa, "What sort of man is your king, my friend?"

"Well, my lord, he's been on the throne for ten years or so—that must put him in his thirties. He's a great conqueror who has brought many new lands under the sway of Hatti."

Yes, Hani thought dryly. *Including some of our vassals.* "But as a man?"

Pirwa looked uncomfortable. "I don't know him, of course. But my father has said... He's said the king can get very angry. That he's temperamental. You don't want to cross him."

Hani stared grimly into his lap. It didn't surprise him that a man of such drive should be intense, but that didn't make his own mission any easier. "The more I know about him, the easier it will be not to offend him," he said in a genial tone. "And we mean him only respect."

"He came to the throne by assassinating his brother-in-law, my lord. And he's been pretty ruthless in ridding himself of enemies. But of course, we admire that strength," the boy said loyally.

"Has he ever rid himself of any foreign ambassadors?" Mery-ra asked from behind Hani.

Pirwa looked around, his eyes widening as if he'd been caught in some insufficiency. "I don't know, my lord."

Hani laughed. With a grunt, Mery-ra swung his legs over the bale that lay between him and his son and squeezed in beside him. "Does he like beautiful things that come from the south?"

"I'm sure he does." The poor lad was starting to get uncomfortable. Perhaps he feared he was giving away state secrets.

"We'll find out all these things in good time, Father," Hani said with a smile.

Pirwa walked on a little quicker.

The two men rode in friendly silence, swaying to the movement of the vehicle.

At last, Hani asked, "Where's Maya?"

"He's asleep in the back of the cart. He said he didn't sleep well last night—he had some sort of bad dream about Sat-hut-haru and the baby, and it has him all nervous."

Hani felt a chill trickle down his spine. Not all dreams were prophetic, but some were. And he didn't know any dream interpreters around there. After a moment, he said with an ill-at-ease sigh, "Well, I guess any letters from home will reach us in the capital."

CHAPTER 3

B Y MIDDAY, THEY HAD CROSSED the Marasshantiya River. It was broad though nowhere near as big as the River of the Two Lands, and it didn't seem to be navigated except by a few small fishing boats floating immobile on the flat silver water. The roads, already impressive, improved, as if frequently traveled, and Hani saw the deep grooves left by the constant passage of cart wheels in the rocky surface. Indeed, they passed people more often now— herdsmen with their flocks, laden donkeys or oxcarts, and an occasional chariot. Hani shaded his eyes with a hand. In the distance, the land rose steadily toward hazy, wooded foothills. He thought he saw a pale shimmer against the forest that might have been a city perched well up above the plain.

To the evident surprise of the young officers, Hani dismounted and walked along with the soldiers, delighting in the action of swinging his legs one after the other and eager to smell the land from up close. He could hear the song of unfamiliar birds twittering in the scrub.

Pirwa drew near to Hani and said, pointing at the horizon, "That's the capital, my lord. We'll be there by nightfall."

"Then let's stop for a moment. I'd like to write a letter, formally announcing our approach. We don't want to cause any nasty surprises."

Hani called Maya to him and bade him to prepare for dictation.

The little man, somewhat taken off guard, climbed out of the cart and seated himself cross-legged in the road. Hani observed with amusement the surreptitious look of distaste the secretary shot at the dirt before he set out his writing implements and readied his ink. Clearly, sitting in the road didn't answer to his ideas of scribal dignity. But he said neutrally, "Ready, my lord."

Hani crouched beside Maya and said in a low-enough voice that neither Pirwa nor the soldiers could hear, "We're going to send two letters, son. One to the king, advising him of our imminent arrival and begging for an audience to present our queen's respects. Her own letter, which we brought with us, we'll present in person. Then one to Prince Hattusha-ziti. Remember him?"

"I do, my lord. What are we going to say?"

"The second letter to our friend is this: we remind him of his previous discussion with us and say that Kemet is finally hoping to effect a rapprochement. Ask him to intercede on our behalf and to attest to our good faith with his king. Let's add something more personal and say I hope we'll have the pleasure of seeing him while we're in his beautiful city." Hani winked. "That should soften him up."

Maya set to work, his head bowed in concentration,

and finally, he handed his father-in-law a neatly written sheet of papyrus. "Is this satisfactory, Lord Hani?"

Hani took the letter and read it over. "Perfect, my boy. Write Prince Hattusha-ziti's name on the outside, and put my seal on it, and we'll get Pirwa to deliver it for us."

Maya beamed modestly and set to writing the address. Then he rose and, with a final brush at the seat of his kilt, said, "I hope he'll get this before we arrive."

"Even if he doesn't see it today, we certainly won't receive an official audience immediately." Hani remembered how long Aziru, the king of A'amu, had waited for an audience with Nefer-khepru-ra—nearly a year. *Let's hope the formidable Shuppiluliuma isn't so slow making up his mind.*

Pirwa was sent into the city in one of the Egyptians' light, fast chariots. As Hani watched the plume of dust billowing from behind the horses until the lad disappeared from sight, he thought about all the things that could go wrong with his coming audience. The queen's request was, frankly, insane. Everyone knew that Egyptian royal women were never married out to foreigners. It was too much honor for a so-called barbarian, even a king. *How can I convince them that I'm serious—that it's neither a trap nor a mockery—without telling them too much about the internal situation in the Two Lands?* Hani heaved a deep sigh. He had asked himself that over and over and had yet to come up with an answer.

His father, sitting in the cart above him, said, "This is going to be a real test of your diplomatic skills, my boy." Mery-ra smiled, but his eyes were serious. "If the king refuses, it will be a huge insult for our country."

Hani shot him an equally bleak smile. "Let's just hope

that in expressing his disapproval of the message, he doesn't kill the messenger."

✦

Maya was the first to spot Pirwa's return, and it was none too soon. The walls of the Hittite capital were clearly visible a league or so away as the boy galloped up alongside Hani's cart.

"The king's chamberlain said Our Sun looks forward to receiving you, my lord. And the chamberlain says he will happily vouch for you," Pirwa called breathlessly.

"So our friend Prince Hattusha-ziti is the chamberlain, is he? Not a bad supporter to have," Lord Mery-ra commented. The three scribes were sitting side by side on the baggage, and Maya was uncomfortably squeezed by the two broad men beside him.

"*Our*" *friend?* Maya thought, annoyed. *It was Lord Hani and I who met him.*

Hani rose in the awkward confines of the cart and rubbed his hands briskly. "Let's get the chariots unpacked, Menna. We're going to enter in style!" he said with a gap-toothed grin at the officer who walked alongside the cart.

The long shadows of a summer afternoon stretched across the plateau. The party had emerged into what appeared to be a vast, widely spaced fruit orchard, and the shade of the trees cast purple slats of darkness over the gilded earth. Ahead, the walls of Hattusha rose, tier over tier, atop the great thrusting rocks of its hilltop. The setting sun smelted its mudbrick walls to bronze, and against the indigo of a darkening sky, it resembled some city of the gods. *Iyah,* Maya thought. *That's a formidable-looking place.*

Beside him, Lord Mery-ra beamed as he shaded his eyes from the glare. "Just as I remember it. Sometimes the things you recall as spectacular turn out not to be so impressive, but this is quite a city. The men of Kheta may not have as appealing statues as we do, but they know how to build."

There was something a little ominous about it, Maya thought uneasily. Its ponderous, barbaric weight seemed to have incarnated the savage countryside itself. *Once those gates close on us, we'll be at their mercy.* That reality had never sunk in before, although he had been sealed within many a city in Djahy and Kharu. But those had been vassals of the Black Land. Kheta was the kingdom Maya had grown up considering the enemy.

Eventually, the chariots had been unpacked and reassembled, the horses harnessed, and Pirwa and Hani mounted the lead vehicle. Maya would have liked to join his father-in-law, but Hani had assigned him to a third chariot along with Menna, who drove, while Lord Mery-ra occupied the one before him, Pa-ra-mes-su as his charioteer. They had all bedecked themselves in their best finery, the soldiers in their padded aprons and leather-mesh overskirts and the scribes in clean shirts and their finest wigs. Hani put on all his gold of honor over a fancy beaded *weshket* collar, until he could hardly turn his head for the glittering abundance of it. Lord Mery-ra had donned his finery as well. Maya felt a little naked, although he could afford some nice pieces of jewelry, thanks to his mother's skills. He stared around at his countrymen, who had suddenly transformed from a hot, tired, bedraggled bunch of travelers into a rich legation worthy of the Black Land, and his heart swelled with pride.

As soon as the company was ready, they set off at a sedate pace, growing ever closer to the fantastic city at the mountains' hem, which sharpened in detail as they approached. Against the dark forests behind rose the same square towers and scalloped crenellations as the governor's palace at Ura had displayed. Pirwa gazed at it reverently, his freckled face rapt. *No doubt he feels about Hattusha the way I feel about Waset,* Maya thought.

Then just as the horses began trudging up the steep slope that fronted the city, the sun dropped below the horizon. In deepening twilight, they passed under the tall arched gate flanked by lions, through the black tunnel beneath the parapets, and into the city of the Hittites.

⚜

"You're the delegation of Egyptians?" said the officer waiting on the inside of the vast wooden doors. "I have orders to escort you to the palace." He sealed the gate behind them with a big lens-shaped seal pressed into a lump of clay then proceeded to the front of their procession and, with a small company of soldiers at his heels, led the march through the darkening city by the light of several torches.

The public ways were emptying for the night, and it had grown quiet except for the echoing clop-clop of their animals and a low rumbling of wheels on the sloped, stone-paved street. Hani couldn't see much but the walls of close-packed houses flickering in the torchlight and a slit of orange brightness from shuttered windows here and there. It had the look of a modest neighborhood. Every so often, patches of deeper darkness suggested that the blocks were not so densely settled as they appeared but rather interrupted at intervals by barren stretches of rock too bony and steep to build on.

A very strange place. Let's hope a hard land hasn't made the people hard.

Before long, they came to another wall with a gate that stood open, but instead of exiting the city, they passed into a second quarter similar to the first.

"I remember this," Mery-ra said in a low voice, drawing next to Hani's chariot. "The whole city is divided by walls like this. So if the enemy breaks into one district, he can be stopped from going any farther. I think they're that afraid of being overrun."

Hani chuckled. "By whom? Us?"

"Some kind of barbarians from the north."

"I thought *they* were the barbarians from the north," Menna said from Mery-ra's side.

"Don't underestimate these people, my boy," Hani cautioned him. "They're far from savages."

They crossed the city for what seemed like an endless time, mounting higher and higher through increasingly rocky and sparsely settled neighborhoods, where the houses seemed to be larger. At last, they gathered at the base of what appeared to be a vast wall of scrub-infested stone.

Pirwa pointed overhead. "The royal citadel is on top of this cliff, my lord. We'll have to leave the horses and chariots here and go up by litter or on foot."

"What about the donkeys?" Hani asked uneasily. He wasn't about to separate himself from the treasures they had brought so far.

"They can navigate it. The path is too steep for wheels, though."

As Hani and his party dismounted, the officer who had guided them through the dark maze of the capital approached. "You'll have to leave your soldiers here, my lord. You can take a few officers for an escort, but foreign troops can't enter the royal precinct."

"I understand. They can stay with the horses, wherever you have a mind to put them."

Litters appeared from somewhere, and Hani and Maya ensconced themselves in the first. Mery-ra occupied the second, and the rest of the secretaries and staff prepared to walk the dim path scratched into the stone. The Hittite soldiers spaced themselves out and held torches aloft to aid the climb, but Hani's stomach was in his mouth as their bearers hoicked up the litter and began the swaying ascent. He thought he'd never experienced anything that felt so physically dangerous.

Maya gulped uneasily. "You don't suppose this is a way of getting rid of us, do you, Lord Hani?"

Hani laughed, but it was a nervous noise. "I guess these people do it all the time." *Although maybe not in darkness...*

At last, the vertiginous climb up the face of the cliff ended at a yawning gateway arched in the odd fashion of the Hittites. Soldiers threw it open, and the procession moved into a modest courtyard with another lion-guarded gate opposite. The travelers dismounted while the donkeys were led off to the side along with Menna and Pa-ra-mes-su, who didn't want to leave their gifts unsupervised. Hani and his father and son-in-law were gestured respectfully to the inner gate. Pirwa accompanied them, a pace behind.

There, an unexpected figure awaited them.

"Prince Hattusha-ziti!" Hani cried, relieved to see a familiar face in the radically unfamiliar surroundings.

"Lord Hani, my friend," the chamberlain said, coming forward with welcoming arms.

Behind him stood a stout middle-aged man with mild brown eyes and a politely impassive expression. Only his large arched nose seemed to lend any character to a forgettable face.

"My secretary," the chamberlain said with a nod. "If there's anything you need, just let him know." He slapped Hani familiarly on the back and gave him a knowing look then tipped his head to their guide. "Pirwa, you got them here safely. Your father will be proud."

The youth nodded shyly and melted backward into the shadows.

"So," Hattusha-ziti said in a low voice near Hani's ear, "your government has decided to exchange enmity for friendship at last, eh?"

"I pray that may be the case, my prince." Hani counted on the ambiguity of his reply to dissemble his own vague fears. The result of his mission *could* be friendship—or civil war, with a foreign power dragged in.

"You can stay in guest apartments here in the citadel, if you like, or join your men in the Upper City. We've accommodated them at a caravansary used by merchants, so they won't have to be separated from their horses. Our Sun will receive you tomorrow."

"I thank your king for his hospitality, my lord. Considering the hour, I think we'd better plan to stay the night here at least this once." Hani didn't think he could face a descent and remounting of that dreadful staircase so soon. His stomach growled.

Hattusha-ziti smiled. "And, considering the hour, I feel sure you gentlemen would like something to eat. I'll show you to your room, and Kurunuwa here will have a meal brought up to you."

The chamberlain led them across the courtyard into moonless darkness illumined only by torches around the periphery and left them with a friendly bow. Hani, Maya, and Mery-ra found themselves in a large, low-ceilinged room lit dimly by a central brazier and a scattering of lamps. The small windows were shuttered, and the room was quiet except for the faint sound of crickets from outside.

"We're all in here together, are we?" Mery-ra asked, looking around him. There were, in fact, three beds around the walls, on three sides.

"So it seems." As best as Hani could see, the place was far from luxurious but well furnished, with a handsome rug and surprisingly heavy tapestry coverlets. A fair-sized table occupied the fourth wall of the room, with nicely carved stools. It had the look of a guest room, all right—serviceable and impersonal. Shuppiluliuma wasn't trying to impress them.

Before long, a servant had brought them an ample meal of cold meat and bread and pickled vegetables along with a ewer of wine. Mery-ra gave a cry of delight and dived for a slice of turnip, which he devoured with a smack of the lips.

Hani laughed. "So this is where you learned to love them, eh? I wonder where our toilet articles have gone. Surely not with the soldiers."

But the men's traveling baskets had been thoughtfully

placed in a corner. They stripped off their jewelry and good shirts, kicked off their sandals, and more comfortable, attacked the meal. By the time they had reduced it to a pile of scraps, Hani was ready for bed.

"May the lord of the horizon give you both a good night," he said, rising from the table. "I've got a royal audience tomorrow morning, and I need to be sharp." The tightness in his stomach was a harbinger of full-blown fear. The morning would be trying. He would need to be more than sharp.

"Will we be going with you, my lord?" Maya asked hopefully.

"I don't think so, son. These will be delicate negotiations, and the king may not want anyone present to witness them. You and Father are free to sightsee or whatever you want to do. We may move into the same inn as our troops in the afternoon. I don't want to be dependent on King Shuppiluliuma if the talks don't go well."

"If we don't see you by midafternoon, should we run for our lives?" Mery-ra chuckled, his belly bouncing.

But Hani was profoundly serious when he said, "I think you should, yes."

＊

Strips of bright daylight had filled the guest chamber when Maya finally sat up and rubbed the sleep from his eyes, only to find that Hani had slipped from the room before the others awoke. Maya slid out of bed and pushed open the shutters, letting a flood of golden sun pour into the bedchamber. From outside, he heard distant voices and the clack of numerous footsteps coming and going. Clearly, the life of the palace had begun for the day. He drew a deep breath in front of one of the two windows, unable to see anything but the sky, and regretted that they were so high placed. *These accursed tall men of Kheta.*

Lord Mery-ra yawned with a roar and stretched his arms. "Has Hani gone yet?" he mumbled, scratching his belly sleepily.

"He has, my lord. It must be midmorning. I suppose he's in the king's presence as we speak."

The old man swung his feet to the floor with a grunt. "May the Hidden One be with him and inspire his words. He's having to argue an almost-impossible case." He shook his head. "What is our queen thinking?"

"I'm not sure thinking is what she's doing," Maya growled. "What I don't understand is why Lord Mai and the others support her."

"Why, the same reason we all have, my boy. She claims she's working to restore the Lord Amen-Ra to his place in the heavens."

"But Lord Hani says Lord Ay is doing the same thing without the violence. He's reopened the temples, after all. Ay is a vile person, but I don't know that I disapprove of his campaign. Slow and peaceful certainly seems wiser than fast and violent." Maya expelled a heavy breath and scratched his head. The situation was all too confusing for his moral sense. If even his father-in-law was conflicted, small wonder he, a simple royal scribe, had his doubts.

"After breakfast, I have some errands to run, son. You'll have to entertain yourself for a few hours."

"Oh?" Maya couldn't think of what sort of errands Lord Mery-ra could have in a foreign city the morning after his arrival. Perhaps, as Maya had feared, Hani had assigned him some important fact-finding mission. "Can I go with you?"

"No, no. It's nothing important, my boy. Just enjoy the sights until I get back."

A short while later, Maya observed the old man toddling across the courtyard and out the inner gate toward the entrance.

Maya stared around. The palace was considerably more impressive by day than it had been in the darkness, with a vast, sunbaked expanse of pavement stretching out around him, bordered with solid-looking buildings. Servants and officials crossed briskly in all directions, and more than one followed Maya curiously with their eyes. He was powerfully tempted to do his Bes impersonation and stick out his tongue. Instead, in Lord Mery-ra's footsteps, Maya made his way to the external gate, which was flanked by two fierce stone lions. He noted with approval that their tongues stuck out.

Guards stood posted at the gate on the outside, their spears in hand, but no one made a move to stop him as he crossed the smaller entry court and walked with an insouciance he didn't feel through the tunnel of the outer gate. He relished the chill of the stone after the reflected heat of the courtyard. Finally, he stood on the edge of the path down the cliff. Maya had to admit it didn't look quite so horrific as it had seemed by darkness, because in fact, the path was wide enough for two pedestrians to pass in comfortable safety. *Or maybe safety isn't the word,* he thought with reluctance as he set foot cautiously on the sloping trail. Below him, the city stretched out, sprawled over the rocks like a coating of lichen, swelling and falling with the topography, cut by sharp rills and pierced by naked rocks. He felt he could see to the ends of the earth.

People were coming and going, as if the descent were nothing. Below him swayed a litter that might have contained Lord Mery-ra, and he hastened his steps. It wasn't that he actually wanted to overtake the old man, but he felt with a twinge of resentment that he had been left adrift to make his way in a strange city where he hardly understood the language. A little company would be reassuring. He could wait until Mery-ra had completed his errands.

It seemed to take a very long while to make the descent. Other people passed him at a brisk pace, but Maya didn't feel too secure on the worn stone slopes and steps. At last, he emerged into what they called the Upper City, although it was emphatically "below." By that hour, more people were milling in the streets. Soldiers led chariot horses to some unknown destination, and merchants conducted their donkey trains. Still, that part of the capital was sparsely inhabited.

"Where has Mery-ra gone?" he murmured, annoyed.

Someone was getting into a litter not far away, and it set off up the path to the citadel. *That's the one that brought Lord Mery-ra down, I think. He must be on foot now. I'm sure I can catch up to him. But in which direction has he gone?*

Maya hustled downhill toward the interior wall that separated the Upper City from the rest of the place. Once he had passed through the gate, the crowd became downright lively. Perhaps it was a market day. He craned his neck around, looking for someone in Egyptian clothing, but it was impossible to see more than a few cubits in any direction. *I probably shouldn't be doing this. It makes me look needy. If he'd wanted my company, Lord Mery-ra would have asked me along.* Still, he had to admit to a certain curiosity. And it relieved his boredom. He realized he was so fixed on the idea of finding Lord Hani's father that he wasn't noticing much about his surroundings. So much for sightseeing.

Alongside the wall that pressed in against the street to his left stood a public fountain with a basin several cubits tall, surrounded by women—some with long hair, others with veils over high caps. He climbed onto the rim, disregarding the looks of amusement from the women drawing water around him. From that vantage point, he could see over the heads of the crowd, and sure enough, he spied at less distance than he had feared a flash of white linen. It was Lord Mery-ra. The old man was flowing with the crowd toward whatever market was their destination, then he suddenly veered right, into another street.

Maya pushed his way through the sweaty bodies of men and donkeys, eliciting some exasperated objections. But he was able to force a path to the intersection. The side street was much less filled with people, and ahead, Mery-ra trundled along purposefully. Maya slowed down, suddenly embarrassed at the idea of being spotted dogging the old man's steps. He realized how flimsy any justification he could offer would be if his quarry should turn around and see him creeping surreptitiously in his wake.

All at once, Mery-ra stopped before a door. He stood for a moment, as if girding himself for a difficult task, then he straightened, hitched up his kilt, and knocked. A moment later, the door opened, and a person invisible to

Maya seemed to invite the old man in. Mery-ra disappeared into the darkness of the building.

"I wonder whose house that is." *Someone Mery-ra knows from fifty years ago? Or is he on a mission for Lord Hani?*

Maya stood staring at the blind house front, curiosity sparking in his thoughts. *What if I... but no. That's wrong. This is Lord Hani's father.* Still, he had just enough resentment left in him to overcome his sense of propriety. There was only one way to know what the old man was up to with this clandestine meeting. It might be nothing, or it might be the proof of what Maya feared most—that Mery-ra was replacing Maya in Hani's confidence.

Fighting down a sense of guilt, Maya strolled to the doorway. Pedestrians passed him with only a glance. As if to rest, he leaned against the heavy wood and pressed his ear to the door. From within, he could hear faint masculine voices speaking Neshite. Hardly a syllable was comprehensible. He thought he picked out the words "Are you ready," then the voices trailed off into silence, as if the speakers had entered another room.

Maya straightened. Passersby were looking at him curiously by this time, and his face grew hot. *That was unworthy, Maya, my boy,* he told himself sternly. But the worst part was that he didn't know any more than he had before. *How can I get any closer?* There was no garden wall to climb over, even if he didn't consider it below his dignity to break into a stranger's house.

Embarrassment finally overcame him, and he turned with a curse and made his way back to the main street. There, he let the crowd push him farther down to the square where the market appeared to be taking place. He used his few words of Neshite and an array of hand gestures to buy a pomegranate, a compact wedge of cheese, and a round loaf of bread that could have fed four people comfortably and headed for some quiet cross street where he could sit and eat his lunch in peace. Out of what he realized was a shameful inquisitiveness, he plopped himself down in a doorway on the street where Lord Mery-ra had disappeared.

The sun was starting to move across the meridian, and the shadows of the surrounding houses were ebbing away like the tide, leaving Maya stranded in the hot sun. He got to his feet and tucked the remaining bread under his arm. "Where is Mery-ra? Lord Hani is probably back from his audience by now," he murmured.

He had decided to return to the citadel when, down the street, the door opened, and Mery-ra himself emerged. His face averted, he started up the paving toward Maya with his rolling gait. Maya wasn't sure what to make of his expression, which had a glassy-eyed blankness about it.

Deciding to take a bold approach, Maya called out to him, "Lord Mery-ra! Imagine meeting you here!"

The old man looked up, as if awakened from a reverie, and said, "Ah, Maya, my boy. What brings you to this remote neighborhood?"

Are his eyes wet with tears? "Oh," Maya said carelessly, "I had just bought some lunch in the market and pulled into a quieter street to eat. I thought I should be getting back to meet Lord Hani, and... there *you* were. Have you eaten?" He extended the remains of his loaf.

"Yes, thanks, son. Let's go back together, then." Mery-ra's wide mouth stretched in a smile, but there was something suspicious about the way his eyes didn't quite meet Maya's.

What's going on, I wonder?

They fell into step together and made their way back through the Upper City to the base of the citadel, where they mounted a litter. A moment later, they were rising up the precarious path to the palace, where they would find out how Hani's embassy had gone.

The chamberlain's secretary came to conduct Hani to his audience before his father or Maya awoke. Hani hadn't slept well, his mind occupied with formulating what to say and how to structure convincing arguments that would win over the Great King of Kheta. That was made more complicated by Hani's no longer being sure he wanted to see the mission succeed. The conflict left a dull hole in his middle—no matter what the king's answer, Hani would lose.

Clad in his finest beveled wig and all the gold he could pile around his short neck, he set off in the secretary's wake toward King Shuppiluliuma's throne room, a vast, squat structure of two stories. The lower one had a sort of long porch across the front, still shaded from the morning sun to its rear. A pair of staircases rose to a stoop above, where impressive cedar doors flanked by soldiers marked the room in which the king held court. The secretary bowed himself away, and with a deep breath, Hani marched alone up the stairs. One of the saffron-clad guards demanded his identity, and once he had produced his credentials, he was bidden to enter.

It took a moment to regain his sight because the sparingly lit room seemed dark after the morning glare. The small windows were unshuttered, but the place was so vast that hardly any sunlight penetrated as far as the middle, and torches flared around the edge of the royal dais. About Hani, a forest of elaborately painted wooden columns stretched, and because of the expanse, the ceiling seemed low, although it was not. The space pulsed with something heavy and ominous—or perhaps that was only Hani's mood.

A majordomo appeared from nowhere to lead Hani toward the throne on the other side of the hall. There, the Great King sat upon his ornate carved chair.

Not yet daring to raise his eyes, Hani prostrated himself until a deep, gravelly voice said, "Rise, messenger."

He found himself in the presence of a man who was fairly young but already hard-faced. Shuppiluliuma's brown hair was brushed into a long mane over his shoulders, and he glittered with gold jewelry, gold embroidery, and gold paillettes all over his robes that made him flicker like some burning demon in the semidarkness. On his head was the strangely simple cap that was the crown of his people. A handful of men stood about him, soldiers and older civilians—including Hattusha-ziti—who were presumably councilors, and his queen sat beside him.

"Speak, emissary of the queen of Mizri," the king said, fixing Hani with a look that seemed to penetrate him to the core and read his very soul. Its cold fire promised a terrible end for those who displeased him.

"Great King, I bring you the respectful wishes of my

queen, who desires to knit closer relations with the land of Kheta, where the sun god is also worshiped."

The king tipped his head slightly, never a smile breaking the flinty gravity of his expression.

"You will find in this letter the expression of her esteem, and of course, we have brought gifts befitting your rank. She also extends to you this invitation." He began to recite from the letter the text he had memorized. "My husband is dead, and I have no son. I have heard that you have many sons. Send us one of them to be my husband, and he will reign beside me, and Kemet and Kheta Land will be as one."

At first, the king barely registered any reaction but continued to stare at Hani with his fierce eagle's gaze. Then he asked quietly in a brittle voice, "Is this a joke?"

Hani saw with trepidation that the king's face had grown a violent shade of crimson. Shuppiluliuma and his queen exchanged unreadable looks.

"No, My Sun, I assure you. She is absolutely serious. At the moment, her mother is on the throne, but when Ankhet-khepru-ra dies, Lady Meryet-aten hopes to reign in her stead. Since it is traditional for royal women to marry and perpetuate the divine line, she must seek a consort. But she refuses to consider a commoner, and therefore she turns to the other great power of the earth, a people devoted, like us, to the worship of the sun, for a man of royal lineage who is her equal." Hani's heart was pounding. He could well imagine how improbable that had to sound to the Hittites.

"Whose queen is she, then, if her mother is on the throne?" Shuppiluliuma's wife asked. She was a strong-jawed, keen-looking woman, a worthy match for the king.

"Her late husband was her father's coregent, Ankh-khepru-ra Smenkh-kha-ra, my lady. She is now considered the formal queen of her mother, for ceremonial purposes. But she believes she must think of the future."

Wrinkling her nose in ill-concealed disapproval, the queen of Kheta sat back. Hani knew how the Hittites abhorred anything that smacked of incest.

A moment of considering silence settled in while the courtiers at the king's side shuffled uneasily.

Finally, Shuppiluliuma said, "I've never heard of anything like this." He shot a look toward Hattusha-ziti, his brows drawn down into a grim line. "Do you know aught about it, cousin?"

"Nothing, My Sun." Hattusha-ziti looked surprised, his eyes wide.

"Our queen was aware you were desirous of forming closer relations with the Two Lands, thanks to the mission of Prince Hattusha-ziti last year," Hani said in his smoothest, most flattering voice. "Her father was not interested, but she has seen the wisdom of your openness. Our great kingdoms should live in peace—trade and cooperate against common enemies like the *hapiru*. This is her sincere desire, My Sun. There is no hidden agenda here."

The Great King exchanged suspicious looks with his wife again. "And what does this queen look like? How old is she?"

"She is twenty-one, My Sun, and a truly beautiful young woman. She would be sure to please any man fortunate enough to wed her." Hani declined to mention what a bronze-willed fanatic Meryet-aten was. In fact, any husband of hers would have his hands full.

Shuppiluliuma fell silent again, his suspicions chasing one another visibly across the granite of his face. Finally, he growled, "And he would reign beside her, eh? And their children would succeed them on the throne of Mizri?"

"My Sun has understood me perfectly."

"Let me think about this. Bring your gifts tomorrow, and we'll discuss it further."

The king rose abruptly, and he and his queen departed through the door behind the throne with a swirl of spangled skirts. The courtiers followed in a colorful crowd, but Hani could almost feel their incredulity like a solid mass, a train dragging at their heels.

He prostrated himself once more, and the majordomo escorted him down the long, carpeted path to the door. The great cedar panels opened, and he stepped out of the throne room into the glare and heat of midmorning.

⁂

Maya and Lord Mery-ra dismounted from their litter in the outer court of the citadel, with its deep-red stone paving. Throughout the ascent, the old man had been sunk in his own thoughts, and Maya longed to ask what he had been doing that put him in such a pensive mood. But the secretary suppressed his curiosity, lest it be too obvious he'd been following Hani's father. Still unspeaking, they made their way into the larger court, where to Maya's surprise, they encountered Lord Hani standing in the middle, his eyes unfocused, while servants and scribes milled about him.

"Hani, my son. Are you all right?" Mery-ra called.

Hani looked up and cast his squinting eyes around

until he saw his father and son-in-law approaching. He smiled, but it was a preoccupied expression. "I am, Father. Although I'm still not sure if our mission is. Let's go back to our room, shall we? I'll tell you all about it and eat something—they summoned me before I even got any breakfast. I'm afraid we can't go down to the city to join our men until we've handed the gifts over to the king, and that won't happen until tomorrow."

"So, he wants you to come back, eh?" Mery-ra said. "That sounds like a good sign, unless he just wants to collect our queen's presents before he kicks you out."

Maya asked eagerly, "Did he show any interest, my lord?"

But Hani declined to talk until they had shut themselves into their quarters, and a slave had been dispatched to find him some lunch.

Once the three men were seated at the big table and Hani had polished off a meal of cold meat, bread, and plenty of beer, he said, "Shuppiluliuma was skeptical, of course. He seemed at first to think Lady Meryet-aten was playing some sort of terrible joke on him. But he said finally that he wanted to think about it. I left her letter with him, and I'm to bring him our gifts tomorrow—surely that will convince him we're in good faith. I think his queen may have been less favorable to the idea than he. He's ruthlessly ambitious, but she may be thinking about what could happen to her little boy."

"Ah, the *tawananna*. It's vital to get her approval. She's as important as the king—independently powerful, not just because she's his wife," Mery-ra said sagely, as if he knew all about the Hittite power structure.

Fighting back annoyance, Maya said, "I don't think I'd want *my* son to head off into the unknown like that, into a country that's always been hostile." He tried to imagine letting little Tepy or Mai-her-pri sail off to a distant kingdom torn with political strife... and couldn't.

"Well, I have to say the king looked interested. For anyone as bent on his country becoming a great empire as he is, this must be a very tempting offer. And at least if our own royal house is any indication, things may not be so tender and loving among him and his sons." Lord Hani looked thoughtful. Then he brightened and asked, "What have you two been up to?"

"Oh," Lord Mery-ra said vaguely, "just looking around, remembering."

Hmm, Maya thought. *"Just looking around," eh?* He left Mery-ra's words unchallenged, though, and said with a show of innocence, "And me? Sightseeing, my lord. Picking up a few impressions for my Tales. I got something to eat in the market, then I ran into Lord Mery-ra. Nothing very interesting."

CHAPTER 4

To Hani's surprise, he slept like a stone that night. Perhaps the tension of waiting for his audience had been released, even though he didn't have an answer to the queen's proposal yet. However, from the greedy gleam in Shuppiluliuma's eye, Hani was confident ambition would outweigh the Hittite's reservations.

The next morning, he watched his father and Maya set off for the city below in two different litters. Then he found Menna and Pa-ra-mes-su, and they loaded the diplomatic gifts on four beautifully decorated carts that were provided for them, Hani himself bearing the casket with the prince's special bracelets. In their dress uniforms, the two officers accompanied him to the building where the throne room was housed, and a parade of slaves appeared to carry the treasures up the stairs and through the tall cedar doors.

They proceeded down the aisle of the vast hall by the light of the torches, which glinted sumptuously on the golden objects. From the shadows, musicians struck up a pompous fanfare, as if the treasures were some imperial personage making his obeisance. The bearers piled up the gifts at the foot of the dais while Hani and the soldiers made their prostration. Hani rose to see the king watching him appraisingly, his narrowed eyes cutting from time to time to the growing heaps of riches at his feet.

"Receive, I beg you, O Great King, these tokens of my queen's esteem for you and your *tawananna* and the land of Kheta," Hani intoned in a loud, formal voice. "They are but a taste of the wealth you and Kemet will share when sons of Kheta sit upon our throne." *May the gods not strike me dead for calling down such a fate upon our Black Land,* he thought, almost ashamed. But that was his job.

He bowed and extended the jewel casket, opening the lid as he proffered it. The bracelets glinted seductively. "And this is a special gift for your son from one who hopes to become his bride."

Shuppiluliuma shot a sideways glance at his wife and began in his deep, gritty voice, "This reassures me somewhat that your queen is serious in her request. But I find it hard to believe that there is no heir in Mizri. The last thing we want is to be found opposing your legitimate succession."

Just a little more gold would no doubt resolve that moral scruple, Hani thought dryly. "My lord, I can swear to you that our king has no sons. But"—he felt he had to be honest or risk some violent disillusionment later in the negotiations—"it is true that there is an heir designated, a young boy who is thought by many to be the son of the previous king and queen, but who is, in fact, the son of a serving girl."

Hattusha-ziti was watching Hani with an interested gaze.

The king snorted and said in a sarcastic voice, "I see things are not so limpid as we might have hoped, emissary. Who is the boy's father, if he is known?"

Hani dared not lie. He would surely be found out, and the wrath of the Great King would fall upon him and his queen. With a sinking feeling in the pit of his stomach, he said simply, "It is suspected the former king, Nefer-khepru-ra, is his father, My Sun."

"By a serving girl, eh? In our land, such a bastard isn't eligible for the throne."

"Nor in ours." *Usually. Unless the king chooses him.*

Shuppiluliuma fell silent, his brows contracted. After a moment, he said, "Does this boy have supporters? Will there be a war if your queen tries to claim the throne?"

Hani had a sudden vision of a civil war in which the Hittites played a deciding role, in which they conquered his fellow Egyptians, maimed them, slew them—all those good people whose only sin was to have accepted the Aten. *My own son.* A deep shiver of horror tunneled down his back like a shearwater whose advancing wake proclaimed its imminent eruption from the River. *This must not happen.* Queen Meryet-aten had no idea what she was inviting in. Shuppiluliuma was a violent, ambitious man who wanted more than anything to conquer every land that ringed the Great Green. *How can I hand my beloved homeland over to such a one?* He wanted to say, "Ha-ha. Sorry. I didn't mean it. You were right—this is a joke." But the words were out. The gifts were delivered. He was not his own man and, as a diplomat, had never been.

Shuppiluliuma didn't wait for an answer. He said loudly, as if to announce it to all the courtiers encircling

89

him, "Hattusha-ziti will return with you to Mizri, and before anything definitive happens regarding an agreement, he will give me his report."

When Hani and his two officers finally emerged from the throne room and stood alone in the blinding sun of midday, Pa-ra-mes-su said with a dubious twist of the mouth, "I don't feel as good about this as I once did." His brow was knit in a somber frown. Like his companion, he had not understood the king's words, but the translator had conveyed their gist.

"Me either," Hani said in a low tone. "But we must obey our queen."

"Are these people really going to restore the Hidden One, do you think, my lord?" Menna asked doubtfully. "Or do they just want to take us over?"

Troubled, Hani blew out a sigh. "I wish I knew. I'm afraid Lady Meryet-aten has been badly advised. But you heard the king. Hattusha-ziti will come back with us and investigate the situation before the prince is sent. Perhaps he'll feel uneasy enough to counsel stopping the plan."

Pa-ra-mes-su gave a pondering hum. "I think Lord Har-em-heb should hear about this, don't you, Lord Hani?"

"I do. I'm going to be sending letters tonight, and I'll include him. Is he still in Ta-nehesy?"

"I don't know, my lord. But the garrison commandant will send it on to him if you address it to Waset."

Since the gifts had been delivered, the two officers decided to join their men in the city below, so Hani marched on alone to the guestroom.

⚜

Maya was put out that the two army officers were to accompany Lord Hani to his second audience. *Surely a pair of secretaries would be a more peaceful escort.* But protocol was what it was. He realized he was going to leave Hattusha without ever seeing the Great King or the throne room. He might as well have stayed in the Upper City with the soldiers and staff, for all the good it would do his Tales. Certainly, his prowling the town in the footsteps of Lord Mery-ra wouldn't be very interesting. He might have to embroider a bit and create some adventure that would excite the children and fan their admiration for their father—unless he could find out something more about the old man's secretive meetings. *There could be more to this than meets the eye. I owe it to Lord Hani to pursue it.*

At the moment, he was elbowing his way down the same street he had visited before, because that was once more where Mery-ra was headed. Maya knew the way by this time. He knew the house. He knew the door in a middle-class neighborhood. *What, by all that's holy, does the old man have to do with this place? He was an army scribe when he was here fifty years ago—a general's secretary.*

He pressed himself against the wall, hidden by the passing bodies of taller people. In fact, he needn't have bothered to hide, because Mery-ra wasn't looking right or left. Instead, he lumbered purposefully straight to the address. As they had the previous day, someone invisible opened the door, and Lord Mery-ra, with a strange look of eagerness and trepidation, entered. Then the person leaned out and cast a furtive look around before he shut the door behind him. The tubby silhouette and heavy beak gave him away—it was Lord Hattusha-ziti's secretary.

Yahyah! That's interesting! A government official—the chamberlain's right-hand man—and Lord Mery-ra is meeting with him in secret. I'll bet Prince Hattusha-ziti is in there too. What are they up to behind Lord Hani's back?

As he had before, Maya beat his way back to the market square, which was rather less crowded than the last time, and bought some olives and bread. As before, he turned down the street where Lord Mery-ra's mysterious assignation was taking place, seated himself on a doorsill shaded by the house behind his back, and ate lunch.

What could have provoked that eager, fearful look and all this secrecy? And what's the chamberlain's secretary doing there? Surely, if Mery-ra were merely visiting an old friend, he wouldn't have been at such pains to keep me away. Yet what else could it have been? A secret confab on Lord Hani's behalf? He laughed. "A meeting of spies?"

Somehow, that thought took hold of him. The Mery-ra he knew was a jovial, loving old soul who seemed ingenuous to a comical extent. But in fact, Lord Hani said he had been a spy. *A spy...*

Is he feeling out the Hittites for Lord Hani and the queen? Or is it the other way around?

Hani had shared everything about the political situation at home with his father—who had his own sources anyway. That nephew of his lady friend, for example, was always passing on court gossip. *Is it conceivable that the great-grandfather of my children is somehow traducing the Black Land?*

The thought made him so nervous that he popped up from his spot on the doorsill. The house had heavily shuttered windows on the street—but the shutters were open a crack to admit light and air without exposing the interior to the gaze of passersby. Maya eyed them. They were too high for him to see inside, but if he could jump only a little bit and wedge his fingers between the parted panels, perhaps he could pull himself up. More than once, he had advanced Lord Hani's mission by some small act of daring like that.

Maya waited until just a pedestrian or two was in the street, then he launched himself upward and grabbed the wooden sill of the window. The shutter swung back on his knuckles. He stifled a cry of pain but hung on. A women emerged from a nearby house and gaped at him, sputtering with disbelieving laughter, before she made her way down the street.

Bes help me. I must look ridiculous. A foreigner, a dwarf, hanging from a window, my feet a cubit from the ground. Maya felt a wash of burning anger harden his determination. *Let this humiliation not be in vain.*

With enormous effort, he drew himself upward, all his weight on his trembling bent arms. The shutters opened backward into the room, and he toppled headfirst over the edge.

His writing case fell off his shoulder with a clatter, and he froze, cowering, afraid that some servant would come running. His wig rolled across the floor. But except for the sound of faint voices from elsewhere in the house, not a noise broke the musty silence. The room seemed to be nothing more than a stairwell, with red-painted walls and a few large jars stored under the wooden stairs. The light from the open window revealed a worn and slightly grubby space. Maya's heart pounded. *What might the Hittites do to*

93

me if they found me inside a person's house? They would think
he was the spy. Suddenly, his idea to listen in seemed a
terrible one. He quietly scooped up his wig, plopped it back
on his head, and settled his scribal gear on his shoulder.

He was tiptoeing toward the door, his stomach in his
mouth, when he heard heavy footsteps creaking on the
floorboards above. Lord Mery-ra's loud, strongly accented
voice rang out in Neshite, "I'm willing to do whatever is
useful to you all, my boy. Just send me a message." Maya
detected a metallic clink, as of silver being pushed across
a table.

Ammit take him! The old man's in their pay! Maya
thought, horrified.

The footsteps started down the stairs. Another man
said in a quieter, higher-pitched voice, "We're already in
your debt."

Maya couldn't understand the rest of it and no longer
cared. He scuttled for the door and fumbled up the bar,
practically hurling himself outside. He brushed himself off,
and to settle the terrified tingling of his hands and feet, he
began to walk hurriedly, although he had no destination.
It was all he could do not to speak, arguing with himself.
*Caught in the act! All you gods, I can't credit my ears! Lord
Hani will never believe me!*

At last, he circled back to the neighborhood he had
left, too preoccupied to have seen a thing. Just as he came
around the corner from the direction of the market street,
the door of the house where Lord Mery-ra had spent the
morning opened, and Maya scampered back out of sight.
In a moment, the old man passed by the intersection,
oblivious to all around him, his eyes red but a big smile

stretching his mouth into a happy crescent. He dashed at his nose and began to move up the slope toward the gate into the Upper City.

You look mighty pleased at having betrayed your country.

Maya slid out behind him, well covered by the crush of larger bodies. Mery-ra churned his way along, rocking from side to side, his broad back and coppery Theban skin making him an easy target, while Maya glided in his wake.

Act natural, he told himself. Maybe you can learn more.

At the gate, he called out, "Lord Mery-ra! Hold up!"

Mery-ra turned hastily and waved. "Maya, my boy. Where did you go this morning?"

"Oh, just around. Looking for details to go in my Tales. You know." He watched the old man's eyes closely as he added, "How about you?"

"Just sightseeing. Reliving my time here long ago."

That's a lie. You're as guilty as a cat in the cream, my lord. "Willing to do whatever is useful" to the enemies of Kemet.

Together, they made their way through the Upper City, hailed litters, and began the slow ascent to the citadel. Maya's mind was working furiously. He didn't want Lord Mery-ra to be involved in anything. *How could I ever tell Lord Hani what I suspect? But why else would the old man be meeting with the secretary of a high official? Why would he lie about his whereabouts all morning every morning unless he's hiding something?*

And why would he hide something unless he has something to hide?

⚜

Three days passed at the slow pace of negotiations, and

on the fourth, Hani trudged once again up the ceremonial stairs to the throne room and made his way down the middle of the dark, flame-guttering colonnades. He prostrated himself and rose heavily to his feet to see Shuppiluliuma seated alone, without his queen. Instead, a tall, muscular youth stood at his side, one fist on his hip. Hani spotted the gift bracelets glittering on his forearms, the perfect complement to his blue tunic—he had obviously dressed to set off the cuffs. Just below the dais, Hattusha-ziti was positioned, his lean, ruddy face studiously expressionless.

The king fixed Hani for a long beat with his raptor's eye. "Here is what we'll do, emissary. My son Zannanza will accompany you to the border but will not set foot in Mizri until Hattusha-ziti has made his report to me. If I'm satisfied by what he says, Zannanza will cross the border with you and take his place beside your queen." He slipped a sideways glance at the prince. "If not... we'll see."

He's decided to do it, Hani told himself. *No matter what the report reveals. He wants Kemet for his own. And who wouldn't?* "My Sun is wise. I'm sure Lord Hattusha-ziti will find the situation to his liking."

Hani shot a quick look at the chosen groom. He was a good-looking young man with thin lips and a stubborn jaw—probably a little younger than Queen Meryet-aten—athletic and sun reddened. There was an absence of innocent excitement about him that worried Hani a bit. The boy already had the hard, smug look of a conqueror. *Meryet-aten will have met her match.*

"Give us a few days to prepare his escort and put together what he'll need for an appropriate entrance. Then you can all head back to Mizri overland. Zannanza will wait for you outside Tsumur."

Tsumur—Simurru—was the last major settlement before the border with Kemet. *If they're going to wait outside the city, it's because there will be a huge number of people and carts. We'll be moving at the pace of oxen.* Hani felt he should be happier that his mission seemed to have succeeded, at least conditionally, but instead he experienced a dull sense of resignation.

He bowed himself from the audience and headed back to the guest room to remove his jewelry. There, he encountered his father and Maya, who themselves seemed just to have returned.

"How did it go, my lord?" Maya cried eagerly.

Hani explained the arrangement. "If Hattusha-ziti likes what he sees, then Prince Zannanza will cross the border with us, and we'll lead him to Waset to meet the queen."

"Why Waset?" Maya scratched his head.

"Because we don't want Lord Ay to know there's a Hittite on his doorstep, planning to claim the throne," Mery-ra, who had remained strangely quiet up to then, said with a chuckle.

"Here comes the civil war, then," the secretary said gloomily.

Hani, equally glum and preoccupied, tried to sound cheery. "What were the two of you up to this morning?"

Maya's eyes immediately grew round and evasive.

Mery-ra said, "Oh, just looking about. Seeing what's new since I was here last."

Hani noticed Maya shooting the old man a strange,

skeptical look, but the secretary said with forced casualness, "Me, too, my lord. Just sightseeing."

Something's going on, Hani thought with amusement.

Mery-ra popped to his feet and said in a clear dismissal, "I think I'll take a little nap, boys. I'm not as young as I used to be. All this tramping around takes it out of one."

"Maya and I will leave you, then. We can go see if any diplomatic pouch has arrived."

Hani drew Maya after him into the corridor and closed the door behind him. He wanted to get well away from the other staff before he said what was on his mind. Together, they headed toward the stone-paved courtyard and emerged into the blinding light of midday. Hani drew his son-in-law against the wall and asked in a low voice, "Why were you making that strange expression when Father spoke, Maya? Is there something I need to know? Are the two of you not getting on?"

Maya drew a deep breath as if to gird himself for something he'd rather not do, then all his words came out in a rush. "Lord Hani, I've been watching your father— quite by accident at first—and he's *not* sightseeing. Every day, he goes directly to a house in the Lower City and spends the whole morning inside—with Lord Hattusha-ziti's secretary! He's in their pay and has promised to do whatever they need him to. Just before you arrived today, I saw him get out a clay tablet and a stylus and stick it under his bed. I'll bet anything he's in there right now, writing a letter in Neshite."

Hani remembered the tablet his father had thrust behind his back before they had left Kemet. He pondered this new information, having no idea what to make of it but inclined to take it skeptically, given Maya's jealousy. "He's probably visiting some old acquaintance from fifty years ago."

"But I overheard him, my lord. Silver changed hands." At Hani's look of surprise, Maya hastened to add, "It's a long story. Only, think of it, Lord Hani. Why would Lord Mery-ra be so secretive about his whereabouts? Why would he keep telling us that he was sightseeing, when the only sights he could have seen were in the salon of that house? Why would he meet with that secretary—a royal official— of all people? It just looks strange to me."

Hani laughed a bit uneasily. "Well, strange, perhaps. I'm sure there's some harmless explanation."

"I hate to say this, because I have the utmost respect and affection for your father, Lord Hani, but he's said before he was a spy up here, remember? Is it possible he's contacted someone and is... is spying again?"

What by the Lady Ma'at is the boy talking about? "Do you mean spying on us for Lord Ay? If he's spying, it's because the king has told him to, Maya. There's nothing illegitimate about that."

"Or reporting to the Hittites about us? They're definitely involved. I don't know." Maya looked uncomfortable. "I'm not accusing him of any crime, but you've told him everything about the Haru in the nest's real parentage, for example."

"And I told King Shuppiluliuma, too—or almost everything. He would eventually find out anyway." Hani stroked his chin, curious but not troubled. "I'll ask Father this evening what was going on. And now, how about some lunch, or have you eaten?"

Maya admitted he had eaten some olives and bread, but he seemed eager enough to join Hani in another small meal.

Hani called one of the slaves who had been assigned to them and ordered some lentils and onions, which they devoured in the nearly empty staff dining hall.

As Hani sopped up the last of the juice with his bread, Maya laid a hand on his forearm and said earnestly, "I hope you don't think I'm being officious, my lord. I just don't want anything, however innocently intended, to jeopardize your mission or... or endanger you."

Hani smiled. "I can't imagine what harm a spy could do to our mission, frankly, other than trying to block our discussions with Shuppiluliuma. And they've already taken place. Anyway, I think we can rely on Father to be an honest and honorable man, Maya. He would never hide from me anything except an order from the king. There's undoubtedly a perfectly mundane explanation for his actions." But he remembered the words his father had said before they left the farm: "There's a lot you don't know." He rose. "Now, let's go find the mail."

When dusk had fallen, the three scribes met in the Upper City to share the evening meal at the garrison tavern with their escort. The common room was heavy with smoke and the smell of roast goat from the central fire, where a kitchen boy turned a whole kid on a spit. From the low, soot-blackened ceiling, the laughter and talk of the soldiers echoed loudly. They sat at long tables, a dozen men or more on a side on heavy benches. Hani, his secretary, and his father found a space at the lower end of a table, where the obliging soldiers squeezed aside to accommodate them. It was rather compacted to be comfortable—and hard on the backside—but at least the level of noise in the room made it possible to converse privately.

"Let's see those letters from home, Maya, my friend." Hani held out a hand. He took one of the papyrus packets, broke the seal, and unfolded it. As he read, his stomach knotted with unease. Finally, he let his hand drop and faced the others, dry-mouthed. "Listen to this. Ptah-mes says war seems to be breaking out in the Two Lands."

Maya gasped.

Mery-ra shook his head sadly. "It had to come to that, son. Ay was probably afraid to let his enemies grow any stronger."

"Where does that leave us, then, my lord?"

Hani heaved a sigh. "I don't know. I just don't know. It depends on who wins the war, I suppose." He picked up the letter again and continued reading. "He says it isn't yet to the point of open battle, but the king's troops have been patrolling the streets in Waset. People are under curfew. Lord Si-mut seems to have disappeared. Ptah-mes isn't sure if he's fled or..." He and his father exchanged looks of dire suspicion.

"We probably know the answer to that," Mery-ra said darkly. "What about Little Shu?"

That was the old man's name for Nub-nefer's brother—after the male twin of the primordial gods—because of Amen-em-hut's resemblance to his sister. He was Third Prophet of the Hidden One, right after Si-mut.

"I don't think he's going for the priests yet in any big way. I guess he can't afford to alienate them, just after giving them back their jobs and winning most of them over to his side. But Si-mut was one of the leaders of the queen's party." Hani read to the end and laid down the papyrus, staring unseeing at the tabletop. "I just hope the family is safe."

No one said anything, but their pensive and anxious expressions spoke eloquently of their agreement.

In resignation, Hani unfolded the next letter and saw with a warm swelling of the heart that it was from Nub-nefer, although the hand was Amen-em-hut's.

Dearest Hani, he read. *I can't tell you how we long for your return. There are soldiers in the streets, and it's a very chilling presence. I just hope the king doesn't seal the borders.* He read on, his heart stopping in his mouth as the words sank in. *Something very sad has happened. Sati has lost the baby. He was stillborn just a few weeks before he was due. She's inconsolable, as you may imagine, and seems to be sinking more and more into a kind of lethargy. She hugs Pa-miu and weeps all the time and cries out for Maya. Is there any chance he could come home? I know that by the time this letter reaches you, some weeks will have passed, and maybe she'll be better, but I'm really worried about her. She's almost to the point of neglecting the other children. I've brought her home so she can be around people, at least.*

The letter continued, but Hani's eyes kept slipping off the words. The thought of his little swallow weeping and mourning her baby without her husband's comforting presence wrung his heart. At last, he handed the letter to Maya and said gently, "You'd better read this, son."

Anxiety cast a sudden shadow over Maya's face like a cloud sliding in front of the sun as he accepted the papyrus and bent to read it. Above the secretary's head, Hani exchanged sorrowful looks with his father. "Sati's baby," he formed silently with his lips.

Maya gave a cry of anguish and stared up at the two men, tears wetting his lashes. "She needs me, and I'm not there!" he choked out.

"I don't see why you can't go back right away, Maya. Our negotiations are finished, and we're just waiting on the king's preparations. But that could take a while. Go."

Maya, unable to speak, swung his legs around and slid off the bench. He ran from the mess hall under the curious eyes of some of the soldiers.

"Maybe I should go with him," Mery-ra said under his breath. "He'll need to book a passage, and his Neshite is still shaky. Then I suspect he'll have to transfer somewhere in Kharu. Surely we aren't letting Hittite vassal ships into our harbors. We don't want him to end up in Keftiu or someplace."

"If you want, Father. I'm sure he'd be grateful."

The old man hauled himself up from his seat. As he passed his son, he clapped him on the shoulder with compassion, and Hani gripped his hand for a moment. Together, they could get through the family sorrow.

Summer was closing down there in the north, and while the heat was still oppressive on the sunbaked plains, the atmosphere became pleasanter once they reached the mountains. If the donkey train that had borne Queen Meryet-aten's gifts had been impressive, Prince Zannanza's cortege of luxurious household items and rich clothes took up an even more breathtaking space, packed on oxcarts.

Ten of his young companions accompanied him—each with his own baggage—and innumerable slaves and guards. There must have been hundreds of people. Hani wasn't sure how they would be received at the border, even with him and the two officers to pave the way.

While the prince and his friends rode in two-wheeled carriages pulled by matched white mules, Hani and Hattusha-ziti traveled together on one of the baggage carts. Unlike the prince, the diplomats were not to be accompanied to Kemet by so much as a secretary or a body servant. Theirs was an utterly confidential mission, and Hani's staff and military escort would remain at Simurru until they all made their definitive journey home together. They couldn't risk an indiscretion—or worse—that might alert the king to the Hittite's presence in the Two Lands.

At first, neither of them spoke much. From his pensive silence, it was clear that Hattusha-ziti had personal reservations about the royal marriage, but like the professional he was, he never said a word critical of his king. Hani forced himself to act cheerful about the union and optimistic regarding the political situation at home, but it struck him painfully what a lie both performances were. In fact, he wasn't sure how to conceal from the chamberlain how violently divided things seemed to have become in the Two Lands.

Lady Meryet-aten wouldn't be happy either. Before he had set out from Hattusha, Hani had sent the queen a message by fast courier to apprise her of the coming of Shuppiluliuma's emissary and to suggest that he be quartered in Waset rather than flaunted under Ay's nose at the capital. She would be disappointed that Hani didn't return with the prince in tow—perhaps worse than disappointed. The queen had been champing at the bit for years to arrange the union, and she would have to postpone her victory once more. Hani resigned himself to being a scapegoat for both sides.

CHAPTER 5

A T SIMURRU, THE CAPITAL OF the Hittite border state of A'amu, the prince's party along with Hani's staff made camp to wait for their emissary's word, while Hani and Hattusha-ziti continued alone. Just south of Batruna, the two men crossed the border into Egyptian territory. After a few more *iterus* overland, they picked up a ship at Gubla and set sail. Between dread of his meeting with the queen and grief at Sati's sad plight, the voyage was a gloomy one for Hani.

⁜

For Maya, too, the journey home was grueling—not because of any mishaps but because the days seemed to be swelling and boiling all over like water in a pot left too close to the fire—multiplying, pullulating. Time had ceased to have any particular proportions. Maya could believe that he would never set foot on the Black Land again and that the rest of his life would be a featureless cycle of simmering sky and heaving water.

He thought miserably of Sat-hut-haru, inconsolable over the loss of their son—*a son*—and deprived of the support of her husband. He had failed her, just as he had failed his mother. *Oh, neither one of them will reproach me. They'll generously repeat the same excuse I've made for myself—how my work for the king is so much more important than their little concerns.* But his heart told him he was at fault. *How can I make it up to them?* His eyes prickled with tears.

Lord Mery-ra, too, seemed preoccupied, far less garrulous than his usual self. Perhaps old age was finally draining his cheerful energy. They'd had a harrowing few months, even for a man in his late thirties like Maya.

Or is it a guilty conscience?

At last, after what felt like a million years, their ship docked in Per-nefer. The sailors heaved out the stone anchors and slid the gangplank to the shore, and Maya stepped once more upon the beloved soil of Kemet. He felt he could have fallen to his face and kissed it. He stared around him with relish. The Inundation had come and gone. The marshes of the Lower Kingdom were swollen and teeming, tasseled with green reeds and jeweled with bright birds—Lord Hani would know what they were—the fields flooded to either side. *Home.* Maya asked himself in anguish of soul how he could ever leave his homeland and his loved ones again.

Maya and Mery-ra engaged a ferry for the week-long journey upriver. Every sunrise brought Maya closer to Waset and his family. He wondered if he should stop off in the capital to see his mother, but Sati's need was more urgent. His mother had many years of life and eyesight

107

ahead of her, he hoped, before the issue of the workshop became pressing. The image of his wife hugging her sister's cat and weeping was too much to bear.

❖

At last, the two travelers burst through the gate of Hani's house. A'a greeted them with delight, but his grin turned to surprise. "The master of the house isn't with you?" he cried.

Mery-ra said, "He's coming later. Where are the girls?"

"In the garden, my lords."

As weary as he was, Maya dropped his baggage and jogged through the garden toward the pavilion, where he could see flashes of white garments. "Sati! Sati, my love!"

He found all the women of the family gathered on the porch of the pavilion—Baket-iset on her couch, Neferet and Bener-ib playing with the children, even their cousin Mut-nodjmet sitting with an arm around Sat-hut-haru. Nub-nefer was shelling dried cowpeas, which spilled into her basin with a cascade of *plinks*. They all looked up at the sound of Maya's hasty steps crunching on the gravel, and Sati sprang to her feet and flew to her husband.

"My lion!"

She threw herself on him and squatted to level their heights, but Maya, enfolding her in his arms, saw with a pang that her usual sparkle was gone.

"Thank all the gods you're back," she murmured in a trembling voice into his shoulder.

Maya said fiercely—and only just realized it was true—"I'll never leave you again, my love, even if I have to transfer out of the foreign service."

The three children old enough to walk came swooping

down on their father, led by Tepy. "Papa! Papa!" they screeched in excitement, and Maya felt scalding tears well in his eyes. *Never. I'll never leave them again.*

"Here's Papa!" Neferet cooed to little Web-khet as she helped the girl toddle unsteadily to her father's arms.

Maya and Sat-hut-haru were buried in the wriggling mass of ten-year-old Tepy and their three smaller children, and to Maya's relief, Sati hugged them to her bosom. He had feared more than anything that loss might have killed her taste for motherhood.

The other women dabbed their noses and brushed at their eyes. Nub-nefer helped Baket-iset blow her nose, and Maya could see relief all over their faces.

"Sati's best medicine has come back," Baket murmured. "She'll be all right."

To the rear stood Mery-ra, an indecipherable look of sorrow on his square-jowled face.

⚜

Several weeks unrolled. Then at Nub-nefer's urging, Maya and his family decided to take a little holiday in the capital to visit Aha and Pipi and their families—and In-hapy, of course. Maya felt it would do Sat-hut-haru good to get away from the scene of her tragedy for a week or so. Lord Mery-ra decided to come along.

The trip to Akhet-aten unrolled more or less pleasantly but not untainted. The children played together, Tepy keeping watch, lest the little ones get under the sailors' feet. Sati managed to post a smile on her face during the days, but at night, when they docked at whatever village the sunset caught them passing, and she and Maya had retreated to the little pavilion and pulled the curtains about them, he could hear her struggling to conceal her sniffs as she lay beside him. Maya felt overwhelmed and helpless—almost exasperated in the face of a situation he couldn't remedy. He exhorted her to be strong for the other children and assured her they'd make another baby.

"But it won't be him," she said in a quavering little voice. She was like someone sinking up to their chin in quicksand who wouldn't catch at the hand that was offered them.

What can I do? he asked himself wearily. *What more can I do?*

Five days on the River passed with the adults speaking little, while the children entertained themselves. *Thank the gods Tepy is so grown up and responsible,* Maya thought with pride and relief, because he was too preoccupied to want to play games or tell stories.

They slid up against the bank with a thump, and the sailors cast the anchors and extended the gangplank. Maya noted with satisfaction how many admiring glances were shot at the handsome little boat with its Bes-head prow. He shepherded the family to land—Web-khet, the smallest, in his arms and Mery-ra at his heels—and they all trooped off to Lord Pipi's home, where they would be staying. They had brought a servant to carry the baggage after them.

As they walked, the two men fell behind a bit.

"Lord Mery-ra, are you well? I see you unusually silent lately," Maya said, watching the old man carefully. Not that he expected an answer, but curiosity was eating him up. The sudden change of humor almost certainly had something to do with Mery-ra's mysterious activities in the capital of Kheta Land.

"Fine. Fine, son." Mery-ra flashed him a big grin that didn't quite touch his eyes. "I'm just sad for poor Sat-hut-haru. It's hard for a woman to go through something like that when her man's not around."

Annoyance chilled Maya's smile. *So it's my fault, is it? And where were you while your children were growing up, my lord?* He said dismissively, "She's strong. She'll get over it."

He was still in a grumpy mood when they arrived at the house of Sati's uncle. It was surprisingly nice, Maya thought, for the feckless younger brother of Lord Hani. He was amazed the lower-level scribe had been able to save enough to build such a prosperous-looking place. Although perhaps the gold Pipi had received for the sale of his two horses some years back was still keeping him afloat.

Pipi and Nedjem-ib came bursting through the gate to welcome them, all shrieks of laughter and enormous hugs. Nedjem-ib squeezed Sati to her bosom and held her there while she murmured words of comfort in her ear. The children jumped excitedly all over their great-uncle, who could be counted on for a good time, since he was pretty much just a big ten-year-old himself. Then the master and mistress of the house led the way inside, and rooms were assigned, and the servant girl set out a cold snack of roasted sedge nuts, which had already been decimated in the kitchen by Pipi's eleven-year-old twins. The chatter mounted, and Maya saw with relief that Sati was genuinely distracted from her preoccupation.

"My love," he said under his breath, "I need to check

111

whether Lord Hani has any mail at the Hall of Royal Correspondence. I leave you here in good hands, right?"

She assured him she would be fine, and he dodged toward the door.

Maya set off, feeling guilty over the relief that flooded him. He had to escape for a while the oppressive atmosphere of grief that followed his family around. No question but that a week or so spent in the jovial company of Pipi and Nedjem-ib and their children would do Sati good.

He turned in to the familiar warren of low buildings at the edge of the royal complex and made his way across the court. "I'm here to collect any mail the Master of the King's Stables may have received during his absence," he said loftily to the secretary on duty in the reception hall.

The man excused himself and disappeared into the back rooms. A moment later, he returned with an armful of folded papyrus packets spilling out of a leather pouch. "These are for Lord Hani. I'll thank you to bring back the bag," he said sourly, as if Maya had never done business in the chancery before and was likely to run off with the king's property.

Maya eyed him with contempt but managed to say with no particular inflection and only the hint of a lifted nose, "Of course. That goes without saying, my good man."

He had emerged from the cool, shadowed hall into the sunlight, Lord Hani's mail pouch over his shoulder, when he heard a voice he knew. He looked up to see a lean older man and an officer approaching—Lord Ay and General Har-em-heb, walking side by side in conversation. *They're back?* he thought, disconcerted. He saw nowhere he could dodge without being spotted. Maya froze until they had reached him then made a profound bow, his nose to the ground.

"Ah," the God's Father said with cheerful surprise. "Hani's secretary, is it not? You're home from the north, then? How did it go?"

Maya was conscious of Har-em-heb fixing his eyes on the distance in careful absence of expression.

"Only me, my lord. Lord Hani is coming later. There was a... a family emergency."

Lord Ay's brow buckled in concern. "Everything's all right, I hope?"

His charm was seductive, but Maya refused to share his private sorrow with that awful man, even if Ay was the father of the king. "Yes, my lord. I'm honored by your interest." He itched to get away before Ay asked him any specific questions about Hani's undertaking.

"Well, our own mission was successful. Isn't that so, Har-em-heb? The rebels were crushed, and Ta-nehesy returned to peace."

"Yes, my lord," Har-em-heb said, still as expressionless as stone.

Maya writhed inwardly with discomfort. "I rejoice to hear it, my lord." *Why is he telling me this?*

"Yes, yes." Ay cast a bright-eyed glance at Har-em-heb, who stared pointedly into space. "Now, we just need to restore our homeland to peace, eh."

"Er, y-yes, my lord," Maya stammered, unsure what Ay referred to but suffering an unpleasant suspicion.

With a friendly smile, the God's Father moved on toward the Hall of Royal Correspondence. As they passed, Har-em-heb shot Maya a glance from the corner of his eye and flicked a finger, unseen by his companion, in what might have been a warning to silence. Maya gaped after them, uneasy. There had been an unvoiced message to that conversation that he didn't feel he had fully understood. But it reinforced the reality that Lord Ay knew exactly what Hani was up to on behalf of the queen. *Is he just biding his time until he can crush us all—like the Nubian rebels—with one blow?*

Still pondering that possibility, he made his way under the Window of Appearances down the glaring, dusty processional way southward toward Lord Pipi's house.

As soon as he entered, Maya saw that the family had eaten lunch without him. The little tables were still out in the salon, and crumbs, bones, and fruit peels littered them. The volume of noisy conversation drifting in from the porch mounted to toothache level in the effort to surmount the cacophony of the children, who, led by their uncle, were marching around, banging on wooden bowls and bronze pots. Maya felt suddenly the overwhelming urge to disappear again. In fact, he wanted to slip off privately to his mother's workshop and ask a few questions. Months had passed, and no one had done anything about the murder of Ipy. Maya was sure his conscience must be signaling its distress as well as Mery-ra's. He snagged the last piece of bread on a table, stuffed it into his mouth, and made his way quietly back to the vestibule. No one need know he had even returned if they didn't see the mail pouch.

But Mery-ra spotted him tiptoeing away and called, "Where are you off to, son?" He toddled toward Maya, his eyes shiny with curiosity.

"Oh," Maya said airily, "I have an investigation to carry out for Mother. A murder, in fact."

The old man brightened. "Would you mind if I came with you? I'm just underfoot with all the women exchanging gossip in there."

Oh, so I should let you come with me, but you didn't want me along on your little jaunts? A working-class boy has no secrets from an aristocrat? Is that it? But he realized how unhandsome such a thought was, and he said generously, "Of course not, my lord."

The two men made their way through the higgledy-piggledy, garbage-strewn streets of the capital. In the early afternoon, most of the workers were sleeping off their lunch—if they'd been lucky enough to have any. Cicadas blared from the trees in hidden gardens.

"You know, that's something I never saw any of in Hattusha—gardens. Not even at the palace," Maya mused.

"I think you're right, my boy. Perhaps with the woods so close all around, they don't feel the need for greenery the way we do."

"Although I never got to see any private houses. Maybe they have gardens in their courtyards or something." Maya shot a penetrating look at Lord Mery-ra from the corner of his eye, hoping to catch him off guard.

But Mery-ra said blandly, "I don't know. Maybe so."

Come on, my lord. You know very well. Maya fell silent.

With Mery-ra huffing and puffing in the heat, they turned toward the River just before the white walls of the palace rose into sight and passed down the little lane between warehouses and small craftsmen's establishments.

Finally, Maya beat on his mother's bronze-studded gate and called out, "Mother, it's me, Maya. I'm back."

As the old Nubian doorkeeper slid back the bolt, Mery-ra asked under his breath, "Does she know where you've been?"

Maya shook his head.

"Little master! Welcome home! We haven't seen much of you lately." The doorkeeper waved them in, a big grin of delight on his face. "Mistress In-hapy is in her workshop."

And there she came—pulling off her apron as she pushed under the fly-mat—from within the shadowy open door of the workshop. Maya could hear the familiar noises of sawing and filing, the whoosh of workmen blowing on the fire through their long pipes, and the hiss of red-hot metal quenched in water.

"Maya, my love! I haven't seen you for so long!" Maya's mother threw her short arms around him and kissed him greedily then bobbed a bow to Mery-ra. "My lord, what do we owe this honor to? Are you in need of some gold work?"

"No, no, my dear lady. I'm just here with Maya. He's ready to investigate your murder for you. We only arrived this morning from—from where we've been." Mery-ra beamed his gap-toothed grin and slipped his thumbs into the waistband to hitch up his kilt, which was sagging below his broad belly, as it tended to do.

"Oh, Maya, you didn't have to rush. I told you not to worry about it. We've had Ipy's funeral already—I paid for it myself—and finding his killer can't bring him back." His mother smoothed the scarf that covered her hair in an unconscious gesture. "Although I do miss him. None of the others is ready for as much responsibility as he was. He was a great help to me. And especially now, when we have such a big royal order to be filled."

Maya winced. *It should be me who is her great help.* "Sati lost our baby. I guess you knew that. I came home early to be with her."

"Hani's still in—overseas," Mery-ra added.

"I did know, my dear. Lady Nub-nefer told me. I'm so sorry for you both. Can I offer you gentlemen some beer? A few dates?"

"Let's go inside the house, and you can tell us something about Ipy's death."

On her bowed little legs, Maya's mother led the way across the work yard to the door of the house. It, too, stood open against the heat, with only a mat hanging over it. Inside, it was still stuffy—but at least in the shade. She gestured for them to have a seat. *And of course,* Maya thought in annoyance, *there are no stools, only cushions on a masonry bench. How many times have I offered to buy her stools?*

"Well, my love, the last time I saw Ipy, he was putting the finishing touches on a pair of truly splendid cuff bracelets." His mother settled her skirts over her knees. "We were told they were for the palace, and I believe it. We spared no expense—gold, silver. They were inlaid with precious stones in sacred signs. Of course, I don't know what they said, but the effect was dazzling—red symbols on blue and turquoise. Even some yellow faience. I'm sure the king has never owned a more beautiful pair of bracelets."

Lord Mery-ra and Maya exchanged looks of puzzlement. Those sounded suspiciously like the bracelets Lady Meryet-aten had offered to her chosen fiancé. "Who ordered the bracelets, mistress? Some servant of the king's household?" Mery-ra asked neutrally.

"I suppose he was. Who else could afford such pieces? Although they seemed rather large for a woman. But then our sun god has gained quite a lot of weight lately..."

Maya pondered that information. Perhaps they were different bracelets altogether than the ones he and Lord Hani had delivered to Kheta, despite the striking similarity. *But perhaps not.* "Could it have been the queen who commissioned them, Mother?"

"Why, I guess so. Certainly someone in the royal household." She looked back and forth between them. "They paid us up front, every *deben* we asked, with no haggling."

"And Ipy made them, you say, mistress?"

"He did. Design and everything. They were as beautiful as any pieces I've ever seen come out of the workshop. The man was a master craftsman."

Lord Mery-ra looked innocent. "Perhaps it was a diplomatic gift for some foreigner."

"That's certainly possible," Maya's mother agreed.

Maya said, "You were telling us that Ipy was finishing these pieces up, and...?"

"Oh yes. That's a lot of work for one man. He often stayed late working on them—well after me. This one evening, I had gone into the house for dinner when he left. And the next day, another of the workmen found him knifed, right out there in the street." Her voice trembled a little. "He called the police." She dropped her eyes.

"It was probably the police who did it," Mery-ra growled.

"Oh, they're not so bad under the new chief," In-hapy said with her usual optimism. "It was that Mahu who was so mean and disrespectful. But it has me worried—right out in front of the shop. I'm afraid for the others to come and go after dark now."

"Do you have a sketch or anything of the bracelets? Like the cartoons you work from?" Maya asked.

"Why, yes, son." She got to her feet and excused herself. Maya could hear her rapid bare footsteps pattering across the court. In a moment, she returned with a whitewashed board about a cubit across and handed it to him. On it were sketched in much-scraped-out and redrawn lines of diluted ink a flattened-out version of a cuff. The sacred signs had been fitted artistically into the borders in a way that was not only legible but beautiful as well. Even an illiterate would appreciate it—though only a scribe would know what it said: "All of them will come to it," over and over. The line was from a harper's song performed at funerals.

"How strange," Lord Mery-ra said, pushing back his wig and scratching his head. "It's not uncommon to write a prayer, a charm, or a wish for long life or health into a piece of jewelry to protect the wearer. But what does this mean? It sounds like a reference to death."

Could these have been the bracelets given to the prince? Maya asked himself, almost sure that it was so. He hadn't really seen them all that clearly inside their case, in the half darkness, but he had glimpsed the colors and a bit of elegant script. *Yet why the cryptic message from one who wished him well?* "I wonder if Ipy's death had anything to do with these pieces. Maybe whoever killed him thought he was carrying them on his person."

Mery-ra's tufty eyebrows were drawn down in thought. "Mistress, would anyone even have known that Ipy was working on them? You have a large workshop."

Ammit take it, I should have thought of that. Maya hoped he hadn't made himself look foolish and unprofessional by overlooking such a thing.

"I suppose so, my lord. The servant or whoever it was came into the shop to talk about the design and show us the words he wanted written, and of course, I had Ipy in to hear the discussion. He was going to do the work, after all. The servant would have recognized him as my chief artisan."

The hair rose on Maya's arms. "Are you sure they wouldn't think *you* were involved, Mother? In that case, you're in danger too."

"Oh, I made it clear as we talked that it would be Ipy's project, deferring to his ideas and all. Don't worry about me, son. If they haven't tried anything in all these months, they won't now. Although…"

"What, Mother? Did someone threaten you?"

"No, no. But the competition between workshops has gotten really bitter. I've never seen the like in all my years as a goldsmith. The workmen are always yelling taunts at one another. Sometimes they stand outside and shout, trying to provoke one of my men to come out and fight. I think all the royal business that has come our way has made us a target." In-hapy forced a smile. "But that's just the way young men are. That doesn't mean they'd kill anybody."

Still, Maya felt distinctly uneasy. *Yet another reason I should never have left my family for so long.*

✦

Maya's brood returned from the capital almost at the same time that Hani finally made it home to Waset.

Nub-nefer flew to him from the inner door and threw herself into his arms. "Hani, my love! Thank the gods you're back!"

Hani enfolded her like the precious treasure she was to him. "My dove," he murmured into the lily-scented crown of her wig. "I can't tell you how much I've missed you all. You've had to face too much alone these months."

"I know you had your duties, Hani. Isn't your guest with you?" Nub-nefer looked around, still holding Hani's upper arms. It seemed she had received his letter.

"Oh yes, but like the discreet fellow he is, he said he would prefer to wait in the garden until I had greeted my family. How are the children?"

"Baket-iset is her usual cheerful self. She's eager to see you. Neferet and Bener-ib are here for a few days. The boys are still in the capital, I suppose." Her smile faded into concern, her big dark eyes pools of sorrow. "Sati's not doing well at all, and it's been months. She'll seem fine one day, and the next, she's weeping uncontrollably. I don't know what to do for her."

"I guess it helped that Maya came back early?"

Nub-nefer led Hani through the salon toward the shady porch where his eldest daughter's couch was set up. "Undoubtedly. Thank you for that." Her smile grew rueful. "But you know, my love, for all his virtues, our good Maya isn't the most understanding of men. Sometimes he acts as heartbroken as she, but at others he seems to expect Sati to pull herself out of her sorrow by an act of will."

Hani sighed, sadness a heavy blanket over his heart that seemed to drag it to the ground. They had their own history of loss, and he had to say he understood his daughter. As cheerful and optimistic a person as he was by nature, there had been times when he had simply been unable to draw up from within himself the strength to resist misery. Like a bird caught in quicklime, the more he had struggled, the more trapped he'd seemed to become.

"I guess we should let our guest come in and introduce himself. He'll probably want to bathe and relax until dinner," he said finally, imagining Hattusha-ziti impatiently drumming his fingers in the kiosk. "I'll see Baket on my way in."

But the Hittite was standing on the path next to the fish pool, staring at Qenyt-ta-sherit, Hani's heron, who was poised in the water on one burnished leg, staring back. Hattusha-ziti looked up as the couple's footsteps crunched toward him over the gravel and folded in a courtly bow to the mistress of the house, a hand over his heart. "My lady, I thank you for your hospitality. I know this must disrupt your family, but it seemed better for the success of our mission not to stay at the palace." A wry smile twitched at the corner of his mouth.

"You are welcome to our home and to our land," Nub-nefer said graciously. "I've instructed the servants to draw you a bath and prepare your room. Before you leave, we'll celebrate your arrival as it deserves." She took the emissary's hand. "Permit me to show you to your quarters, my lord. I'm sure you're tired after such a long journey."

The exceedingly tall Hattusha-ziti let himself be led by the tiny mistress of the house, and the mismatched pair disappeared through the salon and into the back of the house. A moment later, Hani heard their footsteps clumping up the stairs. Nub-nefer's voice kept up a pleasant patter, punctuated now and again by Hattusha-ziti's deeper one. *I can always trust her to show the perfect mix of respect and friendliness,* Hani thought, filled with the warmth of pride.

He mounted the step of the porch and called out to his eldest daughter, who had been waiting patiently.

"Papa!" she said, beaming. "I'm so glad you're back." Her eyes followed Hani's as he made his way to her couch side and leaned over to kiss her, and her voice fell to a whisper. "How did it go?"

Hani tried not to reveal his ambivalence as he said, "Probably well. Did you see our Hittite go past?"

"Yes, I did, but I don't think he saw me. Mama was leading him at a pretty brisk pace, and he seemed to be sunk in his own reflections."

Hani leaned closer and asked quietly, "What did you think of him?" Baket-iset had such a refined intuition about people that he thought of her as his oracle. He had never known her to be wrong in her basic judgments.

"I haven't spoken to him yet, of course, but he seems like an honorable man. His friendliness is genuine, I think." She looked up at her father. "He'll do whatever he has to do to attain his ends, though—ruthless but in the service of his principles. What do *you* think about him?"

"I agree with you, my swan. He's every bit the professional diplomat—his concern is always the welfare of his country." *However, in a way, that makes him more predictable.*

"He's certainly big," Baket-iset said with a smile. "Are all the Hittites that tall?"

Hani laughed. "No, he's tall even there. But they're a race of big men, no question." He added with a mischievous grin, "We're smarter, though."

Suddenly, Mery-ra appeared in the doorway. "Smarter than what? A crocodile?"

Hani opened his arms to his father, who embraced him eagerly. "A certain kingdom to the north. How was the trip back, Father? Have you recovered from the journey?"

"Oh yes, my boy. I doubt I'll ever go that way again, so it was nice to see my old haunts. Was I right about those rocks?" He winked at Baket-iset.

"Right, as usual, revered parent," Hani conceded with a laugh. "We're going to have a party to see our guest off the day before he leaves, so don't make any arrangements with Meryet-amen for dinner." Meryet-amen was Mery-ra's widowed lady friend.

"Ooh, a party!" Neferet cried as she emerged onto the porch with Bener-ib at her heels. "Welcome back, Papa! Mama said you'd be out here."

Hani greeted his youngest daughter tenderly and hugged her shy friend as well. He wasn't sure what else to call her, although the girls' love for each other was deeper than friendship. "You ladies are well, I hope? No more plague at the palace?"

Neferet shrugged and gave a deep, philosophical sigh. "Now and then. But what can you do?"

The family exchanged news for a while, until Mery-ra

said, as if he had been pondering it all along, "Can we even have a party with the curfew going on? I don't see people wanting to leave before it's dark."

Hani shot him a tense look. "Has it come to that, then? We heard rumors."

Nub-nefer joined them. "Yes. Things are quite strained, even here in Waset. Lord Ptah-mes said the capital is even worse. People are almost afraid to leave the house except to go to work." She slipped an arm around Hani's waist. "Our party may have to be a family affair."

This is it, then, Hani thought, his stomach sinking like a rock. *The civil war has begun. Hattusha-ziti is going to have a lot to tell his king, and no festivities are going to mask that fact.*

He forced a cheerful smile. "Well, there are plenty of us here to make a convivial gathering. I had hoped to invite Lord Mai, Amen-em-hut, and some of the other priests— they could make a better case for the queen's cause than I, but now..."

"Amen-em-hut and his family can come and stay the night, don't you think, my love?" Nub-nefer looked up at Hani with a pleading smile. She missed no chance to enjoy her brother's company.

"If they're willing."

"Lord Ptah-mes could come too," Neferet said. "He's family."

That thought somehow never failed to stop Hani in surprise. "Of course, my duckling. He's certainly welcome to spend the night."

"He should have our bedroom," Nub-nefer said, looking around with a gaze fixed on the distance, her forefinger to her lip. Hani could see her already working out the practicalities of the evening. "Maya and Sati will certainly take up one room. Hani, the girls and we can sleep on the roof terrace. You, too, Father, and we'll give our foreign guest your apartment."

"It'll be fun!" Neferet cried, nudging Bener-ib. "Like staying at the farm."

"Well, to work, everyone. Nub-nefer, give us our assignments." Mery-ra rubbed his hands eagerly.

"First of all, I guess we need to send our invitations." Hani's uneasiness began to ebb under the rousing prospect of a festive occasion. "Now let's just hope that by the time our friend leaves, there's something to celebrate."

Sati had been doing so well. With the presence of all the family and the excited planning for the party, she had given herself over to the moment and was looking forward to helping her mother play hostess. But then something changed.

"Maya, I'm not going to the party," she declared dully that morning when they woke up, as if she had already been pondering the question for hours and had reached a decision. "It's not right. There's nothing to be happy about."

That bleak, dark-ringed look Maya dreaded was back in her eyes. She rolled away from him and pulled the sheet over her head.

"But, Sati, my love," Maya cried, swinging his feet to the floor. "This is important to your father. Can't you make a little more effort? It will be good for you to forget about our loss for an evening. We have to keep living, after all."

He heard little squeaks and hiccups, and her shoulders began to shake. Maya felt close to despair. He touched her back. "Come on, my love. Think of the children. They need their mother. *I* need you."

"I feel like I killed him," she said in a tiny voice shaking with misery. "I killed our son, Maya. Why didn't I die with him?"

A quiver of fear rippled up Maya's neck. Sometimes people really did go at their own hand to join a dead loved one. Merciful gods, he couldn't bear it. "Listen, my dove. I have to work for Lord Hani this morning. Why don't you come with me? I think it would be good for you to be with your mother today."

She protested loudly, curling into a defiant ball beside him, her hands over her head, but Maya strode to Sati's side of the bed and whisked the sheet off her. "I'm your husband, and I'm giving you an order. We're going to your parents'. The children will be fine with the nurse. You shouldn't be alone. Come on, now. Let's get dressed. I'll call the serving girl."

How much of this can I stand? Maya asked himself raggedly as they marched down the street to Lord Hani's house. *If there was ever any person I couldn't imagine sliding into a funk like this, it's Sat-hut-haru, always so cheery and effervescent, taking such delight in her children. What's happened to her? She's not the same woman I married.*

He had carried offerings to the temple of Mut, had bought Sati amulets of Ta-weret, the Great One, and had prayed to his own patron, Bes—but there she still was.

It's been months. The whole thing left him with a sense of helpless anguish. *What am I supposed to do? I have work to accomplish. I can't stay home all day, guarding her, lest she… Dear gods forbid.* He made an apotropaic gesture.

A'a admitted them to the house, his toothless grin melting off as he saw Sati's strained expression. "The master and mistress of the house are in the salon," he said neutrally, catching Maya's eye.

They made their way through the vestibule, Maya's steps brisk and determined. He had almost talked himself into righteous anger, although the better part of him knew his wife couldn't help herself. But it put a burden on him and the children. He was conscious of Sati's great silence behind him, as if she were holding her breath.

Lady Nub-nefer entered, all smiles, her arms outstretched, then she saw her daughter's expression, and her own transformed into one of tender sorrow. "My little girl, it's not a good day, is it?" She folded her middle daughter to her bosom and held her close. Sati clutched at her, shaking soundlessly.

Maya's face grew hot with shame at this demonstration of the motherly bond. *How could I judge my wife so harshly, knowing—or at least guessing at—the rupture of that bond she suffered?* He hung his head, feeling a telltale prickling in his nose.

Suddenly, Lord Hani was beside him, a hand laid upon his shoulder. "Go to her," he said quietly. "It's you she really needs."

Maya went up to Sati and put an arm around her hips. She turned her ravaged face down to him, and he gestured with a tip of the head. Sati followed him to a stool, he pulled another up to it with a screech, and they both sat down and leaned into each other. Tears began to dribble down Maya's face. *How could you be so unfeeling?* he castigated himself, wrapping her in an embrace. *The woman you love is suffering.*

He was remotely conscious of Hani and Nub-nefer quietly tiptoeing from the room onto the porch.

✲

Hani stood sad and helpless beside Nub-nefer as Maya and Sat-hut-haru clung to each other tearfully. Mery-ra, at the foot of the steps, gazed with compassion, his eyes misty. Sorrow hung in a suffocating cloud over them, and Hani was unable to say anything for a long time, the painful memory of his and Nub-nefer's lost child constricting his throat. The little boy had come right between Baket-iset and Pa-kiki, but he had flown into the West after only a few days among them, before his parents had been able to accustom themselves to his endearing ways, his sweet smile, his tiny hands. At Hani's side, Nub-nefer trembled with the tears she was too strong to let fall, and he wondered how much more devastated she had to have been than him at a magnitude of loss he couldn't really understand—the child had been a part of her for nearly ten months. It would have been too cruel to remind her that almost every family had lost at least one child.

He tightened his arm around her shoulders, and she laid her head against his chest. "Do you remember, Hani, my love?" she murmured. "He would have been thirty-five years old by now."

Hani nodded, suddenly unable to speak. The two of them stood frozen with shared pain.

After a moment, his wife said, "All Sati has ever wanted

129

is to be a mother. She has so much love she said she can never have enough children."

"She has four of the finest little ones in the Two Lands, my dear. And she'll have more. She's still young," Hani said, conscious of what cold comfort such words provided. He laid his lips on the top of his wife's wig.

At last, Nub-nefer heaved a sigh and said, "We're in the hands of the gods. The Lord Amen-Ra has care of us."

Hani quoted softly the hymn he had heard her sing so often:

"Pilot who knows the waters,

Helmsman of the weak,

Who gives bread to him who has none,

Who nourishes the servant of his house..."

And she, the god's chantress, broke quietly into song to finish the verse in her sweet voice:

"The lord is my protector,

A helper strong of arm,

Amen, who knows compassion,

Who hearkens to him who calls."

She squeezed Hani's hand and said in a faltering voice, "She'll get over it someday. We all will."

But Hani's heart was leaden. He hadn't been able to spare his little swallow this pain, any more than he had managed to protect Baket-iset from the malice that had blighted her life forever—any more than he could avoid whatever diplomatic disaster was coming for the Two Lands. He felt very small, and the weight of the world seemed to bow down his shoulders.

CHAPTER 6

Hani had introduced Prince Hattusha-ziti to Lord Mai, who would be able to fill him in eloquently on how the queen's supporters saw the future playing out after the Hittite marriage. The emissary would be the guest of the high priest for the next week or so, while other supporters of Meryet-aten paid him court and tried to convince him of the feasibility of their plan. And that left Hani some time to devote to the murder of In-hapy's foreman. Maya, torn between his duties to his mother and his wife's need for his presence, was finally convinced—with a somewhat less than perfect grace—to stay in Waset. But at the last moment, he came pattering up the gangplank of Hani's yacht just as the sailors prepared to heave it aboard.

"Maya, my boy," Hani said in surprise. "Did you change your mind?"

"There's nothing I can do for Sati that her mother and sisters can't, Lord Hani." Maya was breathing hard after what had clearly been a rapid trip to the banks of the River. He looked almost guilty, as if he feared his father-in-law would judge him for abandoning his grieving wife, and said defensively, "I'm not sure she even cares whether I'm there."

This is all hard on the poor man, Hani thought in compassion. *It's hard on Sati in one way, but it's hard on Maya in another. He's locked on the outside of her sorrow, yet he has grief of his own.* "You're more than welcome, my friend. This is really your investigation, after all."

They made their way up the sloping stern of the boat and seated themselves under the shade of the kiosk. Hani stretched out his legs and gave a sigh of satisfaction as the yacht angled into the current and took off at a gallop. A wedge of ducks beat heavily into the sky from the malachite waters and, wheeling in midflight as if one thought directed them, sailed toward the marshes. Hani watched admiringly, almost enviously. No one said anything for a long interval of enjoyment.

At last, Maya spoke up. "Do we know who found Ipy's body? Maybe they noticed something about the wound or the way he fell that might give us a clue."

"I was thinking that too. Maya, you knew Ipy, didn't you? What sort of person was he?"

"I haven't been around him much for years, my lord. But he always struck me as a nice fellow—modest. No airs. He wouldn't be one to get up anybody's nose."

High praise indeed from Maya. "I wonder if he had debts or was playing around with someone else's wife."

Maya shrugged. "Hard to imagine. He never struck me as a ladies' man—he seemed to be working all the time."

Five days later, they set foot on the dusty streets of the capital. Although it might have been his imagination, Hani thought Akhet-aten already seemed strangely deserted, as if the mere rumor of its abandonment had begun to empty it. Or perhaps it was the chilling effect of knots of soldiers at nearly every intersection. The guard platforms that punctuated the processional street were all manned, as if some spectacle were under way, and there was no possibility of forgetting that martial law held sway in the City of the Horizon.

The position of the sun declared it was midafternoon, the hottest part of the day, and a few artisans were making their way back to work after their siesta, but the scribal cadre was nowhere to be seen.

"Let's head directly to your mother's workshop," Hani said. "We can check the mail at the chancery on our way back to Lord Ptah-mes's. I'm not sure anyone has returned to the Hall of Royal Correspondence yet."

They turned their steps toward the River and the warehouse district and before long were knocking at the bronze-studded gate that defended the goldsmith studio.

In-hapy herself greeted them. "Ah, Lord Hani. Maya, my son!" she cried, her eyes brightening with pleasure. "The porter is still sleeping. Come in. Come in." She stepped back and let the men pass inside the broad work court. From within the open door of the workshop, quiet metallic noises already sounded—tapping, clinking, and a prolonged hiss.

"Perhaps we could talk to the man who found Ipy, mistress," Hani said. "Or see if anyone else here knew of anything that might have made him a target."

"Of course, my lord. Talk to anyone you like. I'll send Pi-ay to you right away." In-hapy waddled away obligingly to the workshop, as if she and her men had nothing better to do than answer questions.

"Do you think this Pi-ay might have seen something, Lord Hani?" Maya asked under his breath.

"We can't know until we ask him. I'd like to think the police have already questioned him, but who can be sure?"

A moment later, a compactly built little man who might have been in his early forties appeared at Hani's side. He still had his teeth and a full head of mostly dark hair that flipped up at the front in an unsubduable cowlick. Hani saw a flicker of nervousness in his light-brown eyes. No one wanted to get involved in a criminal investigation.

"In-hapy tells me that you were the one who found the body of your colleague Ipy. Is that true?" Hani gave him a friendly smile, hoping to put him at ease.

"It is, my lord. I was on my way back to work early in the morning, and there he lay, sprawled in the street with a knife in his back." The man swallowed hard.

"He'd lain there all night, and no one had found him?" Maya demanded skeptically.

"I don't know, master. I don't know when he was killed."

Well said. This man is smart. "How was he positioned? Where had he been struck?"

"He was facedown, his head pointing right at the gate here, as if he were on his way in or had turned back for something. He'd been stabbed in the back, between the shoulder blades." The man reached behind himself and poked his own back with a thumb.

Maya pressed him. "Did it look like he died quickly, or had he crawled?"

The goldsmith stroked his chin. "I couldn't say, master.

He was stretched out rather neatly. He didn't seem to have fought. That's for sure. Somebody must've come up behind him."

Or else it was someone he knew and didn't fear to turn his back on.

"What kind of knife was it?" Maya asked.

"I... I don't remember. I was so horrified I hardly noticed."

Maya was grilling the man aggressively, Hani saw with amusement, and the fellow was starting to get nervous, casting his eyes toward the workshop as if he thought In-hapy might rescue him.

Hani decided to shift the focus of the questions. "What's your job here, Pi-ay?"

A proud smile twitched at the goldsmith's lips. "I'm the filigree man. I lay out the wire borders for enamel work and filigree decorations. Granulation too. All that decoration that gives a piece its value. Texture, you know?"

"Highly skilled." Hani was genuinely admiring. "How well did you know Ipy?"

Pi-ay gave an ironic bark, and for the first time, a cloud of pain drifted across his broad features. "We'd worked together for twenty years—since he joined the workshop as an apprentice. Though lately, the mistress had made him a kind of foreman over the rest of us."

"It's my understanding she was hoping to leave the business to him, since her son here wasn't interested. Is that the case, do you know?" Hani asked with an innocent lift of the eyebrows.

The goldsmith shrugged, his mouth twisted to one side dubiously. "Maybe. Nobody told me in so many words."

I'm like some poor lark tugging at a worm that doesn't want to come out of the ground, Hani thought, chuckling. *This fellow certainly isn't volunteering any information.* "How old a man was Ipy? What sort of person was he?"

"Oh, midthirties, maybe five years younger than me, I'd say. Don't know why the mistress would put somebody that young over the rest of us. I've worked with the mistress or her husband longer than him—since I was a boy. Ipy came along later."

Hani asked, "Did that go to his head? Was he an arrogant sort who might have made enemies?"

"Everybody liked him," Pi-ay admitted. "Had a knack for making people like him. We were friends, and everybody says I'm hard to get along with." He looked up at Hani with mild defiance, as if daring him to disagree.

"So, you don't know of anyone who might have had it in for him?"

"Not here, no. Unless one of those hyenas from another workshop went after him." Pi-ay's expression grew unpleasant, and he spat on the ground. "Competition's gotten so fierce I wouldn't put it past them to kill somebody. Trying to get our jobs, you know? Everybody wants the king's commissions. The palace has started piling up treasures for her tomb, whenever she—you know."

"Really?" Hani said, startled.

"Oh yes. There's only so much royal business, and Mistress In-hapy has had most of it for a long time. Some people are getting impatient. They're always harassing us, hanging around, trying to scare us."

"That's what Mother said," Maya confirmed.

Hani shot him a thoughtful look. *Things are that bitter, eh?*

"Did you pull the knife out of him when you found him?" Maya asked.

"No, master. The *medjay* did that."

Too bad, Hani thought. *We might have told from the angle of the knife whether his murderer was tall or short, at least.* Hani wasn't sure the man had any more to offer that might be relevant. "Did Ipy leave behind a family?"

"He did, my lord. A wife, Hemet-min, and six children. And his father. The old man's"—the goldsmith lifted an eyebrow significantly—"not all there. Ipy's widow, Hemet-min, is a lazy slattern. I don't know how the family will manage with *her* trying to keep them together."

A pang of sorrow for the bereaved woman pierced Hani. *All that responsibility, and now her breadwinner is gone. Slattern or not.* "Thank you, my man. You can get back to your work."

Hani and Maya thanked In-hapy for her cooperation and made their way out into the lane. Hani stared for a moment at the street in front of the gate, trying to imagine a stabbed man lying there—praying for help, perhaps, or, as his life ebbed away, wondering what would become of his loved ones. The earth had been swept, and no traces of violence remained.

As they walked on, Hani said soberly, "Perhaps we should offer the family a little something. Maybe the widow could hire someone to help her with the household."

"I can't imagine that Ipy wasn't well paid, my lord. In fact, I think his eldest son works for Mother too. Surely they don't lack for food."

"I'd like to talk to this Hemet-min, in any case. She may know something about the Osir that would have offered another motive for his murder. But we'll wait till this evening. We can catch the son, too, when he's home." Then Hani stopped in his tracks. "Oh, wait—I forgot to ask your mother where Ipy lived."

"I know, Lord Hani," Maya assured him in a manner that smacked a little of smugness. "Mother sometimes sent me to take things to him after hours when I was a youth."

Hani, with nothing particular to demand his attention for once, drifted down the narrow street, observing the workshops and stalls that had not yet packed away their wares for the night's curfew. Maya, at his side, barely stifled a yawn.

"You can go on home if you like, son," Hani said affably. "I'm just ambling here, with no objective."

But Maya protested, "No, no, my lord. It's not boredom—I just didn't get much sleep last night. Some rope was slapping in the wind against the mast, making noise."

Thinking they might make a nice gift for Neferet and Bener-ib, Hani bent to examine an array of large bowl-shaped covered baskets set along the edge of the street. But the proprietor came rushing out from the interior of his shop, sandals flapping. "Oh, don't open those, my lord. They're not for sale."

"Then perhaps you shouldn't set them out in front." Hani grinned.

"They contain my real wares." The man, a scrawny, middle-aged specimen with his thinning hair cut in a wig-like bowl, rubbed his hands and wiped them on his kilt, which looked as if it had been used as a towel before. He leaned over one of the baskets and whisked the lid off.

A rank animal odor hit Hani's nose. At his side, Maya tottered back, fanning the air before his face as if to disperse the effluvium. Within the dark interior of the basket, something began to move—a smooth, sinuous rope of living flesh enameled in vague patterns of buff and brown. It drew itself up and up, its malevolent black eyes fixed on Hani's. The shopkeeper stuffed the emerging reptile into its basket and slammed the lid down.

Hani reeled back, pulling Maya with him. "By all the gods, man! You can't leave deadly snakes out here on the street. Some curious child might have opened the basket."

"Whoever heard of anyone buying snakes anyway?" Maya cried in disgust. "There are too many of them already."

The man shrugged, his mouth pursed as if at a good joke. "You'd be surprised, my lord. They catch rats. They eat other worse snakes. You can train them to dance…"

"I can't imagine there's a huge market in snake charmers," Maya grumbled. "And that was a cobra. What worse snakes is *he* going to eat?"

The merchant shrugged. "They make medicine out of the venom." His thick lips spread in a sly smile. "They buy them to kill enemies."

Hmmm. "That can't be legal," Hani said dryly.

"But I don't know what people are going to do with them when they buy them, do I now, my lord? Maybe those people are just going to catch rats."

His nose wrinkled with distaste, Maya said, "Snakes don't seem very smart to me. How can you be sure one's going to kill the person you want him to anyway? Do you show him a picture and say, 'That's the one'?"

The man laughed obsequiously. "My lord is a man of jest. No, you train it by making it associate food with some symbol or garment or something that your target is going to be wearing or carrying. Blue and green colors are best. Then let your legless one get good and hungry and turn him loose in the victim's vicinity, and he'll find that symbol, and that's the person he'll approach. Then of course, your target will react with fear, and it'll make the snake afraid, and he'll strike." He added, "There's no guarantee, of course. I'm not responsible for the fellow after he leaves my shop."

As beautiful as they were, in their fashion, snakes were not Hani's favorite creatures—ever since he had seen one empty a nest of helpless baby birds. The idea of deadly snakes being sent after people to kill them made the bile rise in his gorge. Fighting down his disgust, he said nothing. *Of course, the snake is just an innocent animal fulfilling his nature. The cobra is sacred, even. It's the murderer who's the real reptile.* Eventually, he asked, "What sort of lure do people use to mark their prey?"

"Oh, a sash or a piece of jewelry. A leopard skin—see how easy it would be to target a priest? Something with strong patterns and some color contrast. I can show you a few, because I have to train the cobra using the real thing or a copy."

Hani was constantly amazed at the energy people put into nefarious activities. But his curiosity was aroused. "Very well. Show us. We're not keeping you from going home to dinner, are we?"

"No, no, as long as we aren't caught by the curfew. I'm

always happy to show off my children." The man looked pleased, no doubt expecting a sale. He picked up the cobra's basket and brought it inside with him.

Hani and Maya followed him into the dim interior of the shop. The shopkeeper stuck his serpent under a long table and lit a lamp. Then he slid out yet another basket—square, like a chest—and laid it on the table. "You see, my lord? Here's the sort of things we use. Snakes are actually rather intelligent." He extracted a *weshket* necklace of turquoise faience, a sash with fringed and embroidered ends, a bit of leopard pelt, and a small painted piece of papyrus. The last object caught Hani's eye, and he held it flat with his fingers while he studied it for a moment. He heard Maya's breath catch, and his own heart stepped up its beat. Before him lay a painting of In-hapy's beautiful inlaid gold cuffs, which the queen had given to her Hittite fiancé. It was curled as if it had been rolled around a man's forearm to resemble a real bracelet.

Hani stared at it, the hair on his arms rising. He didn't know what to think, but he couldn't help but feel it was an important clue of some sort. "And you didn't know that these people who asked you to train a cobra to target a specific person had murder on their mind?" he asked pointedly. "It seems to me these objects make you an accessory to their crimes, my friend."

The man blanched and slammed the basket shut. "You're *medjay*? Great One, protect us..." He started to back away, as if intending to run.

But Hani stepped between him and the door and continued smoothly, "No, but I do have some influence with the king. Perhaps if you cooperate and give me the information I need, I can plead on your behalf."

"Anything, my lord. I'm just an honest man trying to make a living, as my ancestors have before me." The merchant cringed and clasped his hands in anxiety.

"This picture—who brought it? Who asked for a snake trained to attack the person wearing such a bracelet?"

"I... I don't know, my lord. A bureaucrat or high-level functionary, I think. It's been a long time now. I thought he wanted to assassinate some enemy of the king, you see. How could I know—"

"No doubt that was it—an enemy of the king." Hani saw Maya's expression of contempt on the other side of the merchant. "Do you get many orders from the palace?"

"No, no, my lord. Rarely. But then how would I know, if some well-dressed servant came along?" The snake man looked as if he wanted to turn into a serpent himself and crawl liquidly away into a hole to hide.

"What did the man who ordered it look like?"

"Lean, good-looking. About sixtyish, I'd say. A whiff of the military about him."

Ay. "I'll take this." Hani rolled up the mock bracelet and stuck it into the waistband of his kilt. "After the functionary brought you this object, you trained a snake accordingly, right? Did the man ever pick it up?"

"Oh yes, my lord. It was a beautiful specimen."

On an impulse, Hani pulled the faience sealing ring from his finger and thrust it at the merchant. "Here. Go turn the rest of them loose in the desert. They deserve to live with dignity, not as criminals."

"May Meret-seger and Wadjet bless you, my lord!"

Hani and Maya finally detached themselves from the merchant's grateful bobbing and regained the street, where twilight was settling in. The lane was empty, and lamplight glowed from the high windows here and there where families had sat down to dinner. An owl swooped overhead like a pale, silent shadow—he, too, seeking his meal.

"*Yahya!*" Maya said under his breath. "That was interesting." Hani could see the whites of his son-in-law's eyes glitter as he turned to look back at the serpent shop.

"A whole new profession I knew nothing about." But Hani's thoughts were galloping elsewhere. "Was the queen trying to get Prince Zannanza killed when she gave him those cuffs? If so, why, after risking so much to marry him? And why not find a more direct and reliable method?"

"Maybe it isn't the queen. Maybe someone else knows about the bracelets and has decided to turn them against the prince. He's still in danger."

In his absorption, Hani's stride had lengthened until Maya was almost trotting to keep up. Hani felt a swelling urgency. Something was beginning to make sense at last. "You're right. Maybe someone else had the bracelets made and added them to the diplomatic gifts in the queen's name. I could never figure out why they would be inscribed with something as lugubrious as 'Everyone will come to it,' but if they were intended from the first to be an instrument of death..."

Maya, starting to breathe heavily, nodded in understanding. "And I'll wager we know who that someone is, don't we, my lord? A certain God's Father. The description fit him perfectly."

"That seems very likely." Hani absorbed the idea.

"But there are no cobras in Hatti Land or even Kharu. If one suddenly appears, it will be glaringly obvious that an Egyptian is behind it."

"Can he intend to wait until the lad is here in Kemet before he makes his move?"

Hani made a considering moue, his eyebrows knotted. "He must. That would explain why no one attempted anything on our party in Kheta Land. They're going to target the prince himself."

The hour was getting late, so rather than return home, Hani and Maya trudged back into the warehouse district near the palace, where many of the royal workmen had set up their residences when the capital moved from Waset. The heat of the day had abated, and all around them, laborers were making their way back to their homes for dinner and an early bedtime.

What a hardship on all of them, Hani thought with a shake of the head. *Hundreds of people who could ill afford such a move but who could afford even less to lose their jobs.*

The goldsmith's house was a featureless cube of shabby, unwhitewashed brick with a trampled little court. For a man who had to have earned a fair sum for his highly skilled labor, it didn't look very prosperous. But then six children and an old father would have divided the amount into small parts.

A stringy girl in early adolescence opened the door to them. Her Haru lock looked as if it hadn't been re-braided since she was six. Other children peered down from the parapet of the roof. Maya looked around with a wrinkled nose as the two men entered the vestibule.

"Is your mother in, my girl?" Hani asked in a kindly voice.

She nodded listlessly and disappeared into the shadowy salon. A few moments later, a haggard young woman of thirty or so entered, a baby on her hip and her dress strap peeled down to nurse. She had about her the nervous, exhausted air of one who was so harried she was in danger of flying apart completely.

"What is it?" she said.

"My name is Hani son of Mery-ra, and this is Mistress In-hapy's son. Our condolences, mistress. May the Osir Ipy enjoy a happy eternity in the West. We're trying to find out who killed him in order to appease his *ba*."

"Who asked you to get involved?" she cried. "Don't we have enough trouble?"

Hani was taken aback. Families were usually delighted to think someone was going to find their relative's killer. He and Maya exchanged glances.

"Mistress In-hapy. She thought very highly of your husband. She said to give you this."

Hemet-min stared expressionlessly at the big bag of grain Hani slipped into her free hand. "T-Thank you, my lord," she stammered as if uncomprehending. "Thanks to Mistress In-hapy. I... I don't know how we're going to manage anyway—all these mouths."

At that moment, a thunder of footsteps sounded down the stairs of the small house, and two skinny children, their knees black with grime, came clattering down, yelling at each other.

"Mama! Mama! He hit me!"

"She took my ball!"

The girl carried a dirty-faced toddler around the middle so that his feet trailed the floor, and her brother tugged at the little one's arm as if to pull him away. Flies clustered around the smaller boy's rheumy eyes.

"You're going to hurt him!" his big brother cried.

"Stop!" The girl whipped around to avoid the boy's grasp.

The toddler looked dazed and finally began to cry. The room shattered into a din of screaming and yelling, and even the baby on Hemet-min's hip broke into wails. The woman's face was so wild and exhausted that Hani's heart went out to her.

"Be quiet, all of you, if you don't want a beating!" she cried in a breaking voice. "Be quiet! Mother of the gods, take me away from this!"

The adolescent girl who had answered the door reappeared, calling, "Mama, Grandfather is out in the street. A neighbor brought him home."

Hemet-min put down the baby and the grain sack and rushed to the doorway. "You just left him out there alone? What if the soldiers get him?"

"Hu-may is with him. He just shat on the neighbor's step."

Hani said to Maya under his breath, "I think this may not be a good time to talk to her."

Maya raised a wry eyebrow that said, "There's an understatement."

They retreated toward the door. Just inside the gate, they encountered Hemet-min and a boy who seemed about twelve trying to wrangle a naked, reed-thin old man toward the house. The grandfather looked confused, his weepy, flyblown eyes unfocused and his mouth hanging open. The stench made it clear what he had done.

Hani heaved a deep sigh of compassion, seeing the future of his own beloved father. "Go in with your daughter now, my grandfather. It's getting late," he said, taking the old man gently by the stick-like brown arm. But clearly Hemet-min was as much an object of pity as her father-in-law. Tears had begun to deform her face, and she dashed helplessly at her eyes as she scooped up the snotty-nosed baby. "What am I going to do with him? Ipy was always busy, never home, and now it's worse. It's *his* father, Ammit take it. I can't stand it anymore." Her voice rose, wobbling dangerously.

Hani helped her guide the old man toward the door, where the children, in a swarm, crowded in behind their grandfather, sniggering and shoving. The rolled mat over the doorway dropped in the oldest boy's face, and the lad pushed his way inside after the others, leaving Hani and Maya alone at the gate.

Silently, Hani led the way out into the street. They needed to get back before the watchman came by and caught them out after curfew. Darkness had already settled softly over the rooftops, and the first stars appeared in the sky like fireflies. After the painful disorder of the dead man's house, it was hard to remember how peaceful a summer evening could be. Several neighbors were sitting on their doorsills, their legs stretched out wearily, gossiping. Another woman with a scarf on her head leaned down from her terrace. He had a feeling he knew what they were discussing.

"Whew. Somebody didn't manage their household very efficiently," Maya said disapprovingly. "If Mother had known about this, I'm not sure Ipy would have been the man she chose to run her business."

Hani felt little inclined to criticize the desperate family. "It's hard to say. How are they going to make a living now when the oldest boy is so young? He must not earn much as an apprentice. And Hemet-min can't work while she's trying to keep up with all those little ones."

They walked on in silence, their footsteps on the packed earth the only sound until a brief, distant thunder of passing chariot troops on the main road rumbled by. A chill tingled up Hani's spine. "Normally, there would be grandparents or aunties around to take care of those children. But nobody who lives in this city of the damned is from here. Their relatives are probably in Waset."

Maya let out a tense breath between his teeth. "You know, Lord Hani, I don't want my family to sink into that kind of chaos. Sat-hut-haru is tired and lonely. I think that's why she's taken the loss of this child so hard. I should be there to help her. And of course, the stress of soldiers in the streets everywhere doesn't do her any good."

Hani shot him a sharp glance from the corner of his eye. *Is he trying to tell me something?* "I know what you mean, my boy. I sometimes feel guilty about that too. It's just that I may be able to do more good where I am." In fact, he felt his conscience had been stretched so thin during this assignment that it might never snap back to its normal shape. *No, after this mission is over, I'm resigning.*

⁕

By the time Hani and Maya returned to Waset, a week had passed, during which Lord Mai and the other high-placed partisans of the queen had presented to the Hittite emissary all the reasons their cabal should win and why a union between Kheta and the Black Land would be beneficial to both sides. Hattusha-ziti was once more at Hani's, filling one wax tablet after another with notes in the strange sacred pictures of the Luwian system. It struck Hani as a useful precaution, since virtually no one in the Two Lands was likely to be able to read it, him included.

"Were the priests eloquent, my lord?" Hani asked with a smile.

Hattusha-ziti closed the wooden frame of his tablet and pushed it to one side. "Indeed. Especially your fervent brother-in-law. They all had a little trouble explaining why the soldiers at every corner weren't a sign of danger, however."

Hani could think of no reply. The Hittite wasn't a fool—nor was he an optimistic zealot like Amen-em-hut and Mai. Troubled, Hani blew out a breath through the nose. "I'm sure you'll make an honest report."

"As honest as I'm able, given the information I've gleaned," the Hittite said evasively.

"Lord Hattusha-ziti, in the days left to you, it might help relieve your mind to speak to the physicians of the royal women. They were present at the exchange of babies and perhaps above anyone else can testify to the reality of what I've told you."

"An excellent idea, if they're willing to divulge such a thing to a foreigner like me."

"I'm sure they will be. They're very much in favor of the bonds your country and ours are hoping to forge," Hani assured him.

Hattusha-ziti's lips spread in his thin, conspiratorial smile. "Can we do this without being seen by the king or her people?"

"Easily, my lord. The doctors happen to be in Waset at the moment."

Hattusha-ziti expressed his satisfaction, and Hani called for the litter. "Why don't you ride, for greater privacy? It isn't far, and I have no problem walking. If anyone sees us passing, they'll think it's my father in the litter."

The Hittite laughed. "Your father is quite a fellow. He reminds me of my own father—no longer among us, alas."

Hani grinned, pleased. Once more, he warned himself not to fall too far under the charm of these foreigners, who—like him—were out for the good of their own land. And the thought of his father left him with a vaguely uneasy feeling. "There are plenty of things you don't know," Mery-ra had said.

They made their way to Ptah-mes's villa in the southern suburbs, where the servants, accustomed to Hani's presence, welcomed them.

"Is the mistress of the house in?" Hani asked.

"She is, my lord. And the master too."

Hani thought good manners demanded that he greet Ptah-mes first, and he was happy to do so. He realized how he missed the sardonic humor and experienced advice of his friend and sometime superior. To the doorkeeper, he said, "We'll speak to Lord Maya first, then. Please tell him we have a foreign guest."

The man disappeared into the house.

Hattusha-ziti said in a low voice, "I don't suppose this Maya is the commissioner in Azzati?"

"He is, my lord. Or rather, he was. He's now the treasurer—and also the husband of the *sunet* we're here to see."

The Hittite nodded.

A moment later, the servant returned and said with a bow, "The Master of the Double House will see you, my lords."

The vestibule was filled with petitioners of one sort or another—taxmen come to report their collections, secretaries, and those humble folk who sought an exemption. But Hani and his guest were led directly into Ptah-mes's elegant salon, where he sat on his chair of audience, bedecked in all his fashionable splendor, the small flat scepter of authority resting in the bend of his arm.

His severe face lit up at the sight of Hani, and he rose, his pleats unwrinkled. He laid aside the scepter as he stepped down from the dais, extending his hands. "Hani, my friend. It's good to see you." Hani sensed Ptah-mes wanted to ask how the mission to the north had gone, but instead he turned graciously to Hattusha-ziti and said with a tip of the head, "I believe you are the king of Kheta's chamberlain, are you not, my lord? We met last year in Azzati. Welcome to my humble residence."

Hani smiled within. The villa was far from humble, but to a grandee like Ptah-mes, perhaps it seemed so. His friend was clothed in his usual crisp, spotless garments, a large bunch of gathered linen falling from the waistband of the kilt in front, in the latest fashion. Not many people could wear it so well as the tall, slim Ptah-mes. A colorful *weshket* collar lay upon his shoulders, and inlaid bracelets clasped

151

his forearms below full, pleated sleeves. Hani wondered with amusement if he'd been sitting around, awaiting a prestigious foreign visitor—but Ptah-mes would consider receiving petitioners at home a fully formal occasion.

"How can I help you?" their host asked, drawing the two men after him into the garden.

"Lord Hattusha-ziti has come to the Black Land to look over the political situation, my lord. His king is hesitant, fearing that there may be some circumstances that would endanger his son."

Hattusha-ziti said to Hani, "He knows about my mission, eh?" Then he turned to Ptah-mes. "Please see in this hesitancy no offense to your queen, but I'm sure you understand Our Sun's concerns, Lord Maya."

"By all means." Ptah-mes drew them to chairs and bade them sit. "Hani has made you aware of the political situation, I suppose?"

Hattusha-ziti said smoothly, "I'm hoping this trip will clarify it."

"Lord Mai and others of his persuasion have spent the last week explaining everything to him. Before he leaves, I thought we might have him talk to Neferet and Bener-ib about the identity of the Haru in the nest."

"An excellent idea."

Anything else Ptah-mes might have had in mind to say was interrupted by the thunder of bare feet on the stairs and the appearance of the two young *sunet*s.

Neferet, as always, burst into the room in an explosion of energy. "Papa!" she cried in delight. "What brings you here? It seems like aaages since we've seen you." She threw her arms exuberantly around him, and Bener-ib did likewise in her shy way.

Hattusha-ziti shot Hani a wry smile of surprise. "They're your daughters?"

"Neferet is, my lord. Lady Bener-ib is her colleague and like one of the family." He could feel heat stealing up his cheeks. It had not, perhaps, been altogether honest to withhold that information from the Hittite, but he had feared that it might look a little too neat—that Neferet's testimony might seem too coached.

Never one to let others speak for her, Neferet said proudly, "We're the king's physicians."

"And witnesses of the crown prince's birth," Hani added.

Ptah-mes watched the exchange in blandly observant silence.

Hattusha-ziti's eyes narrowed a little, as if he were weighing the validity of twenty-three-year-old female doctors. Certainly, Hani realized, there were no such things in Kheta, although there were certainly prestigious female practitioners of magic. His recollection was that medicine was fairly primitive in that northern kingdom anyway.

"Neferet, my duckling, could you and Bener-ib describe for our guest what happened the day of the crown prince's birth?" he asked, drawing the girl toward him.

"Of course, Papa." She stood in the center of the seated men and cleared her throat, not with unease but as a kind of professional storyteller's gesture. "Bener-ib and I were students at that point, my lord, studying under Lady Djefat-nebty, the royal *sunet*. She had us join her and the midwives for the birth of the queen—now the king's—seventh child."

"Life, prosperity, and health to her," Ptah-mes interjected in a tone so dry it might or might not have been sarcastic. His expression betrayed nothing.

"I had been told that if she gave birth to a daughter, I was to go into the room down the corridor where King Nefer-khepru-ra's sister was also giving birth and exchange the two children—I mean if hers was a boy."

Hattusha-ziti watched her recital with interest. Hani prayed that she wouldn't go too far and reveal the full identity of the prince's grandmother.

"The queen's child was a stillborn girl, and Lady Sit-pa-aten's was a son. So I switched them out. And the queen never knew. The boy became the Haru in the nest, and everybody thought he was the son of the king and queen." She finished off with a satisfied grin that bared the gap between her front teeth.

"Only..." Bener-ib piped up in her girlish voice, "it wasn't really Lady Sit-pa-aten at all."

"No. She turned out to be a servant! And the late king was the father!" Neferet looked around in triumph.

The Hittite sat in silence for a long time, digesting the information, then asked, "Do you swear that what you have told me is true, mistress?"

"Oh, yes, my lord. I swear on my mother's *ka*. May Ma'at put scorpions in my ears and unravel my navel if I'm not telling the truth."

Even though it's not the whole truth. Hani, relieved at the girls' perfect performance, felt he could finally let out his breath. Ptah-mes discreetly concealed a smile behind a small cough.

Raising his eyes to Neferet, Hattusha-ziti asked, "How many people know this story?" He seemed very serious.

"Not too many, my lord," Hani answered him before Neferet could launch into some other long explication. "My family. The high priests of Amen-Ra and some of the military. The king's father, no doubt. And of course, Queen Meryet-aten, who was present. Certain others of the actual witnesses are no longer with us."

"And Lady Djefat-nebty," Neferet added, "but she's on our side."

"What happened to the real mother?"

Hani said, "She's still alive, my lord. And in my employ. But her tongue has been cut out, so she can't testify."

Hattusha-ziti rose to his feet, and out of courtesy, the others did too. "I want to see her. Is that possible?"

"Of course, my lord."

"Maybe you'd want to talk to Lady Djefat-nebty," Neferet suggested in an eager voice.

"She's in Sau now, isn't she?" Hani asked skeptically, hoping not to encourage such a long journey for a few minutes' interview.

"Actually, Papa, she's back in Akhet-aten, because—*doot doo-doot!*" Neferet lifted her hands to her mouth, like a trumpeter. "Lord Pentju has been named vizier of the Upper Kingdom!"

CHAPTER 7

H ANI AND PTAH-MES EXCHANGED WIDE-EYED looks of astonishment. Hani felt as if a carpet had been jerked out from under him, leaving him dangerously off balance.

Observing their expressions, Hattusha-ziti asked, "And who is Lord Pentju?"

"Djefat-nebty's husband," Hani replied quickly. That was a promising development in itself but nothing he wanted the Hittite to think about too closely. Because it, like the appointment of Ptah-mes to the Double House, suggested that Lord Ay was moving the kingdom away from the Aten, incorporating one-time enemies into his daughter's government—weaning them, in short, away from the party of his granddaughter and the Hittite marriage. Pentju had been a secret zealot of the Hidden One, in whose name he had committed desperate violence. And now the former vizier Nakht-pa-aten, who had been a little too open about his opposition to the God's Father, was out of favor, and

Pentju, who had dissembled his enmity, was in. Ay had co-opted even him.

As the men stood staring at one another in uncomprehending silence, Hani thought with a sinking in his middle, *This gambit is finished before it's begun. Nobody will accept a foreign king anymore. Nobody will even accept Lady Meryet-aten and her bloody revolution. Hattusha-ziti will tell his king it's a bad idea, and they'll send young Zannanza home. The queen will blame me and have me killed and thrown into the River without burial.* He would have said he bowed to that likelihood fatalistically, but a chilly sweat bathed his temples.

At last, his face grave with reflection, Hattusha-ziti said, "Perhaps we should get back to your house, Hani, and have a word with your mute servant."

They took their leave of Lord Ptah-mes and the girls and made their way through the garden, which was sinking into twilight. The curfew would descend soon. Hani was deeply preoccupied.

As they crunched down the gravel path side by side, the Hittite asked in a low, tense voice, "What is the significance of this Pentju? I see we have a complicated situation here, my friend. Would you care to explain it to me a little more forthrightly than you have?"

"Forgive my seeming lack of candor, my prince," Hani said apologetically. "It appears things are changing rapidly, even since I set off for Kheta. The king's father is co-opting the supporters of Lady Meryet-aten with a promise to restore the glory of the King of the Gods, thereby cutting out from under her the reason most of her followers had joined with her."

Hattusha-ziti absorbed the news in silence. Finally, he said, "This will thrust our prince into a dangerous situation, will it not? A civil war he has very little chance of winning."

Hani heaved a huge breath and nodded. He could feel the Hittite's eyes upon him, unblinking.

"How many of the queen's supporters know the identity of the crown prince's father?"

"Few know the real circumstances, my lord, although most assume that he's the son of the late king and his queen. Needless to say Lady Meryet-aten would rather it didn't become public."

Hattusha-ziti nodded, but he added a little cynically, "Although being illegitimate disqualifies him from kingship anyway, does it not?" He folded his long body into the litter.

Hani's skin crawled with unease. It was getting harder and harder to put a smooth face on the unraveling political situation, and his increasing distaste for the idea of a Hittite marriage made it that much more difficult to give it his best effort.

They said nothing further as Hani strode alongside the litter-bearers toward his house. At a certain point, they passed a troop of soldiers marching grimly down the nearly deserted street. Their officer gave Hani a dark, suspicious look, and with a smile and an apologetic wiggle of the fingers, Hani hastened his steps. The curfew must have begun.

Once they had entered his vestibule and he had kicked off his sandals, he asked the porter in a quiet voice, "Can you call the mute girl for me please, A'a?"

"Yes, my lord." The old man made a little bow, more

for appearances in the presence of a guest than because such formalities were much observed in the household.

As he hustled off, Hani called after him, "Is the mistress of the house here?"

"No, my lord. She's at Lady Sat-hut-haru's, helping with the children. Lady Baket-iset is with her, and Lord Mery-ra is at his lady friend's house. They'll all be staying the night."

So we're alone. Perhaps that's better. Hani showed his guest to a seat in the finest carved chair—a little luxury that had been his treat to himself when he received his second set of gold of honor. Its legs were shaped like duck heads instead of the usual lion paws, and he had fallen in love with it.

He settled himself beside Hattusha-ziti, who sank into the low-seated chair. The Hittite stared off into space with an unreadable expression. Hani said nothing.

Eventually, the servant girl who was the mother of the crown prince appeared in the doorway. In addition to her beauty, she had the perfect manners of a court-trained lady's maid and was clever with her hands. She had become a real help to Nub-nefer in running the house. They called her Meret-seger, after the goddess—the Lover of Silence.

"Come in, my girl," Hani said with a smile of encouragement.

She slid gracefully toward them and waited with an intelligent cock of the head.

Hani lowered his voice. "This gentleman wants to ask you about the birth of the Haru in the nest."

A light of something feral—*fear? anger?*—flickered across her face, but she gave a little bow of acquiescence.

Hattusha-ziti, his gaze earnest and penetrating, stared her in the eyes and asked, "Is it true you are the mother of the crown prince and that his father was the late king?"

Meret-seger's face darkened. She nodded.

"Did they reduce you to muteness to keep you from telling anyone?"

Another nod followed. Her mouth grew thin with the effort to hold back tears.

"And who are you?" Hattusha-ziti was almost talking to himself.

But Hani spoke up in a low voice. "My lord, she is... she is the daughter of the late King Neb-ma'at-ra by a servant. He never recognized her."

"That will be all, then, my dear," the Hittite said, and the girl bowed and departed.

The two men were left staring at each other, unspeaking.

At last, Hattusha-ziti said with a deep sigh, "Were you ever going to tell me the full truth, Hani?"

Hani lowered his eyes uncomfortably. "I am a servant of the queen, my lord." *And there you have it, Hani, my boy. You can't be a diplomat and a wholly honest man at the same time.*

"I think I won't need to speak to any more of your leaders after all. Nakht-pa-aten seems no longer to be the vizier anyway. I'll meet with your queen out of courtesy, then we can return to Amurru." Hattusha-ziti rose and, with a preoccupied tip of the head, headed for his bedchamber.

❖

By the time Hani and Hattusha-ziti reached the capital, the full weight of Hani's exhaustion lay squarely across his shoulders—an exhaustion not so much physical as moral. *Will I ever be able to draw an honest breath again, dear Lord Djehuty?* he wondered. He reminded himself that he was obeying his queen and that his activities were approved by Lord Ay, which meant—in theory, at least—the king. Yet he felt it had been an age since he had last spoken frankly to anyone. The simple truth seemed to have dropped from his professional vocabulary.

He sighed, and Hattusha-ziti, at his side, shot him a glance from the corner of his eye. They followed the majordomo down the hall of the queen's luxurious apartments.

This won't be pleasant.

In her private audience room, the young Great Royal Wife was waiting for them in complete regalia, already standing, her fists clenching and unclenching at her sides. As soon as Hani appeared in the doorway, she hurried forward and cried urgently, "Where is he, Hani? Did the king of Kheta agree to my offer?"

Hani made a full court prostration, as much to buy himself time to cover his confusion as to honor the queen. *Has she not received my message?* He hauled himself to his feet and said in a bland voice, "He is receptive, my lady. But he has commissioned his emissary, whom you see beside me, to investigate the political environment before deciding."

Hattusha-ziti acknowledged Hani's introduction with a nod. "My Sun is hesitant about sending his own flesh and blood into a volatile situation, my queen. I am his chamberlain and a kinsman. He has asked me to get a feel for the lay of things before he makes a decision."

Meryet-aten's eyes blazed, but there was as much

desperation as anger in her face. She lunged at Hani. "What do you mean? He hasn't sent the prince?" she almost shouted, her voice rising to a near hysterical pitch. "Hani, don't fail me like this!"

All at once, seeming to realize how out of control her words sounded, she turned and walked away a few steps, breathing heavily, then faced them once more, and her manner was calmer. "I trust Hani is informing you of the situation, emissary. He has told you about the spurious origins of the so-called heir to the throne?"

Meryet-aten was a singularly beautiful girl, with her mother's high cheekbones and hypnotic eyes and her father's pointed chin and full, curved lips—a living reminder of her royal pedigree. She was young, Hani reflected—younger than Neferet—and already manipulating thousands of experienced older men in the service of her ambitions.

"He has, my queen," Hattusha-ziti said silkily. His eyes, too, flicked up and down over her, missing nothing.

"Hani can't have told you this because he didn't know about it, but they want me to marry the Haru in the nest. Look how insecure they are about his legitimacy—they need me to reinforce his bonds with the royal family."

Hani went stiff but managed to control his face. *Ay's been busy. He knows exactly what she's doing and is taking up his own counterpositions, like the good military man he is.*

"But I will not marry this commoner, emissary. I will not unite the blood of the sun with that of a servant." Meryet-aten drew herself up regally, and even more than the red sash or the gilded vulture headdress, her demeanor proclaimed her a queen.

Then her hauteur melted, and the desperate girl peeked

out. She wrung her slim hennaed hands. "You see why we must hurry. Every day that passes brings us closer to the irrevocable. Once I'm married to that child, and he's on the throne..." She looked pleadingly from one face to the other.

Hattusha-ziti replied to the queen with an admirably neutral expression, "We'll be returning to Kheta right away, my lady, and I'll certainly report to My Sun how things stand in the Two Lands. Then he will make his judgment."

"Go, then. And hurry, I beg you. Hurry. Hurry."

Hani and the Hittite bowed their way out through the tall golden doors, which seemed to open magically at their approach. *She never received my letter,* Hani concluded grimly. *Either it was intercepted, or the messenger himself defected. Our spy at work?*

They made their way across the vast courts of the queen's palace and out the pylon gate. Hani wondered if the unimaginable luxury of the building had undermined the emissary's negative evaluation at all. Such wealth would certainly weigh strongly in the king of Kheta's decision, he suspected. With Shuppiluliuma's son on the throne, this would all be his.

In silence, they made their way to Hani's litter, where it awaited them outside the north wall. It was midday, and the late-summer sun ignited the whitewashed brick to a blinding glare. Hani almost regretted that he had turned the litter over to Hattusha-ziti until they made their way into the shady park that fronted the temple of the Aten. From there, they angled toward the embarcadero, which was swarming with vessels large and small, like mosquitoes around a sweaty body.

Not until they stood upon the deck of Hani's boat did either of them say a word.

Hani began tentatively, "She's a beautiful young woman, isn't she? I think Prince Zannanza would find her very tempting."

"Yielding to temptation is not always a good thing, Hani," the emissary said dryly.

"You can't deny that the succession is extremely troubled and that war is probably coming. I'm not sure I can recommend this marriage to My Sun. It might prove to be a disastrous entanglement for us, who have no real stake in the outcome."

Hani heaved a sigh. "I understand completely, my prince."

✦

They arrived back in Waset five days later, just in time for the planned farewell party. By the time twilight of the following evening had fallen, with its curfew, all the nonresident guests had arrived. Hattusha-ziti had been coached in the fine points of party etiquette, and his long graying hair wreathed with flowers and adorned with a cone of perfumed fat, he acquitted himself like the master diplomat he was. Amen-em-hut descended upon him and excitedly refined his description of the benefits of an Egyptian-Hittite union.

When Hattusha-ziti finally offered his excuses and managed to exchange a few words with his hostess, Amen-em-hut made a beeline straight for Hani, his eyes alight with the gravity of the moment and his handsome face flushed. "I can't thank you enough for inviting us, Hani. This is an important occasion—important enough for me to miss a meeting with Lord Mai and some of the other opposition leaders. Here's where our friend will hear the voice of the people." The priest took his brother-in-law by the arm, as if to keep himself from flying away in his excitement. "He'll see that this is not just the queen's personal plan."

Hani fought down his misgivings and, smiling wordlessly, refilled Amen-em-hut's cup with some of the wine of Gubla Lord Ptah-mes had brought as a gift. It occurred to him that Nub-nefer's well-born brother was hardly "the people." Hani saw that his chief problem as host was going to be to keep the priest from their foreign guest long enough for Hattusha-ziti to talk to others.

Ptah-mes was at his most elegant and charming, making everyone feel worthy of conversation without dominating anyone, despite his superior social status. Hani realized that, after twenty years of friendship and their relationship by marriage, Ptah-mes had never dined at his house before. But his presence, too, was crucial to illustrate the seriousness of Queen Meryet-aten's case. He was Master of the Double House of Silver and Gold, after all. Hani sighed. What a pity that even this warm and wonderful gathering of family had its political agenda.

The porch was open to the mild late-summer evening, its steps twinkling with moringa oil lamps. A pleasant breeze drifted down from the ceiling ventilator, and the servants stirred it with their fans of trimmed palmetto. In the corner, hired musicians played softly, and laughter and happy conversation rose louder and louder as beer and wine flowed. Directing the serving girls when to circulate with trays of food, Nub-nefer flitted about, both genial

165

welcomer of friends and perfectly organized mistress of the feast, in her floral necklace, a fringe-like wreath of flowers gracing her brow.

She's the golden treasure her name proclaims, Hani thought, his heart brimming. *I'm nothing without her.*

Hani had just dropped the bones of a succulent roast duck onto his plate and twiddled his fingers in the bowl of scented water at its side when A'a slid in from the vestibule. His face was grim. A wave of fear buffeted Hani. *Oh no. What's happened? Surely none of the grandchildren.* He saw Maya's eyes cut toward him, anxious under the laughter.

"My lord," the gatekeeper whispered in his ear, "there are soldiers outside. Their officer asked to speak to you."

Hani could hardly swallow. He slipped as unobtrusively from his chair as a big man could and followed A'a to the vestibule. There, he saw General Har-em-heb standing in full battle dress. At first, relief permitted Hani to unclench his muscles—he had expected Lord Ay's forces to be at the door, ready to drag him and Hattusha-ziti off to prison—but Har-em-heb's expression was somber and his clothing blood-spattered.

"What is it, my boy?" Hani asked under his breath.

"Ay has struck, my lord. Lord Mai and others of our leaders, including the former vizier Nakht-pa-aten, have been seized and... and executed summarily."

Hani was speechless. He stared at Har-em-heb, who stood breathing hard with emotion. "When? Where?"

"Within the hour. They had all met at Mai's house, and someone must have betrayed them. I was there, my lord, with the troops. It was agonizing. I managed not to swing my sword against the priests, but I couldn't defend any of them either, or I, too, would have been cut down. I thought it was better that some of us survived." Har-em-heb, usually so sure of himself, seemed to seek Hani's approval of his action. An unaccustomed pallor drained the bronze of his cheeks. He was deeply disturbed by what he had seen. That was clear.

"You did the right thing. What happens now?"

"The resistance is ended. There won't be any Hittite marriage. Lady Meryet-aten won't take the throne. She wasn't there, but her name was on the death list. They'll find her."

Hani fell silent. He heard footsteps running into the room and, glancing back, saw Maya approaching anxiously. "It's not the children, son. I'll tell you in just a minute." To Har-em-heb, he said, "Was our Sun God aware of this, I wonder?"

The general fixed on him a gaze of ill-concealed disgust. "Her seal was on the orders, my lord."

The orders to kill her own daughter. But probably no one had even read the command to her. She would have trusted her father's assurance of its urgency.

Maya had picked up the gist of the conversation and was gawking. "The queen is dead, then?"

The general shook his head slowly. "No, but everyone else. I can't stay—I just wanted you to be aware."

Hani clapped him gratefully on the arms. "Thank you for letting me know. The Hittite emissary is in the salon as we speak. I must tell him."

His heart heavy with reluctance, Hani made his way back into the lit salon, where the sounds of merrymaking trailed off at his grave reappearance. Nub-nefer's face was frozen with dread. One by one, the others ceased talking and fixed their fearful eyes on Hani's.

He cleared his throat nervously. *How much to say?*

"My dear ones," he began, "that was our friend Har-em-heb here to tell us that... Lords Mai and Nakht-pa-aten have been put to death—"

A gasp of horror arose.

"Along with others who were gathered together." Hani hoped to the gods his friend Mane hadn't been among them.

"I was supposed to have attended that meeting!" Amen-em-hut gasped, his mouth hanging open in shock.

His wife clutched at him with a squeal of horror.

Everyone broke out with questions, but Hani, not wanting to try to face inquiries to which he had no replies, took Hattusha-ziti by the arm and conducted him into the empty vestibule, shutting the door behind them. "My lord, I apologize for leading you into this."

The Hittite looked both unnerved and cynical. He had to know well how little appreciated his presence in the Two Lands would be at such a moment if Ay were to become aware of it—assuming that Ay didn't know already. "I suppose that's the end of my mission," he said. "I must tell My Sun."

"The queen still has supporters in the army and among many civilians." Hani knew he must sound desperate to the point of unreality.

"I certainly can't counsel my king to take such a bride of blood, Hani. I'm sorry. If Prince Zannanza had been married to your queen, he too, might have been dead."

"This was a total surprise to me, Hattusha-ziti. Believe me."

The emissary heaved a sigh. "I believe you. We had a civil war not too many years ago as well. Things can change suddenly." He forced a smile that was strained but not hostile. "We tried, my friend. You and I wanted peace between our kingdoms, but the moment just wasn't ripe. Perhaps we'll live to see it yet." He held out his hand, and Hani clasped it. "I think I'll go on up to my room and prepare for our departure tomorrow. Your hospitality is deeply appreciated."

Hani followed Hattusha-ziti back into the salon, where the Hittite bowed politely to the company, his face an expressionless mask, and disappeared up the stairwell. The guests all gaped at Hani, waiting for an explanation.

"That's honestly all I know," he said limply. "The queen's name was on the list, but she wasn't present, so she escaped."

Lord Ptah-mes watched silently while the others clamored and speculated. His black eyes caught the lamplight for a moment and seemed to blaze. He was clearly thinking hard—perhaps wondering about the safety of his children, who were fervent resisters.

The marriage alliance with Kheta was dead. Hani therefore embarked with a weary sense of wasting his time on the long return trip to Simurru, where Prince Zannanza awaited them. The Great King's son wouldn't be happy.

The Hittite emissary seemed preoccupied with the same thought. He was always pleasant, but the depth of his absorption was evident. They spoke little on the ship that took them to the land of A'amu, and Hani could well imagine how depressing it must be for Hattusha-ziti to contemplate the reception he was undoubtedly going to encounter.

Maya had decided to stay home—with his father-in-law's blessing. Sat-hut-haru needed him. Some days, she seemed to be regaining her verve, but others, she appeared to be sliding back into tearful withdrawal. That, too, weighed on Hani. And with the political situation so tense, it seemed advisable to leave someone in addition to Mery-ra to watch over the women and children. In the back of his mind rankled the possibility that his father might have been trying to undermine his mission in Kheta. *Who betrayed the meeting of Mai and the priests?*

A seeming eternity had passed before the two diplomats stepped onto dry land at Simurru and set off toward the forests inland, where the princely tents were set up. Fall was in the air—just a hint of crispness in the mornings. The sky along the coast was veiled with a high haze, like a promise of returning rains. *Yes, the Storm God's season is approaching,* Hani told himself, *and it won't be long before the ships abandon the waves until spring, but for now, the days could hardly be more pleasant.*

Hani and Hattusha-ziti finally rejoined the encampment of Prince Zannanza on the skirt of the highlands overlooking the capital city of Aziru. The fine weather and the memory of Aziru of A'amu, who had been both an adversary and a house guest years ago, improved Hani's mood. *How could a man's little problems outweigh the beauties the good gods have prepared for us?* It seemed the caravan had turned into a hunting party, and Hani thought it a highly successful one at that, judging from the pelts stretched out to dry on lines. At least the prince, too, was in a good mood.

"Well, how does it look, Hattusha-ziti?" he asked when the two emissaries met with him. His face was flushed from the autumn spent outdoors, his eyes bright with expectation.

Hattusha-ziti shot Hani a quick glance and drew a deep breath. "My prince, the political situation in Mizri is dangerous. Civil war is already breaking out, from what I've seen, and many leaders of the party favorable to our alliance have been put to death. There is, in fact, another candidate for the throne, and he has powerful supporters. I fear I must tell your father that I cannot counsel him to go through with this marriage."

Zannanza's dark eyes grew opaque, and he turned away, his nostrils tense. Hani could almost perceive the cold radiating from him, like the smoke of an icy flame. "That's not what the Great King wants to hear, Hattusha-ziti," the prince said between his teeth.

"I must speak honestly, my lord."

The chamberlain managed a neutral tone, but Hani realized he was nervous. Even this cool, experienced diplomat was reluctant to cross the volatile prince. For his part, Hani stood in silence, hoping his existence would go unnoticed—his could only be an inflammatory presence.

"I must speak honestly, too, cousin," Zannanza said, his anger dangerously coiled. His back was still to them. "I will countermand your counsels. You have no right to take this from me." He turned brusquely to face them. "My father wants this marriage, and he shall have it."

He spun on his heel and stalked away between the tents, trailing his fury.

Hattusha-ziti's face had grown crimson, but he was expressionless. Hani could only guess at the emotion that had brought the blood to the Hittite's cheeks, because even Hani, breath suspended, wanted badly to slink away. He should never have witnessed the dressing down of a colleague.

After a painful moment during which neither of the men spoke, Hattusha-ziti said levelly, "I'm going directly to Hattusha. There's no need for you to accompany me, Hani. I'll be back with the king's decision in two weeks or so."

"As my lord desires," Hani said with a respectful nod, thinking, *I'd rather be anywhere than pent up with Zannanza in a bad mood.* A slick of cold sweat was forming on his temples.

Hattusha-ziti turned abruptly and disappeared, and a brief time later, horses whickered and wheels rumbled as the Hittite's chariot galloped out of camp. He was traveling at the speed of a messenger of the gods. *He really might make it back in two weeks.*

Hani drifted to his tent and sat heavily on the edge of the camp bed. He wished his father were with him. Hani needed to talk frankly to him and get some answers that could bring peace back to his heart as it fought off suspicions. In his enforced inactivity, he began to think yet again about Sati and her grief and the little grandson he would never hold in his arms. Embedded in the present moment of his incipient failure, the thought made him very heavy of heart.

✦

Amazingly, Hattusha-ziti returned in only a few weeks' time, as promised, but he was drained looking, and his horses were blown. Hani suspected that Shuppiluliuma had met him somewhere closer than the capital. "The king is determined to go ahead with this marriage, and his desire is our law," he told Hani.

Hani thought he detected an undercurrent of anger in the chamberlain, his smooth, diplomatic facade notwithstanding. Perhaps Hattusha-ziti was so tired he couldn't perfectly control his face.

"Despite everything you told him?" Hani asked in surprise.

The Hittite nodded, his lips compressed. "We are to accompany the prince to Mizri with his escort. Our Sun himself will bid goodbye to his son at the border. We are to await the king's arrival then depart immediately."

He took his leave. At a discreet distance, his secretary awaited him, and after a few words together, the heavyset man bowed and headed off toward the royal encampment. Before Hani retreated to his compound, he saw the scribe standing at the flap of one of the courtiers' tents.

The very next day, Zannanza announced that there would be a lion hunt. Apparently, he wanted to celebrate his victory over the forces of skepticism. His attitude toward Hattusha-ziti was cheerfully gloating, but the chamberlain maintained his dignity, imperturbable. Hani sighed. The more he saw of human nature, the less optimistic he felt. The next time the gods had had enough of men, Sekhmet might well consummate her destruction of the race with no reprieve.

Because Hani couldn't easily avoid it, he was a part of the day's hunt. He had no desire to turn the prince's nearly frustrated ambitions upon himself and the Egyptian delegation by refusing, but neither had he any intention of casting a spear at some innocent wild beast. His presence would be merely symbolic. Hunting was for young people anyway.

Hattusha-ziti pleaded exhaustion after his journey and remained in the camp.

Someone had reported seeing a lion in the Barga Mountains, which rose behind the city, dark and wild, shaggy with the age-old cedars that were the envy of the world. *Perhaps I'll see some birds,* he thought, resigned, as he hauled himself into a chariot with Pa-ra-mes-su. Once they had spotted their prey, the hunters would dismount and proceed on foot into the underbrush among the trees. At the head of their procession, massive dogs strained eagerly at their leashes, baying with excitement. One after another, the six chariots and numerous slaves on foot set out. Donkeys with empty pack saddles plodded along, prepared to bring back the carcasses of whatever game they killed, and Hani was relieved that some of his soldiers as well as a few Hittite troops accompanied the party—he didn't feel altogether sure of the prince's goodwill, and hunting accidents were easy enough to stage.

Zannanza and his people were in high spirits, laughing and bantering, excited by danger and the chance to prove their manhood. It was a fine day, with a light, pleasant breeze blowing off the sea, perfumed with cypress and savory aromatics, and a glorious sky as blue as faience. Even Hani felt his optimism returning. *Who could hang on to their gloom under such conditions?*

The road was hard packed by centuries of ox carts making their way to and from the great stands of cedar trees, and the men and vehicles made good progress across the coastal plain. After climbing gently and steadily since sunrise, by midmorning, they reached the edge of the black forest that lapped the hems of the mountains. The cedars spread above them like vast sunshades, the tallest trees Hani had ever seen, their lacy green crowns interlocked so that hardly any sunlight could enter. The trunks were of such enormity that several men at once couldn't encircle them with their linked arms, and the branches were twisted and spread horizontally in tiers, leaving to each forest giant a territory that might have harbored twenty palm trees planted close together. The temperature dropped noticeably as they entered the penumbra of the forest.

Hani sucked in a deep breath of awe and pleasure, delighting in the resinous fragrance that poured into his lungs and the play of an occasional sunbeam. He was glad he had come after all. Birds twittered a welcome here and there in the branches, and he caught the flash of a yellow body through the feathery greenery. *A serin,* he told himself with pleasure. *What a joyful little fellow!*

He wasn't surprised that the local gods themselves dwelt in these mountains—they were divinely beautiful.

At last, the party made camp in a clearing.

"There's supposedly a lion around here," Zannanza announced to the men. "We'll send the dogs out, and if they find something, we close in on it on foot. Don't bother with deer or anything small. We're after the king of the forest!" He looked quite exalted, his cheeks bright with excitement.

Hani knew how potent the symbolism of striking down a wild animal was, how it foreshadowed the subjugation of Chaos by Ma'at, but it still pained him to think of such a majestic creature being killed for sport. However, he dutifully dismounted and picked up a spear from the pile thrown with a chord of clangs into the midst of the party. They were extra sturdy, with broad bronze points and crossbars—hunting spears meant to bring down something larger than a man. Some of the soldiers shouldered their bows in case a long-distance kill should be required.

Prince Zannanza led the huntsmen in a prayer to the god of the hunting bag and gave the order to send out the dogs. Their handlers immediately set off into the brush in all directions, almost running at the heels of the eager hounds. The other hunters stood about with feigned casualness as the beaters crashed through the brush, everyone tense— eager and fearful at the same time. As for Hani, his heart was pounding fast. He just hoped they found the lion before the lion found them.

Time passed. The baying of the dogs became fainter. The mosquitoes had descended on Hani, feasting on his sweat-salted skin, and he swatted absently, wishing something would happen to relieve the tension of expectation. Then from somewhere in the invisible green near-distance came a rough, panting, bellowing roar—more like a demon than a living creature. Immediately, the men snapped to attention, and the distant dogs began to bark hysterically. Zannanza and his young courtiers set off at a run, and Hani's party flowed in after them.

Hani, who was one of the older hunters and certainly the most reluctant, let the others gain ground while he hung back. That roar set his neck atingle with an atavistic sense of peril. He prayed quietly for the lion to escape, even though he knew what kind of mood that would put the prince in.

Ahead, the dogs barked in a frenzy, then came a *gnarr* that seemed to rumble up from the earth itself. A dog screamed. Men shouted. Hani beat his way through the brush and rushed up to see a black-maned lion cornered against the bole of an enormous tree, his muzzle corrugated in a snarl. Wary, the lion growled and swiped at the animals with a mighty thorned paw if they came too near. But the armed men had begun to close in on him, and he didn't know which way to turn. Prince Zannanza and several young courtiers approached him in a crouch, their spears drawn back. They yelled and whistled in the same wild furor as the animals, their long hair streaming like the manes of two-legged lions. The prince drew ahead of his men, and everyone seemed to understand that the kill should be his.

Suddenly, the lion rocked back and forth on his haunches. Hani had a terrible premonition of what was about to happen. Before he could even cry out a warning, the animal sprang with the force of the Inundation bursting over the rocks. He hurled his immense weight directly at the prince. Zannanza screamed as the lion bore him to the ground with a savage roar. They fell with a crash, the man writhing under the animal's mass. The prince yelled in terror and tried to force the cat's gaping jaws away from his face. Blood rose in scarlet lines where the great claws had raked his arms. His hands were red to the wrists. The men around him were stunned for a moment, afraid to stab at the animal for fear of hitting the prince. Slaves and dignitaries came running and stumbling over the undergrowth. Hani yelled hoarsely from the rear, "Do something!"

The lion rose to his feet for a moment, as if in triumph, one paw holding down the hapless hunter. He resettled his massive jaws around the head of his victim. All at once, an arrow sprouted from the beast's chest, and he reared back, gnashing his teeth in pain. Zannanza lay like a rag at his feet. The men rushed at them and again brandished their spears. His heart hammering, Hani darted in and, grabbing the prince under the armpits, dragged him away from his attacker. Hani could feel the heat radiating from the lion, smell the foul breath of a carnivore on his face. He scuttled back with his burden in desperate haste until he tripped and fell backward. Terror washed over him like a salt wave.

But with one last failing roar, the lion, too, fell and lay still. The men speared it again and again, vindictive and fearful. Others came running to Hani and the prince, who sprawled, limp, at Hani's feet, his shocked and bloody face staring up sightlessly.

"Dear gods, no!" one of the Hittites cried in horror. He knelt and lifted the youth's shoulders then jerked back as if a viper had bitten him. From between Zannanza's shoulder blades, he yanked out a broken arrow. It was bloody all the way up to the middle of the shaft. The prince had been shot. The courtier, his long, sweaty hair plastered to his face, stared up at Hani with eyes full of reproach.

From their posts in the trees, the archers, Hittite

and Egyptian, dropped to the earth, staring aghast at the scene that greeted them. In a circle of crouching, whey-faced men, Prince Zannanza hung lifeless in the arms of his countryman. At his feet stretched the dead king of the forest, its jaws streaked with gore.

Hani's heart pounded in his ears, his face clammy with dread. *Dear gods! Could this be any more awful?* he thought in horror. *What will happen when Shuppiluliuma finds out? Will he hold us men of Kemet responsible?* He was ashamed that his first thought wasn't sorrow for a young life snuffed out so needlessly but fear of the political ramifications.

Almost before anyone could react, one of the Egyptian archers threw down his weapon and pelted wildly toward the forest, leaping the bushes with the agility of the desperate. But a Hittite beater grabbed him roughly by the arms and manhandled him back into the circle of hunters as he struggled and cried out in fear. He fell to his knees among the assembled men, his eyes wide with fright. "Lord Hani, I-I shot him by accident! I was aiming at the lion. I swear."

Even without understanding the words, the Hittites comprehended his anguished expression and the bow he had discarded. They moved toward him with a menacing rumble, weighing their spears in hand.

"This man has murdered Our Sun's boy!" one of the courtiers cried. "Kill him!"

"Wait." Hani stepped between the luckless archer and the crowd of angry foreigners. Beneath his wig, his hair was standing on end with fear—for himself and for his land. "This was clearly an accident. He was trying to save the prince's life."

"Stand aside, emissary. Your treachery has been revealed," the Hittite growled. Hani recalled that the man had been introduced as one of Zannanza's second-rank brothers. Behind the prince, the other hunters drew their knives and raised their spears, and Hani had a terrible vision of him and the trembling archer being cut to ribbons by a vengeful mob. He would never see Nub-nefer again. His dismembered body would remain unburied, and he wouldn't enter a blessed hereafter.

At that very moment, an authoritative voice roared from behind him, "What's this I hear?" It was Hattusha-ziti. Someone had had the presence of mind to run for him as soon as the tragedy had unrolled, and he came striding through the brush to where the stunned hunting party stood around the body of Prince Zannanza.

Everyone tried to speak at once.

"My cousin, this foreigner shot our prince in the back," the victim's brother shouted in a rage.

But Hani protested, "The lion had attacked the boy, my lord. This man was trying to save him, to kill the lion—which, in fact, he did. It was a calculated risk."

Somber faced, Hattusha-ziti walked over and, squatting, examined Zannanza's bloody body. He took the piece of arrow, which had no doubt been broken as Hani had dragged the prince backward, from the other man's hand, stared at it, and threw it into the brush. He turned to look at Hani and the archer, who was shaking and wild-eyed. "It may have been an accident, or it may not. But the man must pay for a life. The life of a prince." He faced his own men again. "Tie him up. We'll take him to the king."

Hani grabbed the Hittite by the sleeve and cried in a

tense undertone, "My prince, it isn't just. This man had only the best intentions."

Hattusha-ziti avoided Hani's eye and said neutrally, "The law is the law, Hani. Perhaps the king will only demand a fine."

But Hani knew well that a man such as Shuppiluliuma would exact more than a fine for the death of his son. And Hani had to admit he himself would have been sufficiently furious and grief-stricken not to be satisfied by anything less than blood if someone had killed Pa-kiki or Aha. *Unless it was an accident... then I'm not sure what I would do. Would my heart hold enough forgiveness to let such an act go as mere human weakness?*

Hittite soldiers bound the young archer's arms behind him and hustled him away wailing, leaving the Egyptians staring at one another, stunned and apprehensive.

At Hani's shoulder, Pa-ra-mes-su asked under his breath, "Is there nothing we can do, my lord? If these people put our man to death, it could mean war."

Hani replied gloomily, "I'm afraid it already means war."

CHAPTER 8

THE GREAT KING OF KHETA appeared the next day with a full retinue and all the pomp an emperor could muster. Hani realized he must have left the capital immediately after his chamberlain—if, in fact, they hadn't met somewhere closer. The king had intended for the prince to depart for Kemet even before hearing his emissary out. He had wanted the marriage at any cost.

Hattusha-ziti intercepted the royal cortege on the road near the camp and drew the king into his tent.

A moment later, a furious voice exploded from within, "By the thousand gods, man! What are you telling me? They dared to kill him right out in the open?"

Hattusha-ziti's murmured reply was inaudible.

The king roared, "That was no accident, you son of a dog. That was murder, pure and simple. You and that Hani were responsible for him. The officers and soldiers, his brother. Where were you all, dammit? Where were you?"

His voice rose to a howl then grew strangled, and Hani realized with pity and horror that the king was in tears.

The flap of the tent started to move, and Hani dodged back to his encampment. He didn't want to be seen as eavesdropping. Shuppiluliuma would likely put Hani to death—probably slash off his head personally—if he encountered the diplomat in that moment of raw grief.

Hani made his way to the officers' tent and called out quietly, "Are you there, Menna? Pa-ra-mes-su?"

Sure enough, the flap opened, and Menna's face appeared. "Lord Hani. Come in."

Hani ducked his head and entered. Quarters were cramped. The tent was no luxurious emissary's pavilion but an austere military lodging with feeble light percolating through the leather sides and a rank, onionish odor of sweat. Menna and Pa-ra-mes-su had clearly been talking as they tried to stay out of sight of the Hittites. Their expressions were grim and apprehensive.

"Is it true the Great King himself is here?" Menna asked, his eyes darting around as if he were afraid somebody was listening.

"He's just arrived, it seems. And he's angry. He's not likely to be satisfied with a fine."

"That's what I feared," Pa-ra-mes-su said and blew a big breath out his nose as if he had been holding it. "But they have to know it was an accident. Our archer did take down the lion, after all. Anyone could have hit the man in the creature's paws like that."

"I noticed none of the Hittites ran in to try to help him," Menna said pointedly.

The regiment commander was brave and would not have hesitated, just as he hadn't when he'd nearly given his life to protect his commandant years ago in A'amu.

Hani said, "I think we should be packed up and ready to go. One of the prince's young friends might decide to return the favor with an arrow in the back. I'll make some kind of abject apology in our country's name and hope these people don't decide to invade our vassals and carve their man price out of our hides."

After a cautious look around from the doorway, Hani took his leave and made his way inconspicuously to his tent, his thoughts whirring like the wings of a flock of starlings taking off.

Strangely, the most horrific image that haunted him from the day of the accident was that of the dead lion bristling with vengeful spears, his majestic head looking not murderous but reproachful, his massive paws helpless. The pelt had been too massacred to bother saving for a trophy, although Menna had reclaimed the arrow in the lion's breast as a grisly souvenir.

Hani found it hard to breathe at the tragic waste of lives in a matter of moments. But perhaps the death of the prince had been a good thing after all, better than the success of Hani's mission would have been. *Thank you, mighty one,* he addressed the beast silently. *Because you wanted to live, you may have saved the Two Lands from a terrible fate.*

Hani sat down on his camp bed, his forearms on his thighs, and pondered events. Despite every appearance of an accident, it was altogether possible that Lord Ay had found a way to stop the queen's marriage in the most absolute manner. In fact, that would explain why Hani's caravan had suffered no attacks en route to Hattusha—their opponents had preferred to wait until the stakes were higher. Yet that meant that someone in Hani's party had colluded with Ay, kept him informed of the negotiations, and seen to it that an opportunity had arisen when the assassination of the bridegroom might have the look of a mischance. Perhaps they'd even suggested the hunt. It occurred to Hani that the prince had to have been shot well before the lion—he was lying on his back by that time and presented no target. *If he was pierced, let's say, in the instant the lion took him to the ground, we wouldn't even have noticed in the terror of the moment, with everyone yelling and watching the animal. It clearly didn't kill him right away because he was still struggling.* But then Hani realized the youth's movements might have been merely convulsive. Hani rose to his feet and, his hands behind his back, began to pace reflectively from one side of the tent to the other.

Was there, in fact, a plot to kill Prince Zannanza before he ever reached Kemet? Did someone spy on members of the Hittite delegation or milk them of information that resulted in this tragedy? Hani found it hard to imagine that anyone among his men—handpicked for loyalty to the queen's project— was such a hardened enemy of the marriage between Hatti and the Two Lands. He tried to think back to the days they had spent in the capital. *Whose behavior was suspect? Someone in my staff or among the soldiers had to have been seen in conversation with a son of Kheta Land. We were always together. No illicit contact could have gone unnoticed.*

In spite of himself, Hani remembered Maya's suspicions—Mery-ra had been engaged in some sort of mysterious visits to a private house in the company of a Hittite royal scribe and had taken pains to keep Maya away. That was unlike him. For him, the more family around, the better. Mery-ra had been seen with the scribe in the street, still, it seemed, hoping not to be witnessed. Then he had left early. Hani visualized the bland, jowly face of Hattusha-ziti's secretary. *That inoffensive-looking man, a villain? A spymaster?* He pushed the idea out of his mind. *What interest could Father have had in seeing this mission fail?* Unless he, like Hani, had begun to realize the danger the alliance with Kheta posed for the Two Lands and had decided to take things into his own hands. *No, that's ridiculous. Father is far too straightforward and honest. He would surely have intimated such scruples to me.*

But then... A lump rose in Hani's throat. *Father was apparently a spy in Kheta all those years ago. Is it possible he's actually renewed his old contacts and let himself be drawn into somebody's grudge? Is he working for Ay?*

The thought left him chilled. Hani would have to confront Mery-ra with it when he next saw his father—assuming, of course, he, Hani, made it home alive.

The likelier possibility—the one he seized upon—was that one of the soldiers who had been billeted in the Upper City with the horses and pack animals had been working against the marriage on the sly. Hani would have to talk to Menna and Pa-ra-mes-su. If the escort had been investigated, as Hani had been told, surely all the men had dossiers. One of the officers would know.

But why does it even matter? he asked himself hopelessly. *The damage is done. Shuppiluliuma won't listen to stories of defectors in our ranks. He'll take the whole horrible accident as malice on the part of Queen Meryet-aten. Some scheme to make a fool of him and his kingdom. An act of war.*

❖

The young archer was tortured, and Hani could do nothing to stop it. The most painful aspect of it was that the Hittites threw his still-living body on the prince's funeral pyre, and as he screamed in his final agony, a part of the man's soul was lost forever. Hani saw the shocked and angry faces of his staff and guards and had to admit he was equally horrified, but any objection would have been likely to bring Shuppiluliuma's wrath down on the whole Egyptian party. Instead, Hani kept his lips sealed, stood with pained diplomatic inscrutability until the two cadavers had disappeared into the roar of flames, then, despite his stomach in revolt, managed to walk away with dignity while the rest of the tall pyre burned to a pile of ashes overnight.

He and his men boarded their boat in silence at Simurru, and at daybreak the following morning, they weighed anchor. Fear, like the ill-fated lion, held Hani in its maw until the vessel had sailed well out of sight of Hittite territory. He tried to let the fresh marine breeze and cerulean sky of autumn work its cleansing, but his heart was heavy with anxiety, grief, and anger.

Did Ay engineer this stroke, even at the cost of an innocent life? He was a military man, and generals habitually sent their blameless troops to their deaths without a qualm. But Ay hadn't looked into the lake of fire and seen a human soul devoured before his eyes. Hani wasn't sure it was a sight that would ever leave him.

Menna and Pa-ra-mes-su came to sit silently beside him. The wind lifting their hair, each of them stared out over the whitecaps without making eye contact, sunk in his private thoughts.

Finally, Pa-ra-mes-su said under his breath, "What should we have done, my lord? At what point did our actions start to become mistakes?"

Hani heaved a huge sigh. "We went astray before we ever left the Black Land, my friend. But the mistake wasn't yours or mine."

The two officers stared up at him, perhaps surprised to hear a diplomat express such criticism of an order, but Hani had lived with his anguish of soul for years. *It's done. You were caught between a blindly ambitious queen and an unscrupulous minister. No path you took could have ended well.* Still, it weighed on him—both the young lives lost and the threat of war that had become a reality. People would die along the border in territories Hani knew well.

"Even though it's easy to imagine how the archer hit Zannanza accidentally, I don't think we can eliminate the possibility that there was some sort of plot against him by someone who wanted to stop the marriage," Hani said under his breath. He couldn't forget the matter of the bracelets and the serpent. *Ay was certainly behind this attempt as well.* "One or more of our people must have been in on it, pressing the Hittites for information. Who could have predicted that the prince would want to go hunting?" He shot the officers a probing glance from the corner of his eye. "Are you sure of all the men?"

"They were investigated thoroughly by General Har-em-heb in person, Lord Hani," Pa-ra-mes-su said. "That bowman, for example—he and his whole family have been zealous for the cause of the Hidden One. Mistakes are always possible, but I would have vouched for any of these people."

Hani nodded, uneasiness a lump of stone in his middle. *Could Father possibly have anything to do with this? No. I refuse to believe it.* But it was getting harder and harder to tell himself that convincingly. He thought of Mery-ra's meetings with the secretary and remembered that same scribe going from tent to tent of the young prince's courtiers.

The journey back to the Two Lands was turbulent. The storm god seemed eager to chase Hani from his kingdom and sent fierce winds and horizontal spatterings of rain to sweep the emissary southward. Only off the coast of Fenkhu did the weather begin to mollify, and Hani was relieved to set foot at last upon the rich banks of the River. He and the officers disembarked for a few days at Akhet-aten.

"I need to make my report, my friends. May the lord of the horizon bless you for your protection." Hani clapped the two young men on the shoulder. His voice dropped. "I wish this could have turned out differently."

Pa-ra-mes-su nodded philosophically. "We'll make our report, too, to General Har-em-heb. I guess he'll have to talk to the archer's family."

Hani heaved a deep sigh. His baggage in the arms of a servant, he set off toward Lord Ptah-mes's villa, intending to bathe and rest a little before braving the disappointed Lady Meryet-aten. He wondered if she was even alive still and, if so, where he would find her.

To Hani's pleasant surprise, Ptah-mes was at home. As it was close to lunchtime, the vestibule was empty of petitioners, and the master of the house was just concluding a solitary meal.

"Hani, you're back!" he cried, rising with his usual grace. "Has anyone told you the news?"

Hani froze, trying to read his friend's expression, but Ptah-mes was too adept at concealing his emotions. "No, my lord. What's happened?"

A sarcastic smile spread across Ptah-mes's lips. "The queen is dead. Supposedly of the plague, but according to those who know, she was executed."

"Ay?" A frisson of fear lifted the hairs on Hani's neck. He had half expected that, but it still horrified him. *Another young life sacrificed.*

"One assumes. The military presence has intensified, especially in Waset. The God's Father seems to have lost patience with our revolutionaries." Ptah-mes gestured for Hani to seat himself at the table, and he, too, took a stool and called to a servant to bring his guest some food. "Rumor has it that his daughter's health is declining fast. He had to act immediately if he wanted to see young Tut-ankh-aten peacefully on the throne. And now he has acted—there is no longer any other candidate."

Hani nodded, cogitating. *Does that mean it's all over?* He bowed over his pot of beer while Ptah-mes stared pensively into space.

Finally, Ptah-mes said, "I received your letter. It all seems like a terrible waste now that there's no bride, does it not?"

Hani set upon his roasted larks hungrily, barely tinged with regret for their lost voices. "The God's Father is a very thorough strategist. I hope he won't feel free to renege on his promises, since no one is forcing him any longer to engineer a return to the old ways. He's pretty much decapitated the priesthood. Are those who remain—who have been restored to their office, for example—still willing to accept him?"

"Probably. For every unrepentant defender of the Hidden One like your brother-in-law, there's an accommodating political appointee like that Pa-ren-nefer, who is succeeding Mai."

"I wonder what Amen-em-hut thinks about all this—whether the execution of the queen is enough of an outrage that it will turn him against Ay or if he's willing to be pragmatic."

The two men sat in silence for a moment. Then Hani, rising, said with an air of determination, "Well, I suppose I don't need to make a report to the Osir Meryet-aten. But it would probably be prudent to talk to Lord Ay—just so he knows I'm still in a cooperative mood. Still loyal to the crown."

"Come by my office when you're finished, my friend. I'm interested to hear what our Sun God's father has to say."

Hani left Ptah-mes to his siesta, work, or whatever he did after lunch, wondering idly where the girls were.

The day was pleasant, not oppressively hot, and Hani would have enjoyed the long walk to the palace except for his anxieties. A vague sense of unease growled in his stomach. Perhaps it was imprudent to stick his head voluntarily into the mouth of the beast. Better Lord Ay forget all about him and his mission. But he knew Ay viewed him as his own man—as in some sense Hani had become—and would expect him to bring the God's Father up to date.

Soldiers were much in evidence around the royal precinct, in all the corridors and public spaces. Otherwise, a strange quiet reigned. The usual musicians and handmaids were nowhere to be seen, and Hani's sandals clopped with unnerving loudness down the polished gypsum halls in the silent wake of the majordomo. He noticed that the palace personnel were adorned with the accouterments of bereavement, but nothing of deep sorrow seemed to inform the general sense of solemnity. At last, Hani was conducted to the smaller private audience room where Ay frequently met with him. The doors closed behind him like the mouth of a snare, and Hani was conscious of having lost any hope of safety if the God's Father should wish him ill.

But Ay seemed no more angry than he was grief-stricken. Seated upon his chair in an easy pose, he held out his hands. "Well, Hani, here we are. Almost at peace at last," he said with a cheerful grin that belied the mourning scarf around his head. "Tell me how things went, my friend. I know only that an unfortunate accident has robbed our late granddaughter's bridegroom of his life."

"My condolences on the loss of Lady Meryet-aten." Hani felt he had to insert forcibly the basic courtesies of commiseration. For all the God's Father's affability, that told Hani something unsettling about Lord Ay.

"It was a shame her life was the price of reunification, but that's something soldiers—and, I suppose, former military scribes—understand. Often, one must die to save the greater number, eh?"

Hani would have had to admit such a truth, but Ay's cynicism in the face of his own granddaughter's execution was breath-snatching. Hani said neutrally, "No doubt, my lord. I can't imagine such a decision was easy on our Sun God."

Ay shrugged. "The Lady of the Two Lands is a mother, but she's also a pragmatist. She could see this coming a long time ago." His reddish-brown eyes glittered with dark humor. "And so we have peace."

"Civil peace. But now there's war with Kheta."

"Border skirmishes," Ay said dismissively. He looked up, and Hani could have sworn he winked. "It must have been a failure to communicate."

Hani wasn't sure how direct he could be with the God's Father. He decided to edge into the topic. "I was surprised no one made an attempt to stop us on our way to Kheta, my lord."

"But Hani, you're the king's loyal friend, are you not? Why would I have stopped you?" Ay crossed his legs and let the sandal dangle from his foot.

"You can't have wanted to see our mission succeed. To see a foreign pretender opposing your grandson for the throne."

"Ah, that. Let's say I prefer to know what my enemy is up to. Who could be sure what Shuppiluliuma had planned up there in his rocky fastness? But then suddenly, his intentions became only too clear, as if the Lord of Light had directed a revealing beam at him." Ay spread his lips in his foxy, engaging smile. "You see the power of patience?"

"Is that why you waited until the last minute to remove the prince?"

Ay's narrow eyes grew round and innocent. "But I had nothing to do with that, my friend. As I've said before, I wanted the government to have no part in anything that could be construed as provoking a war between us and Kheta."

Now it was Hani's turn to gape in surprise. "It wasn't you—us—who arranged the fatal hunting accident? It really was a terrible mistake?"

"If it was deliberate, it wasn't my doing. I thought it was you and was going to offer you my congratulations for your finesse."

Hani stared into space, trying to make sense of what he had seen and what Lord Ay had just told him. *Was it an accident after all?* The coincidence seemed too fortuitous. Surely Ay wasn't so pleasing to the gods that they would arrange things for him to such perfection. And they were at war, which, despite the God's Father's dismissal, seemed grave enough. Finally, Hani said, "Forgive me, my lord, but what if Prince Zannanza had made it alive to Kemet? If his death was an accident, it might just as easily not have happened."

"He wouldn't have had much relevance without the late queen as his bride, though, would he?"

Hani acknowledged that reality with a tip of the head. *So. Ay was so determined to stop this marriage that he targeted both young people.* Either death would have ended the planned alliance, but how much more securely the deaths of both. Hence the cobra as a second line of defense.

"Fortunately," the God's Father said pleasantly, "there's no lack of nubile princesses in the royal family. Lady Ankh-es-en-pa-aten will replace her older sister as the Haru in the nest's bride."

Hani murmured his congratulations.

Eventually, Ay made it clear with a smile and a gesture that the audience was ended, and Hani backed from his presence in a profound obeisance.

Once he had regained the corridor and the majestic gilded doors had thundered shut behind him, he realized he still had boiling questions he had dared not pursue. *What did Ay mean by "a failure to communicate"? Was it, in fact, someone other than Ay who had deliberately caused the accident—maybe one of his henchmen? Someone who had misunderstood his mandate, perhaps?* That confirmed the likelihood that there had been a betrayal among Hani's staff or military escort.

In a pensive mood, Hani left the palace and crossed the street into the warren of low buildings that marked the Hall of Royal Correspondence. He passed the various chancery offices and that of the viziers and came at last to the heavily guarded precinct of the Double House of Silver and Gold, where he hoped to find Ptah-mes.

The Master of the Double House was just leaving when he saw Hani approach. "Ah, my friend. I have a small task to perform at the office of the vizier. Walk with me if you have the time. We can converse as we go."

They crossed the courtyards one after the other, seeing more soldiers than the usual scribes passing busily from building to building. It was too silent. The echoes seemed to be louder than normal against the dun brick walls, as if in an empty house. Hani's flesh crawled. He felt an urgent need to get home and be sure the family was safe. In scarcely more than a whisper, he filled his former superior in on what Lord Ay had revealed.

The two men entered the hall of the viziers, where the receptionist rose and bowed. "The vizier of the Southern Kingdom is expecting you, Lord Maya."

"Pentju has already taken up his duties?" Hani murmured.

Ptah-mes nodded, a dry smile on his lips. He entered the vizier's office, and Hani waited in the cool, dark hall, watching idly the motes of dust float in the streaked sunlight that descended from the high clerestory windows. After a moment, Ptah-mes returned, and they retraced their steps. His expression gave no indication of whether the meeting had been pleasant or distressing.

Once they entered the confines of the Double House, all the life that had drained from elsewhere in the chancery seemed to have concentrated itself. Immediately, petitioners surrounded Ptah-mes. Other people milled about, waiting for an audience, or strode to and fro down the corridors, caught up in their business. As Hani and Ptah-mes walked, from time to time, someone approached and dropped a deep bow to Ptah-mes, a question about the treasury on their lips. Ptah-mes replied in his cool, polite manner, and as soon as the petitioner was satisfied, he and Hani continued on their way. Hani had to smile. Civil war or no, the government needed gold to continue.

Suddenly, someone cried, "Lord Hani!"

They stopped and turned as a youth of about twelve or thirteen ran to them and grabbed Hani's hands. It was Hani's former student Amen-mes, his star pupil at the royal Kap, where Hani had taught languages for nearly a year—and Ptah-mes's grandson, who had never met his grandfather. "My lord, it's wonderful to see you again. I so miss our Akkadian lessons." He was a serious boy, but his face was alight. "Do you think we can start again sometime?"

Hani smiled and clapped him on the shoulder with a

paternal hand, controlling the urge to glance at Ptah-mes, whom he felt stiffen at his side. "That's up to the king, son. Nothing could please me more. You were an exceptional student."

The youngster beamed and turned to look at the man accompanying him. Hani had seen the boy's father once before, at Lady Apeny's funeral. By now, he was in his late thirties or perhaps forty, Hani judged—tall, well-dressed, and noticeably similar in features to his father, Ptah-mes, although rather heavier. Hani observed that his arms were shaved. He remembered his friend's firstborn was a priest of Amen-Ra, and it seemed he was once more in service. No doubt his head was shaved, too, under the expensive wig.

"Lord Hani, this is my father, Djehuty-mes son of Ptah-mes. Father, this is Lord Hani, who taught us our Akkadian." The boy looked happily back and forth between them.

But Djehuty-mes was staring at his own father. Both were frozen into strained expressions of courteous hostility. Ptah-mes had drawn up to his full height and leaned back a little as if to avoid so much as touching the air his son had breathed. Djehuty-mes looked more ambivalent, his black eyes wide with something that might have been longing, while his mouth was taut. A long, uncomfortable silence that Hani and the boy dared not break stretched out between them.

At last, Djehuty-mes said in a stifled voice, "Father."

"Ah, you acknowledge my paternity, do you?" Ptah-mes replied coldly. His nostrils were stiff. Whatever else he felt, he was certainly angry.

Djehuty-mes seemed to struggle with himself. "Congratulations on your new post."

"In the service of a heretic? You should be disapproving, judgmental, in our fine old family tradition."

Ptah-mes's son seemed to blanch, and his arched eyebrows drew down. Ptah-mes showed not the slightest emotion, but Hani suspected his sarcasm hid a deep hurt.

"*He's* your father, Papa?" Amen-mes cried with disbelief, as if he had expected some hideous demon, not this handsome man in fashionable clothing.

But his father didn't answer, having eyes only for Ptah-mes. They were like two suspicious dogs sizing each other up, not daring to break their fixed stare—yet there was a certain goodwill in the priest, Hani thought. *I believe he wants to be reconciled. At least he's speaking to Ptah-mes.*

By way of justifying himself, Djehuty-mes said, "The king is restoring the worship of the Hidden One. She isn't her husband. Things are changing."

Ptah-mes, his hooded eyes inscrutable, said nothing but tipped his head in a gesture of assent so clipped it was almost mocking.

All you gods, make him warm up, Hani thought urgently. *This could be their chance to heal that rift.* But Ptah-mes, for all his virtues, wasn't one to bend.

The goodwill that had opened in Djehuty-mes seemed to be closing already under his father's rebuff. His lips thinned in a look Hani had often seen on Ptah-mes. "Well, life, prosperity, and health to you, Father. Enjoy your little concubine, as she no doubt enjoys your gold," he said acidly and made as if to move on. "Come, Amen-mes."

Hani's face heated with a flush of outrage on Neferet's behalf, but he refused to let himself intervene in the conversation with so much as a *hmph*. The priest and his son moved off into the distance with a determined clop of sandals.

Hani and Ptah-mes were left standing in the middle of the hall like two silent statues.

Finally, Hani said in a low voice, "So, that's your eldest boy."

"Yes. The hypocrite-in-chief."

The words seemed more than a little harsh to Hani, but he bit his tongue—nothing was more private than a man's relationship with his children. He groped for something to say but could only manage, "My business at the palace is done, my lord. Will you forgive me if I go? I'd like to get packed and be off to Waset tomorrow."

Ptah-mes, who was staring blackly into space, seemed suddenly to notice Hani and forced a smile. "Mine is done too. I'll see you before you leave, I hope."

As he walked quickly on, Hani reflected on how little he envied his friend, who, despite his great affluence, led a lonely, conscience-tortured life. He told himself sadly, *Better is bread with a happy heart than wealth with vexation.*

CHAPTER 9

THE FOLLOWING DAY, AFTER LUNCH but before the afternoon petitioners had begun to fill the vestibule, Hani and Ptah-mes sat at table, finishing the last of a ewer of exceedingly fine wine from the north. Ptah-mes put on an affectation of good cheer, but Hani felt he was still troubled by the encounter with his son the previous day. Knowing his friend as he did, Hani suspected the man was recriminating over his intransigence.

A discreet cough made them look up. Ptah-mes's doorkeeper stood in the entry to the vestibule. "Lord Maya, there's a young boy at the door. He asked to see you. May I send him in?" The porter hovered indecisively, his hands clasped taut before him.

Ptah-mes exchanged curious looks with Hani then said, "Yes, of course."

"Should I leave, my lord?" Hani asked quietly, starting to rise.

"No, no. I can't imagine what it can be about. Some tradesman's delivery boy, no doubt."

But Hani wasn't surprised when Amen-mes entered the salon with hesitating steps. He caught sight of Hani from the corner of his eye but, without any sign of recognition, went directly to Ptah-mes's feet and bent in a deep bow, his hand to his mouth.

Ptah-mes said nothing, but his color leached out suddenly.

"My grandfather," the boy murmured. He was visibly girding himself for a difficult exchange, and Hani had to admire the youngster's courage. "I... I wanted you to know that I'm not mad at you, even if Father is." His voice trembled a bit with intensity. "I've always wanted to meet you."

Ptah-mes seemed caught without words for a moment, then he said, "Have you, now?"

Once more, Hani started to his feet, ready to slide unobtrusively away.

Amen-mes said with the earnest innocence of youth, "Grandmother always told us you were a good man, just wrong. And you're a friend of Lord Hani too. You can't be as bad as Aunt Mut-em-wia says."

Ptah-mes laughed—a sharp, bitter noise. Hani had met Ptah-mes's eldest daughter. He could well imagine her trying to poison her nephew against her father, whom she resented not only for his apparent collaboration with the Atenist regime but also for his marriage to Neferet.

"I may or may not be, actually," Ptah-mes said. His voice had softened, and he held out a hand to the boy, who drew nearer. "At any rate, I certainly won't contaminate you. I'm very pleased to meet you at last, Amen-mes."

Hani said with a smile, "Did your aunt tell you your grandfather's wife is my daughter?"

"Mut-em-wia and Father said she was out to get your gold, Grandfather. That she was a bad person. But if she's your daughter, Lord Hani..." Amen-mes hung his head, confused and conflicted.

"In fact, Neferet is a very good person. She's a *sunet* who takes care of sick people," Ptah-mes said. His features had begun to relax somewhat. "Would you like something to eat, my son?"

Amen-mes seemed to fight with himself but said finally with unconcealed pleasure, "Yes, Grandfather. Thank you."

Ptah-mes called a servant to bring some fruit, and the boy gratefully bit into a dried plum.

Hani began again, "My lord, perhaps I should—"

But Ptah-mes forestalled him. "No, no, Hani. You're a friend of this lad."

Hani had a suspicion that Ptah-mes was ill at ease and would probably prefer not to be left alone to carry on a conversation with Amen-mes, so Hani resettled himself in his chair. "Perhaps you'd like to show your grandfather how well you can speak Akkadian," he suggested.

The boy cleared his throat self-consciously and murmured under his breath, "*Shulmu.*"

"*Peace* to you too," Ptah-mes replied in the same language.

"Do you speak Akkadian, Grandfather?"

Ptah-mes gave a dry, self-deprecating smile. "Speak? Not well. I used to read and write it passably." He shot Hani a glance. "I haven't been in a position to need it for some years. I always had colleagues like Hani, who were much more proficient."

No one seemed to know what to say for a long, uncomfortable space of time.

At that moment, they heard the sound of the gate shutting and Neferet crying in her loud, exuberant voice, "Oh? Papa's here? That's wooonderful!"

She burst into the salon, her arms spread wide, and threw herself on Hani with a force that would have made a less solid man totter. "Papa! You're back! I thought we'd never see you again." She turned. "Lord Ptah-mes! It's good to see you, too, but it's only been a little while." She snickered as if at a shared joke.

Then Neferet saw the boy standing goggle eyed between the two men. "Who's this?"

"My grandson," Ptah-mes said with the merest twitch at the corner of his mouth, as if he were afraid to be happy about it.

"Oh. Hello." She beamed at the boy, a grin splitting her face. "My name is Neferet. What's yours?"

The lad looked back and forth between his grandfather and the girl. "I'm called Amen-mes son of Djehuty-mes," he said in a polite, grown-up voice. Hani thought the youngster was having trouble putting this cheerful, shaven-headed young woman together with the stories his family had told him about her.

"Have you seen the house yet?"

"No, my lady." Amen-mes cast shy eyes at his grandfather, silently asking for permission.

Neferet linked arms with him and drew him toward the inner door. "I'll show you around. It's really beautiful.

Lord Ptah-mes has such good taste. And I want to show you what I brought today." She put up her hands and made pleading eyes, her tongue hanging out like a puppy's. The boy gaped, as if not sure how to react to a grown-up who did such things. She cast a glance back at her husband and laid a finger to her mouth, quelling a laugh. Together, the two young people disappeared into the rear of the house, leaving Hani and Ptah-mes staring after them.

At last, Ptah-mes turned to Hani, a sheen of perspiration on his face. The grandee seemed without words.

"This may be your way back to the family, my lord," Hani said quietly. "This boy has no prejudices and will meet you as you are, not as his aunt tells him you are."

Ptah-mes, breathing rather heavily, said nothing. Hani could only imagine what emotions had to be roiling under the expressionless surface.

Later that afternoon, Hani took his leave of his host and, with a grateful hug of his daughter and her friend, set off for Waset at last. His journey home, after all, was not yet over.

❖

With aching relief, Hani finally walked in his door and took Nub-nefer in his arms. Her warmth and the perfume of lilies she always seemed to radiate were like the balm of sleep after an exhausting day—every anxiety seemed to evaporate, and even his physical weariness abandoned him. He had been on the road for endless weeks, and the month of Peret was upon them there in the Black Land, with its release from the heat, its crystalline skies, and its visiting birds from the north.

"There's a civil war of sorts," she told him, "but it doesn't seem to affect our daily lives much. We just stay out of sight of the soldiers. They say the infantry and cavalry are fighting one another somehow."

"Yes, I just heard that in Akhet-aten, my dove. The young queen has been assassinated."

Nub-nefer drew back a pace and gave Hani a piercing look. "They told us she died of the plague."

The two exchanged cynical sniffs.

"How are the children? How is Sat-hut-haru?"

"Better, I think. It's as if a boil has burst in her. These things just have to work their way through."

Hani smiled with relief then a little mischievously. "I'm sure Maya's glad."

"I'm sure he is." Nub-nefer gave her rich, warm laugh that Hani had missed so cruelly.

They drifted hand in hand onto the porch, where Hani faced down a possessive Pa-miu to greet his eldest daughter and sat on the edge of her couch. The cat returned to claim his lap.

"I had a dream last night about your friend from Kheta Land, Papa," she told him. "He was looking pleased with himself—I don't know why."

"I don't either. He's in trouble with his king." Hani chuckled, but then the gravity of the situation resurfaced in his heart, and his amusement chilled. *And so am I and all of Kemet.*

"Are you hungry, my love? Lunch is ready if you are," Nub-nefer said, rising.

Hani patted himself on the belly. "You know me—I'm always hungry." He pushed Pa-miu from his legs, and the animal drifted off in a huff while Hani directed his steps into the salon. The servants followed with Baket-iset's couch.

After a restorative meal of cow peas and fat pork, Hani pushed back from the table with a sigh of contentment, all anxieties forgotten. "How I've longed to taste home cooking. You certainly get the best out of the cook, my dove. I do love the flesh of the pig."

"It's very low class, you know," Nub-nefer reminded him with an affectionate pinch of the cheek. "If poor people can afford any meat at all, it's pork. I'm sure Lord Ptah-mes never serves it. Or Maya."

Cringing under a dull pang of sorrow, Hani remembered Ptah-mes's encounter with his son. "That's not the only pleasure Ptah-mes denies himself." He told his wife and daughter about the meeting and the subsequent visit of young Amen-mes.

"Perhaps it will all turn out for the best, then, Papa," Baket-iset said with her usual optimism.

"I hope you're right, my swan." Hani stood and stretched with a satisfying roar. "I think I'll go say hello to Sati and Maya before I finally sink into such complete relaxation that I won't be able to force myself up again. The grandchildren will wonder where I've been."

A little stroll sounded welcome after such a substantial meal. Hani had just opened the gate and was walking out when he saw a litter standing a few cubits away. From it emerged a leg then a whole man, broad and fleshy and dressed in the most unflattering fashionable garments, with a stiff, pleated apron flaring before his knees.

"Father!" Aha cried, seeming genuinely pleased. "I'm

glad I caught you in. Were you leaving?" He embraced Hani, who reciprocated with a hearty hug.

"Nothing that can't wait. I just got back from abroad. We see too little of you, son—you know how your mother refuses to go to the capital. She'll be delighted."

The two men walked side by side up the gravel path to the porch, where Aha stopped and cleared his throat self-consciously. "Yes, well. I should be seeing more of you both soon. We're no longer going to be living in Akhet-aten. I've, er, got a new post. I'm now First Overseer of the Cattle of Amen-Ra."

It took Hani an instant to know how to react. *Should I praise my firstborn for the promotion, or should I gloat because the boy has found his way back to the Hidden One's fold?* He decided on the former. "Why, that's wonderful, my lad! We're very proud of you."

An embarrassed blush rose up Aha's jowls despite his air of self-satisfaction. "I got to thinking about what you had said, Father—about the worship of the Aten slacking off when the present king dies. And the rumors are running that the court will move back to its old locations, and the Great Temple of the Aten may be closed. It seemed it might be a good opportunity to look for a post elsewhere."

Hani beamed, amused but sincerely delighted. "I think it was an excellent choice. Your experience must have made you very attractive to the priests of Amen."

"Yes. And Mother's connections, of course."

Of course. Now Aha was courting the hierarchy of the god he had cast off as zealously as he had embraced Nefer-khepru-ra's new god. And suddenly, Nub-nefer's familial association with the cult of the Hidden One was a source of pride rather than shame. *Human nature,* he thought with a silent chuckle. "Well, I think you did the right thing. And they're lucky to have you."

With identical grins, they entered the vestibule. Nub-nefer appeared in the inner doorway, her eyes wide with surprise. "Back so soon, Hani? Did you—" Then she saw her son. "Aha, my love! What brings you here? Nothing wrong with the children, I hope." She ran to her firstborn and threw her arms around his broad middle. "We don't see enough of you."

"You'll be seeing more of me from now on. We're moving back to Waset."

She shot Hani a stunned look and cried to Aha, "How wonderful! What's the occasion?"

And Aha explained everything to her.

Nub-nefer's face grew more and more transfigured with joy, but she managed to avoid any words resembling "I told you so." Instead, she embraced her son once more. "Are you going to build a house, my sweet?"

"Actually," the young man said smugly, "there are so many empty ones here at the moment that I was able to find quite a luxurious villa for a ridiculously small amount of grain and a few goats. We could never have built such a place for so little. You must drop by and see it. Most of the renovations are done, and Khentet-ka and the children are coming as soon as I give them the word."

"It will be wonderful to have you among us more frequently." Hani clapped Aha on the shoulder. "And to see more of the grandchildren."

"Yes, that's what I was thinking, Father. They hardly

know you—especially you, Mother. And they can play with Pa-kiki's little ones. It will be perfect."

Hani noticed he made no mention of Sati and Maya's children. "Do you mean Pa-kiki is moving back to Waset, then?"

"Not yet, but he told me that he's been put in charge of all the scribes at the Waset garrison. His general has become some kind of court official—companion to the Haru in the nest, 'sole friend,' or something." Aha beamed and squeezed his father's shoulders conspiratorially. "My little brother is moving up the ladder, eh, Father? He's one of us, after all. I've encouraged him to snap up some villa among those that are so cheap at the moment rather than moving back to their old place. It was totally unsuitable."

Hani and Nub-nefer sneaked looks of amusement at each other.

Hani thought, *Har-em-heb wants to stay out of the conflict between his infantry and Lord Ay's cavalry.*

His hands on his hips, Aha looked around him at the familiar salon, with its frieze of papyrus and worn, painted lily-bud columns. "You know, you could do something nice with new murals and lighten the old-fashioned look a little. I can recommend some good workmen."

Hani forced himself not to catch Nub-nefer's eye. "We're happy with the old look, son. You wouldn't want to shock Grandfather, would you? It was he and Grandmother who had these painted when Pipi and I were children," Hani said, suppressing a smile. Aha was still his old self, desperate to look up-to-the-minute. But at last, that had worked to the good.

"If you'll excuse me, son, I was just on the way to see Sati. She's doing better. Do you want to join me?"

"Oh, not right now, I think. Let me stay and talk to Mother. I haven't seen her in a long time."

Hani embraced his firstborn, and with a wink at Nub-nefer, he made his way through the garden and out the gate, into the brightness of a winter afternoon. Not far down the lane, he encountered his father on foot, toddling along with his rocking gait toward the house. The basket of fresh fish under the old man's arm told Hani that Mery-ra was on his way home from his generous lady-friend's house.

"Ah, revered parent. Let me help you carry that."

"Hani, my boy. You're back." Smiling broadly, Mery-ra handed over the basket. They directed their footsteps back toward the gate. "How was your trip?"

But something else was on Hani's mind. He lowered his voice. "Listen, Father, there's something I've been wanting to ask you. When you were in Hattusha—"

"Could we talk about this later, son? I need to get these to Nub-nefer. She specially requested them, and Meryet-amen gave me orders. You know how women are." Mery-ra looked suddenly very busy. His smile didn't fade, but it grew fixed. He patted his son's shoulder, turned, and hastily hammered on the gate. As soon as A'a pulled back the bolt, Mery-ra dodged inside and pulled the heavy panel shut behind him.

Hani, left standing in the street with a basket of fish over his arm, said, "I guess he doesn't want to talk about it."

⁜

Hani spent the rest of the day with his second daughter and

her family, delighted to find her more her old, laughing self. The children climbed all over her, as if they realized their mother had returned from a dark and distant place and was theirs once more.

"Will you stay for dinner?" Maya asked.

But Hani rose and tugged down his shirt, which had bunched up over his belly as usual. "Ah, my children, it's later than I realized. I need to be going."

After a last round of kisses and "Don't go, Gamfather," Hani reached the door.

Maya called after him, "May I walk with you, my lord? It's such a beautiful day."

Hani assured him he was welcome, and they set off into the late afternoon. The streets were quiet, workers still at their places of labor. Only the bray of a recalcitrant donkey and a distant chant of children's games broke the stillness. It seemed so peaceful. No one would ever have divined that war racked the Two Lands.

Eventually, they reached the point where their paths diverged. Maya saluted and set off with a jaunty step back toward his home, while Hani proceeded alone, lost in thought. His thoughts were troubled by the idea of the trained snakes, which had never really left him since that day he had learned about the connection with Ipy's bracelets.

Suddenly, he noticed how long the shadows were getting and hastened his pace.

I'm not sure I believe Ay had no connection to Zannanza's death. He would have wanted to be sure the wedding was still off even if his granddaughter escaped, and if the hunting "accident" shouldn't work either, he had the serpent to fall back on. It's all a single strategy at work. But there was still a problem. *How did those bracelets find their way among the queen's gifts in the first place? Someone she trusted wasn't loyal after all. The mysterious spy again.*

Only one person could have provided that accurate drawing of the cuffs so long before the pieces were even completed. *Ipy himself must have been involved. That's why he was killed—he knew about the plot against Zannanza.*

Yet many things didn't fit together. Hani wanted to talk the murder case over with Mery-ra, but if his father had a connection with the death of the Hittite prince, Hani wasn't sure he dared. For the first time in his life, he felt he couldn't trust the old man, and the thought filled him with sorrow. Maya's suspicions had infected him despite himself.

At last, he decided he needed to revisit the late goldsmith's house. As soon as he reached home, he told Nub-nefer his plans, and hastily gathering some clean linen, he took off toward the quay, on his way yet again to the City of the Horizon.

En route, Hani snagged his son-in-law, who was still at the dinner table, and they boarded Hani's yacht for the unplanned trip downriver.

⚜

Five days later, they trudged side by side down the lane where Ipy had lived. It was the end-of-week holiday, and neighbors were relaxing on their roof terraces or in the doorways. It seemed that, for the most part, this was a self-respecting block, where women swept the street in front of their gates, and householders trimmed their fruit trees.

But not everyone. If Hani had thought the chaos of

the house of mourning was a temporary condition, his illusion was dispelled by the second visit. Even from the street, he heard the screams of fighting children and the hoarse, despairing shouts of their mother. Maya shot him an alarmed look.

"Shut up! Shut up, I said! Mother of the gods, have mercy!" Hemet-min's wild voice rose into a scream. The sound of a pop followed, and a child wailed.

Hani took a deep breath and knocked on the heavy gate. A moment later, the eldest boy stuck his uneasy face through the crack. When he saw it was Hani, he opened the gate wider. "My mother is busy," he said dully. His eye was ringed with a dark bruise, as if someone had clouted him.

Hani gave him an amiable smile. "You can probably help me, my boy. Your name is Hu-may, isn't it? You worked with your father at Mistress In-hapy's goldsmith shop, right?"

"Yes, my lord." The boy didn't seem sullen so much as cowed.

"Did he draw this beautiful sketch?" Hani tugged from his waistband the snake man's colored drawing of the cuffs and let it curl around his wrist.

Hu-may stared at it expressionlessly. "No. I did."

Maya gave a squawk. "You're just a lad," he cried in amazement. "Did you really do this beautiful picture?"

"Yes, my lord." The goldsmith's apprentice dropped his eyes as if ashamed of his skill.

"Why, son?" Hani asked gently. "Was it part of your work for Mistress In-hapy?"

The boy shrugged, uncomfortable. "The man paid me to do it."

A crash, as of pottery smashing, resounded from within the house, and Hemet-min shrieked, "There, you've spoiled Grandfather's porridge! What's he supposed to eat? What's your baby brother supposed to eat? I don't have enough milk for all of them. You selfish little oaf! Scoop it up! That's *your* dinner now."

Hu-may flinched and gnawed his lip. He was a skinny, smallish lad of about twelve or thirteen, with a ferrety face, too haggard for a child's. *He works hard all day then doesn't get enough to eat,* Hani thought sorrowfully.

"I just copied it from the cartoon," Hu-may said as if in apology.

"What man was this who asked for a copy?"

The boy shrugged apathetically.

"I hope he gave you something for it, at least," Hani said with feeling. "How is it your family seems so poor? Your papa must have been well paid."

"We're not poor," Hu-may said.

Hani and his son-in-law exchanged puzzled glances. *I guess Hemet-min is so overwhelmed with everything she just can't keep up with the household.* "What did the man look like? Do you remember?"

"Rich. Old. He talked to my father, and my father told me to do it. The man gave us a big sack of grain and a goose. His servants did."

Probably more than even such a nice piece of work is worth. Good for Ay. "What sort of man was your father, Hu-may?" Hani asked in a gentle tone.

"He'd never hit us," the boy said, not raising his eyes. It seemed that was different from his mother.

"Is there anybody who can help you now? Any family?" Maya asked.

Hu-may shook his head.

The pace at which Hani was able to drag information out of the lad was painful. In the background, Hemet-min shrieked angrily at one of the children, who screamed back at a flinch-worthy level of volume. Suddenly, the old grandfather drifted out of the doorway, tottering with empty-eyed determination toward the gate. He didn't seem to be aware of the people there but made as if to push past them and leave the yard. Hu-may drew him back, taking a fleshless brown arm wearily in his hand, as if that happened with some frequency. "No, Grandfather. Don't go in the street."

At least the old man had on a loincloth. But he was none too clean, some sort of dribbles daubing his hollow chest and his wispy hair greasy and matted. Hani saw Maya eyeing Ipy's father with horror, perhaps seeing his own future—or giving thanks that his family would never let him come to that.

"Can you think of a reason anyone might have had to kill your father?" Hani asked.

The boy shook his head, his face shriveling with misery. After a moment of struggle, he said in the trembling, small voice of a much younger child, "I miss him."

Hani, his nose twinging with tears, wrapped a paternal arm around Hu-may's bony shoulders and whispered, "Be strong for your family, my lad. You're the man of the house now." He fumbled from the pouch at his waist a string of glass beads. "This is nothing so fine as you and your fellows make, but at least you can buy something for your grandfather's dinner." He pressed them into the boy's thin hand.

The lad's eyes seemed to come to life for the first time. He fell to his knees and babbled, "Thank you, my lord. I... I..."

"Perhaps you could save your mother some anxiety and get something nice for the children too," Hani said in a kindly voice. He lifted the boy to his feet. "If you think of anything that could help us, let me know, son."

He and Maya took their leave. They walked in silence down the lane, Hani's heart heavy.

"Why doesn't she get a servant to help her? A wet nurse? I can't understand why the household seems so poor. The children don't even look as if they have enough to eat." Maya shook his head.

"I don't know, son. I wonder if Ipy gambled."

They fell silent once more, only the dry thud of their footsteps on the packed-earth street accompanying them.

Eventually, Maya said, "So the man who commissioned the bracelets was rich and old, eh? Sounds like the God's Father, all right."

Hani nodded, thinking that anyone over twenty probably looked old to a twelve-year-old. But there was nothing in the lad's words that contradicted the likelihood of it being Lord Ay. Still, something seemed odd. The identification was too neat. *Would Ay have carried out all these low-level transactions in person?* If it had been a servant who paid the boy, then the mastermind could have been anyone. Anyone at all.

CHAPTER 10

A T MIDMORNING THE NEXT DAY, Ptah-mes was at his office in the Double House, and his villa was empty of all but servants, who went about their tasks with silent efficiency. Hani sat pensively by himself, trying to force the facts to make sense. He was so lost in his thoughts that he hardly noticed Maya had come down the stairs and appeared at his side.

"Still trying to figure out who betrayed the prince to his death?" Maya hoisted himself onto a stool.

Hani glanced up and nodded thoughtfully. "Ay said it wasn't him, but he mentioned something about misunderstanding orders. Did he have an accomplice on our staff who overstepped his mandate? Somebody among us must have been working for the God's Father just independently enough to give Ay deniability."

"You know what I think, my lord," Maya said a bit sniffily.

"Father." Hani knew he was resisting the obvious

conclusion. "But what could his motives have been? And he had left before the fatal hunt."

"If he was a professional spy back in his prime, Lord Ay might well have called him back into service, knowing you'd never suspect him." Maya had obviously been giving it some thought, and he made his case with the energy of the convinced. "He would have done it out of duty, just as you obeyed the queen out of duty, whatever he thought of the orders."

Ammit take it, the boy's right, Hani thought, his stomach sinking like a lump of lead to his feet. *That's exactly what a professional would have done.* "But if he was just keeping an eye on me for Ay—the king—why would he have been meeting with a representative of the Hittites?" He stared at Maya almost defiantly, but his confidence crumbled at the certitude he read in his son-in-law's eyes.

"He must have understood that his mandate was to, er, stop the marriage at any cost, my lord. Perhaps the best cover was to seem to be helping the men of Hatti."

Hani fell silent, staring into space. "To pretend to sell us out. That would be why he was so eager to get out of the country before the death of the prince revealed his true allegiance." He wanted his heart to feel lightened. There was nothing dishonorable in any of it. But a little part of him whispered, *What if he really was betraying us? You've told him everything you know about the border vassals over the years.*

Knowing the summer hours of his mother's workmen began with daybreak, Maya set off as soon as it was light to do a little investigation. It had occurred to him that they hadn't interviewed anyone except Ipy's son and the filigree man. Perhaps someone else had observed something or seen Ipy acting suspiciously in the months before his death.

"You can talk to anybody you like, son," his mother told him fondly. "Just try not to keep them so long that it holds up their work."

Maya decided to begin with a bright-eyed young fellow who hadn't worked very long at the shop but seemed not to miss much. He had curly hair and big dimples, showed to advantage by a perpetual broad smile.

"You, my good man. What's your name?" Maya demanded briskly, pulling out his writing tools and sitting cross-legged in a shady corner of the court.

"Pa-shedu, my lord."

"How long have you worked here?"

The young man scratched his head, grinning. "Three years, I think."

Maya looked up at him with withering disgust. "You *think*? If you aren't even sure about that, how much value will any of your testimony have?"

Pa-shedu became properly serious. "Three years and two months, my lord." He shifted nervously from one foot to the other.

"How well did you know the Osir Ipy, my boy?"

"Not well personally. He was higher than me, a master artisan. I'm just a journeyman. But he was always very friendly and nice, not stuck-up like—like some people."

"Had his behavior changed any lately? Did he talk about debts or anything weighing on him?"

"Not to me, my lord. He seemed a little sad or worried, though, like something was on his mind, you know? Usually, he was cheerful like. And actually…"

Maya asked impatiently, "Well, what is it, man?"

"I just overheard this, my lord, so I don't know what he was talking about, but Ipy said to that Pi-ay something about 'What're they up to?' or 'Where's it going?' or something. He looked anxious." The dimpled journeyman smiled expectantly.

"You can't tell the difference between 'What're they up to?' and 'Where's it going?'"

Flustered, the young man amended, "Both. He said both, my lord."

Maya wrote down all the journeyman had to report then looked up. "Anything else?"

Pa-shedu said, "Ipy looked around at where his son was working and said to Pi-ay under his breath, 'Don't say anything in front of'… He meant 'him' or 'the boy.' You know."

"That was all?"

"That was all, my lord. Maybe they saw that I was listening to them or whatever, but they both got busy with their work again." Pa-shedu wiped his nose self-consciously on the back of his wrist.

For all the goldsmith's appealing looks, his fingers were blackened and calloused from handling metal, and Maya thanked the good god Bes that he himself had escaped such a life of drudgery. "That's all, then, my man. You can go back to the workbench now."

Maya kissed his mother goodbye and thanked her.

"Would you like to come for lunch this afternoon, son?

I'm having the girl make minced pork balls and chickpeas. But I know you have lots of things to do for Lord Hani...." She patted Maya's cheek in proud self-effacement.

That's the very least I owe her. "Of course, Mother. I'll see you at the usual hour."

By the time Maya got back to Lord Ptah-mes's house, he found Hani packing his things for the return trip to Waset. "Oh dear. I just told Mother I'd join her for lunch."

"If you want to do that and come on up tomorrow by ferry, you can."

"Oh, maybe I'll just send one of Lord Ptah-mes's servants with a message telling her I can't come." *That will impress her,* he thought with an inward smile. *And I'd rather ride that yacht than a filthy public ferry.*

"Fine, then," Hani said. "We'll down a bite of breakfast and head over to the embarcadero."

Maya couldn't wait to share with his father-in-law what he had learned about Ipy's conversation, but as the men tucked into their meal, Neferet and her friend appeared, laughing and chattering, at the foot of the stairs.

Neferet glanced at the baskets stacked on the floor and asked, "Are you leaving, Papa?"

"Yes, my duckling. As soon as we eat. Care to join us for a bite?"

The two young women pulled up stools and called the servants for a second table and more food.

"How is life at the palace, girls?" Lord Hani asked the *sunet*s as he spread his chunk of bread with soft, fresh cheese.

Neferet replied, "Boooring. Nobody's sick, except the king." She laughed. "I guess we're too good at what we do, eh, Ibet? But that makes me feel better about leaving. I know there'll always be sick people around in Khuit's old neighborhood."

Maya shot her an offended look. "What does that mean, my girl? I happen to live in Khuit's old neighborhood."

Lord Hani and Bener-ib exchanged amused looks, and Maya's face heated up.

"Yes, but you and Sati don't bathe in the River or sleep with a goat in your bedroom, and you keep flies off the babies and all that."

"Is that what they do in the palace?" Hani asked innocently.

Neferet rolled her eyes but couldn't help laughing. "Nooo, Papa. They have a servant shit for them, they're so clean."

"On that unsavory note, we leave you ladies to your breakfast," Hani said, rising. "Maya, are we ready? The dirty River awaits us."

❖

But before Hani could even retreat to the other side of the room to reclaim his basket of linens, a discreet cough stopped him in his tracks. Lord Ptah-mes's elderly doorkeeper stood framed in the doorway of the vestibule, his hands clasped. He looked anxious, although his training was strong enough to conceal all but the slightest trace of it.

"Lord Hani," the porter said. "There's a soldier here to see you. An officer. And several others as well."

A ripple of alarm raised the hair on Hani's neck as he thought about the hostilities breaking out along the border—through his fault, as some might see it. "I'll speak to them in the front garden, my friend. Tell them to wait," he said with an easy-seeming smile.

Maya caught his eye as he headed for the door.

A moment later, Hani emerged onto the porch to find Har-em-heb standing on the path, elegantly military in his scaled corselet, his broad shoulders bare. Pa-ra-mes-su and Menna followed in his wake, looking serious.

"Lord Hani," the general said, clasping Hani warmly by the forearms. "It's been too long since we've seen each other."

"I agree," Hani said in relief. "How are things going with the Haru in the nest?"

"Well, my lord. The boy is very eager to learn the arts of war—the best he can. As you know, he's lame. Although not as bad as his sister and queen."

"Poor lad," Hani said sincerely. "Poor both of them—such nice-looking young people."

"He's said more than once he wants to see you again. I guess that makes it an order, doesn't it?" He smiled, but then his gaze turned intense. "We've come about something else, though. Menna has made a discovery. Tell him, Menna."

Menna slapped his chest with a fist in salute and stepped forward. His friendly face was grave. From under his arm, he produced a long packet wrapped in linen and held it up. "Lord Hani, I picked these up around the site of Prince Zannanza's death and tucked them away. Maybe I unconsciously thought of myself as destroying evidence that might help convict our man. Then I forgot about them until just the other day."

He unwrapped the linen and exposed two arrows stained

with dried blood, one of which—the whole one—the officer held up. "This is the arrow I pulled from the breast of the lion." He passed it to Hani, who took it distastefully between his thumb and forefinger. "And this"—he held up the two pieces of the broken shaft—"is the one that shot the prince."

Hani took the second arrow. He glanced at the tattered fletching then, noticing something, held the first one up beside it. A smile twitched at the corners of Menna's mouth.

"They're not the same," Hani said.

Har-em-heb and his adjutant exchanged looks.

"No, they're not," the general said. "This one"—he tapped the first arrow—"is ours. That poor archer who said he was aiming at the lion really hit him. But this one"—he held out the murder weapon—"is Hittite."

Hani stared at Har-em-heb, frozen. "*They* killed him? One of their archers must have taken a shot and told no one when he saw the result. Let our boy suffer the penalty."

"So it appears," Har-em-heb said. He let Hani absorb that truth.

Nothing about that journey was as it seemed.

"Of course, it's too late to get our man exonerated. They didn't waste any time executing him," Pa-ra-mes-su said.

"At least it might soften Shuppiluliuma's appetite for war." Although Hani couldn't imagine the Great King of Kheta relinquishing his grudge over a little thing like evidence. *Who could prove that the Hittite arrow struck the prince and the Egyptian arrow the lion and not the other way around?* Except, of course, the murder weapon was broken by being dragged over the ground as Hani had tried to pull the victim to safety. Although even that could be explained away, given sufficient motivation.

"I suppose you could report this to Lord Ay, but I don't know what he could or would do." *It must just mean that his strategy involved bribing a Hittite soldier to do the job. As he hinted to me, he didn't want it to be so obvious that the Two Lands were behind the murder.*

"That's no doubt true," Har-em-heb replied with a slight sneer. "And in any case, I certainly shouldn't be the man to report it. We're on even worse terms than usual since this civil war broke out. I've tried my best not to get involved, but I am an infantryman, after all. And there's tension between us over the Haru in the nest." He dropped his eyes, and his voice trembled with hostility. "Ay had the nerve to berate Mut-nodjmet for not giving me children. What sort of monster could be so cruel to his own daughter?" He breathed heavily for a moment then mastered himself. "Anyway, I just wanted you to know about this. There's no justice in the world."

Hani smiled, optimistic despite himself. "Oh, I don't know. Lord Amen-Ra sees all, and justice will be done here or hereafter. 'Pilot who knows the waters, helmsman of the weak...' He sees, my friend. He sees."

Har-em-heb smiled, too, though it held a wistful edge. "Keep our little king-to-be in your prayers, Lord Hani. He's showing interest in the Hidden One, and I'm trying to guide him gently in that direction. I think our hour is coming, even without a Hittite alliance."

Har-em-heb clapped Hani on the arm, and Menna saluted with a grin. For all his brisk, nearly hard military manners, the general was almost tender when he spoke of children.

As the three officers disappeared through the gate, Hani stared down at the arrows in his hand, pondering the clever thoroughness of Lord Ay's strategy, with its feints and layers. But then another idea awoke within him. *Or was someone in the Hittite party behind it? Lord Ptah-mes seemed to think Shuppiluliuma wanted an excuse to attack our vassals. Would he have sacrificed his own son to gain one?* And another question rose in him more painfully: *Could that have had anything to do with Father's secret discussions?*

Hani returned to the salon, pensive, to find that the girls had finished their meal and disappeared. Maya looked up.

"That was Har-em-heb with interesting news about the death of our Hittite prince," Hani said. And he proceeded to tell him what Menna had discovered about the fatal arrow.

"I bet you're right, my lord. Their king did in his own son to give him an excuse to invade our vassals!" Maya cried fiercely. "The barbarian."

They sat in silence for a moment, absorbing what that could mean.

Maya said finally, "Of course, an Egyptian could have bribed the archer to kill the boy just as easily. It's usually their enemies who kill people, after all. Someone in the Two Lands who didn't want to see the Hittite alliance concluded."

"Which could be either of us in this room—or any other member of the family!" Hani managed a strained laugh, though his humor died quickly on his lips. His lighthearted words had brought him too quickly to the painful subject of Mery-ra's political alignment. "I'm not sure there's any point in passing this along to Lord Ay—what if he's the perpetrator? The cobra bracelets make that the likeliest solution. On the other hand, he may find out some other way. Even though he dislikes him, Har-em-heb has to work closely with his father-in-law on matters military. And I'd hate the old fox to believe I was withholding information from him."

Maya grunted sympathetically.

"I think I need to stay another day at least. I want to talk to Ptah-mes about this. See if he recommends reporting to Ay or not." Hani turned to his secretary. "Maya, my boy, feel free to join your mother for lunch after all, if you haven't already made your excuses."

"All right, my lord. I forgot what she said she was having, but it sounded tasty. And, well, I feel like I owe her some attention."

"That's my boy. 'Double the food your mother gave you. Support her as she supported you.'" *Your father too.* The thought had become a complicated one, full of pain.

They unpacked their baskets, and Hani and Maya settled in for some correspondence.

Later in the morning, just as the winter sun was sailing the heights of the heavens, Maya departed for his mother's house, and at about the same time, the girls came back. They and Hani had lunch together in the absence of Lord Ptah-mes, who still hadn't returned from the Double House.

But he did show up later that afternoon for his meal. Neferet and her friend had eaten and drifted back to work by the time he sank wearily into his chair. Maya had yet to return from his mother's, and only Hani and his host were left in the salon as the servants went about, silently placing the tables and laying out food. Hani wanted to bring Ptah-mes up to date on his interview with Lord Ay and all that had happened subsequently.

Once they were alone, Hani revealed what he'd learned. "I'm debating whether the God's Father will expect to get a report on this latest fact. He may decide to obliterate me if he thinks I've discovered his secret." His mind slid unhappily to the murder of Ipy.

Ptah-mes greeted the news with a raised eyebrow and a thoughtful pursing of the mouth.

"I'm not sure you need to meet with him, Hani. At most, you might drop him a hand-carried note. I doubt if he cares one way or the other—who's going to prosecute him for a political assassination? And if he's involved, he certainly won't pursue it with the Hittites."

"Probably not." Something else was on Hani's mind. He hesitated, wishing Nub-nefer and Baket-iset were there to counsel him. But Ptah-mes, as the former commissioner of foreign affairs, had a realistic view of information gathering. "My lord, I have something very private to tell you. Something that gives me great pain even to think about. I would appreciate any insights you might have on the matter."

Ptah-mes's smile faded, and he leaned toward Hani. "Be assured, my friend, nothing you say will ever pass my lips."

Reluctantly, Hani recounted Mery-ra's mysterious activities in Hattusha, his precipitous departure, and the suspicions Hani had begun to harbor about his father's involvement with the death of Prince Zannanza.

Ptah-mes listened silently. Then he said, "Would it be so terrible if he *had* had a hand in this affair, Hani? Would you have preferred to see a Hittite on the throne of the Two Lands?"

With a deep sigh, Hani admitted he would not have. "If he was serving our side—even as that's represented by Ay—I can make my peace with it. But if it was Shuppiluliuma himself who engineered the accident through Father's intervention... If he was somehow betraying our mission to an enemy... No, I just can't believe that." He looked up at his friend. "Perhaps I'm a credulous fool, but he's my father. I can't accept that he would lie to or betray anyone."

Ptah-mes's face looked strained, almost sad. "How long have you been in the diplomatic corps?"

Hani let out a bitter bark of laughter. "You're right. It's what we do."

Ptah-mes sat back with a caustic smile. "Explain nothing. Inform no one about what you're up to. Do your job, no matter your opinions. I'm sure that's exactly what he has done all his long life. In fact, why don't you ask him? If his conscience is clear about it, he may well tell you."

"And if not?" Hani asked, remembering Mery-ra's attempt to evade him.

But Ptah-mes didn't answer.

Some hours later, well after Lord Ptah-mes had returned to his office, the porter appeared in the door of the salon to say, "My lord, a woman is here to see you."

To Hani's surprise, the visitor was In-hapy. From her face, he knew immediately that something was wrong.

"What is it, mistress?" He thought anxiously of all his family who lived in Akhet-aten to whom something might have happened.

"Forgive me, Lord Hani," she said humbly. "I don't like to disturb you or Lord Maya by coming to his house, but I thought my son would be here by now. He left my place a while back, and in the meantime, something came up that I figured you would want to know. One of my senior workmen has disappeared. I told my Maya he hadn't been at work yesterday or the day before, but then I found out more."

Despite her usual easygoing temperament, In-hapy looked desperate. "I've lost two of my most important artisans in a matter of months—just when we're trying to finish that big royal order for the late king's tomb. We have to start years in advance, you know. Almost as soon as someone comes to the throne. And after less than two years, here we are facing the funeral. I don't want to think ill of colleagues, but I wonder if it isn't those rowdies who have been harassing my men who are behind this. They may have kidnapped him—or worse."

"Who is it, mistress?"

"Pi-ay, the filigree man. How am I going to replace him, Lord Hani? I can't turn a royal order over to my journeymen." In-hapy looked as worried as Hani had ever seen her.

Hani didn't like the sound of what she'd told him. Perhaps Ipy's death had *not* been related to the bracelets. Someone was targeting the goldsmith shop, it seemed, and In-hapy herself could be the next victim.

"Do you want me to find out what happened to him too?"

"I hoped you would, Lord Hani. These deaths have to be related, don't they?" She gave a rueful smile, embarrassed, and tucked a sprig of hair under her scarf in a self-conscious gesture. "Look at me—assuming you'll get involved, where you've really no responsibility at all."

But Hani nodded and laid a hand on her shoulder. "You did well. Someone needs to discover the man's fate. I'll walk you back, In-hapy—if someone has a grievance against your workshop, you need to be doubly careful. Is Maya not at your shop?"

"No, my lord. He set out right after lunch. I thought he was with you." The little goldsmith looked up, her brow furrowed with anxiety, as she no doubt feared something had happened to her son too.

"He's probably on his way," Hani reassured her.

He left word of their destination with the gatekeeper in case Maya should reappear in his absence, then he followed the goldsmith into the street. Through the narrow back alleys, her little feet pattered tirelessly at a pace that Hani could barely keep up with.

"You're worried about your son, aren't you?" Hani said softly. "I'm sure he's fine, my dear. Maya knows how to take care of himself."

She shot him a strained smile and said, "Forgive me, my lord, but all these deaths have me upset. If someone is targeting my workshop..."

"Do you think we should talk to some of your competitors?"

To his surprise, In-hapy looked horrified. "Oh no, my

lord. It's important that we all keep up at least a facade of comradeship, or life in the guild will become impossible. It wouldn't be any of the masters anyway. I'm sure it's just young workmen."

In silence, they pounded down the dusty, garbage-strewn lanes. The workday was almost ending, and men shouldering their tools and pack animals loaded with cargo passed them at both shoulders, flashing in and out of the shade of reed awnings. In-hapy's route was different from Hani's accustomed path. She kept to the inland side of the great processional way until the last minute then cut directly across toward the River just before the street ended at the wall of the temple of Aten. At her bronze-studded gate, she called out, "Open up. It's me."

The old Nubian pulled back the panel, his face distraught. He greeted his employer and Hani then said under his breath, "Has our mistress told you, my lord? Another goldsmith dead."

"She has, my friend. But perhaps he's not dead. As I understand it, no one has found a body. What's his family said?"

"He has no family to speak of, Lord Hani," In-hapy said. "He's a widower whose daughters are grown and married and still live in Waset."

"Then there's no point in talking to them yet."

Hani and In-hapy made their way across the work yard toward the open door of the studio.

"What can you tell me about Pi-ay? Was he well liked? A good worker?"

In-hapy looked reluctant. "I wish I could say he was well liked. He was a wonderful craftsman but a rather solitary person, as if he thought he was too good for everyone else. You had to know how to manage Pi-ay, you know? I suspect he worked on independent projects on my time. Sometimes he would disappear for half the day, just like that. Told no one where he was going, asked no one's permission. I try to be understanding about the workmen's needs, and he was such a good goldsmith I let him get away with a lot. He'd been here since before my husband died, my lord. One of the first people we hired when we inherited the shop from Turo's father. I think Pi-ay rather assumed that gave him rights."

"So he might have had enemies who would wish him harm. He might have provoked a fight, let's say, with workmen from another studio." But then something occurred to Hani. "If you say he was frequently absent for long parts of the day, what makes you think he's not just doing the same thing now?"

"He was gone all yesterday and the day before, and neither did he come in this morning. Thinking he might be sick, I sent one of the apprentices to his house after lunch, and he's not there either. His landlady hasn't seen him for days. I'm very much afraid that…" In-hapy swallowed with effort.

Hani reassured In-hapy of his help then took his leave. On his way out, he spoke to several of the workmen, but none of them had seen or heard anything.

He noticed young Hu-may crouched by the forge, watching him with his usual sorrowful expression, and smiled at the boy kindly. *Poor lad. Touched twice by death in only a few months.* And he realized with a sinking heart that he was already thinking in terms of deaths.

CHAPTER 11

Early the next morning, Maya went for a stroll—
or rather something more intense. He needed to be
alone to think before he and Hani headed to the chancery
to begin their day's work. Lord Hani had filled him in on
the latest about Pi-ay's disappearance as soon as Maya had
entered Ptah-mes's house the previous evening, but Maya
had other preoccupations. He strode down the alleys in a
more and more distracted state, stumping along at a pace
that suggested considerable urgency—even though he was
heading nowhere in particular. His mind was churning.
Images of Sat-hut-haru clinging to him, pleading in a small
voice for him not to leave, ate away at his already-shredded
tranquility. *This can't go on. I have to find some job that won't
take me away from Waset all the time.*

Then there was his mother and first of all, her safety.
*If these ruffian competitors are killing off her men, how safe
is she?*

Everyone whispered that the government would move
away from Akhet-aten as soon as the present king flew into

the West, but Maya didn't know if that meant it would go back to Waset or to Men-nefer, a week downriver. He didn't want to take Sati away from her mother's and sisters' company, yet he couldn't imagine Lady Nub-nefer ever leaving the City of the Scepter, since the liturgy of the Hidden One had resumed, and she had taken up her duties once more as a chantress of the god. So whatever Maya found to do had to be in Waset.

But the truth was he could hardly bear the idea of leaving Lord Hani's employ. Nowhere else would he be treated with such respect and affection, such humor and fairness, such trust, such affability, and such love. Maya's nose began to burn at the thought of what his father-in-law meant to him. He adored the man—more than his own father, whom he hardly remembered. Hani had seen to it that a promising student of no birth at all had had the means to continue his education then had employed him. He'd taken him on adventures overseas and helped to polish him, and finally, he had given Maya his daughter's hand in marriage, never objecting once to his son-in-law being just a boy from the working class. *I could never say to that man, "I'm going to leave you after all you've done for me,"* he realized and dashed at his nose. *I've spoken bravely about retiring from the foreign service, but I don't see how I can. It would be heinous ingratitude.*

Iyah! Is there any solution to this problem?

Later that morning, Hani took his secretary to the office to begin making notes on all the things he needed to look into. He wanted to be able to close out his post in such a way that his successor would know just where to begin. They spent the entire morning with scrolls spread out all around them on the floor. Hani had no idea who would take his place when he finally got up the courage to leave. He couldn't think of anyone with the same depth of field expertise since Mane had retired. The years since Lord Ptah-mes's removal from office as high commissioner had seen everything but the bare minimum of activities drift to a haphazard end, leaving the younger generation of diplomats without much practical experience. The kindest thing Hani could do for whoever replaced him as roving emissary would be to leave a detailed summary of where things stood, what overtures had been made, what treaties were in place, and what rulers to look out for.

The state of the records confirmed Hani's perception that the late Nefer-khepru-ra had really had no coherent foreign policy. And his successor hadn't had time to institute one, assuming it was even on her agenda. *What is Ay's attitude toward diplomatic relationships?* Hani wondered. *He's a military man. Will he prefer to settle differences with arms?* Hani's hopes—to see the Two Lands go forward with honesty and efficiency into the world of its peers—would depend on Ay's direction, at least until little Tut-ankh-aten was old enough to set his own policies.

By the end of the morning, Hani felt he had had enough bureaucratic chaos for one day. He stood up, arching his back, and said, "Maya, my friend, what if we paid your mother a quick visit? Maybe something new has turned up about Pi-ay's dea—disappearance." He really expected the goldsmith's body to have washed up on the riverbank.

But what a distraught In-hapy told them when

they arrived was just as disconcerting. Ipy's widow had disappeared.

Hani and Maya exchanged looks of shock.

"This can't be the work of rival workshops, surely. Why would they have targeted a woman who had nothing directly to do with your studio, Mother?"

"I don't know, son. But that makes three people in a very short time. I've told the men to walk home two by two now."

Maya said in concern, "Maybe you should live somewhere else for a while. I'm sure Lord Ptah-mes would have room."

"No. No, son. I'm safer here with this heavy gate and a doorkeeper on guard. I don't want to leave the place until we find out what's going on."

"Maybe the real issue is the inlaid bracelets after all. Ipy might well have told his wife about them, and Pi-ay certainly would have seen the cuffs as his friend worked on them." Hani stared around as if he expected to see some clue right before his eyes. "How is young Hu-may taking it?"

"He's very worried. All the responsibility of the family falls on him, unless his mother shows up again. He was late for work this morning and came to explain why. The poor boy was in tears. It's been several days since they've seen her, apparently. I don't know why he didn't say anything sooner."

In-hapy called Hu-may from the workshop, and he loped toward them across the court—a skinny, sad-eyed creature who looked nowhere near his age. Yet he was a hard-working, talented youngster. He might have looked forward to a prosperous future, but the weight of his responsibility seemed to be crushing him. *How is a young boy supposed to find a wet nurse for his baby brothers?*

"Hu-may, Lord Hani wants to find your mother and help your family stay together," In-hapy said kindly.

Hani laid a fatherly hand on Hu-may's shoulder. "Can you help us, son? I'd like to ask you some questions."

The boy nodded, and In-hapy, with a knowing look at Hani, disappeared into the doorway of the workshop. She motioned for Maya to follow, leaving Hani and Hu-may alone in the court.

"Tell me whatever you know about your mother's disappearance, my lad. When did it happen?"

"Four days ago. At night, my lord. Because when I woke up in the morning, she wasn't there. The baby crying was what woke me up, so I don't know if she had fed him in the night at all or not." Hu-may, half incoherent with distress, rubbed his nose with a wrist. "All the clothes were gone too. I know that because I had to get dressed in the morning before I went to work, and I didn't see anything except my kilt. Or maybe she had left everything at the laundryman's." He looked up in misery at Hani, despite the hope-filled words.

"Let's say the clothes were all at the laundry. Why might your mother have left the house in the middle of the night?" *Anything could have happened to a woman alone, abroad at that hour.* "Did someone come to the door—maybe call her to help a neighbor?"

The boy wrinkled his forehead in thought and said hesitantly, "There may have been a knock, my lord. Or rather a scratch or tap. I barely woke up, and later, I thought it was just something I'd dreamed. But perhaps somebody came for her after all."

Yahya! "Then do you think she maybe just hasn't come home yet?" Hani suggested. "Perhaps she went to help a sick neighbor and has stayed with her until she's out of danger." He had to admit Hemet-min didn't seem like the sort who would run down the block at midnight to take on another responsibility, but that would certainly be the most benign explanation. "What do you think?"

"I... I don't know, my lord. I'm afraid she's dead. Everybody's dead." The boy's assumption was filled with such hopelessness that it split Hani's heart.

"One last thing. Do you have any relatives anywhere, my boy? Anyone who might be considered legally responsible for you?"

To his disappointment, the lad shook his head mournfully. "No, my lord. Mother is from some town upriver, and Father's brother died a few years ago. That's why Grandfather is with us."

"Thank you, Hu-may. You've been very helpful. Very grown up. We'll see to it that someone helps you. We'll find a wet nurse for the little ones." Hani wondered how the boy had fed the suckling baby for so many days—perhaps a compassionate neighbor. He gave Hu-may a squeeze around the narrow shoulders and, with a heavy heart, watched him trot across the work yard and disappear into the door of the studio. *I'll ask if Nub-nefer is open to taking them in,* he thought reluctantly. *The poor little hatchlings.*

Maya decided to stay at his mother's for lunch, so Hani returned alone to Ptah-mes's residence.

That evening, Hani recounted to his host over dinner

the unfortunate plight of Ipy's children. "Unless someone reports finding a body, we can't even be sure their mother is dead. If the murderer threw her into the River, we may never know."

"Corpses seem to be multiplying," Ptah-mes said dryly. He deposited a wing bone neatly onto his dish and dipped his fingers into the small bowl of scented water that sat beside it.

Neferet looked deeply troubled, her straight dark eyebrows knotted. "This is so sad. Who will take the poor little ones in? Just one—maybe you could find somebody. But six and that old man? It's impossible."

"Well, I'm going to talk to your mother. Since all you children are grown and out of the nest, maybe..." Hani had to admit he didn't much look forward to having all those singularly ill-behaved little ones underfoot at his age, although it seemed like the least one human being could do for another. "Perhaps we could build on to the roof terrace to make more room for that big brood and give the children some privacy."

But Neferet said with spirit, "No, Papa. Here's what we'll do. Bener-ib and I will take them in. There's more than enough room for them here and even more in Waset. We can hire a wet nurse for the babies and a nanny for the other children to keep them occupied while the oldest boy works. By the time he can earn a man's wage, the others won't be any trouble."

Hani was so taken aback that he could think of nothing to say. He shot a quick glance at the master of the house, but Ptah-mes had donned his inscrutable face and dropped his eyes discreetly to his plate.

"Wait, my duckling," Hani finally managed to say. "Don't you think you need to consult your husband about this first? And Bener-ib? It will mean an enormous disruption for them—and expense."

But Neferet had latched on to the idea and pursued it with stubborn enthusiasm. Her little eyes snapped, and she planted her hands on her hips. "Lord Ptah-mes always tells me I can do anything I want with his gold. And this is what I want. Ibet doesn't mind. Do you, Ibet?"

The other young *sunet* shook her head dutifully.

Hani turned horrified eyes to his host, mortified to have been a party to such an abuse of hospitality. "You don't have to say yes, my lord. Neferet must learn some boundaries."

Ptah-mes gave a thin smile. "I did tell her she could do what she wanted. And I suppose that, after all the homeless puppies, kittens, and lame donkeys, we might have foreseen this." His smile became more genuinely amused. "She may do as she likes. The children won't be underfoot. There's plenty of room for them to have their own nursery."

Hani was at least as surprised by his friend's reaction as by Neferet's idea. "You've proved your generosity yet again, my lord," he said in admiration. He remembered that Ptah-mes had once had a family of seven children in his household, as hard as it was to imagine the silent discipline of the place disrupted by running and shouting.

"If you were willing to take them in under conditions of hardship, how could I do less when it costs me nothing, Hani? Your daughter is an example to us all."

Neferet sprang from her stool and threw herself on her seated husband with such impetuosity that he nearly toppled backward before he could brace himself. Hani could see by Ptah-mes's eyes how uncomfortable that made him, but the grandee bore it with perfect aplomb, eventually liberating an arm to give her an awkward pat on the back.

"Thank you, Lord Ptah-mes. I've always wanted little brothers and sisters! It will be such fun!" She detached herself and turned to her friend. "Isn't this wonderful, Ibet? Should we tell them about the other thing now?"

Dear gods, Hani thought. *Something else?* He almost broke out laughing. That was so perfectly typical of his youngest daughter.

"What, my dear?" Ptah-mes asked politely, his face aflame. He straightened his shirt with a self-conscious twitch.

"Whenever the king dies, Bener-ib and I are going to resign from the palace and start our own practice in Khuit's old neighborhood in Waset. We feel that poor people deserve good care too and not just rich people." She looked up at her husband with a guilty grin. "Although rich people are perfectly nice."

Hani exchanged stares of confusion with his friend. "Is this a political statement, my duckling? I thought you were happy that things were moving back to the old ways."

"Oh no. We are. But soon, the king will be a boy, and they'll give him a male *sunu*, and we'll only treat the queen and her ladies, and… it just seemed like a good time to do it."

"Besides, we don't like Lord Ay, and he'll be the regent." Bener-ib looked as determined as Hani had ever seen her. The attentions of the king's father had cost the life of one of Bener-ib's patients, a scarcely adolescent handmaid who had died after giving birth to the child he had forced on her.

The timing of the two *sunet*s' resignation suddenly struck Hani as suspicious. He caught Ptah-mes's eye then said quietly to his daughter, "You wouldn't have anything to do with the, er, transition between one reign and another, would you, little duck?"

"Oh no, Papa. I swear it by Mama's *ka*. May Lord Djehuty peck out my liver and peel my toes if I did. May Bes lick my eyeballs, and... and may—"

"There, there, my girl. I believe you. And I won't even ask if any other human hand has a role in the king's declining health." Suddenly, Hani turned from one dinner companion to another. "Has anybody seen Maya? He was having lunch with In-hapy, but that's been hours."

❖

Maya's guilty conscience impelled him once more to take his midday meal at his mother's. He had started toward Lord Ptah-mes's villa after lunch, but in the wake of a big meal, a brisk walk helped him to think. Every time he let his mind wander, it returned to his conundrum: to stay in the foreign service or to find a sedentary post in Waset. The decision obsessed him. He zigzagged aimlessly through the poorer neighborhoods south of the palace, moving generally in the direction of the affluent suburbs. Without even noticing, he had headed westward, toward the River, and now he found himself at the embarcadero. An endless row of boats of all sizes bobbed along the shallow bank, like horses at their watering trough. Off to his right, in the direction of the royal quays, lay Lord Hani's merry little yacht, with its red-and-green-checked decoration and grinning Bes-head prow. Sailing downriver with the wind in his face, the admiring peasants along the bank staring up as he passed, asking themselves who it could be on that deck, filled him with satisfaction like few other things. If he resigned, he might never walk up the beloved gangplank again.

Sunk in his anguish, Maya almost didn't register what he saw ahead of him, where a crowd of people was milling, preparing to board a long-distance ferry heading downriver. Pushing and jostling as ever, the passengers laughed and chattered and clattered on board with their packages, baggage, crates, and sacks of live geese. Parents with small children tried to herd their little ones safely away from the edge of the water, while low-level officials, not quite important enough to have a royal boat at their disposal, looked around them with contempt at their ill-dressed fellow passengers.

And there among them all stood a thin-faced, slope-shouldered woman of about thirty in the company of a small, dapper man he recognized. It was Pi-ay, his mother's filigree artist—the one who hadn't reported for work in days. *Mother will be relieved.* But Maya's senses pricked up in alert. *Pi-ay is widowed, so who is the woman?* She seemed familiar too. Then he remembered her from errands long ago at the home of Ipy. She was the Osir's widow. *She isn't dead at all! No more than that sly dog Pi-ay.*

Letting himself be buffeted by the passing throng, Maya stopped and watched the couple curiously. They looked happy—laughing and familiar with each other. Maya was scandalized. *Her husband is barely in his tomb before she's out cavorting with another man.*

The crowd behind him shoved and shifted impatiently, and Maya decided he needed to get out of the throng, or he would be pushed aboard one of the ferries bound for the Great Green. He fought his way back up the slope, grumbling irritably about the inconsiderateness of so many people. From the level ground beyond the warehouses, he watched Pi-ay and the woman disappear into the press on the deck of a boat then saw the sailors push off into the current, heading north. Shading his eyes, he kept the vessel in view until it disappeared in a blinding flame of sunset-dazzled water. *Who's keeping her children, I wonder?*

While he stood there, the silvery autumn twilight settled in, and before long, the air held only the memory of light. Fireflies had begun to wink here and there. Maya looked around uneasily. Curfew had him nervous. Those soldiers prowling after dark were more frightening than restless revolutionaries. He shivered and made his way as fast as his short legs would carry him without abandoning dignity southward toward Lord Ptah-mes's villa.

Maya hadn't gone far, however, before he decided, despite the danger, to retrace his steps. He headed back to the area of his mother's workshop at a determined pace, casting his eyes around at every intersection, on the lookout for a night patrol. He had a vague recollection of Pi-ay's address from the errands of his youth and told himself that a little investigation might make it clear what the man had been up to over the last several days and why he hadn't shown up for work.

But when he arrived, he rediscovered what he had

forgotten—that Pi-ay didn't live alone. He had a room in a house owned by an old woman, who appeared at the gate, looking fearful at a nighttime knock. Her narrowed eyes ran Maya up and down as she no doubt wondered who the proud, good-looking dwarf with a writing case over his shoulder—who dared to be abroad after curfew—might be. She seemed to be at a loss for words.

Maya flashed her a warm, trustworthy smile such as Lord Hani might have given. "Good evening, mistress. Is this where Pi-ay lives?"

"I thought you was him, finally," she murmured evasively and made as if to shut the door.

But Maya forced it open and stepped into the courtyard. It was barely light enough to see beyond the circle of the old woman's moringa oil lamp. "I'm a friend of his. He works for my mother. He asked me to drop by and get something he forgot."

"Where is he? That boy come the other day and asked about him too," the woman said, backing up ahead of Maya's amiably insistent advance.

Maya thought the question had been asked with honest curiosity rather than as a test, but he said with a conspiratorial grin, "Don't tell him I told you, but he's with that sweetheart of his."

The mistress of the house gave a disapproving sniff. "Her. What do you need to get for him?"

"Some things related to his work." *Ammit take it, stop asking questions, you gossipy old goose.* "Forgive me, mistress, but I'm out after curfew. The sooner I can get this errand done and get home, the better. My wife will start worrying about me if I don't show up for dinner."

Perhaps it was the mental image of an anxious wife, but the woman seemed at last convinced of Maya's good intentions. She gestured for him to move through the door of the tiny vestibule and into a salon with a single simply painted wooden column. "Up them stairs, young man. I'd go with you, but it's got hard to get up them stairs."

"Yes, them stairs are a problem," he agreed as he trudged up the steep steps. They groaned disconcertingly, even under Maya's negligible weight.

"Straight ahead," the old woman called in her reedy voice. He could see her standing at the bottom, craning her neck, undoubtedly hoping to spot something interesting.

Maya quickly realized that he wasn't going to be able to see a thing, interesting or otherwise, on the dark second floor. "I don't suppose there's a lamp up here?"

She assured him there were both a lamp and a fire-drill in the niche to the left of Pi-ay's door. Maya groped his way across the creaking floor, found he could barely reach the niche, and at last, getting more and more anxious, began to pull the bow back and forth almost solely by touch. *What a bad idea this was,* he told himself testily. *I'm going to be picked up for violating the curfew.* At last, sparks jumped out, and the kindling began to glow. Once a flame had fluttered into being, he held a piece of burning straw over the lamp, hoping there was oil inside, and sure enough, the wick caught, its feeble light casting ominous shadows around the corridor. He pushed his way into Pi-ay's room and pulled the door closed gently behind him.

The space was small and bare, with nothing but a soot-stained brazier full of greasy ash and a cheaply made bed hung with mosquito curtains. At first, Maya marveled at its austerity, since Pi-ay, like Ipy, must have been a well-paid artisan—with no one but himself to spend his wages on. But then he realized the quarters had been stripped. Nothing had been left of Pi-ay's property—not a clothes chest, not a stool, not a spare kilt. He cursed under his breath. The goldsmith wasn't just out for a few days' idyll with a girlfriend. He had no intention of coming back.

The jackal—abandoning Mother without a word like that. And he's having an affair with his friend's widow. I'll bet anything he killed Ipy out of jealousy and now has run away before he's caught. Steaming, Maya lifted the lumpy straw mattress sack from the bed frame, almost hoping he'd find the bloody murder weapon there. And he did.

At least, it was a knife—a plain, single-bladed, bone-handled kitchen knife, so frequently sharpened that only a slim skeleton of its former shape was left. If it had been used to kill Ipy, it had been cleaned. Maya sniffed it and was rewarded with a whiff of onion. *So the lying jackal didn't let the* medjay *take it out after all.* He slipped the blade into his waistband and bloused his shirt carefully to conceal the hilt.

Maya stumped down the stairs, lamp in hand, and found the landlady still watching eagerly. He remembered to smile at her and said, "Thanks. Pi-ay will be grateful." He hustled past her and out the door, still carrying the lamp, his jaw clenched with nerves.

Once into the lane, he cast a furtive glance about and slipped the blade around to his back so that if he passed someone, it wouldn't be visible. There didn't seem to be any soldiers in sight, although it was already too dark to make out much. He wondered if it were better to strike out fearlessly down the processional way like a man with a clear conscience or to creep along back streets and hope not to be seen with a knife in his possession. He decided to creep. Only then did Maya notice he had the woman's lamp. *Let's hope she doesn't report it stolen.*

His thoughts were churning. *Pi-ay has to be the murderer.*

Maya was so preoccupied with his theory that he didn't notice the approach of two sets of footsteps until it was too late to dodge out of sight.

"Who goes there? Don't you know we have a curfew?" Lit by a guttering torch, a pair of big men loomed out of the darkness with a leashed baboon who looked heavier than Maya.

Medjay! Bes protect us.

All Maya could think about was the knife behind his back. His heart beating frantically, he groped for some plausible excuse for his presence. "Am I glad to see you!" he cried. "My nieces and nephews' mother has been kidnapped!" He looked wide-eyed from face to face, trying to ignore the baboon perusing him skeptically, piercing his lies with an animal's infallible instinct.

As if he hadn't spoken, one of the policemen, a villainous-looking fellow, growled, "What are you out on the streets after dark for?"

Maya said testily, "Looking for you, of course. My widowed sister-in-law was seen at the embarcadero with a strange man. He was forcing her aboard a northbound boat. I assume you'll go after him as you should, before he does her harm. He's a short, stocky fellow, about forty, and has a big cowlick that flips his hair up in front."

The two *medjay* exchanged glances, as if weighing the veracity of his statement. "And who are you?"

Maya drew himself up and fingered his writing case proudly. "Maya son of Turo, royal scribe. Hurry, man. They just embarked on a ferry. The children are home alone—I have to get back." *To somewhere,* he added silently in the interests of *ma'at.*

To his immense relief, the policemen and their animal took off jogging toward the river, leaving a curl of oily smoke behind them. His knees weak and his temples beaded with cold sweat, Maya stumbled on. Then he brightened, and his steps grew jauntier. *You're really pretty good at this sort of thing, my boy.*

Hani jumped up at the sound of footsteps in Ptah-mes's vestibule. Maya still wasn't home, and In-hapy's concern of the previous day had infected him.

Sure enough, his son-in-law burst into the salon, breathless. Ptah-mes looked up from where he sat on the floor, writing.

"Lord Hani. Lord Ptah-mes. I guess I missed dinner, eh?"

"I'm sure we've left you something," Ptah-mes assured him with a dry smile. He clapped, and a serving girl appeared. He directed her to bring an array of dishes and a ewer of heated wine.

Maya took a seat at the table with Hani. He rubbed his hands and grinned, looking pleased with himself. "I did a little investigating after I left Mother's, and guess what I found out about our latest murders, my lords."

As soon as the servant had set out Maya's dinner on a small table and he had torn a hungry chunk from his roasted quail, Hani asked—as he knew he was expected to—"What, son?"

"The victims are alive and well, very much in love, and on their way up the River, leaving Hemet-min's brood behind."

Hani's heart dropped. "Surely Pi-ay exercised some pressure on her. Could it be that a mother would abandon her small children, including unweaned babies? Could she have been so desperate to get away?" And something in him answered reluctantly, *Yes*. He wasn't sure whether it would be harder on the little ones to think their mother had died or that she had deliberately run away and left them. In either case, Neferet and Bener-ib would have a lot of love to make up to those children.

"Did they know each other before that Ipy's death, I wonder?" Ptah-mes asked.

"I don't know," Hani said.

But Maya seemed to be more certain. "I bet they were having an affair." He took a sip of the wine, and his expression said he was letting it ignite a delightful path of heat all the way to his stomach. He licked his lips appreciatively, clearly reluctant to let a drop be lost. "And the best part is this. I stopped by Pi-ay's house afterward, and guess what I found." He produced the knife with a flourish. "Of course, this means that Pi-ay killed Ipy, doesn't it, Lord Hani? He had a motive. And he had the weapon in his possession!"

"I... I guess." Hani turned the knife over and over, eyeing it carefully. The much-scoured bronze blade reflected his face in a shadowy golden image. And that wasn't the only thing that was blurry and distorted. *Why didn't the goldsmith throw the knife into the River or let it remain in the body instead of hiding it in his room then leaving it behind, where his landlady would eventually find it?* "It may be after all that the murder had nothing to do with the attempt on the prince."

But then a wave of frustration washed over Hani, and he growled, "I just can't figure this out. How many separate crimes do we have here? How many criminals? Are all these deaths related, or aren't they?"

Maya, wound up in his own story, seemed not to hear. "The *medjay* caught me on the street, and I made them think I had gone out looking for them." He blasted a sudden snort of laughter that sent wine spraying from his nose. Ptah-mes looked up with amusement, and a furious blush of embarrassment rose to light the young man's cheeks as he dabbed his chin. He continued with more restraint, "I sent them to stop Pi-ay. I said he was kidnapping Hemet-min. The boat must have put in somewhere nearby—darkness was coming on fast. They may already have captured our two turtledoves."

As soon as the woman makes it clear she wasn't being taken against her will, the medjay will release them. Hani pondered that. *What exactly is my duty toward the pair?* Unless he could prove they had conspired to murder Hemet-min's husband—in which case she would be put to death anyway—it didn't seem to be his business to drag the woman back to her family. He suspected the little ones would have a happier life with Neferet and her friend.

CHAPTER 12

T HE NEXT DAY, HANI AND Maya spent the morning in the chancery and returned to Ptah-mes's villa around midday. As soon as they entered the gate, shrieks of excitement came from the garden along with the rhythmic *pof-pof* of a ball being batted back and forth. *That's certainly not Ptah-mes,* Hani thought with a silent chuckle. He called, "Neferet? Are you here, my duckling?"

The shouts and laughter ceased, and Neferet cried, "Papa! Come see us!"

Hani made his way toward the dining pavilion, with its grape-loaded arbor. In the space before it, Neferet, Bener-ib, and the children of Ipy were playing a game. The oldest girl had wrapped her legs around Neferet's waist, while one of the younger children rode Hu-may's back. Bener-ib carried another youngster. The "horsemen" threw the ball to one another in a three-cornered frenzy, cheered on by the toddlers. When Bener-ib's diminutive rider heaved it wildly into the bushes, the smaller children rushed screaming after it, and the "horses" galloped awkwardly to a palm tree before the little vigilantes could tag them. Hani remembered fondly how his children had loved the game before Sat-hut-haru grew too old and prim for it. It did his heart good to see the orphans enjoying themselves like any children, without an exhausted mother shouting threats at them.

He waited until Neferet, panting and red-faced, had unloaded her passenger. She threw herself on her father with an enthusiastic hug and would have picked Maya right up, except he warned her off with a raised hand and a look of offended dignity.

"You can get them some fruit juice, Ibet," she called back to her friend. "Hu-may can help you carry it." She turned her grinning scarlet face to Hani. "Papa, you're still in Akhet-aten! See what fun we're having?"

"I do see it, my duck. May Mut the mother of us all bless you for this act of generosity."

"I want to take them down to the farm, but Hu-may can't leave his work, so In-hapy said he could board with her when the end-of-week holiday is over."

"That wretched Hemet-min. Look how many lives she's overturned. What kind of woman abandons her family?" Maya looked disgusted, his fists clenched.

In a reflective voice, Hani quoted, "Do not shout, 'Crime!' against a person when the cause of their flight is hidden."

Neferet said sadly, "I don't think she's necessarily a bad person, Maya. She just couldn't take any more. It's really the same thing as Sati—"

"It's nothing like Sati!" Maya cried, indignant. "She

would never have run away and left her children. Or her husband."

To Hani's surprise, Neferet didn't argue, just shrugged, unconvinced. "The children said Hemet-min wasn't always like this. I mean, she was always lazy and dreamy, but just after the birth of the second-to-last baby, she changed. Sometimes a demon gets hold of a woman in childbirth. You never know."

"Sati would never have done such a thing," Maya repeated hotly. "There was no demon in your sister."

Before the argument could go any further, a harried pounding sounded at the gate. Hani heard Ptah-mes's porter unbolt it. Then came the sound of urgent voices and footsteps in the gravel.

A royal servant burst around the bushes and dropped into a wild bow. "Lady Neferet!" he cried, gasping for breath. "You must come to the palace in the greatest haste. Our Sun God is dying."

⸙

By the time Hu-may and the children returned from the kitchen, tamarind juice in hand, Neferet and Bener-ib had rushed away with their baskets, leaving Hani stunned. He sent the youngsters back to their quarters and drifted into the pavilion, where he dropped with a thump onto a low-backed chair. Around him, the darkening twilight was growing almost chilly, and a few brilliant stars had appeared in a sky of luminous beryl. A dove twittered in the trees then flew away on whistling wings, and the evening was left to the crickets. A great dark silence lay upon all the Black Land. One might object to Ankhet-kepru-ra Nefer-neferuaten's policies, but she was the Haru on earth. The Two Kingdoms were in a moment of dangerous vulnerability. Hani murmured a prayer for her and was almost surprised to realize how sincere it was.

Prince Tut-ankh-aten will succeed her now, Hani thought. *He'll take the throne peacefully. Ay will no doubt be the regent, but terrible though the man is, he'll bring the kingdom back to the traditional ways. And he's more than competent.* A huge weight that had crushed him for nearly fifteen years was about to be lifted. At last, he could serve the king in good conscience.

Hani was finally driven indoors by the gooseflesh that prickled along his arms as evening deepened, and the warmth of day bled away. As he entered the salon, Ptah-mes walked in from the vestibule. He looked tired—less well shaved than usual and with dark pouches beneath his eyes. Around his head was tied a mourning scarf.

Hani froze. "Our Sun God has flown into the West?"

Ptah-mes nodded, and they sank to their knees, touching the floor in lieu of strewing dust on their heads. They knelt there for several heartbeats, staring at each other. Little by little, a smile that Hani would have described as triumphant if it hadn't been so heavily inflected by exhaustion lit his friend's face.

Ptah-mes pulled himself wearily to his feet. "The Atenist nightmare's over," he said. "As if it never was."

Hani barely dared to let the words sink in. His whole world had shifted in an instant.

But so had that of the young king. Tut-ankh-aten had lost his mother. He had taken on the cares of a kingdom.

What is he? Nine or ten years old? May the Hidden One guide him. It will say a lot if he's properly consecrated at the Ipet-isut.

"I've been appointed to plan and carry out the funeral rites, so I won't see much of you for the next seventy days, my friend."

Ptah-mes gave Hani a hand, and Hani hoisted himself up.

"You're a good choice, my lord. You carried out the obsequies for Neb-ma'at-ra, which were one of the great liturgies of our lifetime." Hani fell silent then asked, "Is she to be buried at Akhet-aten?"

Ptah-mes nodded. "Our Sun God had a sentimental attachment to the city. Perhaps her worship of the Aten was sincere, or perhaps she just wanted to be buried near her husband."

Hani remembered the then-queen's spectacular beauty and what a splendid couple the royal pair had made. He was glad the reign of the Aten was over, but he found he couldn't gloat. A unique loveliness had abandoned the world of the living.

"If you'll forgive me, Hani, I think I'll go to bed. Tomorrow will be busy." Ptah-mes made his way up the staircase, and his fashionable sandals with their curled-up toes clopped down the upstairs corridor. Hani wouldn't have minded turning in early as well, but he wanted to wait for Neferet and Bener-ib. Nub-nefer would expect all the latest rumors from the palace.

The night was well advanced before the young *sunet*s made an appearance, and Hani was dozing in his chair, his head halfway to his lap. At the sound of Neferet's voice, he jerked upright.

"Papa! I guess you've heard the news." Neferet bounced over to her father and seated herself on his knees. "Ankhet-khepru-ra has flown into the West—or wherever the Aten worshipers fly."

Despite the flippant words, she didn't look quite as victorious as Hani might have expected. Her usually sparkling eyes were dulled with sorrow.

"Was she still alive when you reached the palace, my duckling?"

"Unconscious," Bener-ib said.

"She'd been sick a long while, but this was sudden. They called in all her children to be with her at the last." Neferet's chin trembled. "It's sad when somebody's mother dies. They were all crying." She lowered her face to conceal the tears in her own eyes.

"The daughters who have preceded her will welcome her joyfully to the Duat." *Although maybe not Meryet-aten.* Hani hugged the girl tight. "Was Lord Ay there?"

"Oh yes," Bener-ib said coldly.

"He looked sad, but he didn't cry or tear his hair or anything. Lord Pentju was there."

Hani pushed his daughter gently off his lap and stood up, stretching. "Your husband is in charge of the funeral."

"Oh, is he?" Neferet brightened. "He's so smart. Now Bener-ib and I can move back to Waset and start our practice for the poor." She seized her friend's little hand, and they exchanged looks of excitement.

"You won't make much," Hani reminded them. "Poor people may pay you in dried beans or in their services. It won't be like working at the palace—that was the most prestigious post in the world. Not many people would give it up."

"Lord Ptah-mes doesn't need the income," Neferet said. "And it will be better for the children to get away from this city."

It took Hani a moment to remember who "the children" were. He considered Neferet and Bener-ib—eager to serve the destitute and take in someone else's orphaned brood—and he was overcome with tenderness and admiration. *God prefers him who honors the poor to him who worships the wealthy.* He understood better his maxim.

❖

Lord Ay wasted no time reorganizing the government, not even waiting until the old king had been buried and her successor officially consecrated. Hani grudgingly approved—those long, drawn-out interregnums were moments of dangerous confusion. But he was surprised when he received a summons from Lord Pentju. His old acquaintance—hardly a friend—the former royal physician, had taken up his duties as vizier of the Upper Kingdom and wanted to see Hani right away. Hani wasn't sure exactly how to react. Nearly two years ago, he had discovered that Pentju was guilty of at least one murder and probably several, including that of Pentju's old schoolmate, Bener-ib's father. But as Lady Djefat-nebty had explained it, sometimes what looked like murder was an act of war. Pentju had been covertly on the side of the King of the Gods, so his deeds had been gestures of rebellion against the Atenist regime. *Does that excuse them in the eyes of the Judge of Souls?* Hani didn't know. What was worse, he didn't know if Pentju was aware that he knew about the murders. The summons could be a fatal trap.

Still, the vizier was the most powerful man in the Two Kingdoms after the royal family, and he was Hani's direct superior until a vizier of the Lower Kingdom could be installed. Hani set off for the Hall of Royal Correspondence, Maya at his side. His stomach was tight with anxiety that he tried to reason himself out of.

But Maya seemed to have read his thoughts. "I hope this isn't about what happened last year."

"Me, too, you may be sure," Hani said with a grim chuckle. He strode along with heavy, purposeful steps through the courtyards of the scribal district, where there seemed to be an unusual hustle and bustle, as if someone had stirred the anthill with a stick. *Maybe the time is coming when I never have to see this place again.*

They approached the door of the vizier's reception hall and were admitted by the sour little guardian, who had served a good many masters over the years of Hani's service.

"I'll see if the lord vizier is receiving," he said with his usual haughty sniff. He disappeared into Pentju's private office, only to emerge a moment later. "Lord Pentju will see you."

Hani and Maya exchanged uneasy glances, and Maya took his seat on the floor among the throng of other petitioners, while Hani proceeded into the office with a sigh of resignation.

Pentju was enthroned upon his official chair. At his side, a cross-legged secretary, a scroll unrolled over his lap, sat silently. The former physician was a tall, massively built man with a perpetually disapproving expression upon his heavy features.

I'm not sure I would want him at my bedside, Hani thought, forcing a silent laugh. He dropped into a deep bow, his hands on his knees.

Wasting no time on courtesies, Pentju said in his rumbling voice, "Hani, you're no doubt wondering why I've summoned you. Let me acquaint you with a few facts. Under the new administration, some changes have been made in the hierarchy. I will be serving as de facto vizier of the Upper and Lower Kingdoms. The God's Father, Lord Ay, will hold an ill-defined role that is complementary and probably superior to mine under the title vizier of the Lower Kingdom. Thus, the ordinary running of the kingdom—including the foreign service, usually directed by the vizier of the north—will now be my jurisdiction. Are you following me?"

"Yes, my lord. There have been times in the past when one man held both offices."

Pentju nodded brusquely. "No one has occupied the office of high commissioner of foreign affairs in the north for some time, and things have grown rather lax up there. Now, in addition, the Hittites have become troublesome once more. As I understand it, you have contacts throughout Djahy and Kharu. And of course, Kheta Land."

Hani gulped. Pentju might or might not be aware of the late queen's dealings with Kheta Land—his piety toward the Hidden One had paralleled hers without his being an actual follower. *How much does he know about the subsequent rupture of her hoped-for alliance and my role in it?* "Kheta? Yes, my lord. Although not very cordial at the moment."

"The former high commissioner has spoken highly of you as a man well-liked by our vassals and allies. A man fluent in many languages and acquainted with the cultures of our neighbors. Upon his recommendation, I am appointing you to serve as high commissioner of foreign affairs under our Sun God Neb-khepru-ra Tut-ankh-aten." Pentju fell silent at last, watching Hani closely. He had the sort of eyes in which the flesh overhung the lids completely, making it look as if there were none. It gave him a piercing, reptilian gaze.

Hani felt as if the breath had been knocked out of him. Of all the possible reasons for the present audience, that was one he had never imagined. Once before, he had come close to being offered the position of high commissioner, but he had resolved to refuse it out of loyalty to Ptah-mes, who had been expelled from the office for opposing King Nefer-khepru-ra. But he could no longer see any reason of conscience to abstain. The one problem was that the commissioner's offices were headquartered in Men-nefer— or had been until the capital had moved to Waset then Akhet-aten.

"Before I give you an answer, my lord, may I ask where the government will be centered? Here in Akhet-aten, Men-nefer, or Waset?"

Pentju frowned a little, more with uncertainty than with hostility, Hani thought. "Of course, the ultimate decision will belong to the king—life, prosperity, and health be to him. But I won't be giving away any state secrets to say that a removal from this City of the Horizon is imminent.

Beyond that, one envisions a return to the double capital of tradition. Ay will occupy Men-nefer as nominal vizier of the North, and I and my offices will be centered in Waset. So the foreign service will be concentrated here—that's a change from tradition, to be sure."

A wave of knee-wobbling relief washed over Hani. He'd been on the verge of retiring from the foreign service in the interests of spending more of his life in the presence of his family—he'd passed too many weary years traveling the world or simply churning up and down the River between his home and his superior's office—but this post would be sedentary. He would send others abroad on mission, yet his place would be in the chancery, right there in Waset, day after day. And he could make his reports to a vizier who was no farther away than the next building.

Thank you, Lord Djehuty! "I accept, my lord."

Pentju rose. "Good. Then that's taken care of. Come over tomorrow, and I'll have some of the secretaries show you around. They're the ones who have kept things together in the absence of a high commissioner. I'm afraid your friend Ptah-mes—er, Maya—will be busy over the next month or two, or I'm sure he'd like to do that himself."

The vizier turned and, stepping down heavily from the dais, exited into his private office. Hani barely gathered himself quickly enough to make a belated bow. His heart was in turmoil but a turmoil of delight—that of a flock of geese whose keeper has thrown a handful of barley into their midst. He wanted to jump up and down and clap his hands like a little boy promised a treat. With a wide grin and a buoyant step, he made his way back to the reception room.

Maya had spent most of the brief duration of Hani's audience wrestling with his conscience. He felt he couldn't face himself unless he finally got up his courage, quit the foreign service, and found a post in the city chancery in Waset, where he could be present for Sati and the children. The constant traveling had been exciting, but the older he got, the more he wanted to watch the little ones grow up and to share life with his wife. It wasn't right that he should tear her away from her mother and her sister to follow the court to Men-nefer. They had been her only support for years, while he was trekking around in A'amu someplace— or Kheta Land. No, no matter how it pained him to leave Lord Hani's employ in the diplomatic corps, he had to do it. His father-in-law would understand. *Hasn't Hani himself dreamed for years of doing the same?*

Lord Hani emerged from the inner door, and Maya took a deep breath, girding himself for the ordeal. Before Hani had even crossed the reception hall, Maya was on his feet, and hitching up his kilt, he met his father-in-law in the middle of the room. Hani was beaming. That took some of the sense of trepidation out of Maya.

Still, his heart was thundering as he said quietly, "My lord, I have something to say, and I hope you won't take it the wrong way. Believe me—no one could be more grateful than I for all you've done for me. If it weren't for the welfare of Sati and the little ones, I would never, ever do this to you. But it is, and I must. I have to leave the foreign service. I just can't abandon the family any longer. My wife needs me at her side. I know I've talked about it before in a vague way, but now I'm serious. Please understand. My loyalty to you is unshaken. I—"

Hani gave his broad, gap-toothed smile, all benevolence, and clapped Maya on the shoulder. "I understand completely, my friend. As you know, I've had much the same desire myself, on and off. But let's step outside, and I'll tell you what my interview with the vizier was about."

Lord Hani herded Maya through the hall, the eyes of the guardian fixed on them in disapproval. He was no doubt eager to sweep them and their whispered conversation out of the silent building.

Maya was disconcerted and somewhat put out. *It's my moment of deep, heartfelt soul-baring, and Lord Hani is usurping it?* That wasn't in character. But he let himself be drawn outside against the wall of the court, into the sliver of shade cast by the wall.

And his father-in-law told him everything Pentju had said.

As he listened, joy unfolded within Maya like a big, happy flower. Wide-eyed, he dropped to his knees and bent to kiss Hani's feet, but Hani, still grinning, stopped him and drew him upright.

"The gods are good, eh, my boy? If you want to continue working for me—and I hope you will—we can both stay right there in Waset with our families. All the children will be there once more, and even Pipi will be in the foreign office with us."

"You'll be his superior, my lord?"

Lord Hani's face fell. "Yes. That won't make him happy. He'll be comparing himself to me constantly. But Father will be pleased to have us both in the city for a change. It's only right we should be there for him. He's getting old."

And so is my mother. Maya sank into reflection upon that unresolved piece of his puzzle.

✦

The next morning, as instructed, Hani returned to the foreign service offices to learn his way around the duties of high commissioner. The appointment still had about it an air of unreality. And of course, the entire chancery would vacate these buildings soon enough, when the government moved. Things had been neglected for several years after Ptah-mes had been relieved of his office, and Hani found—as he had expected—no coherent policies in place at that level any more than he had at his own. He resolved to start by working out with Pentju an overarching set of objectives for the kingdom's foreign relations—then hoping that Ay wouldn't ride them down too brutally.

To begin, he requested a list of personnel—regional commissioners, ambassadors, and roving emissaries like him. At first glance, he saw a few names he knew from experience to be unworthy of their mandate. They would have to go. Others, he recognized as solid men who should be promoted or better employed. *No more revenge firing,* he thought caustically, remembering how often Ptah-mes's talents had been wasted because some superior had taken against him. *Some king.*

The secretaries who were initiating Hani disappeared at midday, and Hani took advantage of their absence to prowl through the archives at random, just to get a sense of the system. He could have a bite of lunch in a while at the beer house rather than go all the way back to Ptah-mes's villa. Hani was squatting with one hand on the lowest shelf when a tentative knock sounded from the doorway. He jumped up and tugged at his shirt.

One of the scribes entered and bowed. "I don't know if you're ready to receive foreign visitors, my lord, but an emissary from Kheta Land is here to speak to you—I mean to the high commissioner. I doubt he knows who that is."

Hani stiffened with dread. *Am I going to have to deal with an angry Kheta even before I know my way around the office?* "Show him in, please," he said nonetheless. He seated himself on the magistrate's chair and having, in a mischievous spirit, swung his feet back and forth a few times like a child, planted his soles on the footrest with a sigh.

A moment later, the scribe ushered in a familiar figure. Hattusha-ziti gave a sweeping bow, and when he arose, his eyes grew wide with surprise. "Lord Hani! You here? I see the late queen didn't put you to death, as you feared." Smiling, he came forward, and Hani rose and stepped down from the dais. They clasped forearms.

"Nor did your king execute you. What brings you to the Two Lands again, my friend? I can't imagine your countrymen feel very kindly toward our kingdom at the moment."

Hattusha-ziti's wry smile was tempered by his serious eyes. "Unfortunately, I'm here to register a formal complaint with your new king. I was just going through the official channels, not realizing you were the high commissioner of foreign affairs these days. That will make the process a little friendlier, I hope."

"There's something I'd like to show you, my lord," Hani said, lowering his voice. "Alas, it's not here right now, but if you want, I'll bring it to you. One of our soldiers picked up the two arrows that day—the one that killed the lion and the one that struck Prince Zannanza. The latter was Hittite, not Egyptian." He fixed the emissary with a piercing look. *His reaction will be interesting,* Hani thought.

Hattusha-ziti lowered his eyes in reflection and said, "It doesn't make any difference now, does it? Your archer has been put to death."

"Perhaps King Shuppiluliuma's wrath would be redirected if he knew."

"Maybe. But toward whom?" Hattusha-ziti looked up with a dry quirk of the mouth. "This served his interests quite well. Better than an outright effort to usurp the throne of Kemet. That wouldn't have meant a war of border skirmishes but a full-blown confrontation between great powers—with our troops very far from their supply lines. Would it have been the end of our imperial adventure?"

Hani pondered the ambiguity of this answer that was a question. Whatever he meant to convey, the emissary spoke with grim passion. Hani said tentatively, "Somebody undoubtedly paid your archer to assassinate the prince. It... It has crossed my mind, my lord, that your king himself might have had a hand in it. Is it conceivable that his desire for an excuse for war might have been so great as to make him willing to sacrifice his own son?"

"I think not. His grief was real. He wouldn't scruple to eliminate a relative who betrayed him, but this lad was loyal—and useful. No, it was probably just an accident, don't you think? Hunting is dangerous."

"Not as dangerous as sending a delegation of your people into the heart of a hostile land racked with civil war."

"My sentiments exactly. Our Sun is very ambitious—that's what makes him great. But sometimes it blinds him to the likely consequences of his actions and his dreams." Hattusha-ziti smiled. There was something hard about his eyes, though, almost rancorous.

He was deeply opposed to the king's plans. I'll bet it hurt not to be able to convince His Sun to accept the evidence of their imprudence.

"So, what can I do for you, my lord?" Hani asked after a heartbeat. "Do you want an audience with the king—or more to the point, his regent?"

"If you please, Hani, my friend."

"Shall I bring the arrows to show you?"

"There's really no reason. Reparation has been exacted. What would it accomplish to cause more blood to flow?"

Hani smiled apologetically. "I guess it's just my nature to be curious. I always want to know who committed such an act against *ma'at* and why."

Hattusha-ziti gripped Hani's hand tightly for a moment. "You *do* know, my friend." He turned and made his way to the door. "If you need me, I'm staying at the beer house near the River."

"Oh, that's a shame upon us. If I weren't someone else's guest, I would certainly lodge you most happily. Let me get you a room in the palace visitors' quarters—you're on an official mission."

But Hattusha-ziti made light of the inconvenience and, with something resembling eagerness, took his leave.

Hani studied the closed door for a moment, as if he could read the Hittite's thoughts through the panel. Then he shrugged. *I wonder what Ay will make of this.*

✦

Ptah-mes showed up late for dinner. Hani, Maya, and the girls were just pushing back from their folding tables when he entered, appearing about as exhausted as a conscious man could appear.

"Oh, Lord Ptah-mes, you look awful," Neferet cried with her usual tact. "Let me make you a sleeping potion, then you go right to bed as soon as you've eaten."

"That would be a kindness, my dear," he said with a blurred smile, then sat down and washed his hands in the basin offered him by a servant.

"I hope preparations for the funeral are going well, my lord," Hani said, desiring badly to tell his friend about his new appointment but not wanting to distract Ptah-mes from his own preoccupations.

"They are, although time is passing with frightening rapidity." Ptah-mes picked at a roast lark. "The problem is that a great deal of gold is also needed to prepare the late king's tomb in haste. Choices must sometimes be made. We're going to have to exact more taxes from the peasantry and encourage the nobility to a little more public-spirited generosity."

With a sideways glace at Hani, Maya said, "Lord Hani will be in a position to contribute more with his new position. He's too modest to tell you, but he's been named high commissioner of foreign affairs in the north."

A wave of heat crept up Hani's cheeks.

"I know." Ptah-mes smiled more warmly. "Or at least,

I knew it had been offered to you. Pentju asked me for recommendations, and yours is the only name I proposed. The office couldn't be held by a more deserving person. Congratulations, my friend."

"Thank you, my lord. Yet another favor I owe you," Hani said humbly, his nose burning. Ptah-mes's generosity over the years had gone far beyond the polite minimum. Hani felt he had to change the subject or risk becoming maudlin. "Where is Ankhet-khepru-ra to be buried? Here or in Waset?"

"Here, for the present. I have a suspicion her *khat* will be transferred to Waset in time. Once this city is abandoned, no one will visit the few tombs in the eastern desert. Ay knows how unpopular the sojourn here was—symbolic of so many unpopular things—and will be sure to turn the little king's back to it while everyone is still enchanted by the new regime."

Ptah-mes finally pushed back his dish, which was still mostly full, and rose to his feet. The girls scurried upstairs to prepare the promised potion in their room.

Maya had just preceded Hani up the steps toward their quarters when Ptah-mes called after Hani, "A word with you, my friend."

Hani turned back to the salon expectantly, but just at that instant, a loud knock sounded from outside.

A moment later, the doorkeeper entered, an expression of concern on his face. "There's a delegation of men and women here to see you, my lord. I know it's late. Do you want me to admit them, or should I tell them to come back tomorrow?"

Ptah-mes sighed. "We'll speak later, Hani." To his doorkeeper, he said, "Send them in."

CHAPTER 13

H ANI MADE HIS ACKNOWLEDGMENT WITH a little nod, but before he could cross the room to reach the staircase once more, footsteps sounded in the vestibule. He turned instead into the nearby hallway that led to the back of the house, thinking he could sit in the garden until Ptah-mes's guests had left. To his annoyance, a great pile of furniture had been stacked in the corridor, and he was unable to get around it. He gingerly lifted a stool from the heap, but then voices in the salon made him freeze. One belonged to Lord Ptah-mes's eldest daughter, Lady Mut-em-wia, as peremptory and intense-sounding as usual.

"Here we all are, Father. You can gauge the seriousness of the reason for our presence by our having come to this city of the damned."

Oh dear, Hani thought uneasily. The woman was harshly unfriendly to her father, and Hani would rather not have heard whatever she had to say, but there was no way he could slip off without a great deal of noise. Hidden by the darkness of the corridor, he turned slowly, careful that no sudden movement should give away his presence. Fortunately for him, neither Ptah-mes nor the seven young people were looking at the door. Hani saw the children drawn up in profile, a small invading army locked eye to eye with their father, who said nothing but stood blank-faced and tense. He had to be wondering what was about to drop upon him.

They were a strikingly handsome family, as Hani remembered. He hadn't seen the four younger daughters since Lady Apeny's funeral years before, but they were all as beautiful as their oldest sister and resembled one another noticeably. Ptah-mes and his wife had been cousins and looked quite a bit alike.

The eldest son, the priest Djehuty-mes, whom Hani had met with his son not long before, spoke up quickly. "We're not here to attack you, Father. We... We feel we need to reconcile, all of us. Mother would have wanted it. The Atenist regime is in the past, and so should our rancor be. If you're willing to be flexible for once, we can be a family again."

But Mut-em-wia said in a harsh voice that almost trembled with intensity, "He won't be flexible. He can't back down. I told you, Djehuty-mes, we're wasting our time. Look, he hasn't even said a word in greeting."

"Don't be that way, sister," the youngest said plaintively. He was a gentle-looking youth, perhaps in his early twenties, with Ptah-mes's hooded black eyes. "We have to give something too."

"Is this about your inheritance?" Ptah-mes asked in a controlled voice.

"There it is—the sarcasm," Mut-em-wia cried with a

bark of accusing laughter. She tossed her perfectly coiffed head.

But Djehuty-mes said in a level tone, "No, Father. This is about a rift that has been allowed to become a gulf. Only a fresh, innocent eye like Amen-mes's was able to penetrate how ridiculous it was. He told me he went to see you, and I started thinking about that. Why had I never done the same after fourteen years? It isn't pleasing to the gods. And how much longer will we have? In two years, you'll be sixty."

Watching his friend's fine, sharp profile, Hani saw Ptah-mes's lips thin but not with anger. He seemed to be absorbing his son's words without defensiveness. Perhaps he was too tired to fight. "What do you want of me?"

One of the younger women said in a voice that was starting to break, "Just to treat us like people you actually care about. Not to be so critical, as if failing to live up to your ideals made us bad."

It seemed to Hani that the children had been guilty of that themselves, but clearly, the confrontation was about more than just the rupture over serving the Atenist government. He wished he could shrink away into invisibility and prayed he wouldn't sneeze or otherwise betray his witness of this sensitive conversation.

"That's why the inheritance seemed so important," Mut-em-wia said, her voice cracking with angry tears. "Cutting us out was such a picture of what you thought of us. Never good enough—only to be tolerated, quick to be discarded. Then you married that little girl. Did you want a daughter? As if you didn't already have daughters. *I'm* your daughter, Father. These women are your daughters. Thank the gods, Mother loved us."

Ptah-mes flinched as if she had struck him. He said in a low voice, "I did love you. I do. I always have." His eyes flickered downward, but he raised them again—courageously, Hani thought. "I've always been proud of you."

Djehuty-mes, who seemed to be making a huge effort at temperance, said, "No one needs to throw accusations. We want to discuss things calmly and factually, everyone. There... There are grievances, as you can see, Father, that go back a long way." He shot his elder sister an admonitory glance.

"I know I haven't been a good father. Tell me how I have hurt you," Ptah-mes said stiffly. "What I have done to earn your hatred."

"You weren't exactly cruel, but you were so demanding," one of the younger daughters began. "Nobody could ever live up to your demands. No one could ever be neat enough or efficient enough or graceful enough. We all felt like failures. And you barely ever touched us. We were like pieces of furniture."

Hani remembered what Mery-ra had told him about Ptah-mes's childhood under an impossibly demanding father and was struck with sorrow. *That's all we know about being parents—what's been shown us.* He blessed his own father yet again. For all his human imperfections, Mery-ra had been a loving and tolerant presence in Hani's life—a man who had trained his children by example, not orders. *Perhaps imperfections are gifts from the gods.*

Mut-em-wia cried in a raw voice, "Yes, you *were* cruel. Isn't it cruelty to be made to feel unloved? Only wanted because one is supposed to have lots of children? We were just logs stacked in your woodpile. It was only Mother you ever loved."

Ptah-mes opened his mouth then closed it. His face was flaming. After a moment, he said, barely above a whisper, "Forgive me."

"It would have been better if you had just gotten mad occasionally. At least we would have known you cared about something." The younger son—whose name, Hani remembered, was Huy—dashed at his eyes. "As it was, you just sliced us up with your tongue like a piece of flint."

Poor Ptah-mes. Hani winced. *He's under attack by seven people at once, without the slightest warning, yet he hasn't tried to excuse himself. And poor children too. They're in such pain. This takes enormous reserves of courage on both sides.* He found Djehuty-mes—with his determination to be fair—admirable. Clearly, his father had left him a good example in something. And he, in turn, had brought up a fine, open-minded young son in Amen-mes.

"That sarcasm. That sigh of disappointment that sent a spear point through my heart—dear gods, the very memory of it still freezes my blood!" Mut-em-wia almost shrieked, clutching at the temples of her wig. "I so wanted to please you, but it was impossible. You say you were proud of me. Why did you never show it?"

"What would you have me do to make it up to you?" Ptah-mes asked in a carefully restrained voice, but his breathing had grown heavy.

Several of the young people burst out loudly at once, and someone said bitterly, "There's no making it up to us now. It's done."

Djehuty-mes patted the air for silence. "We've all

suffered, and as the eldest, I as much as any of you. But we're not here to make accusations about the past. We're here to reconcile. Father has asked just the right question. What do we want of him now? And what does he want of us in return? We must act according to *ma'at* and not try to exact vengeance."

Silence fell over the group.

"Do you want to be put back in my will?"

"No," Mut-em-wia said. "I wouldn't take your gold, knowing we had forced it out of you. Mother left us her estate, and we've married well."

"We must all forgive one another, or there will be no reconciliation," Djehuty-mes warned them. "It's not about pretending the past never existed, but we must forgive."

Huy, his lip trembling, looked around for support from his siblings. "I just want him to show he loves me."

A few of the others nodded. Some lowered their eyes, as if ashamed that adults could be reduced to begging for such a primordial gift. Ptah-mes, his expression unreadable, slowly extended his arms toward the youth, and the boy lurched forward, his tear-streaked face alight. They embraced each other tightly, silently, for a very long time, while the sounds of sobbing rose around them. Hani dashed helplessly at his eyes, overcome.

One by one, each of the children threw themselves on Ptah-mes, then all of them embraced at once. If it had been anyone other than his friend of the bronze self-control, Hani would have sworn the man was crying, his mouth stretched downward, his eyes squeezed shut as if he were in agony.

At last, Djehuty-mes drew away. "Thank you for that

act of humility, my father," he said, his voice unsteady. "I think for a proud man like you, that can't have been easy. I... I admire your courage."

Mut-em-wia exploded in a sob but gathered herself, dabbing at her eyes with the corner of her shawl. "We'll go now, Father. May the Hidden One b-bless you. Dear gods, how often I've cursed you instead."

One by one, the others took their leave until Ptah-mes stood there alone, his back to Hani. Suddenly, his exhaustion seemed to enwrap him once more, and he tottered to a chair, where he leaned over, his face in his hands.

Oh, my friend, please leave by the stairs and not by this corridor, Hani thought in desperation.

After a moment, Ptah-mes raised his head and said in a weary voice, "You can come out now, Hani."

Hani stiffened, horrified. His face burning with shame, he stepped into the room, trying to look as small as a big man could look. "Oh, my lord, I'm so sorry. I had no intention of eavesdropping. I just got trapped in that corridor and couldn't get out without drawing attention to myself."

He tried to fall at his host's feet, but Ptah-mes stopped him with a gesture and rose.

"It's all right, my friend. I know you didn't do it purposely." He clapped Hani on the shoulder. "I'm trying not to care that you've seen me as I am—cruel and selfish."

"I would say, rather, honest and brave. Devoted to *ma'at*. The courage it took not to try to excuse yourself! That would have driven them away forever."

Ptah-mes looked old all at once, his ill-shaven cheeks gaunt and the lines from the corners of his nose to the edges of his lips deeply engraved. He crooked his mouth in a rueful smile. "They needed a father like you—a kind word for everyone." He raised his eyes to gaze, bleakly unseeing, into the room. "Everything they said about me was true. Every single thing."

"But you always thought you were doing right for them, Lord Ptah-mes. I can't doubt that you meant well."

"Then more the fool I." He heaved a sigh. "I'm going up to bed. I'll have the servants clear the corridor. I don't know why they picked that spot to stack things."

Ptah-mes made his way with brittle carefulness to the stairs, and in a moment, his slow steps had faded away. Hani's heart was full of pity. He wondered what light that confrontation had shed on his friend's willingness to take six more children under his protection.

⚜

The time had finally come for the Osir Ankhet-khepru-ra Nefer-nefru-aten's funeral. Hani and Maya traveled alone to the capital, soon to be abandoned, where they were, as always, guests of Ptah-mes and Neferet—perhaps for the last time. Nub-nefer and Sati, who didn't feel she could face a funeral, had declined to join them. To Hani's mystification, Mery-ra, too, begged off, claiming his lady-friend Meryet-amen had invited him to a party in honor of her latest grandchild's birth. Hani had a suspicious feeling his father was avoiding him. Thus, it was just the two of them who joined Pipi and the young *sunet*s among the crowd that watched in somber reflection as a dead king was laid in her house of eternity.

After a forty-year reign that had lasted much of Hani's

life, her father-in-law, Neb-ma-at-ra, had been buried in splendor. But his successors had all died young, and the ceremonies of the royal funeral had become almost commonplace. *I hope this will be the last one for a very long time,* Hani thought. And with a ten-year-old on the throne, that seemed like a reasonable expectation.

Ptah-mes had supervised a truly exceptional ceremony, perhaps mindful that it was the first traditional burial in many years—a symbol that the hegemony of the Aten had come and gone and that the gods of Kemet's ancestors were back on their thrones. After the procession of priests and dignitaries, Hani saw his friend floating around the edges of the liturgy, signaling this participant or that, coordinating the musicians and celebrants, calling in the *muu* dancers and the mourning women, the bearers of sacrifice, and those who transported the burial goods he had amassed— all with perfect timing and seamless coordination.

Someone always does this, Hani thought in surprise, *but I've never even noticed. It's only been the spectacle that drew my eye, and I've given no thought to the hard-working master of ceremonies.*

Ptah-mes was also among the pallbearers who sledged the massive coffin to the door of the borrowed tomb, where the new Osir was housed for eternity. It would be the last burial at the Horizon of the Aten, Hani didn't doubt.

Lord Ay was prominent among the royal family, of course. Yet it wasn't he who opened the mouth of his daughter's coffin, but rather her little son. Ptah-mes had devised a sort of sideways carrying chair so the boy could be raised to the proper height for the gesture, and it also concealed his lameness. Perhaps no other sight could have moved the crowd to such a fever of pious loyalty and the anticipation of better times ahead as that of the royal child in his little blue crown loosing his mother's senses for the joys of the afterlife. The lad's formal coronation would be the next great milestone on the kingdom's journey home.

The following morning, only Hani and Maya met in the salon for breakfast. Ptah-mes was finally enjoying a deserved late sleep, and the girls had disappeared early.

Maya said, "Should we take a look around Ipy's house, now that it's empty? Maybe there's some clue there— evidence of a debt or something that could give us a sense of who might have had it in for him. Assuming it's not Pi-ay."

Hani was distracted by his thoughts, which kept coming back to Ptah-mes and the scene Hani had witnessed between him and his children—and from there to his own father. Something had been slightly abnormal about Mery-ra's behavior since the return from Kheta. Things were ever so subtly tense between him and Hani, and Hani wasn't sure if the problem was his own suspicions or his father's guilty conscience. It took him several heartbeats to respond. "Of course, Ipy wasn't literate. I'm not sure what sort of documentation we'd expect to find. But let's do it quickly. I'm eager to get back to Waset."

Hani thrust Pi-ay's knife through his waistband, thinking that if they had time, he would like to cast a personal glance around the missing goldsmith's lodging too. They set out while the morning was still brisk and their host was sleeping. The back lanes were quiet with a hush unusual for the hour, as if, having served its final function, the bay in the eastern desert that wore the Horizon of the

Aten had turned in its sleep and was preparing to shrug off the little habitation of men.

"Never lose a chance to tell your family you love them. 'Speak sweetly, that you may be loved,'" Hani said to Maya as they strode along. "Every day, I understand a little better what that means."

Maya looked at him askance. "Do you think I don't express my love for them often enough, my lord? Are you trying to say that's why Sati went through such a hard time?"

"No. No, my boy. I'm talking out loud to myself." They walked on. "Maybe that was Ipy's flaw. Who knows? Maybe his wife didn't feel he loved her, so she killed him."

Maya's eyes widened with excitement. "Do you think so? She and that Pi-ay were having an affair and decided to get Ipy out of the way!"

"I'm just making that up," Hani admitted. "I think it's far more likely that they somehow knew about the bracelets, and whoever commissioned them wanted to eliminate anyone who could trace him. That person is undoubtedly Ay."

"Not that the *medjay* are likely to go after him," Maya said with a snort.

"No, but it occurs to me that he wouldn't want the Hittites to find out about the plot against their prince, under any circumstances. The modus operandi is far too similar to the hunting accident not to put them both together as a single two-pronged attack. So the fewer people who know he had a hand in it, the less likely it is to find its way to diplomatic circles."

"You think they're similar?"

Hani shrugged. His thoughts on the subject, he had to admit, were vague and confused. There seemed to be so many possibilities. "Both attempts could be claimed to be the natural actions of animals. And he admitted to me he didn't want anything that would openly implicate our government in a hostile act toward a prince of Kheta Land."

They walked on in thoughtful silence.

At last, Maya said, "Does that put *us* in danger, my lord, if Ay should learn we're investigating?"

Hani didn't answer—he dared not. But he and Maya exchanged looks of understanding and walked on.

As they turned down the narrow street where Ipy had lived, Hani froze. Something was wrong. The gate was hanging open, swinging a little with a dry creak in the faint breeze that rustled the palm fronds. It was a desolate sound.

He put out a hand to stop his son-in-law and whispered, "Someone has broken in."

CHAPTER 14

Maya gawped. "Should we call the *medjay*, my lord?"

"We'll have the element of surprise if anyone's still there. But it's daylight anyway—any burglars have probably left. Come on."

They approached quietly, and Hani kicked the gate wide open with a swift blow of the heel just in case a lookout was hiding behind it. But nothing happened except that the panel tottered on its pivot pole, swinging back and forth for a moment with a squeal. He entered the court cautiously, Maya at his side, looking menacing. They stared around the trampled bare court, which was still strewn with discarded household items and broken homemade toys. Silently, they moved toward the doorway. It, too, hung ajar into a melancholy darkness.

Hani slipped off his sandals to walk more quietly, and Maya followed suit. Hani's heart had begun to pound with expectation, even though he knew it was likely no one was within. They looked around the small salon then tiptoed into the inner court, where a summary outdoor kitchen stood under a reed matting for shelter from the sun. Hani found something sad about the cold oven and scattered ashes on the hearth. Once, surely, this had been a happy home.

A heavy, sickening smell of decay filled the little courtyard. He lifted the lid of a pot near the hearth and saw a mass of molding lentils still inside. *It was a sudden departure,* he thought. *But at least she left food for the children.*

Hani hesitated to use Pi-ay's big knife at his waist for defense—he didn't want to kill anyone. He found a tall wooden mortar beside the oven, with its heavy pestle as long as a half-grown boy. He drew the pestle out carefully and hefted it. *The perfect club.* Maya picked up a stone quern by its leg to use as an awkward but intimidating weapon.

They approached the staircase. Fortunately, it was masonry, and no creaking treads would give away Hani's considerable weight. Up they tiptoed. Hani heard Maya's nervous breathing behind him. At the top, a narrow corridor extended for a short way, ending in a ladder that led to the roof terrace. Two doors stood in the dark hall to Hani's left. One yawned open, leaving a long, pale streak of sunlight across the stairwell, and from within came sounds of rifling and throwing things. Hani exchanged looks with Maya and laid a finger to his lips.

They sprang into the room, their weapons brandished. The person within gave a scream and cowered, her hands over her head. It was Hemet-min.

Hani dropped his club, nonplussed. "Mistress, forgive us. We thought someone was burgling the empty house."

The woman, who was on her knees, looked up fearfully. Around her sprawled chests and baskets, empty or overturned, as if she had been searching for something without success. She seemed to recognize Hani at last and lowered her hands, looking confused. "What—?"

"I'm Hani son of Mery-ra, and this is Mistress In-hapy's son, Maya. Do you remember us? We came to offer our condolences some months ago, but I think you were distracted." He squatted beside her in a nonthreatening pose.

Hemet-min's eyes slid from one to the other then away.

"Talk to me, my good woman. Where did you go?"

She sat back on her heels. At first, she seemed reluctant to speak, then she said with some spirit, "To my family in Gebtu. What business is it of yours?"

"Pi-ay went with you, didn't he?"

"So?"

"Did the two of you have an affair?" Hani pressed.

"Why should I tell you?" But after that flash of resistance, she said, hanging her head, "We'd known each other for a long time. He and his wife used to be our friends. When I was widowed... he promised to take me away, to start a new life."

Leaving your orphaned children behind? Hani thought, but he said instead, "Did the two of you kill Ipy, mistress?"

She looked up at him, her eyes round. It looked like innocent shock, but he couldn't be sure. "No. Why would you think so? I loved him."

Hani slid Pi-ay's knife from his waistband. "Why would Pi-ay have hidden this murderous-looking blade in his room?"

The woman scrambled to her knees and snatched at the knife. "Why, it's mine. He had it because he wanted to save me from myself. I tried to take my life." Her gaunt face abruptly stretched with misery and shame. "After Ipy died, I was so desperate and overwhelmed that I was afraid I'd try something on the children." She covered her eyes with her hands and folded double to the floor, as if she were worshiping, her shoulders shaking with silent sobs.

Maya shot Hani a skeptical stare, but Hani felt the woman couldn't have counterfeited such disarray. He said gently, "Help us identify your husband's killer. Put his *ba* to rest, and perhaps your own soul will be more at peace."

She lifted her face. "I didn't kill him. I didn't. And neither did Pi-ay. He and Ipy were friends. A lot of people didn't like Pi-ay, but Ipy did. He liked everybody. They spent more time together than he ever spent with me. Toward the end, he was never home, working all the time." Tears trickled down her face. "He left me to do everything by myself. Then he was gone altogether. Mut the mother of us all—I couldn't live like that. With all those children—he kept giving me more and more, but it was me who had to nurse them and change them and feed them. Then that old father of his. Alone—I was all alone. Don't you see why I wanted to die? And Pi-ay said he'd take me away. We could just live together in happiness, without... without all that."

Behind her head, Maya's face was grim with condemnation, but Hani's heart was heavy for the woman. In her desperation, she had lost her reason, it seemed to him. Like a child, Hemet-min appeared not to understand that her actions had consequences for others. He said gently, "What about the children, mistress? It wasn't their fault they were born."

She reached toward Hani's hand as if to clutch it, beseeching. Her overflowing eyes were desperate with hope. "Someone has taken them. Don't you see? I knew they would. One of the neighbors. The king, maybe. And Hu-may's almost a man. He can support them. I wished them no harm. I love them too."

Maya snorted and said harshly, "You're deceiving yourself, woman. That's not the way to show love. They were more likely to have turned to begging or be impressed for forced labor."

"To relieve your mind, my daughter has taken them in." Hani squeezed Hemet-min's hands reassuringly. "They'll have a comfortable and much-loved childhood. But they think you're dead."

Hemet-min looked at the men with confusion, as if she were waiting for them to tell her what to do. Hani was reminded of a cornered animal growing wilder and wilder. Something more than a little mad flickered in her eyes.

He said gently, "Do you know who murdered Ipy, mistress?"

She shook her head. "I'd kill them if I knew. Then he'd love me again, like he used to."

"Did he have any debts? This household seemed poorer than that of a highly paid artisan should have been. Might he have crossed some violent person? Any problems at work?"

The woman shook her head again, but her eyes were glassy, making Hani wonder if she knew any longer what he had said. "I was setting some of his pay aside and changing it for copper *debens*—hiding them. I wanted to be able to start a new life if things kept getting worse and I couldn't take any more. That's why I came back. I had forgotten them. Pi-ay told me to come back for them. But... But I can't find them."

Hani pursed his lips in thought and heaved himself to his feet. *Has the woman broken any laws? Taking food from her children's mouths? Abandoning them? Against the laws of ma'at, undoubtedly, but she's done nothing men call illegal.* He said, "Then we'll leave you to your search, mistress. May the lord of the horizon give you happiness."

Without exchanging a word, he and Maya descended the stairs and made their way through the gate. Gloom sat heavily in Hani's belly like a stone. He thought he'd seldom heard a sadder tale of human weakness in his life.

Maya murmured, "Do you believe her, my lord? Do you think she's as innocent as she says?"

"I think she's telling the truth as she sees it, but she's a troubled and incoherent soul. May the Weigher of Hearts be gentle with her. Her children are better off without her."

"Pi-ay may have brought his own punishment down on his head by running off with that woman." Maya looked grimly satisfied at the thought.

"Unless he killed a man who was apparently his friend, there's no reason to want him punished."

"Oh, Lord Hani, how could you not think he did it?" Maya cried in frustration. "Why would he run away and leave a high-paying job unless he was afraid he'd be caught?"

Hani sighed. "Father is always saying to trust my gut feeling. I guess that's what I'm doing, my friend."

And he thought he'd been served another lesson about how not to show love to one's children.

Suddenly, Maya slapped his forehead, as if something had occurred to him. "I'll bet it was about those copper *deben*s!"

"What's that, son?"

"I completely forgot to tell you—weeks ago, before the funeral, I went back to Mother's workshop alone, remember? I talked to some of the workmen, thinking maybe one of them might know what Ipy was involved in. One fellow had overheard a conversation between him and Pi-ay, and Ipy had said something like 'I don't know what they're up to' and 'Where is it going?'"

Maya was so excited he was practically bouncing up and down. "It must have been that hoard she had amassed that he was talking about. It sounds like he found it. You can see that he'd wonder why his children seemed to be going hungry, knowing how much he brought home every week. Then he found the copper and confronted his wife, and they fought, and she killed him with that knife. Then Pi-ay took it home to hide it."

Hani, who felt a bit assaulted himself by the sudden rush of hypotheses, said only, "Hmm." Whatever unfortunate things she had done, he didn't think Hemet-min and her husband had fought in the street in front of the workshop.

They walked on, Maya seeming to grow more and more frustrated by Hani's silence. At last, they stopped, Hani sunk in thought.

"What was that town where she said her family lived?" he asked.

Maya replied brusquely, "Gebtu."

Gebtu was a modest-sized settlement but bustling with commerce. There, the gold caravans from the eastern desert loaded their precious cargo onto River ships, and merchants bound for Pwenet set out toward the banks of Pa-yom A'a-en-mukhed, the eastern sea. The town was on the way to the City of the Scepter, and only five or six hours of travel separated Gebtu from Waset—once there, they would be almost home.

"I want to see if we can find Pi-ay, and I'd like to talk to him alone, before Hemet-min rejoins him."

Maya's snit seemed to fall away, and he said eagerly, "We'd better leave right away, then, my lord. She might take ship any minute."

Hani, amused to see the immediate dissolution of Maya's bad mood, changed direction at the next corner, and they set off at a brisk pace for the River.

"According to Pi-ay, the police pulled the knife from Ipy's back, though," Hani mused.

But Maya gave a snort. "We have only his word for it, my lord."

The *iterus* flowed by as the red-and-green yacht slipped up the current, propelled briskly ahead by its broad sail. Hani squinted at the water, with its blinding sparkle. Villages slid past on their left, fringed with palms and green fields, where workers bent over the black earth. On the right, the barren Red Land stretched away, haunt of jackal and hyena and the ghosts of the unappeased dead. *Forgive us, Master Ipy. We want to give you justice, but it gets less likely with*

291

every day that passes, and soon we'll have to go back to work for the king.

After they'd spent some while in reflective silence, Maya asked, "What if we're completely wrong? What if Lord Ay did it after all?"

Hani shot him a glance. He hadn't completely abandoned that idea himself. "Let's find out what we can about this pair, and if nothing's conclusive, we know where to fall back."

Maya shrugged. "I'd rather it was that crazy she-cat of a Hemet-min," he admitted. "Or her flip-haired lover. What a pair. Those poor half-famished children left behind as if they were stray kittens…"

"I'm not sure she's even capable of understanding what she's doing. Pi-ay? Him, I can't figure out. Is he genuinely in love or just making a point over a man he was jealous of?"

"Maybe we'll find out soon."

They fell once more into silence. Gradually, the warmth of the day and the glare of the late-afternoon sun on the water lulled Hani more and more into a drowsy state. He wasn't sure whether he was dreaming or not as a fox with a saucy tail and immense ears seemed to trot across his vision. His eyes fluttered open. *Of course it was a dream,* he realized with a silent chuckle. *There are no foxes on a boat.*

After four days of fine sailing, buoyed by the joyful knowledge that every *iteru* brought them closer to Waset, the two men disembarked at Gebtu. The little port was swarming with soldiers—guards for the donkey trains of gold and gems that poured in daily from the desert mines. Roped together, gangs of half-starved foreign captives passed shuffling through the streets, headed for the mines—hellholes of furnace-like heat, from what Hani had heard. They could expect work no Egyptian would have undertaken unless he was sent there as a convicted criminal—and there were those honest soldiers and civilians who had had the misfortune to be captured in war, doomed to live out the Lake of Fire on earth. Hani wondered if his countrymen and their vassals would soon be sweating away in the silver mines of Kheta. *Will there be anything I can do for them as high commissioner?*

"How are we ever going to find Pi-ay in a strange city?" Maya asked, staring around him at the pack donkeys and heavy carts that thronged the streets, threatening to submerge him. He pushed back his wig and mopped his forehead.

"People of a profession usually marry into a family of the same profession, so maybe Hemet-min comes from a line of goldsmiths. Let's ask around."

They directed their first question to a royal scribe, who stood at the foot of a gangplank where longshoremen were carrying heavy cloth-covered baskets aboard a cargo boat. He annotated every basket carefully, even peering beneath the cloth to ensure its contents. After a moment of concentration during which it was unclear whether he had actually heard Hani, he lowered his piece of potsherd and replied, "No lack of goldsmiths in this city of gold, my lords! The king will part with the metal cheaper here than anywhere before it has to be carried all over the kingdom. Most of the workshops are down that street to the left of the gate"—he gestured with his pen—"and you'll find more behind the market."

"Thank you, my colleague. You've saved us a lot of time."

The town itself was set back from the River port—a walled square of desolate mudbrick, taken up mostly by the temple of Min in the center. As they walked, Hani saw there was a curious haphazardness about the place. He suspected that it wasn't very large, despite the people who thronged the water's edge—at most, a thousand souls who resided permanently and hence needed a house. But then the Red Lands pushed very close to Gebtu, and it was unlikely its exiguous farmlands could support a larger population. He and Maya strode down the straggling road the scribe had indicated. Dust blew fitfully in little curls above the earthen surface, and Hani's feet were already tawny with it to the ankles. The town was a busy yet joyless place—stained, perhaps, by the hopelessness of the prisoners who passed through it on the way to their living hell.

Hani and Maya came to a scattering of several modest but high-walled houses with heavily bronze-studded gates.

"I'll bet these are goldsmiths' workshops," Maya said, eyeing the fortified entries. "Do we just start randomly knocking?"

"Why don't we split up? It'll go faster. We're looking for Pi-ay. You can honestly say he's your mother's employee who's disappeared."

Maya gave a little salute and turned to the other side of the street. Then rubbing his hands in anticipation, he marched up to the first door.

CHAPTER 15

A BURLY YOUTH WITH A SHAVEN head answered Maya's knock. There wasn't much about him that had the look of the typical goldsmith, including his big, knuckly hands. "What can I do for you?" he asked politely in a bass voice.

"Is this a jeweler's workshop, my good man?"

The gateman nodded but didn't offer to admit Maya.

"I'm looking for a fellow named Pi-ay. A filigree man. He's my mother's most experienced workman, and he's suddenly gone missing. We were told he had come here with a woman by the name of Hemet-min, but that's all we know. Have you ever heard of him? Do you know where he might be?"

The youth shook his head and said, "Sorry," then drew shut the heavy gate.

Maya trudged on to the next house and the next. At every gate, the routine was the same. Nobody knew anything about a Pi-ay or a Hemet-min. Maya was ready to believe that the woman had lied to them, and their destination had been somewhere else altogether than Gebtu.

At the fourth and final gate on his side of the street, a worn-looking older woman opened the gate a crack at Maya's knock. He launched into his story, and as he spoke, he could see her eyes narrow and her mouth grow harder.

"They *was* here. She went back to Akhet-aten for something, and right away, off he goes, the gods know where. Some husband."

"You know them, then?"

"She's my niece." The woman stepped back and let Maya pass inside. "You're not In-hapy's son, are you?"

"I am, mistress," Maya said in surprise.

"We go way back, her and me. Done business for years—she gets a lot of her gemstones through us. So, Pi-ay's one of hers, is he? She's lucky to be rid of him." The woman pulled the heavy gate closed behind them, muttering, "All these people around, you never know. Soldiers and foreigners—you just never know."

They stood inside a small, beaten-earth court. From the open door of the low building behind them rose the familiar sounds of the forge and the *tink-tink-tink* of someone hammering sheet gold into repoussé. The baking air was sour with the smell of heating metal and the flux that helped it solder.

"I swore I'd washed my hands of that irresponsible girl long ago. 'Don't come looking to me for help,' I said." The woman shook her head bitterly. "Few years ago, she begged to apprentice a couple of her brats with me, just to get them off her back, but I refused. They were way too young and bad-behaved on top of that. I knew good and well she just didn't want to have to take care of them all herself.

Let *me* feed and clothe them, see? Shiftless thing. Lazy as a crocodile."

"You knew her husband Ipy has died?"

"Yes, and that's why I took her in this time—her and that new husband of hers, or whatever he is. Out of pity, don't you see. But I could tell something was really gone wrong with the girl. She was always like a child when it come to responsibilities, but she seemed to be all out of touch with reality this time. The king had taken her children to raise at court, she told me. Oh really? And I'm a seven-headed demon. She probably sold them to somebody." The woman snorted.

"And the man Pi-ay?"

"The arrogant jackal turd. Here he is on my charity, and nothing was good enough. I offered him a job, but he didn't like what I set him to do. 'I'm a filigree man,' he says. 'Well, here, everybody does everything,' I says back. I was ready to throw them both out on the street, niece or no, when they up and left."

"Did they say where they were going, mistress?" Maya could hardly conceal his excitement.

"They had a big row, and he sent her, crying like a baby, back to Akhet-aten for something. But then while she was gone, he just disappeared, him and all his belongings—his linen and some tools he brought and that heavy little chest. No idea of coming back is my guess. And good riddance. I hope Hemet-min stays, too, because I'm sure not putting her up for the rest of her days, the lazy baggage." The woman planted her fists on her bony hips and looked implacable.

"And when was this?"

"Maybe a week—maybe not even so long. You'd be

amazed how the mood of the workshop has improved since then."

Maya pondered all her news with a growing sense of elation. "Your niece didn't happen to say who had killed her husband, did she?"

"Killed? She said a fox carried him away! The girl's moonstruck. Can't trust a thing that comes out of her mouth. She may believe it, but that don't make it true, does it?" The woman shook her head with a world-weary roll of the eyes.

"I thank you, mistress. You've been very helpful. I'll tell my mother I saw you."

"Tell her it's high time she come back to see me herself, hear?"

Yahyah! Maya chortled as he returned to the street. *This was a gold mine indeed! Wait till Lord Hani hears about it.*

They had agreed to meet at the port-side entrance to the town at midday and compare their findings. Maya went rolling back with a satisfied gait to find Lord Hani sitting on the doorstep of a house, watching some pigeons on the parapet of the roof terrace opposite.

Hani looked up inquiringly and climbed to his feet at Maya's approach. "No luck at my end. Did you find anyone who knew them, my boy?"

Maya laughed. "Did I! Hemet-min's aunt. She took them in for a while, but apparently Pi-ay was dissatisfied, and after he sent his woman back to Akhet-aten to look for 'something,' he disappeared."

Hani's eyes lit up, and he clapped Maya on the shoulder. "Well done. I don't suppose the aunt had any idea where Pi-ay went?"

"I got the impression he just evaporated, taking his possessions with him. It sounds like he'd had enough of that crazy Hemet-min. She really seems to be—" Maya hung out his tongue and crossed his eyes. "The aunt wasn't even willing to take the children. She said she'd washed her hands of her niece. Wait till you hear this: Hemet-min said the king had taken the little ones to raise! Right—a ten-year-old boy!"

Hani shook his head sadly. After a moment spent staring, squint-eyed, at the street in deep thought, he asked, "Did our widow happen to say anything about who killed her husband?"

Maya threw back his head and laughed. "She said a fox ran off with him! *Iy*, this woman's a real marvel of wisdom!"

Lord Hani's eyes widened with surprise for a moment. "Let's see if we can find a beer house and get some lunch. Then—I hate to say it—I need to go back to Akhet-aten. I want to take some documents home with me to work on."

Disappointment dropped on Maya like a stone, and his face fell. "We're so close to Waset, my lord. We could be there by this evening. Are you sure you have to go back now?"

"You can go on if you want, my friend. I won't need your services. I just want to be able to work at home for a bit so that I don't have to return to the City of the Horizon for a while after that." He chuckled. "I'm hoping the capital will be moved in the meantime, and I won't ever have to see its bleak streets again."

Maya strode along beside Hani, his eyes down, his heart torn in two. He would have given almost anything to sleep in his own bed that night. But if Lord Hani headed back to the capital, he should too. He belonged at his father-in-law's side.

＊

Four days later, in the late afternoon, the two scribes entered once more the elegant salon of Lord Ptah-mes. The master of the house was absent, no doubt trying to catch up on the accumulated work at the Double House, since his duties for the royal funeral had ended. Maya trudged upstairs—still a little grumbly—to unpack his traveling basket once again, while Hani wandered out into the garden.

In the shade of the arbor, he dropped into a chair with a thud and stretched his legs out before him. The shadows were getting lengthier, and the coming evening had tempered the warmth of the sun's oblique late-winter rays. He heaved a vast, weary sigh, reflecting upon the great generosity of Ptah-mes, who had permitted Hani and his family to make his home their own for so many years. One of Ptah-mes's servants came out to see if he wanted any beer and a brief while later returned to set up the stand and pot beside Hani. By that time, Maya, too, had made an appearance and was duly served a beer pot of his own. Tired and wind-whipped from their travels, Hani and Maya sucked silently at their straws.

At last, Hani said, "You know, there's something we've not done that could eliminate Pi-ay's knife immediately as a murder weapon. He said the *medjay* took the knife from the body. Maybe that wasn't even true—maybe he took it home and hid it. But if it *was* true, our kitchen knife can't be the one that killed Ipy. I'd like to do a little asking while we're here."

"How are we going to do that, since our friend seems to have disappeared?"

"He wouldn't admit anything to us anyway. We need to talk to the *medjay*."

"How many people do we know in the *medjay*? Even if Mahu were still here, he certainly wouldn't help you," Maya said skeptically. He was still a little sniffy, as if miffed that his father-in-law didn't seem convinced Maya had found the fatal instrument.

"It's not a person. It's an animal."

Maya stared at Hani, his mouth open.

"Remember our old friend Djehuty's Cub? Baboons live a very long time—decades. There's a good chance he's still on the force. It's only been nine or ten years since we met."

"And what's *he* going to tell us, my lord?" Maya asked dubiously.

"Not Cub himself but his handler. He can tell us the name of the officers who saw Ipy's body." Hani grinned, the picture of cheer. "We need to resolve this before I take up my new duties. I won't have much time afterward. And I'll not be eager to return to Akhet-aten once I get away."

The next day, before anyone else was up, Hani and Maya grabbed a simple breakfast and put on their most expensive-looking jewelry. Then they set off for the three-story tower that headquartered the city police.

As jewel-bedecked as grandees, they arrived at the door of the police barracks, which stood open to the warm breeze of morning. A *medjay* patrolman, his legs wide, was posted there—supposedly at attention, but he seemed to be near to dozing.

"How can I help you, my lords?" he asked gruffly, springing to life. The welcome was certainly more civil than any Hani would have expected under Mahu.

"I'm looking to talk to one of your men, whose name I don't know, alas. He has some information about a case that touches my family." Hani gave the man his friendliest smile.

"Ask the officer on duty, then," the policeman said, indicating the open door with a thumb.

Hani thanked him and, Maya in his wake, entered the small reception hall. No one seemed to be around. Apart from the bold blade of sunlight that sliced into the room from the door, it was sunk in shadow.

Hani called out, "*Iyah!* Anybody here?"

A lean man in his forties who looked vaguely familiar appeared from within. *He's probably arrested me at some point,* Hani thought with a silent chuckle.

Hani repeated his request. "The fellow was a handler for a baboon named Djehuty's Cub. Are they still on the force?"

"That would be Ka-bekhnet. He and Cub are on patrol at the moment, but perhaps I can help you, my lord. What case have you in mind?"

"The better part of a year ago, a royal goldsmith was stabbed to death on a street near the River. I'd like to know whether the policemen who found him saw the knife still in his back or if it had been removed."

At Hani's side, Maya grew tense. Hani squelched a grin—his secretary was clearly eager to indict Pi-ay's kitchen knife.

"I was one of the patrolmen on that case, my lord. A

colleague of the deceased who found him came and got us, as I recall. The knife was still in the man's back—a fairly small and beautifully made dagger with a gilded handle." He looked suddenly suspicious. "How are you related to this case again?"

"The victim was the employee of my son-in-law here's mother. We promised her to try to find out who killed him to appease his *ba*." Hani was surprised the officer had been as forthcoming as he had. It never hurt to look prosperous and powerful when dealing with the *medjay*.

The policeman nodded, apparently satisfied.

"Do you remember in any more detail what that dagger looked like? Any decoration?"

The man looked hesitant for a moment, then he said, "I can show it to you—no reason not to." He turned to the corner of the room, where a stack of baskets and hempen bags lay piled haphazardly. After a brief contemplation, he dived toward the pile and rummaged through a basket then emerged a moment later with a handsome and very expensive dagger. He held it out to Hani. The bronze blade was still stained with the artisan's blood, but the golden handle was clean—a simple hilt narrowed at the waist for a better grip, decorated at both ends with a single row of triangular inlays like a row of teeth—lapis, turquoise, and the red of carnelian. A chill ran up Hani's neck, because he knew the knife. In-hapy's studio had made them years ago as a special gift for Nefer-khepru-ra's friends.

Hani's stomach was fluttering as he said in what he hoped was a natural-sounding voice, "Thank you, my friend. You've been very helpful. We'll leave you to your work. Good to know people like you are looking out for our safety."

The two men took their leave.

As they passed through the door, the officer called out, "You're Lord Hani, aren't you? You and Lord Mahu were always like that!" He crossed his index fingers to indicate opposition then gave a laugh that grew progressively more hilarious until he was practically in tears. Hani couldn't help joining in. In fact, his collisions with the former police chief did look funny in retrospect, as frightening as they had seemed at the time. He had often wondered what the average policeman really thought of Mahu and his obsessions.

Riding the crest of this shared memory, Hani said jovially, "May the lord of the horizon grant you a pleasant afternoon," and he and Maya set off down the street.

After they had gone a short way, and Hani had finally recovered from his laughter, rumination settled back down on him, a vulture that couldn't be shooed away for long. He said to Maya, "I guess we'll have to discount that knife at Pi-ay's as the murder weapon after all."

Maya, who had watched his father-in-law's hilarity with a look of shock, seemed reluctant to be convinced. "Why would anyone hide a kitchen knife under their mattress unless it had some louche history attached to it?"

"Where *would* you keep a big thing like that if you only had one room and no proper kitchen?" Hani strode along for a space, Maya pattering at his side, then he said under his breath, "Did you recognize that dagger, my friend?"

Maya stared at Hani, his face frozen in concentration. Eventually, he murmured, "It looked familiar."

"Your mother and some of her workmen made six of them for the king to give six of his friends. This was right at the beginning of Nefer-khepru-ra's solo reign or maybe even when he was still coregent. Remember? One of them was used to kill Abdi-ashirta, the bandit king in A'amu."

His eyes growing round, Maya nodded, as if the light had dawned at last. "Yes, it comes back to me now. But who—"

"Who indeed. Most of the men who received the daggers are dead by now."

"Unless Ipy had made one for himself. He did make some of them, didn't he?"

"Yes. It's possible, then Hemet-min would have had access to it. But it would be a pretty expensive object for an artisan to possess. Although the labor was his own," Hani admitted. "Is there any chance your mother would have made him a gift of the materials as part of his pay?"

"I can ask her this afternoon, my lord."

When Ptah-mes came home that evening, Maya was at his mother's. Hani and his friend settled in the pavilion side by side, watching the ducks waddle in a purposeful line toward the fishpond.

Hani filled Ptah-mes in on how their double investigation had progressed—or not progressed—while the latter had been absorbed with the royal funeral. Finally, Hani told him about the chance discovery of the trained cobra and the purpose of the special bracelets that had been gifts to the young prince. He concluded, "I still don't know whether the fateful arrow was an honest error, my lord, or if it was the first prong of Ay's attempt to assassinate Zannanza. Ay assured me it isn't. But then how much can we trust anything he says? Still, he's almost certainly the one behind the plan to train the cobra and lure it to his prey. Notice how both attempts were designed to make it look like an innocent animal was the culprit. He's a thorough master of strategy, after all."

Ptah-mes stared for a moment into his lap, his expression pensive, then he said, "Ay didn't commission the bracelets, Hani. I did."

Hani's eyes widened with astonishment. He could hardly believe he had heard his friend correctly, and for a moment, words seemed stuck in his throat. A chill flickered up the back of his neck. "You, my lord? But why?"

Ptah-mes stood and brushed down the pleats of his pristine kilt, as if to clear his lap of invisible crumbs, then reseated himself. He stared at Hani with no shame. "Because he needed killing. Ay didn't seem to be doing it—and I wasn't sure why."

"I think," Hani said cautiously, "he didn't want to start a war with the Hittites, who were already suspicious of our good faith." *Although Ay doesn't seem to care now that that war is a reality. Such an eventuality must have occurred to Ptah-mes as well.*

"A calculated risk, no more frightful than civil war. Rather less so, in fact, because it would only be our northern border, far away, that would suffer. But it was imperative that no son of Kheta Land sit on our throne. You've met Shuppiluliuma, as I've observed him for years. A more dangerous man, I can't imagine. This whole scheme of the queen's was insanely imprudent. When I saw no sign of Ay acting, I took it upon myself. Then he arranged the hunting accident." He raised his eyes and fixed Hani's with a frank stare. "Which is better, my friend? A struggle that would cost thousands of lives—or one man's unfortunate encounter with a wild animal known to haunt our land? Who could prove any mortal had a hand in it? It was easy enough for me, the Master of the Double House of Silver and Gold, to insert the bracelets among the gifts the queen chose from my storehouses."

Ptah-mes's argument was the same as Ay's, Hani observed. Better one person should die than many. He sat for a moment, staring at the floor. That certainly rearranged his theories. Once so prudent, Ptah-mes had grown more and more reckless with time. *However...* "Forgive me, my lord, but I thought you felt some loyalty to Lady Meryet-aten."

"I supported her religious position," Ptah-mes said with a sigh. He clearly understood Hani was referring to an indiscretion he had once committed out of a desire for the queen's favor. "I, too, wanted to see the Hidden One reestablished. But when I saw Ay moving in that direction without bloody revolution, my personal sense of gratitude had to step aside. I think you would agree that a conscience cannot be bought—forever." He smiled thinly. "You've been my inspiration when it comes to conscience, Hani. You and Apeny."

Hani dropped his gaze, touched, then looked Ptah-mes in the eye. "Well, it seems we needn't pursue the cobra scheme any further. Ay got what he wanted. Perhaps that young archer was his creature after all. How hard would it have been for him to use a Hittite arrow? It's impossible for me to believe it was a simple accident."

When Hani filled Maya in on the solution to the cobra mystery, the secretary's jaw dropped, and his eyes grew wide with shock. "Lord Ptah-mes did it? I'm stunned."

"Me too. But there you have it. He had defected from the queen's party, like so many of us." Hani lifted a rueful eyebrow. "Or as so many of us wanted to."

"So *he* was the rich old man, not Ay. Well, well."

"I guess he—or probably a servant—commissioned the bracelets too. It doesn't surprise me. Apart from the royal family, there aren't many people who could afford such pieces."

"What if Zannanza never wore them?"

Hani gave a bark of laughter. "What vain young man wouldn't have—a special gift from his lady love? I don't know when Ptah-mes planned to sic the serpent on him, but our friend was enough part of Meryet-aten's inner circle that he would have known the man's movements once he arrived in our land."

Maya shook his head and blew a deep breath through his lips. "I confess I would never have figured Lord Ptah-mes for an assassin."

"Let's call it an act of war." Hani wrinkled his nose in confusion. "As for Ipy's murderer... I can't imagine that was Ptah-mes." *Although a man of that class would be completely invisible to him. And he was one of the two men still living who was given one of those knives.*

"But Lord Hani, who else would have had a motive?"

Hani chuckled and shot Maya a mischievous look. "You. Ipy was going to inherit your mother's business instead of you."

Maya's eyes flew wide open in horror. "My lord! You can't think that!"

Hani patted him on the shoulder with affectionate reassurance. "Of course not, son. Just pointing out how little we know yet and how we can't jump to judgment."

"Could it have been someone opposed to the Hittite marriage but not working with Lord Ay or Ptah-mes?"

"Certainly. But why would our hypothetical plotter have targeted Ipy, if he had nothing to do with the cobra bracelets? Unless the murder really was part of that intimidation campaign by your mother's rivals."

Maya gave uneasy *hmm*. "I hope not. That might mean Mother is in danger."

"I wish the Hittites hadn't burned the young man's body so fast," Hani said. "I would have liked to see the angle at which that arrow went into his back. It might have told us where it really came from—our hapless archer or somewhere else."

"Dear gods, burning someone's body! How barbaric! Don't they know they denied him an afterlife?" Maya shivered.

Hani smiled sadly. "The men of Kheta believe that souls ascend with the smoke. And perhaps they do. Who's to say there aren't different doors into the hereafter for them and for us?"

Maya shot him a skeptical sideways look, but Hani was too preoccupied to continue the conversation. It was just soaking in: Ptah-mes owned one of those knives.

⁜

Once Hani's yacht drew up to the quay in Waset, Hani and Maya stepped onto dry land as gratefully as if they had spent the last year in some distant corner of the earth. They had sat almost silent throughout the trip—not out of any hostility but because their whole souls were turned toward their destination and the loved ones who awaited them there.

"To think!" Maya said finally with a sigh of satisfaction. "We may never have to go back to that city of the damned! I'm saving to get a piece of land somewhere and farm it. The children so love to visit your country place."

"The Pilot has brought us home," Hani agreed, a beatific smile splitting his cheeks. "I just want to get on my little reed boat and paddle out into the marshes somewhere."

They parted company at the usual intersection, and shouldering his basket, Hani swung down the lane to the southern suburbs. Already, the neighborhood looked livelier, the empty houses taken in hand, the garden walls freshly whitewashed. Palms bowed their tousled heads in gracious welcome. *If cities can suffer, then the pain of our beloved City of the Scepter is healing.*

To Hani's disappointment, Nub-nefer was in service at the temple. He drifted into the garden to wait for her return and for the lunch whose tasty smells were already wafting from the kitchen. He watched the ducks paddle with businesslike concentration around the lily pond. A queue of fuzzy brown-and-yellow ducklings streamed after their mother, quacking. *When they're grown, they seem to have nothing to do with one another,* Hani reflected. *Do they even know which are their own family? Do the parents and children recognize one another?*

He drew back into the shade of the *doum* palm and took a seat on the ground, folding his legs. With a great ripple of wings like a shaking of sheets, Qenyt alighted, her own long legs extended, and waded majestically out into the water. Hani watched her with affectionate admiration. The gentle heat radiating up from the gravel was starting to make him sleepy.

"You're home, son? For good, this time?" Mery-ra asked from behind Hani.

Hani climbed to his feet and gave his father a hug. Despite the big smile, there was a flicker of trepidation in the old man's eyes.

"I hope so. Let's sit down on the bench, Father. I feel like I haven't seen much of you for months." *Ever since we came back from Kheta.* Something had been missing from their old relationship, and that something had been trust. Its absence was a gnawing pain in Hani's soul. Every time he had made the choice not to tell his father about the investigation of the bracelets, he realized he needed to ask Mery-ra about his mysterious activities. But he never had. He had feared what he would learn. They settled side by side on the bench. Hani laid a hand on his father's leg so Mery-ra couldn't pop up and hurry off to some specious task. Hani took a deep breath and dived in.

"I've been meaning to ask you since we were in Hattusha, Father. Where did you go every day up there? Maya said he saw you head repeatedly to a certain address and stay there all morning with Hattusha-ziti's secretary. Did he find an old acquaintance for you?"

Mery-ra looked uneasy, his tufty brows crumpled in something that might have been shame. He dropped his eyes. "That's it, Hani. An old acquaintance."

Intrigued, Hani persisted, "Maya was almost convinced

that you were spying. I nearly began to believe it myself after the death of the prince, when it became clear someone in our party was working against the mission. I thought maybe you were the one in the hire of Lord Ay—or the Hittite king." He grinned to show how little credence he had ever placed in such a theory.

But Mery-ra looked up gravely and stared Hani in the eye. "No, son. In some ways, it's worse than that."

He seemed utterly serious, and Hani felt a cold draft of apprehension down his neck.

"Worse than treason?" he asked in surprise.

His father heaved a huge sigh that seemed to deflate him visibly. "A betrayal, yes. And worse than betraying my country. Hani, my boy, I'm going to tell you a story about something that happened fifty years ago, and I can only beg you not to judge me too harshly."

Hani scooted closer and cocked his head attentively. Curiosity and dread mingled in his gut.

"I was just a young man, maybe Pa-kiki's age. My general was part of a diplomatic mission to Kheta, and I accompanied him as his secretary, of course. But I was also under the orders of the king to feel out less-than-loyal factions in Hattusha who might act on our behalf. An unimportant fellow like me was under no observation, you see."

"You were a spy."

"Yes. Or an agent, you might call it," Mery-ra said quietly. Before Hani's eyes, his face seemed to droop more and more with sorrow. "I was to meet with several members of this opposition to coordinate their efforts, even to promise them our help—covertly, of course. I worked long and closely with them." His little brown eyes looked pleadingly into Hani's. "Among these conspirators was a woman. She, like me, was young and not likely to be suspected—a minor scribe's wife. I don't think he ever realized his wife was working against the king."

A terrible suspicion was brewing in Hani, but he refused to believe it until he heard it from his father's mouth. "I suppose she was beautiful," he said a bit more harshly than he'd intended.

"She was. I was young and far from home for months. We worked very—well, intimately. I... I guess it was inevitable." Mery-ra hung his head. "I'm not proud of it, my boy. I was weak. That's all."

Hani was struck wordless. *My father had an affair? The man I most admire in the world—and whose goodness I've spent a lifetime trying to emulate?* Every particle of him wanted to protest, "Impossible!"

At last, he was able to stammer, "You betrayed Mother? Did you ever tell her?"

"No. No. She never knew. And yes, I guess I did. But it was always and only your mother I loved, Hani. You must believe that." Tears sparkled on Mery-ra's lashes.

He reached out to touch Hani, but Hani drew away, wounded to the core. "Fifty years ago—she must have been carrying Pipi. By all the gods, man! What sort of person deceives his pregnant wife?"

Hani surged to his feet, his heart in turmoil, disgust and pain boiling up his throat until he felt he would gag. He couldn't even look at his father. *Please, great Hidden One. Make his words disappear. Let it be that he never told me this. That it never happened.* Hani could have accepted anything else—selling out the Black Land would have disturbed him less. He had grown up swaddled in the knowledge that his parents loved each other deeply. That *that* had lain unspoken between them for lifetimes was like a violation of everything Hani had cherished. It felt like a dagger blow struck at the innocence of his own childhood.

He could feel a twinging in his nose that threatened tears. "So was it only once, or did you have a relationship?" he asked roughly.

Mery-ra heaved a painful sigh, his eyes still fixed on his lap. He seemed to be sinking lower and lower onto the bench. "I was only there for a few months, son. You could hardly call it a relationship."

Hani snorted. He wanted to yell, "Don't try to excuse yourself!" But he remained silent, a wounded, angry silence that throbbed under the breastbone.

"Then a few days before you were to take off for Hattusha, I received a letter from a man up there I'd never met, a certain scribe named Kurunuwa, saying that Ammi-hatna—that was her name—was failing and had just revealed something to him. That he was... was my son."

"Mut, mother of us all!" Hani exploded. He seemed to have passed beyond anger into purest agony. "So your 'nonrelationship' has flesh and blood, has it?" He hid his face in his hands. "Poor Mother, trusting you all those months at a time you were gone. Is this what's-his-name the only bastard you've dropped, or did you have a 'nonrelationship' on every journey? Whatever happened to 'Beware of a woman who is a stranger. She is ready to ensnare you. A great deadly crime when it is heard'?"

Tears ran openly down Mery-ra's cheeks. He shook his

head brokenly. "That was the only time. I was faithful to your mother, my son."

The sight of Hani's father in tears before him, so slumped over, so contrite—so old—made his heart clench with pity. *Why does this shock me so?* he wondered, striving to breathe. *Why does it make me so outraged? I know many colleagues who have done no less, and I've laughed it off. Why, Mane has a whole other family in Wasshukanni, and I've never cared. I've told myself that was human weakness. But suddenly, it's my own father...*

Mery-ra looked up. A pitiful hope flickered like the reflection of a guttering flame in the despair of his eyes.

"So when you received that letter, you decided you wanted to see her again and meet this unknown son, right? And as luck would have it, I was on my way to Hattusha, so you invited yourself along."

"That's it, my boy. Wouldn't you have done the same? I'm an old man. How many more chances would I have?" Mery-ra spread his big hands in pleading then dropped his eyes. "She had gotten so shrunken, son. So frail. Hardly anything left of all that beautiful hair. It was hard to believe she was the same woman. And that's happening to me too. It was very painful to see her like that..."

Torn in two, Hani breathed deeply, trying to calm himself. He felt as if he'd been tricked personally—his hero had deceived him, betrayed him, let him down. Anyone else could fall but not his father. Yet he tried to put Mery-ra's transgression into perspective.

"I've never, ever been unfaithful to Nub-nefer, Father. And I always thought I was following your example," he said with an air of weariness, not rancor.

"I've failed you, son."

Feeling he couldn't look at Mery-ra a moment more, Hani surged to his feet and walked away, nearly staggering. He had been dealt a blow that left him gasping in pain. *Deceived. Betrayed. Mother dishonored.* He stood staring into the branches of the trees, fanning his outrage, and saw there a pair of *menut* doves cooing to each other. *Fidelity is possible, Ammit take it.*

Suddenly, Hani could bear it no longer. He wasn't a man who maintained a white-hot pitch of anger easily, and he had already burned through his supply. His eyes beginning to shrivel, he knelt in the gravel at Mery-ra's feet and opened his arms. They clung to each other as if in the other's embrace lay the safety of the world, while Mery-ra's tears ran down Hani's neck. It struck Hani with a pang—just as the sight of his old love had struck Mery-ra—how slack and almost fragile his father had become, unlike the solid wrestler's build of years past. *How many times did we reenact this ritual in my childhood, when I was the weak one, and Father's strong arms comforted me?* His tears flowed, scalding away all anger in a magma of love. *Life is too brief to waste on anger.*

"Forgive me, son," Mery-ra snuffled.

But Hani tried to smile through his tears. "You're forgiven, you old rascal. But only because you're my favorite father."

CHAPTER 16

"Hani?" Nub-nefer called from the gate. "Where are you, my love?"

Hani clambered to his feet, brushed down the seat of his kilt, and dashed at his eyes. "In the garden, my dove." He stumped down the path—comfortably barefooted, wigless, and shirtless, as he could never be at Ptah-mes's mansion—to find his wife approaching, her arms outstretched.

"You're back!" she cried joyously. "A'a said you were out here. Welcome home." She encircled him with her arms and laid her cheek against his chest.

Hani breathed in the fragrance of warm, perfumed flesh and oil of lilies that was like a whiff of the Field of Reeds to him. He kissed the part of her wig. "You look so beautiful, my sweet dove. Even more than usual."

"I've been singing for the Hidden One," she explained, gazing up at him with love. They linked arms and walked to the porch. "Are you home for long?"

"I'm home forever," he said with a wide grin of delight.

"Or soon will be." He told her all about Pentju's interview and the new headquarters of the foreign service.

Her kohl-painted eyes grew wider and wider. "Oh, Hani! That's so wonderful! My prayers have been answered."

"What's that?" Mery-ra asked from the path. "I've been praying that lunch would be ready soon. Are my prayers to be answered too?" His eyes were red, but the old joyous, gap-toothed smile lit his face once more.

Hani and his wife laughed. He advanced on his father and swept him into a crushing hug. "Thank you, revered Father. Thank you for being who you are."

Mery-ra returned the squeeze fervently, without the usual quip. He believed, no doubt, he knew exactly what Hani meant. But Hani was also thinking of something else. He said, "An event both painful and happy has befallen Ptah-mes. I'll tell you about it at the table."

"Then let me go fulfill Father's prayer and see if lunch is ready." Nub-nefer set off for the kitchen with a look over her shoulder. She smiled and blew a kiss at Hani, her big dark eyes tender.

Hani described for his father his new mandate and how, henceforth, he and Pipi would be stationed in Waset.

Mery-ra's eyes grew round with delight. "Now, that's an answered prayer, son. I've almost forgotten what my children looked like." A flush of embarrassment rose up his jowls as he realized what he had just said. "I mean—"

"You forget I've met Kurunuwa, although I didn't even realize it. He's Hattusha-ziti's secretary, you know." Hani pictured the scribe's mild, jowly face with its dominating nose. He glanced sideways at Mery-ra, a twinkle of mischief in his eye. "The men of our family may be big, but we aren't a very pretty lot."

Mery-ra returned his look uncertainly, as if he wasn't sure of Hani's tone of voice. Then he saw Hani's grin and relaxed. "It's a natural defense, to be sure not too many beautiful women fall all over us." The conversation had become a trail of pitfalls he couldn't avoid. After a moment, he said with a kind of childlike hopefulness, "He's a nice boy. I think you'd like each other."

But Hani, who secretly agreed, just laughed then rubbed his hands together in anticipation as he saw Nub-nefer leading in the servants with tables and platters of food. How good it felt not to have to suspect his father. It was like the fragrant fat of a festive cone melting over his shoulders.

"It's simple fare, my love," she said apologetically. "I didn't know when you'd be here."

"Perfect. After several weeks at Ptah-mes's villa, I long for something simple."

Hani tucked into the dish of broad beans and onions with a relish his growling stomach seconded.

"You said something has happened to your friend?" Mery-ra prodded as he ripped off a piece of pot-shaped bread.

"I overheard this conversation by accident, and while Ptah-mes is aware of that, I'm sure he'd appreciate keeping it private."

"Tell! Tell!"

"His children all appeared and wanted to reconcile. They said the Atenist nightmare was over, and their rancor should be too."

Nub-nefer sniffed. "I hope they've included our Neferet in their new attitude. I don't want anyone saying she's after his gold."

"I suspect they have. It seems the real acrimony started with their childhood. The inheritance was just a symbol of everything they felt was wrong with their relationship with their father."

"He didn't abuse them or anything, did he? He seems like such a perfect gentleman." Nub-nefer's shapely eyebrows wrinkled with distress.

Hani grew heavy-hearted at the memory of his friend at bay, with the seven angry children attacking. "No. No. He was just... himself. Demanding. Not very warm. All those sarcastic comments that I, an adult, find enjoyably astringent must've stung like a whiplash the hearts of little children, who are so literal. I'm sure he had no idea he had hurt them. But he acknowledged everything without any attempt to excuse himself and made a very touching gesture to show his goodwill. I think their bonds will be greatly strengthened from now on."

"Why, then, that's wonderful. Look at how much closer we are to Aha after he begged our forgiveness. Humility is irresistible." Nub-nefer squeezed Hani's hand.

Staring at his beans, Mery-ra said with a cryptic twitch of the mouth, "And forgiveness is all-powerful. 'You will find it the path of life,' as a wise man said."

Hani laughed while the heat of embarrassment crept up his cheeks. "So I'm a wise man now, am I? I can tell you this much: it's often *difficult*."

"How is your investigation of that goldsmith's murder

going, my love?" Nub-nefer handed around a dish of dried figs and dates, from which the two men helped themselves.

Hani sighed. "Speaking of difficult things! One false trail after another. It's probably either a gang of envious young goldsmiths or that Pi-ay, but he's disappeared. Ay's motive has evaporated, so he's out." He couldn't bring himself to include Ptah-mes on the list.

"Two in a row. It's a good thing they're taking you out of the field and putting you in the office, son. You may have lost your touch." Mery-ra chuckled.

"How 'two,' Father?" Nub-nefer asked.

"He means the death of Prince Zannanza." But Hani said nothing more. He didn't want it becoming more widely known that he suspected Lord Ay.

As they crawled into bed that night, Nub-nefer said, "I forgot to mention the girls are here in town. They've been spending their days cleaning up Khuit's old house for a little dispensary. Lord Ptah-mes bought it for them. I'm just glad Neferet didn't decide to receive patients right in his salon."

Hani, feeling mellow, chuckled. He stroked his wife's cheek. "I can picture her coughing and crippled poor people mingling with Ptah-mes's tax collectors and ministers. Maybe it would be good for those bureaucrats to see what the people they tax so blithely look like. And how they have to spend their last little bag of grain on some eye salve so their children won't go blind."

"Do go see her when you get a chance, my love. She and Bener-ib are doing marvels with those children they adopted."

"I'm delighted—because the little ones' own aunt didn't want anything to do with them."

Nub-nefer snuggled against Hani's chest, and he wrapped an arm around her. "The ways of the gods are mysterious, aren't they? Sati, who wants little ones so desperately, lost hers, and this woman, who doesn't seem to care anything about her children, had so many. Neferet, who never wanted to bear children, has six of them all at once."

"How is our little swallow doing these days, my dove?" Hani's words were growing slurred. The comfort of his bed and the warmth of his wife's perfumed body seemed to be massaging away his grip on consciousness.

"Back to her old self—except matured, I think. She went into this sorrow a happy girl, but she's come out a strong and compassionate woman. You'll see her. Why don't we have them over for dinner tomorrow?"

Hani made some kind of noise of assent, but all at once, the weariness of so many days' travel descended upon him like a shroud, and he sank gently into sleep with a half-formed "I love you" on his lips.

The next day, Hani and his father set out to see the little dispensary Neferet and Bener-ib were setting up in Khuit's ramshackle old house. Neferet's loud, energetic voice rang out all the way to the street as she called orders to the workmen.

"Perhaps she should have been a general, not a *sunet*," Mery-ra commented. "It's not too late to apprentice her to Har-em-heb."

They slipped through the gate, which stood open. The dry little court was littered with boards and bricks, but Hani remembered it as the house of the village healer who had been Neferet's first teacher of practical medicine. He could still see in his imagination the old woman lying dead in her salon, her throat slit.

They pushed under the fly mat into the tiny vestibule to find everything whitewashed and immaculately clean. The earthen floor had been plastered and polished. The salon was equally transformed. Gone were the bundles of dusty herbs festooned with cobwebs hanging from the rafters. No tables full of pots, baskets, or mysterious implements crowded the diminutive room, and no owl-eyed cat presided over the clutter. Only three neatly made beds and a stool occupied the space. Beyond, in the kitchen, Neferet and her friend climbed one after the other up a ladder.

A man said, "You're going to want to put bars in that window."

"Hello, my duckling," Hani called. "It's Papa and Grandfather."

He stuck his head through the door to find Bener-ib seated, teetering, on a shelf that ran along the top of the room—barely tall enough to leave space for her head—and Neferet perching on the ladder just below her, handing things up. Two workmen stood with their hands on their hips, watching. They all turned at the sound of his voice.

"Papa!" Neferet cried with pleasure. "Let Ibet get down, and we'll show you around. Grandfather! See our lovely dispensary?" She clattered down the rungs hastily, while her friend inched with care toward the ladder and turned for the descent.

"It's a good thing one of them is small and agile," Mery-ra said under his breath.

Neferet galloped to Hani and threw herself on him then, more gingerly, enveloped her grandfather. "Isn't it beautiful? This little room that used to be the kitchen is for preparing medicines, and that one is for consultation and for treatments. We won't actually keep patients here, of course, but if they're able to walk, we can treat them here, because if we go to their house, as usual, we may not have everything we need with us, and sometimes things have to be done fast. Of course, we'll go to their houses too. Oh, and that shelf is for our casebooks. And look here—in our niche for the household gods we have Sekhmet, the goddess of healing, and Im-hotep, patron of *sunus*. Mama gave us those."

When Neferet slowed down for a breath, Hani said, "I can see you've thought of everything, my girl. Now all you need is patients. How will people know you're here?"

"The watchman is going to tell everyone in the neighborhood, and the workmen will tell their families, then those people will tell *their* families and friends." She beamed, a great gap-toothed crescent of joy. "I think all the people who used to see Khuit will naturally come here too."

"Better be prepared to hang mouse bones around their necks," Mery-ra said with a naughty grin.

"But you know, Grandfather, that really is a remedy for teething pains. Only, it's the mother's neck. And you have to eat the mouse first. Cooked, I mean."

Hani chuckled. "Thanks be to the Hidden One you and I are safe from such remedies, Father."

"Here's Ibet. Papa and Grandfather came to see what we're doing, Ibet," Neferet said excitedly.

Ibet had just extricated herself from the shelf and entered the room, dusting her hands. She bestowed a shy hug on Hani and Mery-ra, who had become her family.

"Mama and Sati have come, too, and Mut-benret. Pa-kiki is still in Akhet-aten for a while. And Aha? Well, we'll see. He'll be grateful we're here if anyone in his family gets sick."

"I expect you'll have to go to his house if anyone gets sick, my duckling," Hani said, trying unsuccessfully to imagine Aha or his wife descending to that working-class neighborhood. He hadn't even visited Sati at her home. "I don't suppose Lord Ptah-mes has seen it. He probably has so much work backed up that he can't leave the capital."

"Yes, he did, Papa. He said how proud he was of us. Wasn't that nice? We'd barely seen him for ages, even before we came back to Waset, but here he came. I think he turned right around and went back afterward."

It occurred to Hani that his friend seemed to be practicing to be a better, more caring father. The idea touched him somehow. "I'm sure he'll have more time to relax now. Grandfather and I will leave you two ladies to your work, since you have carpenters or someone here." Hani squeezed his daughter around the shoulders and added, although he knew she would pay no attention, "Try to get back before dark, all right? I know the curfew is over, but still, things are unsettled."

"Lord Ptah-mes said to take his litter, but that seems a little faaancy, doesn't it?" she said, imitating her husband's upper-class drawl. "I mean, can you imagine anyone around here having a litter? Except Maya—he'd love to have a litter. He'd have a litter to carry his litter." She snickered wickedly, and Mery-ra gave a snort of laughter.

Hani, trying not to encourage his daughter's mischief, forced down a hoot. "On that note, we leave you, ladies."

They hugged, and the two men took their leave, Mery-ra chuckling as they passed through the court. "Does she know we have the litter?"

"*You* have the litter, august father," Hani corrected him. "And its purpose is medical. I'm on my two properly working-class feet."

Mery-ra gave a *pshaw* of dismissal. "Medical indeed. Age isn't a disease, my boy. Didn't I just make the long trip to the northern edge of the world with you, sleeping rough with the roughest of your young soldiers?"

Hani threw back his head and laughed. "You certainly—"

He stopped abruptly and held Mery-ra motionless with a hand. Ahead of them, a short, sturdily built man of about forty was crossing the street, but at Hani's voice, he looked up and froze. He had a distinctive quiff over his brow.

"Pi-ay!" Hani cried. "Wait! I've been looking for you."

But the goldsmith turned and took off running. Hani kicked away his sandals and bolted after him. "Wait, man. I mean you no harm."

Hani, with his broad wrestler's build and generously fleshed middle, wasn't designed for speed. Still, desperation lent him the relentless wings of a hawk. He thundered down the narrow lane, dodging startled passersby, who, no doubt, had never seen a well-dressed middle-aged scribe in full pursuit.

"Pi-ay! Hold up! I want to talk to you!" he shouted breathlessly.

The goldsmith slipped sideways into an alley and hammered off. His steps were flagging. Hani was close enough to hear the man's breath ripping in his throat.

Hani, too, was reaching his limit. The pulse banged in his temple. Moving his legs grew harder and harder. *I'm going to have to stop.*

But then Pi-ay glanced back over his shoulder in fear. As he did, a scabby dog wandered in front of him. To their mutual surprise and horror, they collided. The man went flying head over heels, while the frightened dog three-footed off with a yipe. Pi-ay lay still for a moment, flat on his face in the street, stunned.

Hani closed the distance between them and crouched at his side, sucking in air. He put a heavy hand on Pi-ay's shoulder and pulled him up to a kneeling position. "Are you all right?" he asked, panting.

Pi-ay straightened himself with a groan and made a gesture as if to jerk away, but he was too winded.

Hani tightened his grip. "Why did you run, my friend? You're not in any trouble. I just have some questions to ask you."

Pi-ay grimaced with pain. His chin and the side of his face were a pulsing red-purple that would surely become a terrible bruise, and his whole front was ocher with dirt and beaded with blood from his scraped skin. "I have nothing to say. Tell Lord Ay I don't know anything," he gasped, his bare chest heaving.

A silent squawk of alarm sounded in Hani's ear. He waited until the thunder of his heart had begun to subside, then he wheezed, "I have nothing to do with Lord Ay. I'm just a relative of Mistress In-hapy. She's worried about you. She thought you were dead."

Hani helped the goldsmith climb laboriously to his feet. His knees were scraped and bleeding.

"Can you walk? There's a healer near here, and we can talk there in privacy."

They hobbled painfully back toward Neferet's dispensary, Hani recovering his breath little by little and supporting Pi-ay, who could hardly bend his legs.

"What are you doing in Waset?" Hani asked him quietly as they limped back the way they had come. "We talked to Hemet-min's aunt in Gebtu, and she said you had run off all of a sudden."

"Why are you after me? Let me just disappear. I don't particularly want to die," the goldsmith said thickly through his bruised lips.

"Why would you die? Is someone after you? Is... Is Lord Ay?"

Pi-ay stopped and grew rigid. He shot a fearful glance at Hani from the corner of his eye. "Please don't let him get me," he whispered, clutching at Hani's shirt. "I don't know anything."

Yahyah! Hani thought. *I'll bet you do know something, and I want to know it too.* He drew Pi-ay toward Neferet's neighborhood with a firm but gentle hand on the back.

As they approached, Hani saw Mery-ra and the four litter bearers standing or squatting in the street outside the *sunets*' gate. Mery-ra pulled away from the wall he had been leaning against and gave Hani a curious stare.

"Let's go back inside. Neferet can clear out her workmen."

"Oh, they all left for lunch. The girls are still here but preparing to leave. I was afraid to go until you returned in case you needed me." Mery-ra toddled alongside Hani, who swept the limping goldsmith before him through the court and into the house.

"My duckling," Hani called, "I have your first patient."

Neferet and Bener-ib appeared from the salon, bright-eyed with eagerness.

"Oh, what happened to you? Come in here and sit down on this bed, and we'll clean you off and put some aloe on you." Neferet led the way into the little dispensary and gestured for the man to sit on the side of one of the beds.

Pi-ay shot a surprised glance at Hani. "Girls?" he mouthed uneasily.

Hani had a feeling that was going to be the reaction of a lot of people when they saw the new neighborhood *sunet*s.

Bener-ib brought a basin and some clean cloths, while Neferet carried in a spiky plant in a pot from outside.

"This will hurt a little," Neferet warned Pi-ay as she wrung a cloth out of the water and began to dab at his tattered knees and chest.

He flinched and gave a hiss of pain.

"It looks like somebody dragged you down the street." Neferet smiled cheerfully. "We'll need some resin, Ibet, and I'll cut us some bandages."

Her friend set out for the former kitchen, while Neferet cut several squares of linen then slit a leaf of the plant and smeared its clear, gelatinous sap all over the middle of one side. When Bener-ib returned with a little

329

pot and an applicator stick, she dabbed a bit of its sticky contents around the edge and pressed the square to one of Pi-ay's knees then the other, where the resin held it in place. Neferet stood back and observed the bandages with satisfaction.

"It's like making meat pies," Mery-ra observed. "Which reminds me—it's lunchtime."

"Now, my girls, could you go on home to eat, as planned, and leave us to talk to this gentleman?"

"Of course, Papa. We won't be long."

The two young doctors departed, whispering and giggling, while Pi-ay stared after them.

"They're real healers?" he asked skeptically after the door had slammed behind them.

"More than that. They're literate and highly trained *sunet*s. They were the late king's personal physicians." Hani doubted the man believed him, but the girls' handiwork would speak for itself. "Now, Pi-ay, tell me what's going on. Why did you drop out of sight? Hemet-min's going to be heartbroken when she gets back to Gebtu and finds you've gone."

Pi-ay shook his head slowly. "Somehow, he found me in Gebtu, my lord. I had to run. That's why I left Mistress In-hapy's in the first place. I need to make myself invisible, or I'm a dead man."

"Who is *he*?" Hani swallowed hard, afraid even to say it. "Lord Ay?"

The goldsmith nodded, furtively glancing around.

"Why?"

"Look what happened to Ipy. That'll be me if he finds me."

A wave of fear if not altogether of surprise rose up Hani's spine. *Ay, the old fox, killed him after all? And maybe in person, judging from the presence of the gold dagger.* Then it crossed his mind that in her madness, Hemet-min must have had a hint from the gods—a fox had, in fact, carried her husband off. Perhaps the two men had spoken and argued in the street that night, then Ipy had turned away, and Ay had thrown himself on Ipy without any resistance from the unsuspecting artisan, who had fallen where he stood. The king's grandfather might be getting up in years, but he was hale—and armed.

"Why did the God's Father kill a goldsmith, Pi-ay? That seems a little below his usual notice."

"Because Ipy knew all about the plan to kill... somebody. And Ammit take him, Ipy drew me into it."

Hani stared uncomprehendingly at the man. *Ay was aware of Ptah-mes's plan? And what danger would that have put Ay in, should it have become known? Were they working together? Unthinkable. Ptah-mes is as suspicious of him as I am.*

"What plan is this, Pi-ay? The one that involved the inlaid bracelets?"

Now it was the goldsmith's turn to look confused.

"The cobra?" Hani pressed.

"N-No, my lord. Do you mean those beautiful cuffs Ipy was working on? I don't know anything about that. This was a necklace. The God's Father approached Ipy about it, but he was already busy with the bracelets—him all alone—and he was afraid he couldn't finish in time, so he asked me to help. In-hapy didn't know about it. He had to do it all after hours so she wouldn't know what he was working on. And me, too, when I could. I often asked to work at a friend's shop during the day so In-hapy wouldn't know what I was up to. I told him we were so busy we didn't have enough room at the forge, and he let me use a little corner of his to do all my soldering. I had to pay him, of course, and Ipy paid me. A lot. But it was all hush-hush."

So that's where all his money was going, even apart from what his wife was hiding. "What was so sinister about a necklace that Ay didn't want anybody to know about it?"

"It was specially designed with roughness on the inside so it would scratch the skin. If you painted it with something poisonous, it would get inside and kill the person."

Hani and Mery-ra gaped at each other.

"Sounds like our friend learned from the little handmaid who tried to poison the king," Mery-ra said with a lift of the eyebrows.

"And they told Ipy, 'Be sure to make it rough. I'm going to poison somebody'?" Hani asked dubiously.

"No, no. He overheard them testing it on their thumbs. He knew his life wasn't worth anything after that, but they left him alone long enough to finish the piece. Then they finished *him*. But they never got the necklace."

"And where is it?"

Pi-ay's face grew pale. "I have it. I've been cutting pieces off it to live."

Hani nodded slowly. Things were starting to fit together—around the edges, at least. "That was in the heavy chest Hemet-min's aunt mentioned?"

"Yes. The night he died, Ipy was carrying a lot of the extra gold he had melted down so it couldn't be identified. I guess he was going to slip it back in among the gold stock at the workshop. When I saw it still on him, I knew what had happened. No drunken apprentices from the other studios would have left that. I... I took it and cached it in the yard with Hemet-min's copper debens. I didn't steal any of it, my lord."

"Listen, Pi-ay, I need to ask you a few more questions, but the two doctors will be coming back. Are you willing to stay at my house for a couple of days and tell me everything you know? Not that you know anything, of course, if anyone should ask."

The goldsmith ran his fingers through his bangs nervously. "Why should I tell you all this? I'd be better off heading to some unknown location."

"Ipy was your friend, my man. Don't you think his *ba* wants justice done?"

Pi-ay snorted. "You think anyone's going to do justice to a person like Lord Ay? He's more powerful than the king."

How sadly true, Hani had to admit. But he said earnestly, "Give me this satisfaction, and I'll see to it you get away to safety. I'm high commissioner of foreign affairs. I can take you off to the north, where no one will find you, and your skills will be appreciated. Do you want Hemet-min to go with you?"

"Ha!" Pi-ay gave a bark of laughter. "Her? I hope I never see her again. I tried to take care of her because Ipy was my friend, but the woman's as mad as a bitch in the moonlight—leaving her children like that. I thought once we talked to that aunt, she'd take them all in, but even Hemet-min's own family's given up on her. She kept telling them I was her husband, but believe me, I feel no responsibility for her or her brood. I guess Hu-may will have to take care of the brats."

Pi-ay looked down, then a shadow of guilt passed over his swollen face. "Maybe I should give him some of the necklace, since it was half Ipy's. But he might get in trouble if he tries to sell any of it, and he's got a small fortune with those scraps of gold."

"We'll discuss everything. Let's get some lunch before we do anything else."

"I need to pick up the chest first—I don't want anyone to steal it or report it as a stolen article. I'd like to melt that necklace down, but I have to find a forge someplace where no one will ask questions." He looked annoyed all of a sudden. "Seems a shame. It's a really beautiful piece of work."

"Where are you staying?"

"At the beer house near the temple of Khonsu."

Hani helped the goldsmith into the litter, and he and Mery-ra walked at its side. The beer house wasn't far, which was a blessing, because Hani found his sprint through the streets had left him stiff and tenderfooted. He decided to accompany Pi-ay to his room, just in case he should decide to bolt, and the two men trudged painfully up the stairs to the little cubicle where the latter had stashed his things. Pi-ay squatted awkwardly then gave up. "It's under the bed, my lord, but I can't get down on my knees."

Hani heaved a sigh and lowered himself flat to the floor then stretched out a groping hand under the bed, his face in the dusty darkness, until he felt the chest pushed up against the wall. He wriggled in a little farther, knowing what his kilt was going to look like when he emerged. Hani was rather too thick to make it an easy maneuver. Suddenly, he heard a faint shuffle behind him and tried to jerk around, hitting his head on the bed frame and knocking his wig askew. With a terrible suspicion, he slid backward and rose to his knees, his belly draped in cobwebs. Sure enough, Pi-ay had disappeared.

Ammit take him, Hani thought, gritting his teeth. He rushed to the door. From the foot of the stairs came a scuffle and a cry of frustration. Even before he could descend the steps, he saw Pi-ay being frog-marched back up them, Mery-ra gripping him by the arms, which he had pinned uncomfortably behind the goldsmith's back.

"Looks like you lost something, son," the old man said grimly. He shoved his prisoner back into the room and slammed the door behind him. "The litter bearers are at the bottom, waiting until he tries again to escape, and they aren't such kindly old grandfathers as I am. They're itching to break a few bones."

"Good thinking, Father," Hani said. And his heart grew warmer to have Mery-ra as his trusted partner once more. He turned and, lifting the light, cheap bed frame, dragged it to the side with a squawk of floorboards, exposing the chest. "Get the necklace, Pi-ay, and anything else you want to take with you, and let's go."

The goldsmith stooped over the chest—which, although not large, was solid—and opened it. Within lay a string of elongated beads in gold and colored jewels with an elaborate pendant in front and a counterpoise in back. The string of the necklace had been cut, and several beads were missing. Hani didn't get a thorough look, but he saw some beautiful colored enamel on the pendant. *Pi-ay's filigree,* he thought admiringly. It occurred to him that very little, if any, of the jewelry would actually touch the skin of a man dressed in a high-necked woolen tunic.

"Who was this for, Pi-ay? The Hittite prince, right?"

But the goldsmith looked blank. "Hittite prince?"

Hani's heart drummed with sudden excitement. "Who, then? Who was Ay going to kill?"

"Why, General Har-em-heb, my lord."

CHAPTER 17

H ANI AND HIS FATHER EXCHANGED stunned looks. Mery-ra murmured in disbelief, "Har-em-heb? I thought he was Ay's son-in-law."

"We'll discuss this later, Father. Pi-ay, get the chest, and let's get home, where it's private."

They bundled the goldsmith into the litter once more, and the bearers set off at a quick march. When they had entered the garden and closed the gate behind them, and Pi-ay had emerged stiffly from the conveyance, Hani said under his breath, "You're not a prisoner, my friend, but I strongly advise you not to run. As soon as you've answered my questions, I'll get you on board a diplomatic ship bound for Azzati, with full letters of recommendation for the commandant there. You can change your name and shave your head, and no one will ever know where you are. The garrison isn't about to let anyone who's after their beloved general get you, no matter how high placed he may be."

Resigned, Pi-ay nodded. With the chest in his arms, he limped into the house ahead of Hani, who drew up a stool for him. The goldsmith gaped around at the villa. Modest though it was, it would have taken decades of his salary to have purchased such a home.

Hani called for Nub-nefer, but the kitchen girl informed him she was still on temple duty. A simple lunch was prepared and ready to serve, and Maya was waiting in the kiosk.

"That's right—I had invited him for the afternoon. We had some work to do."

They trailed outside, a subdued Pi-ay between Hani and his father. The goldsmith's face had begun to turn a ferocious shade of amethyst.

As their steps crunched toward the dining pavilion, Maya jumped up from his seat. "Lord Hani! Lord Mery-ra! I'm glad you're—" He broke off at the sight of Pi-ay. "You found him?"

"Yes, and he's going to tell us everything he knows, because only if I'm pleased with how forthcoming he is will I save his life."

After a copious helping of cracked-wheat porridge and a good deal of beer, Hani said, "Pi-ay, begin at the beginning. When did this business start?"

"Last year, my lord. Some months before Ipy died. Lord Ay came in person to the shop after hours, when Ipy was working there alone. He couldn't refuse to let in the God's Father, could he? Maybe Lord Ay said he was there for the king." The goldsmith turned from face to face, as if to convince his listeners of his improbable words.

"He told Ipy to make this necklace with a rough interior on the counterpoise, pendant, and gold beads—rough enough to break skin."

And of course, Hani thought, *any time Har-em-heb wore his military garb, his shoulders and torso would be bare, vulnerable to the poisoned prickles.*

"But who would wear something so uncomfortable?" Mery-ra asked.

"I guess it only took once, my lord. Anyway, Ay paid him a lot up front, including the gold he'd need, and promised him a lot more if he could do this without breathing a word to anybody. But Ipy was trying to get those bracelets ready and was afraid he couldn't do it fast enough, so he asked me to help him. There were a lot of cloisons to do, which is my specialty." Despite his fear, the man looked proud.

"I worked late with him many an evening, but even so, it was slow, finical going, so—as I told you—I had to take time off and work at my friend's shop during the day. Then one night, Lord Ay came to check how things were progressing. He appeared with some of his henchmen when Ipy and I were both there at the forge. And when they thought they were out of earshot, they started talking about how this was going to work, and how they were going to kill Lord Har-em-heb with it."

Maya's eyes flew wide, and his jaw dropped with shocked incomprehension, but he said nothing.

"Then they realized that Ipy and I had overheard, although we begged and protested we hadn't. Ay pretended to believe us. Of course, he needed us to finish the piece, didn't he? As soon as we had completed it and turned it over to Lord Ay, they killed Ipy. But then they brought the necklace back, said it wasn't sharp enough, and asked if I could rough up the back a little more. They had no idea how much trouble that was going to be, of course. We had cast those prickles right into the sections. To add more by soldering? Work, I tell you. Then to have to file them down so the additions were invisible? They had no idea.

"That's when I disappeared, my lord. I knew what would happen to me as soon as they had it to their liking."

"What if you or Ipy had gone to the police before you were finished with it?" Mery-ra asked, scratching his wigless head.

"They couldn't have touched him, Father. Ay is more powerful than the police."

"So what was he afraid of? Why did these men have to be shut up?"

Hani pondered that question. Pensively, he said, "The only person more powerful than Ay is the king. At that point, the king was his daughter, and she was ill for a long time, as I understand. So she might very likely have done nothing. But as soon as she died, Prince Tut-ankh-aten became king."

"And he loves Har-em-heb. The general has become a kind of father to him. He might well have done something, even to his grandfather. At the very least, he would have told Har-em-heb." Maya, who was catching the gist of the story at last, broke out in a triumphant grin. "And *he* would surely have done something in the king's name! It would have given him great delight to break his father-in-law at last."

"And there we have our motive," Hani finished. "Ay must be getting worried about the amount of influence Har-em-heb has with the little king. Not to mention his control of the infantry. Our friend's becoming a very powerful man."

"He tried to stay out of the conflict between cavalry and infantry, didn't he?" Mery-ra asked.

"Yes, he's too smart to oppose Ay openly. But that doesn't mean that if he whistled, the infantry wouldn't come running to his rescue. And," Hani added as the idea came to him, "Har-em-heb is definitely a supporter of the priesthood of Amen-Ra. His own people are priests of Haru, remember?"

"Maybe somebody told Ay that Har-em-heb didn't really fight the priests when he was sent to kill Lord Mai and the others!" Maya burst out.

Hani nodded and continued, "Whereas if I were Ay, I would want to keep the priesthood carefully under control. Make them happy by restoring the liturgy, but don't let them own too much land or employ too many people. If they become overly powerful again, they become a rival for Ay's influence with the king. Har-em-heb's a real zealot for the Hidden One's cause, not just an opportunist. He must scare the God's Father a great deal."

They all stared at each other in excitement. The theory had the ring of truth to it.

I think we've finally solved this murder, Hani thought. *But of course, absolutely nothing will happen as a result.*

He turned toward Pi-ay, who was staring around him, wide-eyed with apprehension at all these revelations. "You, my friend—you've been very helpful. I'll write you some letters, and off you'll go to safety in Azzati. Just stay completely out of sight, eh?"

"Whatever you say, my lord." He seemed to have lost his uncooperative spirit, which had mostly been fear, Hani thought.

He called a servant to take Pi-ay to a spare room—probably a nicer space than any the goldsmith had occupied in his life. "Try to get some rest this afternoon," Hani told him kindly. "We'll be going to the coronation tomorrow, and while everyone is concentrating on that, you can slip away. Thank you for your help." He turned to go but stopped. "I'll see to it you have some clean clothes, and a servant will bring a jug for a shower. You look like you've been rolled in the dust."

"I have," the goldsmith said somewhat peevishly, and Hani remembered with amusement that he had a reputation for being disagreeable.

CHAPTER 18

ONCE HANI HAD RETURNED TO the kiosk, he, Mery-ra, and Maya sat staring at one another.

"So, Ipy's murder had nothing to do with the gift bracelets or with Hemet-min? Or with those bastards who are harassing Mother's workmen?" Maya asked finally.

"So it seems. I don't know what will become of Hemet-min now. Maybe her aunt will take her in after all."

Mery-ra raised his bushy eyebrows skeptically. "As long as she doesn't decide she wants those children back."

But Hani felt mostly sorrow for the poor woman. Something wasn't quite right about her. He hoped the gods would be merciful.

"What did that man overhear about 'What are they up to?' and 'Where's it going?' I would have sworn he was talking about his wife robbing his pay." Maya stroked his chin in puzzlement.

"Maybe," Hani allowed. "That's still true, after all. Or it could have been about the necklace. Especially before they knew what the textures were for."

Maya let out a hoot of laughter. "It's been a busy year at Mother's workshop." His look of amusement faded suddenly. "I don't know what she's going to do when the capital moves. Probably head down to Men-nefer with the court. That's going to make it even harder for me to take care of her in her old age."

Hani glanced at the little man wryly. Despite her gray hair and work-worn appearance, In-hapy was several years younger than Hani, and he felt his own old age was some distance in the future. But it spoke well of the boy that he was concerned. "I imagine the king will spend time in Waset too. It seems like a good idea to keep a presence at both ends of the Black Land, as they've always done. You could probably talk her into staying here."

Maya nodded without much enthusiasm, his brow wrinkled with anxiety. "You don't think she's in any danger, do you? She was probably right in the house when Lord Ay came to the shop that evening, and if he thinks she saw him…"

"Apparently, he doesn't, or she'd already be dead." At Maya's horrified expression, Mery-ra added, "He didn't need *her* to finish anything for him."

"Father's right. It's been more than a year." Hani finally broke his postprandial inertia and forced himself to his feet. "Well, I think I'll get a little work done and finish organizing my files. After the coronation, government departments will officially begin moving to Men-nefer and Waset. Maya, would you get those scrolls in my room, please?"

As they dispersed, Hani murmured to his father, "I think I need to talk to Har-em-heb."

Since the coronation was a good excuse for a family reunion, everyone but Neferet and her entourage descended on Hani's house. Nub-nefer had prepared a huge array of food, and while sleeping quarters were tight, there was a general air of festival, with overexcited cousins running everywhere.

"You've heard that the foreign service is moving to Waset?" Hani asked his brother as they watched their children and grandchildren at play.

Pipi's small brown eyes opened wide with delight. "Then it's for real? I'd heard rumors, but one never knows what's true and what isn't. Oh, Hani, you can't imagine how happy I'll be to come back to the old hometown. To see you and Father more frequently. And now Mut-nodjmet says she and Pa-kiki will be assigned there too—it's the Field of Reeds on earth! Nedjem-ib will be so happy!"

Hani laughed and put an arm affectionately around Pipi's broad shoulders. "Like old times, eh, little brother?"

They walked, leaning against each other, into the salon, where Neferet and Bener-ib had just appeared, the six children in tow. They were silent for once, staring about them, intimidated by all the strangers who seemed to know one another—and no doubt by the comparative luxury. Young Hu-may watched his former colleague with confusion and doubt. *Does the lad suspect that his mother and the goldsmith disappeared together and wonder why one returned but not the other?*

"Who are these, Hani?" Pipi asked in confusion. "I thought Neferet and Ptah-mes weren't—"

"They're the children of the victim of a crime Maya

just investigated for his mother," Hani said offhandedly. He could imagine Pipi wanting to be part of every case of Hani's since they would be inhabitants of the same city again. *But then,* he reminded himself happily, *I won't have any more missions. I'll be sending off other people from now on.*

"We're going out into the garden to play," Neferet announced loudly. "Anybody want to come?"

Ipy's children trooped after her and her friend, punching one another, sniggering, making donkey ears, and generally being pests, as they were evidently accustomed to do.

Nub-nefer watched them over her shoulder, distracted from a conversation with her sister-in-law. Eventually, she excused herself and made her way toward the porch. She smiled as she saw Hani. "I'm going to watch them play, my love. I don't want them to feel like nobody cares about them."

Hani joined her, beaming. *She is indeed the perfect woman. My pure gold.*

They observed their daughter drawing the little ones up into two teams, as if she had spent her entire life organizing sports. "This team will be—what? The Valiant Hawks? And this team?"

"The Donkey Poops!" One of the Hawks, a boy of about seven, snickered.

Hani realized with shame he hadn't made the slightest effort so far to learn their names.

The children of the yet-unnamed team cried out loudly in protest, and a small one struck at the seven-year-old with his fist.

But Neferet wasn't about to put up with that. "Wait! Do we hit one another? Do we shout insults? No."

But her answer was almost drowned out by a tittering chorus of equal parts "Yes!" and "No!"

"You know what that means," she said in an ominous voice, her eyebrows knotted in a look of menace. The children's giggles turned uneasy. "What happens when somebody hits somebody or makes fun of them or takes something from them?"

Hu-may spoke up timidly. "They go to the Hall of Justice?"

"Yes!" Neferet roared. "They go to the Hall of Justice! Come here, you two, Qen and Shu-roy. We're going to have a trial."

The little boys stepped forward, their naughty grins fast freezing into fear. They still didn't know this strange new grown-up very well, and they'd been struck plenty of times by an angry woman. Hani and Nub-nefer exchanged curious glances.

"Who's going to be the Master of the Hall of Justice?"

"Him," somebody said, pointing at the baby, who sat placidly with a thumb in his mouth, staring around.

"Ah, no, my boy. The Master has to volunteer."

Uneasy silence followed. Several of the grown-ups had drifted onto the porch and were watching with amusement.

Mery-ra toddled over to Hani and whispered, "You remember what happens next, don't you?"

"I'll be the Master of the Hall, then," Neferet cried in a portentous voice. "We'll find out which of these two wretches is guilty."

She positioned the two malefactors side by side and

scrunched her eyes and mouth in a long face intended to be that of a baboon. After a baboonish bark or two, the other children were laughing with a mixture of shock and pleasure, but the two little boys on trial struggled to keep from breaking their serious expressions. Next, Neferet dropped to her knees and began meowing like a cat, rubbing back and forth against the children's legs. Her nieces and nephews were used to that sort of behavior, but Ipy's offspring were dumbfounded. The smaller defendant burst out with a snort but managed to straighten his face.

"Now I remember!" Hani laughed. "We haven't had a trial since Sati was seven or eight. She was too well-behaved after that."

"And even Neferet couldn't fight all by herself," her mother said, grinning.

Neferet's next impersonation was that of a goose. She squatted on her haunches and flapped her elbows, making a raucous squawking noise. With wild eyes, she waddled over to pinch Qen and Shu-roy, who promptly dissolved in hysterical laughter.

"There! Simultaneous," Neferet pronounced, rising to her feet. "They're both guilty. Case dismissed."

While she finally organized the now-joyous children for their game, Hani, Nub-nefer, and Mery-ra drifted back into the salon, while a servant cleared the tables away.

"You certainly had a novel way of breaking up a fight, Father," Nub-nefer said with a warm glance at Mery-ra. "Hani came by his original methods honestly—and I see at least one of the youngsters has remembered her childhood."

"I'm just glad Neferet has found an outlet for her instincts," Hani said. "She has a talent for child-rearing."

"My hippopotamus impersonation was what always broke up you and Pipi." Mery-ra chuckled, a touch of pride in his voice. "Just mention it to Pipi, and he'll still burst out laughing."

Hani thought about the people he loved and how fortunate he was. None of his dear ones had been murdered, none had disappeared, none had abandoned anybody. The Hidden One had piloted them safely through the dangerous shallows. Hani's heart was swollen with contentment.

He passed through the salon and saw his eldest daughter watching him with a luminous smile.

"Everything has turned out well, Papa? Your questions are all answered?"

Hani shoved aside Pa-miu the cat and seated himself on the edge of Baket-iset's couch. "All but one. I'm not completely sure who killed that Hittite prince our late queen wanted to marry. Ay is almost certainly at the bottom of it, but I'll probably never have any proof. He acted as if he thought it was me!"

Baket-iset laughed. "Why would you have done that?"

"Well, Zannanza was a pretty irritating young man. But Ay pretended I had misunderstood my orders. He seemed to think I considered myself to be acting as his agent." Then something came to his mind, and he said with a laugh at himself, "At one point, I even thought your grandfather had something to do with it."

But Baket-iset didn't seem to find anything funny about that. She said with a wise smile, "It was something else, though, wasn't it, Papa? Something more human?"

How does she know? Hani wondered. *How does she*

always know? He squeezed her withered forearm, unable to speak. *My little oracle.*

◆

Later that afternoon, Lord Hani and Maya tried to get a bit of work done, since they would be taking advantage of the extended holiday that accompanied the king's coronation. They took each roll of papyrus and laid it out on the floor of the salon so they could rank them in order of urgency. Maya felt lighthearted, as if a physical burden had been lifted from his back. He found himself easily inclined to laughter, so it was almost impossible not to erupt in merriment at the tuneless rumble emerging from Hani's barely open mouth. That passed for song with his father-in-law, who was as tone-deaf as his chantress wife was melodious.

Suddenly, Hani fell silent and looked up from his stack of papyrus. "Aha said the king is in Waset, preparing for the coronation. He'll be inspecting the estates of the Hidden One while he's here, and Aha has to host him on his tour of the cattle pens. This may be a good time for me to seek an audience with our Sun God."

"Oh?" Maya asked in disgust, picturing Hani's firstborn abasing his fleshy body before the little king and being rewarded for his sycophancy. "Did you need to see him for something?"

"Har-em-heb hinted that Neb-khepru-ra wanted to see me, and even if I haven't been summoned, that's an order. Besides, I need to warn our general about Ay's attempt on him." Hani's little eyes widened suddenly. "I think I have the perfect coronation gift, too—if she's willing."

It took Maya a moment to remember that Neb-khepru-ra was Prince Tut-ankh-aten's throne name, by which he would henceforth be known. "*She*, my lord? A slave?"

"No, no, a free woman. A princess, in fact, although no one but you and me knows that." Hani winked. "What a nice handmaid our Meret-seger would make for a thirteen-year-old queen, eh?"

Maya nodded slowly. "What if someone should recognize her, though? Her life would be worth nothing."

"That's why we need to talk to her first." Hani called out to the servant who was cleaning in the kitchen to find the mute girl, and a moment later, Meret-seger glided modestly into the salon and bowed, some of Nub-nefer's toilet articles still in her hand from her interrupted work.

"My dear girl, I have something to offer you, but you'll have to tell me if you want it and if you think it's safe."

Meret-seger's pretty face grew politely attentive.

"If I give your services to the royal household, you would be able to see your, er, *king* grow up. Would that please you?"

The young woman's eyes grew enormous with joy, and pressing her hands to her heart, she dropped to her knees and bent to kiss Hani's feet. He drew her up kindly, and Maya saw that tears had starred her lashes. *What mother wouldn't want to see her son, at least from afar?*

"I thought you might," Lord Hani said in a benevolent voice. "Nub-nefer will miss you, but I know she'll agree this is the best thing we can do for you. Now"—he shot a glance at Maya then looked back at the girl more seriously—"you must tell me if anyone in the royal household is going to recognize you. Neither of the previous kings is still alive. The midwives are likewise dead, and Princess Meryet-aten.

Our two young *sunets* and Lady Djefat-nebty are all that are left of those who witnessed the birth. But be sure there isn't anyone who might realize what your real relationship to the king is, or they might try to finish the work of silencing you."

She shook her head earnestly, pleading with her big, painted eyes.

She's willing to take that chance, Maya told himself. "Is she safe from Ay, do you think, my lord? He seems to have an eye for attractive handmaids."

Hani looked at the girl for her opinion, and she shrugged, but her eyes were still fixed on his in supplication.

He said to Maya, "It's been ten years since she was seen at court, and she was barely more than a child then. Surely she's changed. And we can't protect her from Ay's roving gaze any more than we can protect any of the hundreds of other young women who serve at the palace. If the king and his queen favor her, that should be her best protection."

At the end of the morning, as soon as Nub-nefer returned from her marketing, where she and Nedjem-ib had laid in a big supply of anything the farm itself didn't produce, Hani called her over and explained his plan.

Her expression grew tender, and her eyes misted over. "What a wonderful thought, my love. It must be like a dream come true for her, even though the king doesn't know who she is and must never know." She stretched up to kiss her husband. "Not just every man would have come up with such a plan, but you have a good heart, Hani."

Hani blushed with schoolboyish pleasure and returned the kiss. Maya, observing, was between being amused and moved.

"Well, then, I'll request an audience, and we'll see where things go from there. Maya"—Hani turned to him—"take dictation, my friend. And we'll send a note to Har-em-heb too."

⁜

The next morning, the steward presented Hani with a letter from the king's chamberlain confirming his audience the following day. Thus, two days after Hani had requested to see the king, he set out across the river—alone except for the serving girl—to the old Per-hay, the house of rejoicing, which was the magnificent pleasure palace constructed for his first jubilee by Neb-ma'at-ra, of lamented memory. He had moved the main capital to Waset at the same time and had spent the rest of his life in its elegant but intimate halls on the west bank of the river. Since then, it had chiefly served to house monarchs traveling to the City of the Scepter for one reason or another. Under the circumstances, that meant it had stood empty for more than two years, last occupied briefly by the late coregent Ankh-khepru-ra.

They sailed into the immense man-made lake that fronted the palace, connected to the River by a channel, and landed at the royal quay. Hani passed through the pylon gate guarded by soldiers in plumes and leopard skins and up the long court with its shady hypostyle of palms. Bureaucrats and servants hustled here and there, never far from the king, wherever he should be.

At Hani's side, Meret-seger cast her eyes around surreptitiously. She had grown up in the palace of the royal harem, and such splendor wasn't altogether new to her. Still, she licked her lips nervously. Hani shot her a look of encouragement. Nub-nefer had personally provided her with cosmetics and given her a big fashionable wig and some of her mistress's own expensive clothing, and with her natural beauty, Meret-seger appeared every bit the princess her birth made her.

"Don't worry, my girl. You look as fine as any lady at court. The little queen will be delighted to have your services," Hani told her with a smile.

They turned in to the main entryway, where more soldiers and a majordomo in splendid dress welcomed them with courtly bows.

"Lord Hani. Our Sun God awaits you," he said and led Hani through the vestibule, into a second colonnaded waiting room.

It had always struck Hani how much more human in scale this house of joy was than the vast, impersonal spaces of the palaces at Akhet-aten. The throne hall was a light-feeling bright space illuminated by high grilled windows and punctuated by two rows of slender columns painted red. At the end, open doors revealed a golden baldachin over the dais where the young king sat in his glittering chair like a god in his shrine. Two Nubian servants with ostrich-plume fans posed at either side of the doors, and next to the throne, on the dais just below it, stood Hor-em-heb in civilian clothes.

Hani and the serving girl proceeded up the center of the colonnaded hall, their sandals clicking on the polished gypsum floors painted with bound captives—the Nine Bows of Kemet's enemies.

"Hani!" the little king cried eagerly, bouncing in his

chair. "I've missed you. Are we ever going to have our Akkadian lessons again?"

Hani managed a hasty prostration and said, even as he rose to face Neb-khepru-ra once more, "That would please me mightily, my Sun God. The command is yours to give."

"Who's the pretty lady?"

"Her services are a gift for your coronation. She is a trained palace handmaid who will make a helpful and discreet servant for Lady Ankh-es-en-pa-aten."

"What's your name, girl?" Neb-khepru-ra asked her. Perhaps it was the reflection of all the gold around him, but he seemed almost to glow, as if the divinity awaiting him in the coronation ceremony had already begun to seep inside. His head was covered by a blue-and-gold *nemes* headdress made to his diminutive size, and a beautiful, jeweled collar lay on his narrow shoulders. He was a child king—a child god, a true Golden Haru on earth.

"She's mute, my lord, but she can hear. Her name is Meret-seger. She has served my family for several years and is as intelligent and good-humored as she is lovely."

The girl seemed to be melting with longing for her divine son on the throne, her eyes misted, her lips trembling.

"What do you think, Har-em-heb?" The little king turned to the general at his side with an almost comically grown-up moue of evaluation on his boyish features.

Har-em-heb smiled. "I think she would make a gracious addition to your queen's entourage, my king. We can trust Lord Hani's recommendation."

"Do I have time to learn Akkadian again, do you think?" Neb-khepru-ra asked his councilor.

"Whatever my Sun God desires. Anything that helps you understand the Two Lands' diplomacy is good."

"That's my will, then. And the other boys too." The little king rose and drew to himself an ornamental walking stick that had lain unobtrusively against the throne. "It's good to see you again, Hani. I want you to serve me."

"He is your high commissioner of foreign affairs, my king," Har-em-heb murmured discreetly. "He will serve you with all his heart."

The majordomo appeared silently from somewhere and guided Hani into a complete court prostration. When he rose, the king and Har-em-heb had gone and, with them, Meret-seger.

Hani followed the functionary out of the throne room and down the long, airy colonnade. Outside the door, in the vestibule, the general stepped forward from the shadows and said under his breath, "You wanted to see me, Hani?"

"Is there somewhere we can talk with no one overhearing?"

Har-em-heb led him out the door of the palace into the tree-shaded court, and together, they made their way to the center of the area, surrounded only by palms. No one could approach them without being seen. They stood in the wavering shade of the fronds, a pigeon calling overhead and the summer breeze strummed by cicadas.

"Where is Lord Ay?" Hani asked quietly.

"In Akhet-aten, preparing the chancery for its move to Men-nefer. Why?"

They drew nearer until their heads almost touched.

"He wanted to assassinate you with a poisoned necklace, although the artisan who was making it has frustrated that attempt. But I'm sure it won't be the last. The God's Father must be afraid of your growing influence with the king."

Har-em-heb gave a harsh bark of laughter. "Of course he is. He'd like to see the boy reduced to complete childlike helplessness and given over to the path of pleasure so he, the old fox, can guide the country. He does everything he can to thwart my attempts to train the lad to rule—including putting him under that kinsman of his who cares nothing for the king and gives him credit for no spine at all." He shook his head in bitterness, his mouth implacably hard. "Doesn't Ay see that he's an old man? This boy will be on the throne long after he's gone. Neb-khepru-ra must be fit to direct the kingdom. But you know the lad, Hani. He'll do the easy thing if he can. Without someone pushing him, he'll drift off into a life of gilded idleness, leaving his kingdom to others to run."

"We'll do what we can to guide him, my friend, and the rest is in the hand of the Hidden One. But watch out for yourself."

"Oh, I do." Har-em-heb wrinkled his nose with disgust, as if he had gotten a whiff of something putrid. "Mut-nodjmet told me he had approached her about giving me a little gift from her hands. It must have been your necklace. Fortunately, she was mistrustful. I ask you, Hani, what sort of father uses his own daughter to commit crimes for him? She's the one who would have been punished if anything had happened to me."

Another way not to show love for your child, Hani thought sadly.

He left the palace sobered but not altogether gloomy.

The new reign still held promise of a fresh direction for the Two Lands. Ay wouldn't live forever.

As he descended the broad steps to the royal quay on the bank of the lake, Hani noticed a tall, middle-aged man with long hair walking in the same direction, almost at his side. Hattusha-ziti was proceeding purposefully, his mouth pursed and his eyes on the ground, and he clearly hadn't noticed Hani next to him.

He's still in Kemet? It's been weeks since he arrived. Hani called out, "Prince Hattusha-ziti!"

The emissary turned and, seeing Hani before him, let a look of pleasure thaw his features. He approached, and they clasped forearms.

"Hani, my friend. I have finally seen your king. It took weeks to gain an audience, and I had to follow him down here."

"How did the audience go, my lord? Are we at war?" Hani asked with an uncertain smile.

Prince Hattusha-ziti returned the smile wearily. "Probably. We're protesting strongly the death of Our Sun's boy after promising him a royal union with Kemet's queen. I doubt we'll see each other again, Hani. Perhaps our grandsons will be friends."

"I can't imagine the present government feels much responsibility for the treasonous promises of the late queen," Hani said with a sigh.

Hattusha-ziti gave a bark of laughter. "No. Well, I've accomplished my mission. I'm glad to have a chance to say goodbye. If all the sons of the Two Lands were as reasonable and clear-sighted as you, we wouldn't have come to this pass. Not to mention my own countrymen."

They slapped each other on the back with real warmth.

"Are you staying for the coronation?" Hani asked.

"No, no. Our two countries have no diplomatic relations at the moment, and my presence might be construed as homage." Hattusha-ziti turned to go.

Hani said, "Do you happen to know a man named Kurunuwa, my lord?"

"He's my secretary. Remember him? Why?"

"He's my brother."

The prince stopped dead, confused, then apparently deciding this must be a joke he didn't understand, he said with a chuckle, "That's what I like about you, Hani. Always ready to acknowledge the humanity of others, even enemies. May Ishtanu, the golden sun and the god of truth, bless you."

Pondering, Hani watched the Hittite's retreating back as Hattusha-ziti clattered down the rest of the shallow steps. Hani called out to him once more, "My prince, who killed Zannanza?"

Hattusha-ziti spun back with a wide, quirked grin on his ruddy face. "You've asked me that before. Someone who loved his country and wanted to spare it a terrible fate, wouldn't you say?"

And with that, the emissary was gone, striding away down the quay.

※

For the first time in nearly fifteen years, the crowning of Neb-khepru-ra Tut-ankh-aten was to take place at the Ipet-isut, under the loving eye of the Hidden One. Bureaucrats and foreign diplomats thronged to the City of the Scepter, joyful and dressed in their finest. Many of the mansions that had stood empty since the relocating of the capital were being reclaimed by their owners.

Aha did well to buy one while the prices were down, Hani told himself. *I don't know where he got his financial sense— he never seemed to listen to me.*

On the day of the great ceremony, Hani and his household stood alongside the processional way. Before them unrolled the avenue lined with ram-headed lions that led from the River to the outermost pylon of the Hidden One's southern temple. They had arrived nearly at dawn for good places, although Hani and most of the other men would soon join the procession. Nub-nefer had already taken up her position with the priests and chantresses who would accompany the barque of the god and the carrying chairs of the Haru on earth and his thirteen-year-old wife.

It was a fine spring day in early harvest season, and there was a lightness, a sense of fresh beginnings among the crowd that seemed to have been distilled into the scent of newly-cut grain straw from the fields inland. It flitted through Hani's mind that now that he would be traveling less and spending more time in the City of the Scepter, he could cultivate his land with greater intensity.

"Well, gentlemen, shall we return to the northern temple and take our places in line?" he finally suggested, eyeing the sun. "Father, let me unfold this stool for you. Neferet will hold the sunshade."

Mery-ra sputtered, "You're making me look ridiculous, son. I'm not an invalid." But he took his seat.

Aha was already striding off through the crowd, eager to be seen among the lay administrators of the god's estates, but as Hani and the others started after him, Pa-kiki said with a touch of melancholy, "I won't be in the procession, Father. I think Lord Ay doesn't trust the infantry, so there will be just a few foot troops participating and none of our scribes at all."

"Why? Because the scribes are more dangerous than the soldiers?" Mery-ra snorted. "Afraid they'll fling ink on Ay's fancy clothes?"

The others laughed. Neferet, always ready to jump into any source of merriment, cried, "Or push their pens up people's noses, or... or—"

"Time to go, my lads," Hani interrupted, grinning. "They'll start without us."

The men waved goodbye to their wives and children and the household servants. It did Hani's heart good to see Sat-hut-haru cheerfully among them, her little ones hanging on to her skirts. Neferet and Nedjem-ib were screaming with laughter over something, while Bener-ib sputtered into her hand. Pa-kiki and his family returned the wave, and in a moment, the crowd had closed behind Hani. Not far away, he spotted with relief his old friend Mane, who would once have been part of the procession but was retired. They exchanged salutes.

Hani and Maya along with their colleagues in the foreign service stood in the shadow of the Ipet-isut's serpentine wall until their time came to join in, but it was nearly midmorning before the head of the procession began to move. First came a body of priests, with sacrificial animals and incense bowls and sacred vessels, Amen-em-hut once more proudly carrying the ram-headed standard of the Hidden One, his handsome face alight. Next was a block of lay administrators of the temple, among whom Hani spied with tenderness and amusement his firstborn. Then came choruses of men and of women singing to the rhythm of their sistra while dancers swooped and weaved gracefully behind them, tossing handfuls of flower petals into the air. Hani had eyes for no one other than his wife, devout and beautiful in her wreath of water lilies.

This is your triumph, my dove, he thought, his heart overflowing. *You've waited and prayed for this faithfully for all these years.*

In the wake of the chantresses, the god himself proceeded majestically on his golden ram-headed barque, borne on the shoulders of eight *wab* priests who shuffled along under the boat's great weight. Smaller barques transported Amen-Ra's wife and son, who would reunite in the southern temple for the first time in fourteen years. Unseen in his gilded shrine, Amen-Ra shed his healing rays upon the crowd, who bowed in a wave like whitecaps in the wind as he passed to the booming beat of drums. Hani's throat clogged with emotion. This day was proof of the greatness of the Hidden One, whose power could never be suppressed.

Pilot who knows the waters, you have brought us safely back to port, he thought as he folded in a bow, a hand to his lips. *Thank you, O compassionate one, for letting us see this day.*

Musicians followed, chariot troops and infantrymen, marching in blocks. Pentju and Ay strode along abreast in their long vizier kilts, and immediately behind them, Ptah-mes, erect and dignified, loaded with his gold of honor; then came lesser masters of important divisions of government.

This is your triumph, too, my friend.

Hani and Maya peeled off and slid into line with their colleagues of the foreign service and other bureaucrats. Pipi was back there someplace. Hani could picture the young king at the end, held high on his carrying chair.

The procession was slow, moving forward at the pace of the *wab* priests who panted under the weight of the god's barque. Every so often, a ritual stop took place, as much to let the sweating bearers rest as to offer prayers and hymns. Although the distance could be traversed quickly at a normal walk, it would take the long procession hours to reach the southern temple. At every moment, the cheering crowd swarmed the edge of the road but were held back by gorgeously garbed soldiers.

The day was growing warmer, but Hani, caught up in the fervor and joy of the moment, barely noticed the perspiration trickling between his shoulder blades. Within his very viscera, the drums pounded relentlessly until he felt almost entranced, part of a great living being with a thousand heads. Maya, at his side, strode along, his chest out and his eyes scanning the crowd for people he knew.

At last, they reached the southern temple, and the vanguard of the procession turned into the allée of ram-headed lions that led to the mighty door of the god's sacred precinct. Over the heads of those before him, Hani saw the snapping banners that marked the temple as inhabited. The gilded panels swung open. The divine barques, the king, and the priests and chantresses proceeded into the court of the temple, while everyone else turned aside to wait in the vast plaza outside. Hani's family still stood in the front row. His father had risen from his stool, trying to avoid the sunshade Neferet held overhead. Beside Mery-ra stood the cheerful, tubby figure of his lady friend, her arm through his. They waved in a broad gesture, and Hani and Maya managed to wade through the dissolving procession to join them. The nurses had rounded up the children, including Ipy's brood, and young Tepy ran to his father, his face alight with pride.

"Gammother went inside with Uncle Amen-em-hut and the priests!" he cried. "Can we go too, Papa?"

"No, son," Maya said. "The only laymen who can go in are the ones selected to represent the people, and they only go as far as the first court."

"What happens inside that we can't see?" Maya's six-year-old, Mai-her-pri, demanded of Hani, who had taken the boy from Sati and perched him on his shoulders to have a better view.

"One by one, they set the crowns on the little king's head, then the Hidden One lays hands on him and changes his *ka* from a human one to a divine one."

Mai-her-pri's voice dropped in awe, although he couldn't have had the slightest idea of what that meant. "*Iyah,*" he breathed.

Despite being unable to repress a smile, Hani forced himself not to laugh. *Do any of us comprehend such a mystery?*

"Look," Neferet said suddenly. "Lord Ptah-mes is going inside too."

Interesting. He must have been chosen to represent the old nobility of Waset in the outer court. His tide has finally come in.

At last, King-Elect Tut-ankh-aten's carrying chair bore

him into the temple—a small, lone figure—and the golden doors clanged shut. When he emerged hours later, he would be a full-fledged king... and a god.

After the ceremony had concluded with an ecstatic greeting of the newly crowned king, the crowds dispersed. Out of deference to the small children and older people among his party, Hani decided to take his boat back to their neighborhood, shortening the walk. As he strolled back toward the quay with his family about him, he, too, was buoyed by a warm wave of optimism. *It's over,* he thought, as he had so often lately. He smiled down at Nub-nefer, who walked at his side, her arm through his. She was still crowned with flowers, her sistrum in her hand.

"My lord!" Maya and his family hustled up from behind Hani. His mother was in town for the occasion, and the little goldsmith waddled alongside him.

"Oh, Lord Hani," she said gratefully, coming up beside him, "thank you and Maya for solving Ipy's murder. The boy wouldn't tell me who the killer was because he said it was a state secret, but Ipy's *ba* knows and must surely be relieved. It's a sad world where a person would kill over a piece of jewelry, isn't it?"

"It certainly is, mistress." As always, Hani was impressed by the maturity and common sense of Maya's mother. "Fortunately, there are a lot of good people too."

"I wanted to tell you, Lord Hani, what I just told Maya. We're going to be moving the workshop back to Waset. They're saying the court will be spending nearly half the year here, and some departments will be here permanently.

What cause have I, at my age, to go starting over in Men-nefer, when I know everybody here—the suppliers and a lot of my private customers? My sisters and their families are here too. That makes sense, doesn't it?"

"It makes perfect sense," Hani said with a smile. "And you can see your grandchildren."

Her face broke out in a complicit grin. "That was the main reason, I have to admit, my lord. Maya's my only son, after all. And now that Sat-hut-haru is expecting again…"

Nub-nefer looked up at Hani with surprise and delight sparkling in her eyes. She rushed forward and embraced her middle daughter, cooing sounds of happiness, while Sati squealed in excited confirmation.

"We're so happy for you, my swallow," Hani added, embracing them both with a tender stretch of the arms. His voice was unsteady. *This is a victory of courage, an act of confidence in the future. Sati is back.* "Baket-iset will be so happy. She's kept us all strong with her faith in you."

Behind his mother, Maya beamed proudly.

In a light and optimistic frame of mind, Hani and his family continued down the processional way to where the land began to slope toward the River. Many of the participants in the funeral peeled off to their various neighborhoods, while an equal number headed to their boats for the journey home, even the short one to the suburban ends of the city. The sense of new beginnings perfumed the golden air of harvest season. What had died with Ankhet-khepru-ra was something not much regretted.

Ahead of Hani walked a group of tall, slim, beautifully dressed people and among them, one who was short and stocky with a shaven head. *Neferet. Which means the rest of them must be Lord Ptah-mes and his offspring and their spouses and children.* He was amazed to see those high aristocrats walking and even more amazed that the three generations walked together. *They're all really trying. And they'll succeed. "The back is not broken by bending it."*

To no one's surprise, Neferet was holding forth with great animation, and the others, especially the grandchildren, were laughing in delight. *There's one who's never let preconceptions stand in the way of seeing the truth.*

Ptah-mes's family approached his splendid yacht, and Neferet bade goodbye to them with a hearty wave, running back up the slope of the embarcadero to rejoin her family. "Where are Ibet and the children?" she called.

"Back there with the other cousins," Nub-nefer said with a fond smile.

A touch on his sleeve made Hani turn. Pi-ay walked, still a little stiff-legged, at his side, unrecognizable in a wig that hid his distinctive hairline. "Should I go now, my lord?" he asked under his breath.

"This is a good time, my friend, while everyone's crowding to the boats. Nobody will notice you. I just hope that Hemet-min finds a place for herself as well. But I guess that cache of copper debens will keep her afloat."

Pi-ay gave a bark of gloating laughter. "She'll never find it. Hu-may has it—he buried it in In-hapy's yard."

Hani stopped walking for a moment and said in confusion, "But you sent her back for it from Gebtu. You already knew the boy had it?"

"Let's just say I sent her back," Pi-ay said a bit unkindly. "He has it because I gave it to him. That was food she'd taken from the children's mouths. Hemet-min was worse than a crow."

"That must be why the boy said they weren't poor, even

though the children clearly weren't getting enough to eat. Well, Bes and the Great One will watch over them. They have a little something of their own now and needn't feel beholden." But he thought of Hemet-min, left alone to face a world she seemed badly equipped to live in. *Watch over her, too, Great Lady.*

"I think Hemet-min's aunt will take her in finally. I was really the problem." Pi-ay looked in embarrassment down at his hands—a goldsmith's clever hands—and said, "How can I thank you? You're saving my life."

"Think of it as passing along the favor you've done these children. Pick up your chest at the house, and get going quickly. Khonsu the Traveler protect you. Perhaps we'll meet again." He clapped him on the back, and Pi-ay strode unevenly off into the crowd.

Hani turned to find his father standing at his side, watching him with his wise little eyes.

"A new beginning, eh, son?"

"For him or for us?"

"For everybody," Mery-ra said with a grin that might once have been complacent. "It's been quite a year."

Hani realized that was precisely so. During the harvest season a year ago, word had first come of his mission to Kheta and all that followed. Much had changed since then.

"Meryet-amen said to give you this." Hani's father pulled a large, round covered basket from behind him. "Her nephew works at the treasury, and Ptah-mes gave it to him to give to you. Don't ask me how your friend knew there was a connection between our families—or why he thought you'd want such a thing."

Hani laughed. "Somehow, he knows everything that goes on at court." Recognizing it as the cobra's basket, he took the woven box gingerly. But the light weight told him it was empty.

"He said to tell you—now, what was it?—'He's gone home.' I don't know who."

Hani nodded with a smile of relief. Another sign that a painful and violent chapter of everyone's lives had closed.

He gazed around him at the merry white-clad crowds streaming toward the River and their homes, at the processional street lined with king-headed lions, growing drab as it emptied out. He squinted up at the pure blue midday sky, which was a little muted by the dust kicked up by a thousand feet but filled with the benevolent light of the Lord Amen-Ra. He glanced behind him at the throng of his family laughing and chattering, the children dancing around their parents' legs, and a deep sense of well-being flowed over him like warm ointment after a bath.

"Who wants Papa to give us some more Tales of the Traveler tonight?" Sati called out in her bright voice.

The children shouted eagerly, and the younger ones jumped up and down.

"Let Aunt Neferet act it out!" Tepy shouted.

Nub-nefer slipped forward between Hani and his father and, smiling up at her husband, slid her arm in his, radiating contentment.

What more could a man ask? Hani thought, his heart full. *I'm sure I don't know.*

THE END

ACKNOWLEDGMENTS

THE AUTHOR GRATEFULLY ACKNOWLEDGES ALL those who have helped her in the production of this book. To the wonderful women of my writers' group, for their critique and encouragement, my thanks. Your input was especially important to this book. To Lynn McNamee and her editorial team at Red Adept—Jessica, Susie, and Irene—profound gratitude (and Lynn, for so many other forms of help). To the flexible and talented gang at Streetlight Graphics for the cover and map. To my cousin and her husband, my technology guru: thanks, guys. To Enid, who urged me forward by her support, I can't thank you sufficiently. And most of all, to my husband, Ippokratis, who put up with the months of fixation it takes to write a novel, many, many thanks.

ABOUT THE AUTHOR

 N.L. Holmes is the pen name of a professional archaeologist who received her doctorate from Bryn Mawr College. She has excavated in Greece and in Israel and taught ancient history and humanities at the university level for many years. She has always had a passion for books, and in childhood, she and her cousin (also a writer today) used to write stories for fun.

Today, since their son is grown, she lives with her husband and two cats. They split their time between Florida and northern France, where she gardens, weaves, plays the violin, dances, and occasionally drives a jog-cart. And reads, of course.

OTHER TITLES BY N.L. HOLMES

THE LORD HANI MYSTERIES
Political intrigue and mystery in Akh-en-aten's Egyptian

Finalist, Best Series of 2021, Next Generation
Independent Book Award

Finalist, Best Series of 2022, Chanticleer
Independent Book Awards

Bird in a Snare (2020) Grand Prize, Geoffrey Chaucer
Award 2021 for best historical fiction before 1750

The Crocodile Makes No Sound (2020) Gold Medal
Adult Fiction 2022 Wishing Shelf Book Awards

Scepter of Flint (2020)

The North Wind Descends (2020)

Lake of Flowers (2021)

Pilot Who Knows the Waters (2022)

THE *EMPIRE AT TWILIGHT* SERIES
Free-standing personal dramas with a touch
of intrigue, set in the Hittite Empire

The Lightning Horse (2020)

The Singer and Her Song (2020)

The Queen's Dog (2020)

The Sun at Twilight (2021)

The Moon That Fell from Heaven (Red Adept, *Vella*, 2021)

The Players (Red Adept, *Vella*, coming soon)

COMING SOON:
THE *HANI'S DAUGHTER* MYSTERIES
Neferet carries on the family curiosity
in the reign of Tut-ankh-amen